THE SHARING KNIFE

BEGUILEMENT

THE SHARING KNIFE

Volume One
BEGUILEMENT

Lois McMaster Bujold

eos

An Imprint of HarperCollinsPublishers

THE SHARING KNIFE, VOLUME ONE: BEGUILEMENT. Copyright © 2006 by Lois McMaster Bujold. All rights reserved. Printed in the United States of America. No part of this book may be used or reproduced in any manner whatsoever without written permission except in the case of brief quotations embodied in critical articles and reviews. For information address HarperCollins Publishers, 10 East 53rd Street, New York, NY 10022.

HarperCollins books may be purchased for educational, business, or sales promotional use. For information please write: Special Markets Department, HarperCollins Publishers, 10 East 53rd Street, New York, NY 10022.

FIRST EDITION

Eos is a federally registered trademark of HarperCollins Publishers.

Designed by Sunil Manchikanti
Map by Lois McMaster Bujold

Library of Congress Cataloging-in-Publication Data has been applied for.

ISBN-13: 978-0-06-113758-7
ISBN-10: 0-06-113758-7-8

06 07 08 09 10 JTC/RRD 10 9 8 7 6 5 4 3 2 1

FIC

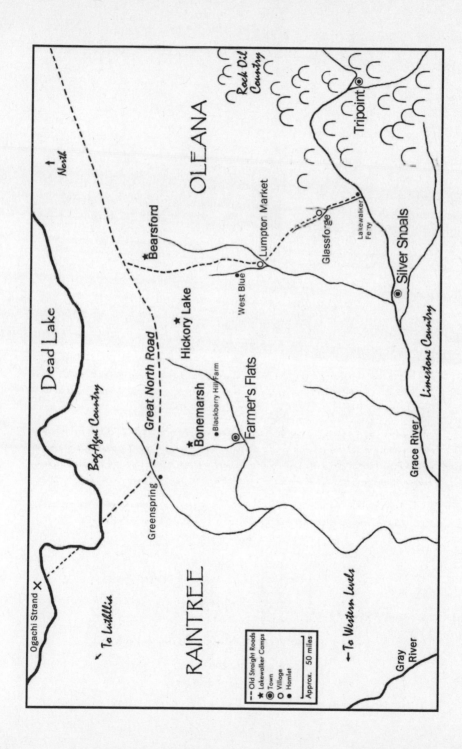

THE SHARING KNIFE

BEGUILEMENT

1

Fawn came to the well-house a little before noon. More than a farmstead, less than an inn, it sat close to the straight road she'd been trudging down for two days. The farmyard lay open to travelers, bounded by a semicircle of old log outbuildings, with the promised covered well in the middle. To resolve all doubt, somebody had nailed a sign picturing the well itself to one of the support posts, and below the painting a long list of goods the farm might sell, with the prices. Each painstakingly printed line had a little picture below it, and colored circles of coins lined up in rows beyond, for those who could not read the words and numbers themselves. Fawn could, and keep accounts as well, skills her mother had taught her along with a hundred other household tasks. She frowned at the unbidden thought: *So if I'm so clever, what am I doing in this fix?*

She set her teeth and felt in her skirt pocket for her coin purse. It was not heavy, but she might certainly buy some bread. Bread would be bland. The dried mutton from her pack that she'd tried to eat this morning had made her sick, again, but she needed something to fight the horrible fatigue that slowed her steps to a plod, or she'd never make it to Glassforge. She glanced around the unpeopled yard and at the iron bell hung from the post with a pull cord dangling invitingly, then lifted her eyes to the rolling fields beyond the buildings. On a distant sunlit slope, a dozen or so people were haying. Uncertainly, she went around to the farmhouse's kitchen door and knocked.

A striped cat perching on the step eyed her without getting up. The cat's plump calm reassured Fawn, together with the good repair of the house's faded shingles and fieldstone foundation, so that when a comfortably middle-aged farmwife opened the door, Fawn's heart was hardly pounding at all.

"Yes, child?" said the woman.

I'm not a child, I'm just short, Fawn bit back; given the crinkles at the corners of the woman's friendly eyes, maybe Fawn's basket of years would still seem scant to her. "You sell bread?"

The farmwife's glance around took in her aloneness. "Aye; step in."

A broad hearth at one end of the room heated it beyond summer, and was crowded with pots hanging from iron hooks. Delectable smells of ham and beans, corn and bread and cooking fruit mingled in the moist air, noon meal in the making for the gang of hay cutters. The farmwife folded back a cloth from a lumpy row on a side table, fresh loaves from a workday that had doubtless started before dawn. Despite her nausea Fawn's mouth watered, and she picked out a loaf that the woman told her was rolled inside with crystal honey and hickory nuts. Fawn fished out a coin, wrapped the loaf in her kerchief, and took it back outside. The woman walked along with her.

"The water's clean and free, but you have to draw it yourself," the woman told her, as Fawn tore off a corner of the loaf and nibbled. "Ladle's on the hook. Which way were you heading, child?"

"To Glassforge."

"By yourself?" The woman frowned. "Do you have people there?"

"Yes," Fawn lied.

"Shame on them, then. Word is there's a pack of robbers on the road near Glassforge. They shouldn't have sent you out by yourself."

"South or north of town?" asked Fawn in worry.

"A ways south, I heard, but there's no saying they'll stay put."

"I'm only going as far south as Glassforge." Fawn set the bread on the bench beside her pack, freed the latch for the crank, and let the bucket fall till a splash echoed back up the well's cool stone sides, then began turning.

Robbers did not sound good. Still, they were a frank hazard. Any fool would know enough not to go near them. When Fawn had started on this miserable journey six days ago, she had cadged rides from wagons at every chance as soon as she'd walked far enough from home not to risk encountering someone who knew her. Which had been fine until that one fellow who'd said stupid things that made her very uncomfortable and followed up with a grab and a grope. Fawn had managed to break away, and the man had not been willing to abandon his rig and restive team to chase her down, but she might have been less lucky. After that, she'd hidden discreetly in the verge from the occasional passing carts until she was sure there was a woman or a family aboard.

The few bites of bread were helping settle her stomach already. She hoisted the bucket onto the bench and took the wooden dipper the woman handed down to her. The water tasted of iron and old eggs, but was clear and cold. Better. She would rest a while on this bench in the shade, and perhaps this afternoon she would make better time.

From the road to the north, hoofbeats and a jingle of harness sounded. No creak or rattle of wheels, but quite a *lot* of hooves. The farmwife glanced up, her eyes narrowing, and her hand rose to the cord on the bell clapper.

"Child," she said, "see those old apple trees at the side of the yard? Why don't you just go skin up one and stay quiet till we see what this is, eh?"

Fawn thought of several responses, but settled on, "Yes'm." She started across the yard, turned back and grabbed her loaf, then trotted to the small grove. The closest tree had a set of boards nailed to the side like a ladder, and she scrambled up quickly through branches thick with leaves and hard little green apples. Her dress was dyed dull blue, her jacket brown; she would blend with the shadows here as well as she had on the road verge, likely. She braced herself along a branch, tucked in her pale hands and lowered her face, shook her head, and peered out through the cascade of black curls falling over her forehead.

The mob of riders turned into the yard, and the farmwife came off her tense toes, shoulders relaxing. She released the bell cord. There must have been a dozen and a half horses, of many colors, but all rangy and long-legged. The riders wore mostly dark clothing, had saddlebags and bedrolls tied behind their cantles, and—Fawn's breath caught—long knives and swords hanging from their belts. Many also bore bows, un-strung athwart their backs, and quivers full of arrows.

No, not all men. A woman rode out of the pack, slid from her horse, and nodded to the farmwife. She was dressed much as the rest, in riding trousers and boots and a long leather vest, and had iron-gray hair braided and tied in a tight knot at her nape. The men wore their hair long too: some braided back or tied in queues, with decorations of glass beads or bright metal or colored threads twisted in, some knotted tight and plain like the woman's.

Lakewalkers. A whole patrol of them, apparently. Fawn had seen their kind only once before, when she'd come with her parents and brothers to Lumpton Market to buy special seed, glass jars, rock oil and wax, and dyes. Not a patrol, that time, but a clan of traders from the wilderness up around the Dead Lake, who had brought fine furs and leathers and odd woodland produce and clever metalwork and more secret items: medicines, or maybe subtle poisons. The Lakewalkers were rumored to practice black sorcery.

Other, less unlikely rumors abounded. Lakewalker kinfolk did not settle in one place, but moved about from camp to camp depending on the needs of the season. No man among them owned his own land, carefully parceling it out amongst his heirs, but considered the vast wild tracts to be held in common by all his kin. A man owned only the clothes he stood in, his weapons, and the catches of his hunts. When they married, a woman did not become mistress of her husband's house, obliged to the care of his aging parents; instead a man moved into the tents of his bride's mother, and became as a son to her family. There were also whispers of strange bed customs among them which, maddeningly, no one would confide to Fawn.

On one thing, the folks were clear. If you suffered an incursion by a blight bogle, you called in the Lakewalkers. And you did not cheat them of their pay once they had removed the menace.

Fawn was not entirely sure she believed in blight bogles. For all the tall tales, she had never encountered one in her life, no, nor known anyone else who had, either. They seemed like ghost stories, got up to thrill the shrewd listeners and frighten the gullible ones. She had been gulled by her snickering older brothers far too many times to rise readily to the bait anymore.

She froze again when she realized that one of the patrollers was walking toward her tree. He looked different than the others, and it took her a moment to realize that his dark hair was not long and neatly braided, but cut short to an untidy tousle. He was alarmingly tall, though, and very lean. He yawned and stretched, and something glinted on his left hand. At first Fawn thought it was a knife, then realized with a slight chill that the man had no left hand. The glint was from some sort of hook or clamp, but how it was fastened to his wrist beneath his long sleeve she could not see. To her dismay, he ambled into the shade directly below her, there to lower his long body, prop his back comfortably against her tree trunk, and close his eyes.

Fawn jerked and nearly fell out of the tree when the farmwife

reached up and rang her bell after all. Two loud clanks and three, repeated: evidently a signal or call, not an alarm, for she was talking all the
time in an animated way with the patroller woman. Now that Fawn's eyes
had time to sort them out in their strange garb, she could see three or
four more women among the men. A couple of men busied themselves
at the well, hauling up the bucket to slosh the water into the wooden
trough on the side opposite the bench; others led their horses in turn to
drink. A boy loped around the outbuildings in answer to the bell, and the
farmwife sent him with several more of the patrollers into the barn. Two
of the younger women followed the farmwife into her house, and came
out in a while with packets wrapped in cloth—more of the good farm
food, obviously. The others emerged from the barn lugging sacks of what
Fawn supposed must be grain for their horses.

They all met again by the well, where a brief, vigorous conversation ensued between the farmwife and the gray-haired patroller woman.
It ended with a counting over of sacks and packets in return for coins
and some small items from the patroller saddlebags that Fawn could not
make out, to the apparent satisfaction of both sides. The patrol broke up
into small groups to seek shade around the yard and share food.

The patrol leader walked over to Fawn's tree and sat down cross-
legged beside the tall man. "You have the right idea, Dag."

A grunt. If the man opened his eyes, Fawn could not tell; her leaf-
obstructed view was now of two ovals, one smooth and gray, the other
ruffled and dark. And a lot of booted leg, stretched out.

"So what did your old friend have to say?" asked the man. His low
voice sounded tired, or maybe it was just naturally raspy. "Malice confirmed, or not?"

"Rumors of bandits only, so far, but a lot of disappearances around
Glassforge. With no bodies found."

"Mm."

"Here, eat." She handed him something, ham wrapped in bread judging by the enticing aroma that rose to Fawn. The woman lowered her voice. "You feel anything yet?"

"You have better groundsense than I do," he mumbled around a mouthful. "If you don't, I surely won't."

"Experience, Dag. I've been in on maybe nine kills in my life. You've done what—fifteen? Twenty?"

"More, but the rest were just little ones. Lucky finds."

"Lucky ha, and little ones count just the same. They'd have been big ones by the next year." She took a bite of her own food, chewed, and sighed. "The children are excited."

"Noticed. They're going to start setting each other off if they get wound up much tighter."

A snort, presumably of agreement.

The raspy voice grew suddenly urgent. "If we do find the malice's lair, put the youngsters to the back."

"Can't. They need the experience, just as we did."

A mutter: "Some experiences no one needs."

The woman ignored this, and said, "I thought I'd pair Saun with you."

"Spare me. Unless I'm pulling camp guard duty. Again."

"Not this time. The Glassforge folk are offering a passel of men to help."

"Ah, spare us all. Clumsy farmers, worse than the children."

"It's their folk being lost. They've a right."

"Doubt they could even take out real bandits." He added after a moment, "Or they would have by now." And after another, "If they are real bandits."

"Thought I'd stick the Glassforgers with holding the horses, mostly. If it is a malice, and if it's grown as big as Chato fears, we'll need every pair of our hands to the front."

A short silence. "Poor word choice, Mari."

"Bucket's over there. Soak your head, Dag. You know what I meant."

The right hand waved. "Yeah, yeah."

With an *oof,* the woman rose to her feet. "Eat. That's an order, if you like."

"*I'm* not nervy."

"No"—the woman sighed—"no, you are not that." She strode off.

The man settled back again. *Go away, you,* Fawn thought down at him resentfully. *I have to pee.*

But in a few minutes, just before she was driven by her body's needs into entirely unwelcome bravery, the man got up and wandered after the patrol leader. His steps were unhurried but long, and he was across the yard before the leader gave a vague wave of her hand and a side glance. Fawn could not see how it could be an order, yet somehow, everyone in the patrol was suddenly up and in motion, saddlebags re-packed, girths tightened. The whole lot of them were mounted and on their way in five minutes.

Fawn slipped down the tree trunk and peered around it. The one-handed man—riding rear guard?—was looking back over his shoulder. She ducked out of sight again till the hoofbeats faded, then unclutched the apple tree and went to seek the farmwife. Her pack, she was relieved to see in passing, lay untouched on the bench.

Dag glanced back, wondering anew about the little farm girl who'd been hiding shyly up the apple tree. There, now—down she slid, but he still gained no clear look at her. Not that a few leaves and branches could hide a life-spark so bright from his groundsense at *that* range.

His mind's eye sketched a picture of her tidy farm raided by a mal-

ice's mud-men, all its cheerful routine turned to ash and blood and char-
nel smoke. Or worse—and not imagination but memory supplied the
vision—a ruination like the Western Levels beyond the Gray River, not
six hundred miles west of here. Not so far away to him, who had ridden
or walked the distance a dozen times, yet altogether beyond these local
people's horizons. Endless miles of open flat, so devastated that even
rocks could not hold their shape and slumped into gray dust. To cross
that vast blight leached the ground from one's body as a desert parched
the mouth, and it was just as potentially lethal to linger there. A thousand
years of sparse rains had only begun to sculpt the Levels into something
resembling a landscape again. To see this farm girl's green rolling lands
laid low like that . . .

Not if I can help it, Little Spark.

He doubted they would meet again, or that she would ever know
what her—mother's?—strange customers today sought to do on her behalf and their own. Still, he could not begrudge her his weariness in this
endless task. The country people who gained even a partial understanding of the methods called it black necromancy and sidled away from
patrollers in the street. But they accepted their gift of safety all the same.
*So yet again, one more time anew, we will buy the death of this malice with one
of our own.*

But not more than one, not if he could make it so.

Dag clapped his heels to his horse's sides and cantered after his
patrol.

The farmwife watched thoughtfully as Fawn packed up her bedroll,
straightened the straps, and hitched it over her shoulder once more. "It's
near a day's ride to Glassforge from here," she remarked. "Longer, walking. You're like to be benighted on the road."

"It's all right," said Fawn. "I've not had trouble finding a place to sleep." Which was true enough. It was easy to find a cranny to curl up in out of sight of the road, and bedtime was a simple routine when all you did was spread a blanket and lie down, unwashed and unbrushed, in your clothes. The only pests that had found her in the dark were the mosquitoes and ticks.

"You could sleep in the barn. Start off early tomorrow." Shading her eyes, the woman stared down the road where the patrollers had vanished a while ago. "I'd not charge you for it, child."

Her honest concern for Fawn's safety stood clear in her face. Fawn was torn between unjust anger and a desire to burst into tears, equally uncomfortable lumps in her stomach and throat. *I'm not twelve, woman.* She thought of saying so, and more. She had to start practicing it sooner or later: *I'm twenty. I'm a widow.* The phrases did not rise readily to her lips as yet.

Still . . . the farmwife's offer beguiled her mind. Stay a day, do a chore or two or six and show how useful she could be, stay another day, and another . . . farms always needed more hands, and Fawn knew how to keep hers busy. Her first planned act when she reached Glassforge was to look for work. Plenty of work right here—familiar tasks, not scary and strange.

But Glassforge had been the goal of her imagination for weeks now. It seemed like quitting to stop short. And wouldn't a town offer better privacy? *Not necessarily,* she realized with a sigh. Wherever she went, folks would get to know her sooner or later. Maybe it was all the same, no new horizons anywhere, really.

She mustered her flagging determination. "Thanks, but I'm expected. Folk'll worry if I'm late."

The woman gave a little headshake, a combination of conceding the argument and farewell. "Take care, then." She turned back to her house and her own onslaught of tasks, duties that probably kept her running from before dawn to after dark.

A life I would have taken up, except for Sunny Sawman, Fawn thought gloomily, climbing back up to the straight road once more. *I'd have taken it up for the sake of Sunny Sawman, and never thought of another.*

Well, I've thought of another now, and I'm not going to go and unthink it. Let's go see Glassforge.

One more time, she called up her wearied fury with Sunny, the low, stupid, nasty . . . stupid fool, and let it stiffen her spine. Nice to know he had a use after all, of a sort. She faced south and began marching.

2

Last year's leaves were damp and black with rot underfoot, and as Dag climbed the steep slope in the dark, his boot slid. Instantly, a strong and anxious hand grasped his right arm.

"Do that again," said Dag in a level whisper, "and I'll beat you senseless. Quit trying to protect me, Saun."

"Sorry," Saun whispered back, releasing the death clutch. After a momentary pause, he added, "Mari says she won't pair you with the girls anymore because *you're* overprotective."

Dag swallowed a curse. "Well, that does not apply to you. Senseless. And bloody."

He could feel Saun's grin flash in the shadows of the woods. They heaved themselves upward a few more yards, finding handgrips among the rocks and roots and saplings.

"Stop," Dag breathed.

A nearly soundless query from his right.

"We'll be up on them over this rise. What you can see, can see you, and if there's anything over there with groundsense, you'll look like a torch in the trees. Stop it down, boy."

A grunt of frustration. "But I can't see Razi and Utau. I can barely see you. You're like an ember under a handful of ash."

"I can track Razi and Utau. Mari holds us all in her head, you don't have to. You only have to track me." He slipped behind the youth and gripped his right shoulder, massaging. He wished he could do both sides together, but this touch seemed to be enough; the flaring tension started to go out of Saun, both body and mind. "Down. Down. That's right. Better." And after a moment, "You're going to do just fine."

Dag had no idea whether Saun was going to do well or disastrously, but Saun evidently believed him, with appalling earnestness; the bright anxiety decreased still further.

"Besides," Dag added, "it's not raining. Can't have a debacle without rain. It's obligatory, in my experience. So we're good." The humor was weak, but under the circumstances, worked well enough; Saun chuckled.

He released the youth, and they continued their climb.

"Is the malice there?" muttered Saun.

Dag stopped again, bending in the shadows to hook up a plant left-sided. He held it under Saun's nose. "See this?"

Saun's head jerked backward. "It's poison ivy. Get it out of my face."

"If we were this close to a malice's lair, not even the poison ivy would still be alive. Though I admit, it would be among the last to go. This isn't the lair."

"Then why are we here?"

Behind them, Dag could hear the men from Glassforge topping the ridge and starting down into the ravine out of which he and the patrol were climbing. Second wave. Even Saun didn't manage to make that much noise. Mari had better land her punches before their helpers closed the gap, or there would be no surprise left. "Chato thinks this robber troop has been infiltrated, or worse, suborned. Catch us a mud-man, it'll lead us to its maker, quick enough."

"*Do* mud-men have groundsense?"

"Some. Malice ever catches one of us, it takes everything. Groundsense. Methods and weapon skills. Locations of our camps . . . Likely the first human this one caught was a road robber, trying to hide out in the hills, which is why it's doing what it is. None of us have been reported missing, so we still may have the edge. A patroller doesn't let a malice take him alive if he can help it." *Or his partner.* Enough lessons for one night. "Climb."

On the ridgetop, they crouched low.

Smoothly, Saun strung his bow. Less smoothly but just as quickly, Dag unshipped and strung his shorter, adapted one, then swapped out the hook screwed into the wooden cuff strapped to the stump of his left wrist, and swapped in the bow-rest. He seated it good and tight, clamped the lock, and dropped the hook into the pouch on his belt. Undid the guard strap on his sheath and made sure the big knife would draw smoothly. It was all scarcely more awkward than carrying the bow in his hand had once been, and at least he couldn't drop it.

At the bottom of the dell, Dag could see the clearing through the trees: three or four campfires burning low, tents, and an old cabin with half its roof tumbled in. Lumps of sleeping men in bedrolls, like scratchy burrs touching his groundsense. The faint flares of a guard, awake in the woods beyond, and someone stumbling back from the slit trenches. The sleepy smudges of a few horses tethered beyond. Words of the body's senses for something his eyes did not see nor hand touch. Maybe twenty-five men altogether, against the patrol's sixteen and the score or so of volunteers from Glassforge. He began to sort through the life-prickles, looking for things shaped like men that . . . weren't.

The night sounds of the woods carried on: the croak of tree frogs, the chirp of crickets, the sawing of less identifiable insects. An occasional tiny rustle in the weeds. Anything bigger might have been either scared off by the noise of the camp below, or, depending on how the robbers buried their scraps, attracted. Dag felt around with his groundsense beyond the tightening perimeter of the patrol, but found no nervous scavengers.

Then, too soon, a startled yell from his far right, partway around the patroller circle. Grunts, cries, the ring of metal on metal. The camp stirred. *That's it, in we go.*

"Closer," snapped Dag to Saun, and led a slide downslope to shorten their range. By the time he'd closed the distance to a bare twenty paces and found a gap in the trees through which to shoot, the targets were obligingly rising to their feet. From even farther to his right, a flaming arrow arced high and came down on a tent; in a few minutes, he might even be able to see what he was shooting at.

Dag let both fear and hope fade from his mind, together with worries about the inner nature of what they faced. It was just targets. One at a time. That one. And that one. And in that confusion of flickering shadows. . . .

Dag loosed another shaft, and was rewarded by a distant yelp. He had no idea what he'd hit or where, but it would be moving slower now. He paused to observe, and was satisfied when Saun's next shaft also vanished into the black dark beyond the cabin and returned a meaty *thunk* they could hear all the way up here. All around in the woods, the patrol was igniting with excitement; his head would be as full of them as Mari's was in a moment if they didn't all get a grip on themselves.

The advantage of twenty paces was that it was a nice, short, snappy range to shoot from. The disadvantage was how little time it took your targets to run up on your position . . .

Dag cursed as three or four large shapes came crashing through the dark at them. He let his bow arm pivot down and yanked out his knife. Glancing right, he saw Saun pull his long sword, swing, and make the discovery that a blade length that gave great advantage from horseback was awkwardly constrained in a close-grown woods.

"You can't lop heads here!" Dag yelled over his shoulder. "Go to thrusts!" He grunted as he folded in his bow-arm and shoved his left shoulder into the nearest attacker, knocking the man back down the hillside. He caught a blade that came out of seeming-nowhere on the brass of his hilt, and with a shuddering scrape closed in along it for a well-placed knee to a target groin. These men might have fancied themselves bandits, but they still fought like farmers.

Saun raised a leg and booted his blade free of a target; the man's cry choked in his throat, and the withdrawing steel made an ugly sucking noise. Saun followed Dag at a run toward the bandit camp. Razi and Utau, to their right and left, paced them, closing in tight as they all descended, stooping like hawks.

In the clearing, Saun devolved to his favorite powerful swings again. Which worked spectacularly bloodily when they connected, and left him wide open when they didn't. A target succeeded in ducking, then came up swinging a long-handled, iron-headed sledgehammer. The breaking-pumpkin sound when it hit Saun's chest made Dag's stomach heave. Dag leaped inside the target's lethal radius, clutched him tightly around the back with his bow-arm, and brought his knife up hard. Wet horrors spilled over his hand, and he twisted the knife and shoved the target off it. Saun lay on his back, writhing, his face darkening.

"Utau! Cover us!" Dag yelled. Utau, gasping for breath, nodded and took up a protective stance, blade ready. Dag slid down to Saun's side, snapped off his bow lock and dropped it, and raised Saun's head to his lap, letting his right hand slide over the strike zone.

Broken ribs and shattered breathing, heart shocked still. Dag let his groundsense, nearly extinguished so as to block his targets' agony, come up fully, then flow into the boy. The pain was immense. *Heart first.* He concentrated himself there. A dangerous unity, if the yoked organs both chose to stop instead of start. A burning, lumping sensation in his own chest mirrored the boy's. *Come on, Saun, dance with me . . .* A flutter, a stutter, a bruised limping. Stronger. Now the lungs. One breath, two, three, and the chest rose again, then again, and finally steadied in synchrony. Good, yes, heart and lungs would continue on their own.

The stunning reverberation of Saun's targets' ill fates still sloshed through the boy's system, insufficiently blocked. Mari would have some work there, later. *I hate fighting humans.* Regretfully, Dag let the pain flow back to its source. The boy would be walking bent over for a month, but he would live.

The world returned to his senses. Around the clearing, bandits were starting to surrender as the yelling Glassforge men arrived and broke from the woods. Dag grabbed up his bow and rose to his feet, looking around. Beyond the burning tent, he spotted Mari. *Dag!* her mouth moved, but the cry was lost in the noise. She raised two fingers, pointed beyond the clearing on the opposite side, and snapped them down against her armguard. Dag's head swiveled.

Two bandits had dodged through the perimeter and were running away. Dag waved his bow in acknowledgment, and cried to his left linker, "Utau! Take Saun?"

Utau signaled his receipt of Dag's injured partner. Dag turned to give chase, trying to reaffix the bow to its clamp as he ran. By the time he'd succeeded, he was well beyond the light from the fires. Closer . . .

The horse nearly ran him down; he leaped away barely before he could be knocked aside. The fugitives were riding double, a big man in front and a huge one behind.

No. That second one wasn't a man.

Dizzied with excitement, the chase, and the aftershock of Saun's injury, Dag bent a moment, gasping for control of his own breathing. His hand rose to check the twin knife sheath hung under his shirt, a reassuring lump against his chest. Dark, warm, mortal hum. *Mud-man. We have you. You and your maker are ours . . .*

He despised tracking from horseback, but he wasn't going to catch them on foot, not even with that dual burden. He calmed himself again, down, down, *ours!*, *down* curse it, and summoned his horse. It would take Copperhead several minutes to blunder through the woods from the patrol's hidden assembly point. He knelt and removed his bow again, unstrung and stored it, and fumbled out the most useful of his hand replacements, a simple hook with a flat tongue of springy steel set against its outside curve to act as a sometimes-pincer. Tapping out a resin soaked stick from the tin case in his vest pocket, he set it in the pinch of the spring and persuaded it to ignite. As the flare burned down to its end, he shuffled back and forth studying the hoofprints. When he was sure he could recognize them again, he pushed to his feet.

His quarry had nearly passed the limit of his groundsense by the time his mount arrived, snorting, and Dag swung aboard. Where one horse went another could follow, right? He kicked Copperhead after them at a speed that would have had Mari swearing at him for risking his fool neck in the dark. *Mine.*

Fawn plodded.

Now that she was finally coming out of the flats into the southeastern hills, the straight road was not as level as it had run since Lumpton, nor as straight. Its gentle slopes and curves were interspersed with odd climbs up through narrow, choked ravines that slashed through the rock, or down to timber bridges replacing shattered stone spans that lay like old bones between one impossible jumping-off point and another. The track dodged awkwardly around old rockfalls, or wet its feet and hers in fords.

Fawn wondered when she would finally reach Glassforge. It couldn't be too much farther, for all that she had made a slow start this dawn. The last of the good bread had stayed down, at least. The day threatened to grow hot and sticky, later. Here, the road was pleasantly shaded, with woods crowding up to both sides.

So far this morning she had passed a farm cart, a pack train of mules, and a small flock of sheep, all going the other way. She'd encountered nothing else for nearly an hour. Now she raised her head to see a horse coming toward her, down the road a piece. Also going the wrong way, unfortunately. As it neared, she stepped aside. Not only headed north, but also already double-loaded. Bareback. The animal was plodding almost as wearily as Fawn, its unbrushed dun hair smeared with salty crusts of dried sweat, burrs matting its black mane and tail.

The riders seemed as tired and ill kept as the horse. A big fellow looking not much older than her actual age rode in front, all rumpled jacket and stubbled chin. Behind him, his bigger companion clung on. The second man had lumpy features and long untrimmed nails so crusted with dirt as to look black, and a blank expression. His too-small clothes seemed an afterthought: a ragged shirt hanging open with sleeves rolled up, trousers that did not reach his boot tops. His age was hard to guess. Fawn wondered if he was a simpleton. They both looked as though they were making their way home from a night of drinking, or worse. The young man bore a big hunting knife, though the other seemed weaponless. Fawn marched past with the briefest nod, making no greeting to them, though out of the corner of her eye she could see both their heads turn. She walked on, not looking back.

The receding rhythm of hoofbeats stopped. She dared a glance over her shoulder. The two men seemed to be arguing, in voices too hushed and rumbling for her to make out the words, except a reiterated, "Master want!" in rising, urgent tones from the simpleton, and a sharp, aggravated "Why?" from the other. She lowered her face and walked faster. The hoofbeats started again, but instead of fading into the distance, grew louder.

The animal loomed alongside. "Morning," the younger man called down in a would-be cheerful tone. Fawn glanced up. He tugged his dirty blond hair at her politely, but his smile did not reach his eyes. The simpleton just stared tensely at her.

Fawn combined a civil nod with a repelling frown, starting to think, *Please, let there be a cart. Cows. Other riders, anything, I don't care which direction.*

"Going to Glassforge?" he inquired.

"I'm expected," Fawn returned shortly. *Go away. Just turn around and go away.*

"Family there?"

"Yes." She considered inventing some large Glassforge brothers and uncles, or just relocating the real ones. The plague of her life, she almost wished for them now.

The simpleton thumped his friend on the shoulder, scowling. "No talk. Just take." His voice came out smeared, as though his mouth was the wrong shape inside.

A manure wagon would be just lovely. One with a lot of people on board, preferably.

"You do it, then," snapped the young man.

The simpleton shrugged, braced his hands, and slid himself off right over the horse's rump. He landed more neatly than Fawn would have expected. She lengthened her stride; then, as he came around the horse toward her, she broke into a dead run, looking around frantically.

The trees were no help. Anything she could climb, he could too. To get out of sight long enough to hide in the woods, she had to outpace her pursuer by an impossible margin. Might she stay ahead until a miracle occurred, such as someone riding around that long curve up ahead?

He moved faster than she would have guessed for a man that size, too. Before her third breath or step, huge hands clamped around her upper arms and lifted her right off her pumping feet. At this range she could see that their nails were not just dirty but utterly black, like claws. They bit through her jacket as he swung her around.

She yelled as loud as she could, "Let go of me! Let go!" followed up with throat-searing screams. She kicked and struggled with all her strength. It was like fighting an oak tree, for all the result she got.

"Well, now you've got her all riled up," said the young man in disgust. He too slid off the horse, stared a moment, and pulled off the rope holding up his trousers. "We'll have to tie her hands. Unless you want your eyes clawed out."

Good idea. Fawn tried. Useless: the simpleton's hands remained clamped on her wrists, yanked high over her head. She writhed around and bit a bare, hairy arm. The huge man's skin had a most peculiar smell and taste, like cat fur, not as foul as she would have expected. Her satisfaction at drawing blood was short-lived as he spun her around and, still without visible emotion, fetched her an open-handed slap across the face that snapped her head back and dropped her to the road, black-and-purple shadows boiling up in her vision.

Her ears were still ringing when she was jerked upright and tied, then lifted. The simpleton handed her up to the young man, now back aboard his horse. He shoved at her skirts and set her upright in front of him, both hands clamped around her waist. The horse's sweaty barrel was warm under her legs. The simpleton took the reins to lead them and started walking once more, faster.

"There, that's better," said the man who held her, his sour breath wafting past her ear. "Sorry he hit you, but you shouldn't have run from him. Come on along, you'll have more fun with me." One hand wandered up and squeezed her breast. "Huh. Riper than I thought."

Fawn, gasping for air and still shuddering with shock, licked at a wet trickle from her nose. Was it tears, or blood, or both? She pulled surreptitiously at the rope around her wrists uncomfortably binding her hands. The knots seemed very tight. She considered more screaming. No, they might hit her again, or gag her. Better to pretend to be stunned, and then if they passed anyone within shouting distance, she'd still have command of her voice and her legs.

This hopeful plan lasted all of ten minutes, when, before anyone else hove into sight, they turned right off the road onto a hidden path. The young man's clutch had turned into an almost lazy embrace, and his hands wandered up and down her torso. As they started up a slope, he hitched forward as she slid backward, shoved her bedroll out of the way, and held her backside more tightly against his front, letting the horse's movement rub them together.

As much as this flagrant interest frightened her, she wasn't sure but what the simpleton's indifference frightened her more. The young man was being nasty in predictable ways. The other . . . she had no idea what he was thinking, if anything.

Well, if this is going where it looks, at least they can't make me pregnant. Thank you, stupid Sunny Sawman. As bright sides went, that one stank like a cesspit, but she had to allow the point. She hated her body's trembling, signaling her fear to her captor, but she could not stop it. The simpleton led them deeper into the woods.

Dag stood in his stirrups when the distant yelling echoed through the trees from the broad ravine, so high and fierce that he could barely distinguish words: *Let! Go!*

He kicked his horse into a trot, ignoring the branches that swiped and scratched them both. The strange marks he'd read in the road a couple of miles back suddenly grew a lot more worrisome. He'd been trailing his quarry at the outermost edge of his groundsense for hours, now, while the night's exhaustion crept up on his body and wits, hoping that they were leading him to the malice's lair. His suspicion that a new concern had been added to his pack chilled his belly as the outraged cries continued.

He popped over a rise and took a fast shortcut down an erosion gully with his horse nearly sliding on its haunches. His quarry came into sight at last in a small clearing. *What . . . ?* He snapped his jaw shut and cantered forward, heedless of his own noise now. Pulled up at ten paces, flung himself off, let his hand go through the steps of stringing and mounting and locking his bow without conscious thought.

It was abundantly clear that he wasn't interrupting someone's tryst. The kneeling mud-man, blank-faced, was holding down the shoulders of a struggling figure who was obscured by his comrade. The other man was trying, simultaneously, to pull down his trousers and part the legs of the captive, who was kicking valiantly at him. He cursed as a small foot connected.

"*Hold* her!"

"No time to stop," grumbled the mud-man. "Need to go on. No time for this."

"It won't take long if you just . . . hold her . . . still!" He finally managed to shove his hips inside the angle of the kicks.

Absent gods, was that a *child* they were pinning to the dirt? Dag's groundsense threatened to boil over; distracted or no, the mud-man must notice him soon even if the other had his backside turned. The middle figure surged upward briefly, face flushed and black curls flying, dress pulled half-down as well as shoved half-up. A flash of sweet breasts like apples smote Dag's eyes. *Oh.* That short rounded form was no child after all. But outweighed like one nonetheless.

Dag quelled his fury and drew. Those heaving moon-colored buttocks had to be the most righteous target ever presented to his aim. And for once in his accursed life, it seemed he was *not too late.* He considered this marvel for the whole moment it took to adjust his tension to be sure the arrow would not go through and into the girl. Woman. Whatever she was.

Release.

He was reaching for another shaft before the first found its mark. The perfection of the *thunk,* square in the middle of the left cheek, was even more satisfying than the surprised scream that followed. The bandit bucked and rolled off the girl, howling and trying to reach around himself, twisting from side to side.

Now the danger was not halved, but doubled. The mud-man stood abruptly, seeing Dag at last, and dragged the girl up in front of his torso as a shield. His height and her shortness thwarted his intent; Dag sent his next shaft toward the creature's calf. It was a glancing hit, but stung. The mud-man leaped.

Did this one have enough wits to threaten his prisoner in order to stop Dag? Dag didn't wait to find out. Lips drawn back in a fierce grin, he drew his war knife and pelted forward. Death was in his stride.

The mud-man saw it; fear flashed in that sullen, lumpy face. With a panicked heave, he tossed the crying girl toward Dag, turned, and fled.

Bow still encumbering his left arm, the knife in his right hand, Dag had no way to catch her. The best he could do was fling his arms wide so that she wasn't stabbed or battered. He lost his skidding balance on her impact, and they both went down in a tangle.

For a moment, she was on top of him, her breath knocked out, her body's softness squashed onto his. She inhaled, made a strained squeaking noise, yanked herself up, and began clawing at his face. He tried to get out words to calm her, but she wouldn't let him; finally he was forced to let go of his weapon and just fling her off. With two live enemies still on the ground, he would have to deal with her *next.* He rolled away, snatched up his knife again, and surged to his feet.

The mud-man had scrambled back up on the bandit's horse. He yanked the beast's head around and tried to ride Dag down. Dag dodged, started to flip his knife around for a throw, thought better of it, dropped it again, reached back to his now-twisted-around quiver, and drew one of his few remaining arrows. Nocked, aimed.

No.

Let the creature keep running, back to the lair. Dag could pick up those tracks again if he had to. One wounded prisoner would test the limits of what he could handle right now. A prisoner who was, most definitely, going to be made to talk. The horse vanished up the faint trail leading out of the clearing that paralleled the course of a nearby creek. Dag lowered the bow and looked around.

The human bandit too had disappeared, but for once, tracking was not going to be any trouble. Dag pointed to the girl, now standing up a few yards away and struggling to readjust her torn blue dress. "*Stay* there." He followed the blood trail.

Past a screen of saplings and brush lining the clearing, the splashes grew heavier. By the boulders of the creek a figure lay prone and silent in a red puddle, trousers about his knees, Dag's arrow clutched in his hand.

Too still. Dag set his teeth. The man had evidently tried to drag the maddening shaft out of his flesh by main force, and must have ripped open an artery doing so. *That wasn't a killing shot, blight it!* Wasn't supposed to be. *Good intentions, where have we met before?* Dag balanced himself and shoved the body over with one foot. The pale unshaven face looked terribly young in death, even shadowed as it was by dirt. No answers now to be squeezed from this one; he had reached the last of all betrayals.

"Absent gods. *More* children. Is there no end to them?" Dag muttered.

He looked up to see the woman-child standing a few paces back along the blood trail, staring at them both. Her eyes were huge and brown, like a terrified deer's. At least she wasn't screaming anymore. She frowned down at her late assailant, and an unvoiced *Oh* ghosted from her tender, bitten lips. A livid bruise was starting up one side of her face, scored with four parallel red gouges. "He's dead?"

"Unfortunately. And unnecessarily. If he'd just lain still and waited for help, I'd have taken him prisoner."

She looked him up, and up, and down, fearfully. The top of her dark head, were they standing closer, would come just about to the middle of his chest, Dag judged. Self-consciously, he tucked his bow hand down by his side, half out of sight around his thigh, and sheathed his knife.

"I know who you are!" she said suddenly. "You're that Lakewalker patroller I saw at the well-house!"

Dag blinked, and blinked again, and let his groundsense, shielded from the shock of this death, come up again. She blazed in his perceptions. "Little Spark! What are you doing so far from your farm?"

3

The tall patroller was staring at Fawn as though he recognized her. She wrinkled her nose in confusion, not following his words. From this angle and distance, she could at last see the color of his eyes, which were an unexpected metallic gold. They seemed very bright in his bony face, against weathered skin tanned to a dark coppery sheen on his face and hand. Several sets of scratches scored his cheeks and forehead and jaw, most just red but some bleeding. *I did that, oh dear.*

Beyond, the body of her would-be ravisher lay on the smoothed stones of the creek bank. Some of his still-wet blood trickled into the creek, to swirl away in the clear water in faint red threads, dissipating to pink and then gone. He had been so hotly, heavily, frighteningly alive just minutes ago, when she had wished him dead. Now she had her wish, she was not so sure.

"I . . . it . . . " she began, waving an uncertain hand at, well, everything, then blurted, "I'm sorry I scratched you up. I didn't understand what was coming at me." Then added, "You scared me." *I think I've lost my wits.*

A hesitant smile turned the patroller's lips, making him look for a moment like someone altogether else. Not so . . . looming. "I was trying to scare the other fellow."

"It worked," she allowed, and the smile firmed briefly before fleeing again.

He felt his face, glanced at the red smears on his fingertips as if surprised, then shrugged and looked back at her. The weight of his attention was startling to her, as though no one in her life had ever looked at her before, really looked; in her present shaky state, it was not a comfortable sensation.

"Are you all right otherwise?" he asked gravely. His right hand made an inquiring jerk. The other he still held down by his side, the short, powerful-looking bow cocked at an angle out of the way by his leg. "Aside from your face."

"My face?" Her quivering fingertips probed where the simpleton had struck her. Still a little numb, but starting to ache. "Does it show?"

He nodded.

"Oh."

"Those gouges don't look so good. I have some things in my saddle-bags to clean them up. Come away, here, come sit down, um . . . away."

From that. She eyed the corpse and swallowed. "All right." And added, "I'm all right. I'll stop shaking in a minute, sure. Stupid of me."

With his open hand not coming within three feet of her, he herded her back toward the clearing like someone shooing ducks. He pointed to a big fallen log a way apart from the scuffed spot of her recent struggle and walked to his horse, a rangy chestnut calmly browsing in the weeds trailing its reins. She plunked down heavily and sat bent over, arms wrapped around herself, rocking a little. Her throat was raw, her stomach hurt, and though she wasn't gasping anymore, it still felt as though she couldn't get her breath back or that it had returned badly out of rhythm.

The patroller carefully turned his back to Fawn, did something to dismantle his bow, and rummaged in his saddlebag. More adjustments of some sort. He turned again, shrugging the strap of a water bottle over one shoulder, and with a couple of cloth-wrapped packets tucked under his left arm. Fawn blinked, because he seemed to have suddenly regained a left hand, stiffly curved in a leather glove.

He lowered himself beside her with a tired-sounding grunt, and arranged those legs. At this range he smelled, not altogether unpleasantly, of dried sweat, woodsmoke, horse, and fatigue. He laid out the packets and handed her the bottle. "Drink, first."

She nodded. The water was flat and tepid but seemed clean.

"Eat." He held out a piece of bread fished from the one cloth.

"I couldn't."

"No, really. It'll give your body something to do besides shake. Very distractible that way, bodies. Try it."

Doubtfully, she took it and nibbled. It was very good bread, if a little dry by now, and she thought she recognized its source. She had to take another sip of water to force it down, but her uncontrolled trembling grew less. She peeked at his still left hand as he opened the second cloth, and decided it must be carved of wood, for show.

He wetted a bit of cloth with something from a small bottle—Lakewalker medicine?—and raised his right hand to her aching left cheek. She flinched, although the cool liquid did not sting.

"Sorry. Don't want to leave those dirty."

"No. Yes. I mean, right. It's all right. I think the simpleton clawed me when he hit me." Claws. Those had been claws, not nails. What kind of monstrous birth . . . ?

His lips thinned, but his touch remained firm.

"I'm sorry I didn't come up on you sooner, miss. I could see something had happened back on the road, there. I'd been trailing those two all night. My patrol seized their gang's camp a couple of hours after midnight, up in the hills on the other side of Glassforge. I'm afraid I flushed them right into you."

She shook her head, not in denial. "I was walking down the road. They just picked me up like you'd pick up a lost . . . thing, and claim it was yours." Her frown deepened. "No . . . not just. They argued first.

Strange. The one who was . . . um . . . the one you shot, he didn't want to take me along, at first. It was the other one who insisted. But he wasn't interested in me at all, later. When—just before you came." And added under her breath, not expecting an answer, "What *was* he?"

"Raccoon, is my best guess," said the patroller. He turned the cloth, hiding browning blood, and wet it again, moving down her cheek to the next gash.

This bizarre answer seemed so entirely unrelated to her question that she decided he must not have heard her aright. "No, I mean the big fellow who hit me. The one who ran away from you. He didn't seem right in the head."

"Truer than you guess, miss. I've been hunting those creatures all my life. You get so you can tell. He was a made thing. Confirms that a malice—your folk would call it a blight bogle—has emerged near here. The malice makes slaves of human shape for itself, to fight, or do its dirty work. Other shapes too, sometimes. Mud-men, we call them. But the malice can't make them up out of nothing. So it catches animals, and reshapes them. Crudely at first, till it grows stronger and smarter. Can't make life at all, really. Only death. Its slaves don't last too long, but it hardly cares."

Was he gulling her, like her brothers? Seeing how much a silly little farm girl could be made to swallow down whole? He seemed perfectly serious, but maybe he was just especially good at tall tales. "Are you saying that blight bogles are *real?*"

It was his turn to look surprised. "Where are you from, miss?" he asked in renewed caution.

She started to name the village nearest her family's farm, but changed it to "Lumpton Market." It was a bigger town, more anonymous. She straightened, trying to marshal the casual phrase *I'm a widow* and push it past her bruised lips.

"What's your name?"

"Fawn. Saw . . . field," she added, and flinched. She'd wanted neither Sunny's name nor her own family's, and now she'd stuck herself with some of both.

"Fawn. Apt," said the patroller, with a sideways tilt of his head. "You must have had those eyes from birth."

It was that uncomfortable weighty attention again. She tried shoving back: "What's yours?" though she thought she already knew.

"I answer to Dag."

She waited a moment. "Isn't there any more?"

He shrugged. "I have a tent name, a camp name, and a hinterland name, but *Dag* is easier to shout." The smile glimmered by again. "Short is better, in the field. *Dag, duck!* See? If it were any longer, it might be too late. Ah, that's better."

She realized she'd smiled back. She didn't know if it was his talk or his bread or just the sitting down quietly, but her stomach had finally stopped shuddering. She was left hot and tired and drained.

He restoppered his bottle.

"Shouldn't you use that too?" she asked.

"Oh. Yeah." Cursorily, he turned the cloth again and swiped it over his face. He missed about half the marks.

"Why did you call me Little Spark?"

"When you were hiding above me in that apple tree yesterday, that's how I thought of you."

"I didn't think you could see me. You never looked up!"

"You didn't act as though to wanted to be seen. It only seemed polite." He added, "I thought that pretty farm was your home."

"It *was* pretty, wasn't it? But I only stopped there for water. I was walking to Glassforge."

"From Lumpton?"

And points north. "Yes."

He, at least, did not say anything about, *It's a long way for such short legs.* He did say, inevitably, "Family there?"

She almost said *yes,* then realized he might possibly intend to take her there, which could prove awkward. "No. I was going there to look for work." She straightened her spine. "I'm a grass widow."

A slow blink; his face went blank for a rather long moment. He finally said, in an oddly cautious tone, "Pardon, missus . . . but do you know what *grass widow* means?"

"A new widow," she replied promptly, then hesitated. "There was a woman came up from Glassforge to our village, once. She took in sewing and made cord and netting. She had the most beautiful little boy. My uncles called her a grass widow." Another too-quiet pause. "That's right, isn't it?"

He scratched his rat's nest of dark hair. "Well . . . yes and no. It's a farmer term for a woman pregnant or with a child in tow with no husband in sight anywhere. It's more polite than, um, less polite terms. But it's not altogether kind."

Fawn flushed.

He said even more apologetically, "I didn't mean to embarrass you. It just seemed I ought to check."

She swallowed. "Thank you." *It seems I told the truth despite myself, then.*

"And your little girl?" he said.

"What?" said Fawn sharply.

He motioned at her. "The one you bear now."

Flat panic stopped her breath. *I don't show! How can he know?* And how could he know, in any case, if the fruit of that really, really ill-considered and now deeply regretted frantic fumble with Sunny Sawman at his sister's spring wedding party was going to be a boy or a girl, anyhow?

He seemed to realize he'd made some mistake, but to be uncertain what it was. His gesture wavered, turning to open-handed earnestness. "It was what attracted the mud-man. Your present state. It was almost certainly why they grabbed you. If the other assault seemed an after-thought, it likely was."

"How can you—what—*why?*"

His lips parted for a moment, then, visibly, he changed whatever he'd been about to say to: "Nothing's going to happen to you now." He packed up his cloths. Anyone else might have tied the corners together, but he whipped a bit of cord around them that he somehow managed to wind into a pull-knot one-handed.

He put his right hand on the log and shoved himself to his feet. "I either need to put that body up a tree or pile some rocks on it, so the scavengers don't get to it before someone can pick it up. He might have people." He looked around vaguely. "Then decide what to do with you."

"Put me back on the road. Or just point me to it. I can find it."

He shook his head. "Those might not be the only fugitives. Not all the bandits might have been in the camp we took, or they might have had more than one hideout. And the malice is still out there, unless my patrol has got ahead of me, which I don't think is possible. My people were combing the hills to the south of Glassforge, and now I think the lair's northeast. This is no good time or place for you, especially, to be wandering about on your own." He bit his lip and went on almost as if talking to himself, "Body can wait. Got to put you somewhere safe. Pick up the track again, find the lair, get back to my patrol quick as I can. Absent gods, I'm tired. Mistake to sit down. Can you ride behind me, do you think?"

She almost missed the question in his mumble. *I'm tired too.* "On your horse? Yes, but—"

"Good."

He went to his mount and caught up the reins, but instead of coming back to her, led it to the creek. She trailed along again, partly curious, partly not wanting to let him out of her sight.

He evidently decided a tree would be faster for stowing his prey. He tossed a rope up over the crotch of a big sycamore that overhung the creek, using his horse to haul the body up it. He climbed up to be sure the corpse was securely wedged and to retrieve his rope. He moved so efficiently, Fawn could scarcely spot the extra motions and accommodations he made for his one-handed state.

Dag pressed his tired horse over the last ridge and was rewarded on the other side by finding a double-rutted track bumping along the creek bottom. "Ah, good," he said aloud. "It's been a while since I patrolled down this way, but I recall a good-sized farm tucked up at the head of this valley."

The girl clinging behind his cantle remained too quiet, the same wary silence she'd maintained since he'd discussed her pregnant state. His groundsense, extended to utmost sensitivity in search for hidden threats, was battered by her nearby churning emotions; but the thoughts that drove them remained, as ever, opaque. He had maybe been too indiscreet. Farmers who found out much about Lakewalker groundsense tended to call it the evil eye, or black magic, and accuse patrollers of mind reading, cheating in trade, or worse. It was always trouble.

If he found enough people at this farm, he would leave her in their care, with strong warnings about the half-hunt-half-war presently going on in their hills. If there weren't enough, he must try to persuade them to light out for Glassforge or some other spot where they might find safety in numbers till this malice was taught mortality. If he knew farmers, they wouldn't want to go, and he sighed in anticipation of a dreary and thankless argument.

But the mere thought of a pregnant woman of any height or age wandering about in blithe ignorance anywhere near a malice's lair gave him gruesome horrors. No wonder she'd shone so brightly in his ground-sense, with so much life happening in her. Although he suspected Fawn would have been scarcely less vivid even before this conception. But she would attract a malice's attention the way a fire drew moths.

By the time they'd straightened out the definition of *grass widow,* he had been fairly sure he had no need to offer her condolences. Farmer bed customs made very little sense, sometimes, unless one believed Mari's theories about their childbearing being all mixed up with their pretense of owning land. She had some very tart remarks on farmer women's lack of control of their own fertility, as well. Generally in conjunction with lectures to young patrollers of both sexes about the need to keep their trousers buttoned while in farmer territory.

Old patrollers, too.

Details of a dead husband had been conspicuously absent in Fawn's speech. Dag could understand grief robbing someone of words, but grief, too, seemed missing in her. Anger, fear, tense determination, yes. Shock from the recent terrifying attack upon her. Loneliness and homesickness. But not the anguish of a soul ripped in half. Strangely lacking, too, was the profound satisfaction such lifegiving usually engendered among Lakewalker women he'd known. Farmers, feh. Dag knew why his own people were all a little crazed, but what excuse did farmers have?

He was roused from his weary brooding as they passed out of the woods and the valley farm came into sight. He was instantly ill at ease. The lack of cows and horses and goats and sheep struck him first, then the broken-down places in the split-rail fence lining the pasture. Then the absence of farm dogs, who should have been barking annoyingly around his horse by now. He stood in his stirrups as they plodded up the lane. House and barn, both built of weathered gray planks, were standing—and standing open—but smoke rose in a thin trickle from the char and ashes of an outbuilding.

"What is it?" asked Fawn, the first words she'd spoken for an hour.

"Trouble, I think." He added after a moment, "Trouble past." Nothing human flared in the range of Dag's perceptions—nor anything non-human either. "The place is completely deserted."

He pulled up his horse in front of the house, swung his leg over its neck, and jumped down. "Move up. Take the reins," he told Fawn. "Don't get down yet."

She scrambled forward from her perch on his saddlebags, staring around wide-eyed. "What about you?"

"Going to scout around."

He made a quick pass through the house, a rambling two-story structure with additions built on to additions. The place seemed stripped of small objects of any value. Items too big to carry—beds, clothes chests—were frequently knocked over or split. Every glass window was broken out, senselessly. Dag had an idea how hard those improvements had been to come by, carefully saved for by some hopeful farmwife, packed in straw up from Glassforge over the rutted lanes. The kitchen pantry was stripped of food.

The barn was empty of animals; hay was left, some grain might be gone. Behind the barn on the manure pile, he at last found the bodies of three farm dogs, slashed and hacked about. He eyed the smoldering outbuilding in passing, charred timbers sticking out of the ash like black bones. Someone would need to look through it for other bones, later. He returned to his horse.

Fawn was gazing around warily as she took in the disturbing details. Dag leaned against Copperhead's warm shoulder and swiped his hand through his hair.

"The place was raided by the bandits—or someone—about three days ago, I judge," he told her. "No bodies."

"That's good—yes?" she said, dark eyes growing unsure at whatever expression was leaking onto his features. He couldn't think that it was anything but exhaustion.

"Maybe. But if the people had run away, or been run off, news of this should have reached Glassforge by now. My patrol had no such word as of yesterday evening."

"Where did they all go, then?" she asked.

"Taken, I'm afraid. If this malice is trying to take farmer slaves already, it's growing fast."

"What—slaves for what?"

"Not sure the malice even knows, yet. It's a sort of instinct with malices. It'll figure it out fast enough, though. I'm running out of time." He was growing dizzy with fatigue. Was he also growing stupid with fatigue?

He continued, "I'd give almost anything for two hours of sleep right now, except two hours of light. I need to get back to the trail while I still have daylight to see it. I think . . . " His voice slowed. "I think this place is as safe as any and safer than most. They've hit it once, it's already stripped of everything valuable—they won't be back too soon. I'm thinking maybe I could leave you here anyway. If anyone comes, you can tell them—no. First, if anyone comes, hide, till you are sure they're all-right folks. Then come out and tell them Dag has a message for his patrol, he thinks the malice is holed up northeast of town, not south. If patrollers come, do you think you could show them to where the tracks led off? And that boy's—bandit's—body," he added in afterthought.

She squinted at the wooded hills. "I'm not sure I could find my way back to it, the route you took."

"There's an easier way. This lane"—he waved at the track they'd ridden up—"goes back to the straight road in about four miles. Turn left, and I think the path your mud-man took east from it is about three miles on."

"Oh," she said more eagerly, "I could find that, sure."

"Good, then."

She had no fear, blast and blight it. He could change that . . . So did he want her to be terrified out of her mind, frozen witless? She was already sliding down off the horse, looking pleased to have a task within her capacity.

"What's so dangerous about the mud-men?" she asked, as he gathered his reins and prepared to mount once more.

He hesitated a long moment. "They'll eat you," he said at last. *After everything else is all over, that is.*

"Oh."

Subdued and impressed. And, more important, believing him. Well, it hadn't been a lie. Maybe it would make her just cautious enough. He found his stirrup and pushed up, trying not to dwell on the contrast between this hard saddle and a feather bed. There had been one unslashed feather mattress left inside the farmhouse. He'd noticed it particularly, while shoving aside a little fantasy about falling into it face-first. He swung his horse around.

"Dag . . . ?"

He turned at once to look over his shoulder. Big brown eyes stared up at him from a face like a bruised flower.

"Don't let them eat you, either."

Involuntarily, his lips turned up; she smiled brightly back through her darkening contusions. It gave him an odd feeling in his stomach, which he prudently did not attempt to name. Heartened despite all, he raised his carved hand in salute and cantered back down the lane.

Feeling bereft, Fawn watched the patroller vanish into the tunnel of trees at the edge of the fields. The silence of this homestead, stripped of animals and people, was eerie and oppressive, once she noticed it. She squinted upward. The sun had not even topped the arch of the sky for noon. It seemed years since dawn.

She sighed and ventured into the house. She walked all around it, footsteps echoing, feeling as though she intruded on some stranger's grief. The senseless mess the raiders had left in their wake seemed overwhelming, taken in all at once. She came back to the kitchen and stood there shivering a little. Well, if the house was too much, what about one room? *I could fix one room, yes.*

She braced herself and started by turning back upright anything that would still stand, shelf and table and a couple of chairs. What was broken beyond mending she hauled outside, starting a pile at one end of the porch. Then she swept the floor clear of broken plates and glass and spilled flour and drying food. She swept the porch too, while she was at it.

Beneath a worn old rag rug, ignored by the invaders, she found a trapdoor with a rope handle. She shook the rug over the porch rail, returned, and stared worriedly at the trap. *I don't think Dag saw this.*

She bit her lip, then took a bucket with a broken handle outside and collected a few live coals from the still-smoldering whatever-it-had-been, and started a little fire in the kitchen hearth. From it, she lit a candle stub found in the back of a drawer. She pulled up the trapdoor by its rope, wincing at the groaning of its hinges, swallowed, and stared at the ladder into the dark hole. Could there be anyone still hiding down there? Big spiders? . . . Bodies? She took a deep breath and descended.

When she turned and held up the candle, her lips parted in astonishment. The cellar was lined with shelves, and on them, untouched, were row upon row of glass jars, many sealed with hot rock wax and covered with cloth bound with twine. Food storage for a farm full of hungry people. A year of labor lined up—Fawn knew exactly how much work, too, as preserving boiled foodstuffs under wax seals had been one of her most satisfying tasks back home. None of the jars were labeled, but her eye had no trouble picking out and identifying the contents. Fruit preserves. Vinegar pickles. Corn relish. Stew meat. A barrel in the corner proved to hold several sacks of flour. Another held last year's apples packed in straw, terribly wrinkly and by now only suitable for cooking, but not rotted. She was stirred to enthusiasm, and action.

Most of the jars were big, meant for a crowd, but she found three smaller ones, of dark purple fruit, corn relish, and what she trusted was stew meat, and hauled them up into the light. A kerchief full of flour, as well. A single iron pan, which she found kicked into a corner under a fallen shelf, was all that was left of the tools of this workplace, but with a little ingenuity she soon had flatbread cooking in it over her fire. The jar of meat proved to be, probably, pork cooked to flinders with onions and herbs, which she heated up after she'd freed the pan of her bread circles.

She caught up on days of scant rations, then, replete, set aside portions made up for Dag when he returned. Clearly, judging from his lady patrol leader and his general build, he was the sort of fellow you had to capture, hog-tie, and make remember to eat. Was he just a goer, or did he live too much inside his own head to notice his body's needs? And what all else was that head furnished with? He seemed driven. Considering the almost casual physical courage he'd displayed so far, it was unsettling to consider what he might fear that pushed him along so unceasingly. *Well, if I were as tall as a tree, maybe I'd be brave too.* A skinny tree. Upon consideration, she wrapped the meat and the preserves in rolls of flatbread so that he might eat while riding, because when he came back, it was likely he'd be in a hurry still.

If he came back. He hadn't actually said. The thought made a disappointed cold spot in her belly. *Now you're being stupid. Stop it.* The cure for bad sad thoughts was busyness, right enough, but she was getting dreadfully tired.

In one of the other rooms she found an abandoned sewing basket, also overlooked by the raiders, probably because the mending that topped it looked like rags. They'd entirely missed the valuable tools inside, sharp scissors and good thimbles and a collection of fine iron needles. Were the blight bogle's—malice's—mud-men all men then? Did it make any mud-women? It seemed not.

She decided she would sew up some of the slashed feather ticks in payment for the food, so it wouldn't feel so stolen. Sewing was not her best skill, but straight seams would be simple enough, and it would put an end to the messy, desolate feather wrack drifting about the place. She hauled the ticks out onto the porch, for the light, and so she could watch down the lane for a tall—for whoever. Needle and thread and fine repetitive work made a soothing rhythm under her hands. In the quiet, her mind circled back to this morning's terror. Dwelling on it started to make her feel sick and shaky again. As an alternative, she wrenched her thoughts to Lakewalkers.

Farmer to a Lakewalker didn't mean someone who grew crops; it meant anyone who wasn't a Lakewalker. Townsmen, rivermen, miners, millers—bandits—evidently they were all farmers in Dag's eyes. She wondered at the implications. She'd heard a story about a girl from over to Coshoton who had been seduced by a passing Lakewalker, a trading man, it was said. She had run away north three times to Lakewalker country after him, and been brought back by his people, then hanged herself in the woods. A cautionary tale, that. Fawn wondered what lesson you were supposed to draw from it. Well, *Girls should stay away from Lakewalkers* was the one obviously intended, but maybe the real one was,

If something doesn't work once, don't just repeat it twice more, try something else, or *Don't give up so soon.* Or *Stay out of the woods.*

The nameless girl had died for thwarted love, it was whispered, but Fawn wondered if it hadn't been for thwarted rage, instead. She had, she admitted to herself, had some such thoughts after that awful talk with Stupid Sunny, but it wasn't that she'd wanted to *die,* it was that she'd wanted to make him feel as bad as he'd made her feel. And it had been rather flattening to reflect that she'd not be alive to properly enjoy her revenge, and even more flattening to suspect he'd get over any guilt pretty quick. Long before she'd get over being dead, in any case. And she'd done nothing that night after all, and by the next day, she'd had other ideas. So maybe the real lesson was, *Wait till morning, after breakfast.*

She wondered if the hanged girl had been pregnant too. Then she wondered anew how the tall man had *known,* seemingly just by looking at her with those eyes, their shimmering gold by sudden turns cold as metal or warm as summer. *Sorcerers, huh.* Dag didn't look like a sorcerer. (And what did sorcerers look like anyhow?) He looked like a very tired hunter who had been too long away from home. Hunting things that hunted him back.

A girl baby. Maybe he was just guessing. Fifty percent odds weren't half-bad, for appearing right, later. Still, it was an encouraging thought. Girls she knew. A little boy, however innocent, might have reminded her too much of Sunny. She hadn't meant to be a mother so soon in her life at all, but if she was going to be stuck with it, she would very well try to be a good one. She rubbed absently at her belly. *I will not betray you.* A bold promise. How was she to keep a child safe when she couldn't even save herself? *Also, from now on, I will be more careful.* Anyone could make a mistake. The trick was not to make the same one twice.

She eventually ran out of ripped fabric, patience to brood, and the will to stay awake. Her bruised face was throbbing. She hauled the repaired ticks back inside and piled them four deep in a corner of the kitchen, because the next room was still a disheartening mess and she hadn't the energy left to tackle it. She fell gratefully onto the pile. She had barely time to register the musty scent of them, and reflect that they were overdue for an airing anyhow, when her leaden eyes closed.

Fawn woke to the sound of steps on the wooden porch. Dag back already? It was still light. How long had she slept? Blearily, she pushed up, eager to show him the overlooked treasures in the cellar and to hear what he'd found. Only then did it register that there were too *many* heavy steps out there.

She should have been overlooked in the cellar —*I could have thrown a couple of those mattresses down there*—She had just time to think *What good is it to not to make the same mistakes twice when your new ones'll kill you all the same?* before the three mud-men burst open the door.

4

When the faint path he was following up into the hills turned into something more resembling a beaten trail, Dag decided it was time to get off it. Groundsense or common sense or sheer nerves, he could not tell, but he dismounted and led his horse aside into the woods to a small glade well out of sight and hearing of the track. He hardly needed to lay on suggestions of not-wandering-away; even Copperhead, with his rawhide endurance and his temper, was so tired as to be stumbling. But then, so was Dag. Feeling guilty, he tied the reins up out of the way of front hooves, but left the saddle on. He hated to leave his mount so ill tended, but if he came back in a tearing hurry, there might be no time to fool with gear. Or to hesitate to ride the beast to death, if needs drove hard enough. *Tomorrow, or the day after, we shall all take a better rest. One way or another.*

He did not return to the trail itself but shadowed the track a dozen paces off in the undergrowth. It was slow work, ghosting like a deer, each footfall carefully laid, constantly alert. Not a mile farther on he was glad of his prudence, freezing in a tangle of deadfall and wild grapevines as two figures came thumping openly along the path.

Mud-men. A fox and a rabbit, at a guess, and he hardly needed his inner senses to tell; they were crude, perhaps early efforts, and marks of their animal origin still showed on their hides, their ears, their misshapen faces and noses. It was highly tempting to try to do something with that combination, awaken them to their true-selves and let nature take its course, but the attempt would cost him his cover, perhaps open him to their master beyond. This was no time for games. Regretfully, he let them pass by, grateful that their clumsy new forms included human limitations on their sense of smell in trade for human advantages of hands and speech.

He first knew he was drawing close to the lair by the absence of birds. *This is a day for absences.* He drew his groundsense in even more tightly as the first yellowing, dying weeds began to rustle underfoot. *I wasn't expecting this till miles farther in.* The lair was much closer to the straight road than he'd thought it could possibly be. It was shockingly clever, in a malice so—supposedly—young, for it to send its first human gulls to take prey so far from its initial bastion. *How did we overlook this?*

He knew how. *We are too few, with too much ground to cover and never time enough.* Widen the teeth of the sweeps, speed the search, and risk clues slipping past unobserved. Go slow and close, and risk not getting to all the critical places in time. *Well, we found this one. This is a success, not a failure.*

Maybe.

By the time he reached a vantage he was crawling like a snail, nearly on his belly, scarcely daring to breathe. Every herb and weed around him was dead and brittle, the soil beneath his knees was achingly sterile, and his tightly furled groundsense shivered in the dry shock of the malice's draining aura. *Indeed, it's here.*

At the bottom of a rocky ravine, a creek wound from his right, ran straight below him, and curled away on his left. Not one living plant graced the cleft for as far as he could see in either direction, although the dead bones of a few trees still stood up like sentinels. A camp, of sorts, lay along the creek side: three or four black campfire pits, currently cold, piles of stolen supplies scattered haphazardly about. On the far side of the creek, a couple of uneasy horses stood tied to dead trees. Real, natural horses, as far as Dag could tell. Ill kept, of course.

The space below might accommodate twenty-five or fifty men, but it was nearly deserted at the moment. Exactly one mud-man was asleep on a pile of rags like a nest. Dag wondered if any of the absent company might be men his patrol had captured last night. Which implied that the patrol might well arrive on its own at any time, pleasant thought. He did not allow himself to dwell on the hope.

Partway up the other side of the ravine a shelf of overhanging rock created a cave, perhaps sixty feet long and shielded in front by a smooth gray outcrop of stone pushing up almost to meet the overhang. No telling from here how far back in it went. Paths ran out either end, down to the creek and up over the rise behind.

The malice was inside, at the moment. So was it mobile yet, or still sessile? And if mobile, had it undergone its first molt? And if it hadn't, how frantic would it be to gather the necessary human materials to achieve that? A malice's initial hatching body was even clumsier and cruder than a mud-man's, which generally seemed to irritate it.

Dag opened his shirt and felt for his sharing knives. He pulled the strap over his head and stared a moment at the twin sheaths. The stitched leather was slick with wear and dark with old sweat. He ran one finger over the thread-wound hilts, one blue, one green, drew and contemplated six inches of polished bone blade. Touched it to his lips. It hummed with old mortality.

Is this the day your death is redeemed, Kauneo my love? I have borne it around my neck for so long. As you willed, so I do. This was a vicious malice, big and getting bigger fast. It would nearly be worthy of her, Dag thought. Nearly.

He drew the second, empty bone blade and laid the two back to back. *They come in pairs, oh yes. One for you and one for me.* He slipped them away again.

Mari too bore sharing knives, and so did Utau and Chato, gifts of mortality from patrollers before them. Mari's current set was a legacy from one of her sons, he knew, and as dear to her as these to Dag. The patrol was well supplied. Who used theirs on a malice was not normally a matter of drawing straws, or heroics, or honor. Whoever first could, did. Any way they could. As efficiently as possible. It wasn't as though there wouldn't be another chance later.

Dag's ground was quivering at the drain from the malice's presence, an effect that would bleed over into his body if he lingered here much longer. Sensitive young patrollers were often so disturbed by their first encounter with a malice's aura, it took them weeks to recover. Dag had been one such. Once.

Now: go. Back to the horse, and gallop like a madman to the rendezvous point.

Yet . . . there were so few creatures in the camp. The opportunity beckoned for a, so to speak, single-handed attempt. Down the ravine side, fly across the creek, up into that cave . . . it could all be over in minutes. In the time it took to bring the patrol up, the malice too might draw in its reinforcements (and where were they now, doing what mischief?), turning the attack into a potentially costly fight just to regain a proximity he had right now. Dag thought of Saun. Had he lived the night?

But with his groundsense thwarted, Dag couldn't see how many men or mud-men might be hidden in the cave with the malice. If he went charging in there only to present his head to the enemy, the difficulties his patrol must then face would grow vastly worse. *Also, I would be dead.* In a way, he was glad that last prospect still had the power to disturb him. At least some.

He lowered his face, fought for control of his hastened breathing, and prepared to withdraw. His lips twisted. *Mari will be so proud of me.*

He started to push back from the edge of the ravine, but then froze again. Down a path on the other side, three mud-men appeared. Was that first one a—where had this malice found a *wolf* in these parts? Dag had thought the farmers had reduced wolf numbers in this region, but then, this range of rugged unplowable hills was a reservoir for all sorts of things. *As we see.* His eyes widened as he recognized the second in line, the escaped raccoon-man from this morning. The third, huger still, must once have been a black bear. A flash of familiar dull blue fabric over the giant bear-man's shoulder stopped his breath.

Little Spark. They found Little Spark. How . . . ?

A more or less straight line over the hills to the valley farm from here was the short leg of a triangle, he realized. He had run two long legs, to get from the farm back to where he'd first lost the raccoon-man's traces, then work his way here.

They found her because they went looking, I bet. It accounted for the rest of this malice's absent company; like the two he'd passed on the trail, they had doubtless all been dispatched to comb the hills for the escaped prize. And the malice and its mud-men already knew about the valley farm if they'd recently raided it. Must have known for a long time; his respect for this one's wits notched up again, for it to leave such a nearby tempting target alone, unmolested and unalarmed, for so long. How much strength had it gained, to dare to move openly now? Or had the arrival of Chato's patrol stampeded it?

The blue-clad figure, hanging head down, twitched and struggled. Beat the back of her captor with hard little fists, to no visible effect, except that the bear-man shrugged her hips higher over his shoulder and took a firmer grip on her thighs.

She was alive. Conscious. Undoubtedly terrified.

Not terrified enough. But Dag could make it up for her. His mouth opened, to silence his own speeding breathing, and his heart hammered. Now the malice had just what it needed for its next molt. Dag had only to deliver to it a Lakewalker patroller—and one *so* experienced, too—for its dessert, and its powers would be complete.

He wasn't sure if he was shivering with indecision or just fear. Fear, he decided. Yes, he could run back to the patrol and bring them on in force, by the tested rules, be *sure*. Because the Lakewalkers had to win, every time. But Fawn might be dead by the time they got back.

Or in minutes. The three mud-men vanished behind the occluding rock wall. So, at least three in there. Or there could be ten.

To get in and out of that cave . . . No. He only had to get in.

He didn't know why his brain was still madly trying to calculate risks, because his hand was already moving. Dropping bow and quiver and excess gear. Positioning his sharing-knife sheaths. Swapping out the spring-hook on his wooden wrist cap for the steel knife. Testing the draw of his war knife.

He rose and dropped down over the side of the ravine, sliding from rock to rill as silently as a serpent.

It had all happened so fast . . .

Fawn hung head down, dizzy and nauseated. She wondered if the blow she'd taken on the other side of her face would bruise to match the first. The mud-man's broad shoulder seemed to punch her stomach as it jogged along endlessly, without stopping even when she'd been violently sick down its back. Twice.

When Dag came back to the valley farm—*if* Dag came back to the valley farm—would he be able to read the events from the mess her fight had left in the kitchen? He was a tracker, surely he'd have to notice the footprints in plum jam she had forced her captors to smear across the floor as they'd lunged after her. But it seemed far too much to expect the man to rescue her twice in one day, downright embarrassing, even. Imagining the indignity, she tried one more time to break from the huge mud-man's clutch, beating its back with her fists. She might have been pounding sand for all the difference it made.

She should save her strength for a better chance.

What strength? What chance?

The hot, level sunlight of the summer evening gave way abruptly to gray shadow and the cool smell of dirt and rock. As her captor swung her down and upright, she had a giddy impression of a cave or hollow half-filled with piles of trash. Or war supplies, it was hard to tell. She fought back the black shadows that swarmed over her vision and stood upright, blinking.

Two more of the animal-men rose as if to greet her three escorts. She wondered if they were all about to fall on her and tear her up like a pack of dogs devouring a rabbit. Although she wasn't entirely sure but what that shorter one on the end might have *been* a rabbit, once.

The Voice said, *"Bring her here."*

The words were more clearly spoken than the mud-men's mumblings, but the undertones made her bones feel as though they were melting. She suddenly could not force her trembling face to turn toward the source of that appalling sound. It seemed to flay the wits right out of her mind. *Please let me go please let me go let me go letmego . . .*

The bear-man clutched her shoulders and half dragged, half lifted her to the back of the cave, a long shallow gouge in the hillside. And turned her face-to-face with the source of the Voice.

It might have been a mud-man, if bigger, taller, broader. Its shape was human enough, a head with two eyes, nose, mouth, ears—broad torso, two arms, two legs. But its skin was not even like an animal's, let alone a human's. It made her think of lizards and insects and rock dust plastered together with bird lime. It was hairless. The naked skull was faintly crested. It was quite unclothed, and seemingly unconscious of the fact; the strange lumps at its crotch didn't look like a man's genitals, or a woman's either. It didn't *move* right, as though it were a child's bad clay sculpture given motion and not a breathing creature of bone and sinew and muscle.

The mud-men had animal eyes in human faces, and seemed unspeakably dangerous. This . . . had human eyes in the face of a nightmare. No, no nightmare *she* had ever dreamed or imagined—one of Dag's, maybe. Trapped. Tormented. And yet, for all its pain, as devoid of mercy as a stone. Or a rockslide.

It clutched her shirt, lifted her up to its face, and stared at her for a long, long moment. She was crying now, in fear beyond shame. She would deal with Dag's rescue, yes, or anybody's at all. She would trade back for her bandit-ravisher. She would deal with any god listening, make any promise . . . *letmegoletmego* . . .

With a slow, deliberate motion, the malice lifted her skirt with its other hand, twitched her drawers down to her hips, and drew its claws up her belly.

The pain was so intense, Fawn thought for a moment that she had been gutted. Her knees came up in an involuntary spasm, and she screamed. The sound came so tightly out of her raw throat that it turned into near silence, a rasping hiss. She lowered her face, expecting to see blood spewing, her insides coming out. Only four faint red lines marked the pale unbroken skin of her belly.

"*Drop* her!" a hoarse voice roared from her right.

The malice's face turned, its eyes blinking slowly; Fawn turned too. The sudden release of pressure from her shirt took her utterly by surprise, and she fell to the cave floor, dirt and stones scraping her palms, then scrambled up.

Dag was in the shadows, struggling with three, no, all five of the mud-men. One reeled backward with a slashed throat, and another closed in. Dag nearly disappeared under the grunting pile of creatures. A shuffle, a rip, Dag's yell, and a mess of straps and wood and a flash of metal thudded violently against the cave wall. A mud-man had just torn off his arm contraption. The mud-man twisted the arm around behind Dag's back as though trying to rip it off too.

He met her eyes. Shoved his big steel knife into the nearest mud-man as though wedging it into a tree for safekeeping, and ripped a leather pouch from around his neck, its strap snapping. "Spark! *Watch* this!"

She kept her eyes on it as it sailed toward her and, to her own immense surprise, caught it out of the air. She had never in her life caught——. Another mud-man jumped on Dag.

"Stick it in!" he bellowed, going down again. "Stick it in the malice!"

Knives. The pouch had two knives. She pulled one out. It was made of bone. Magic knives? "Which?" she cried frantically.

"Sharp end first! Anywhere!"

The malice was starting to move toward Dag. Feeling as though her head was floating three feet above her body, Fawn thrust the bone knife deeply into the thing's thigh.

The malice turned back toward her, howling in surprise. The sound split her skull. The malice caught her by the neck, this time, and lifted her up, its hideous face contorting.

"No! No!" screamed Dag. "The *other* one!"

Her one hand still clutched the pouch; the other was free. She had maybe one second before the malice shook her till her neck snapped, like a kitchen boy killing a chicken. She yanked the spare bone blade out of its sheath and jammed it forward. It skittered over something, maybe a rib, then caught and went in, but only a couple of inches. The blade shattered. *Oh no——!*

She was falling, falling as if from a great height. The ground struck her a stunning blow. She shoved herself up once more, everything spinning around her.

Before her eyes, the malice was *slumping*. Bits and pieces sloughed off it like ice blowing from a roof. Its awful, keening voice went up and up and higher still, fading out yet leaving shooting pains in her ears.

And gone. In front of her feet was a pile of sour-smelling yellow dirt. The first knife, the one with the blue haft that hadn't worked, lay before it. In her ears was silence, unless she'd just gone deaf.

No, for a scuffle began again to her right. She whirled, thinking to snatch up the knife and try to help. Its magic might have failed, but it still had an edge and a point. But the three mud-men still on their feet had stopped trying to tear the patroller apart, and instead were scrambling away, yowling. One bowled her over in its frantic flight, apparently without any destructive intent. This time, she stayed on her hands and knees. Gasping. She had thought her body must run out of shakes in sheer exhaustion, but the supply seemed endless. She had to clench her teeth to keep them from chattering, like someone freezing to death. Her belly cramped.

Dag was sitting on the ground ten feet away with a staggered look on his face, legs every which way, mouth open, gasping for air just as hard as she was. His left sleeve was ripped off, and his handless arm was bleeding from long scratches. He must have taken a blow to his face, for one eye was already tearing and swelling.

Fawn scrabbled around till her hand encountered the other knife hilt, the green one that had splintered in the malice. Where was the malice? "I'm sorry. I'm sorry. I broke it." She was sniveling now, tears and snot running down her lip from her nose. "I'm sorry . . ."

"What?" Dag looked up dazedly, and began to crawl toward her one-handed in strange slow hops, his left arm curled up protectively to his chest.

Fawn pointed a trembling finger. "I broke your magic knife."

Dag stared down at the green-wrapped hilt with a disoriented look on his face, as if he was seeing it for the first time. "No . . . it's all right . . . they're supposed to do that. They break like that when they work. When they teach the malice how to die."

"What?"

"Malices are immortal. They cannot die. If you tore that body into a hundred bits, the malice's . . . self, would just flee away to another hole and reassemble itself. Still knowing everything it had learned in this incarnation, and so twice as dangerous. They cannot die on their own, so you have to share a death with them."

"I don't understand."

"I'll explain more," he wheezed, "later . . ." He rolled over on his back, hair sweaty and wild; dilated eyes, the color of sassafras tea in the shadows, looking blankly upwards. "Absent gods. We did it. It's done. *You* did it! What a mess. Mari will kill me. Kiss me first, though, I bet. Kiss us both."

Fawn sat on her knees, bent over her cramps. "Why didn't the first knife work? What was wrong with it?"

"It wasn't primed. I'm sorry, I didn't think. In a hurry. A patroller would have known which was which by touch. Of course you couldn't tell." He rolled over on his left side and reached for the blue-hilted knife. "That one's mine, for me someday."

His hand touched it and jerked back. "*What* the . . . ?" His lips parted, eyes going suddenly intent, and he reached again, gingerly. He drew his hand back more slowly this time, the lunatic exhilaration draining from his face. "That's strange. That's very strange."

"*What?*" snapped Fawn, pain and bewilderment making her sharp. Her body was beaten, her neck felt half-twisted-off, and her belly kept on knotting in aching waves. "You don't tell me anything that makes sense, and then I go and do stupid things, and it's *not my fault.*"

"Oh, I think this one is. That's the rule. Credit goes to the one who does, however scrambled the method. Congratulations, Little Spark. You have just saved the world. My patrol will be so pleased."

She would have thought him ragging her mercilessly, but while his words seemed wild, his level tone was perfectly serious. And his eyes were warm on her, without a hint of . . . malice.

"Maybe you're just crazy," she said gruffly, "and that's why nothing you say makes sense."

"No surprise by now if I am," he said agreeably. With a grunting effort, he rolled over and up onto his knees, hand propping him upright. He opened his jaw as if to stretch his face, as though it had gone numb, and blinked owlishly. "I have to get off this dead dirt. It's fouling up my groundsense something fierce."

"Your what?"

"I'll explain that later"—he sighed—"too. I'll explain anything you want. You're owed, Little Spark. You're owed the world." He added after a reflective moment, "Many people are. Doesn't change the matter."

He started to reach for the unbroken knife again, then paused, his expression growing inward. "Would you do me a favor? Pick that up and carry it along for me. The hilt and the bits of the other, too. It needs proper burying, later on."

Fawn tried not to look at his stump, which was pink and lumpy and appeared sore. "Of course. Of course. Did they break your hand thing?" She spotted the pouch a few feet away and crawled to get it. She wasn't sure she could stand up yet either. She collected the broken bits in his torn-off sleeve and slid the intact knife back into its sheath.

He rubbed his left arm. "Afraid so. It isn't meant to come off that way, by a long shot. Dirla will fix it, she's good with leather. It won't be the first time."

"Is your arm all right?"

He grinned briefly. "It isn't meant to come off that way either, though that bear-fellow sure tried. Nothing's broken. It'll get better with rest."

He shoved to his feet and stood with legs braced apart, swaying, until he seemed sure he wouldn't just fall down again. He limped slowly around the cave collecting first his ruined arm contraption, which he wrapped over his shoulder by its leather straps, then, fallen farther away, his big knife. He swiped it on his filthy shirt and resheathed it. He rolled his shoulders and squinted around for a moment, apparently saw nothing else he wanted, and walked back to Fawn.

Her sharpening cramps almost doubled her over when she tried to rise; he gave her a hand up. She stuffed the pouch and rolled sleeve in her shirt. Leaning on each other, they staggered for the light.

"What about the mud-men? Won't they jump us again?" asked Fawn fearfully as they came out on the path overlooking the dead ravine.

"No. It's all over for them when their malice dies. They go back to their animal minds—trapped in those made-up human bodies. They usually panic and run. They don't do too well, after. We kill them for mercy when we can. Otherwise, they die on their own pretty quick. Horrible, really."

"Oh."

"The men whose minds the malice has seized, its fog lifts from them, too. They revert."

"A malice enslaves men, too?"

"When its powers grow more advanced. I think this one might have, for all it was still in its first molt."

"And they'll . . . be freed? Wherever they may be?"

"Sometimes freed. Sometimes go mad. Depends."

"On what?"

"On what they've been doing betimes. They remember, d'you see."

Fawn wasn't entirely sure she did. Or wished to.

The air was warm, but the sun was setting through bare branches, as though winter had become untimely mixed with summer. "This day has been ten years long," Dag sighed. "*Got* to get me off this bad ground. My horse is too far away to summon. Think we'll take those." He pointed to two horses tied to trees near the creek and led her down the zigzag path toward them. "I don't see any gear. Can you ride bareback?"

"Usually, but right now I feel pretty sick," Fawn admitted. She was still shaking, and she felt cold and clammy. Her breath drew in as another violent cramp passed through her. *That is not good. That is something very wrong.* She had thought herself fresh out of fear, a year's supply used up, but now she was not so sure.

"Huh. Think you'd be all right if I held you in front of me?"

The unpleasant memory of her ride with the bandit this morning— had it only been this morning? Dag was right, this day was a decade— flashed through her mind. *Don't be stupid. Dag is different.* Dag, on the whole, was different from any other person she'd ever met in her life. She gulped. "Yeah. I . . . yeah, probably."

They arrived at the horses, Fawn stumbling a little. Dag ran his hand over them, humming to himself in a tuneless way, and turned one loose after first filching its rope, shooing it off. It trotted away as if glad to be gone. The other was a neat bay mare with black socks and a white star; he fastened the rope to her halter to make reins and led her to a fallen log. He kept trying to use his left limb to assist, wincing, then re-membering, which, among all Fawn's other hurts, made her heart ache strangely.

"Can you get yourself up, or do you need a boost?"

Fawn stood whitely. "Dag?" she said in a small, scared voice.

His head snapped around at her tone, and tilted attentively. "What?"

"I'm bleeding."

He walked back to her. "Where? Did they cut you? I didn't see . . ."

Fawn swallowed hard, thinking that her face would be scarlet if only it had not been green. In an even smaller voice, she choked out, "Between . . . between my legs."

The loopy glee that had underlain his expression ever since the killing of the malice was wiped away as if with a rag. "Oh." And he did not seem to require a single further word of explanation, which was a good thing, as well as being amazing in a man, because Fawn was out of everything. Words. Courage. Ideas.

He took a deep breath. "We still have to get off this ground. Deathly place. I have to get you, get you someplace else. Away from here. We'll just go a little faster, is all. You're going to have to help me with this. Help each other."

It took two tries and considerable awkwardness, but they both managed to get aboard the bay mare at last, thankfully a placid beast. Fawn sat not astride but sideways across Dag's lap, legs pressed together, head to his left shoulder, arm around his neck, leaving his right hand free for the reins. He chirped to the horse and started them off at a brisk walk.

"Stay with me, now," he murmured into her hair. "Do not let go, you hear?"

The world was spinning, but under her ear she could hear a steady heartbeat. She nodded dolefully.

5

By the time they arrived at the deserted valley farm, both the back of Fawn's skirt and the front of Dag's trousers were soaked in too-bright blood.

"Oh," said Fawn in a mortified voice, when he'd swung her down from the horse and slid after her. "Oh, I'm sorry."

Dag raised what he hoped was an admirably calm eyebrow. "What? It's just blood, Little Spark. I've dealt with more blood in my time than you have in your whole bitty body." Which was where this red tide should *be,* blast and blight it. *I will not panic.* He wanted to swing her up in his arms and carry her inside, but he did not trust his strength. He had to keep moving, or his own battered body would start to stiffen. He wrapped his right arm around her shoulders instead, and, leaving the horse to fend for itself, aimed her up the porch steps.

"Why is this happening?" she said, so low and breathy and plaintive he wasn't sure if it was to him or herself.

He hesitated. Yes, she was young, but surely—"Don't you know?"

She glanced up at him. The bruise masking the left side of her face was darkening to purple, the gouges scabbing over. "Yes," she whispered. She steadied her voice by sheer force of will, he thought. "But you seem to know so much. I was hoping you might . . . have a different answer. Stupid of me."

"The malice did something to you. Tried to." Courage failing, he looked away from her gaze to say, "It stole your baby's ground. It would have used it in its next molt, but we killed it first." *And I was too late to stop it.* Five blighted minutes, if he had only been five blighted minutes quicker . . . Yes, and if he'd only been five blighted seconds quicker, once, he'd still have a left hand, and he'd been down that road and back up it enough times to be thoroughly tired of the scenery. Peace. If he had arrived at the lair very much sooner, he might have missed her entirely.

But what had happened to his spare sharing knife, in that terrible scramble? It had been empty, but now he would swear it was primed, and that should not have happened. *Take on your disasters one at a time, old patroller, or you'll lose your trail.* The knife could wait. Fawn could not.

"Then . . . then it's too late. To save. Anything."

"It's never too late to save something," he said sternly. "Might not be what you wanted, is all." Which was certainly something he needed to hear, every day, but was not exactly pertinent to her present need, now was it? He tried again, because he did not think his heart or hers could bear confusion on this point. "She's gone. You're not. Your next job is to" *survive this night* "get better. After that, we'll see."

The twilight was failing as they stepped into the gloomy shadows of the farmhouse kitchen, but Dag could see it was a different mess than before.

"This way," Fawn said. "Don't step in the jam."

"Ah, right."

"There's some candle stubs around. Up over the hearth, there's some more. Oh, no, I can't lie there, I'll stain the ticks."

"Looks flat enough to me, Little Spark. I do know you should be lying down. I'm real sure of that." Her breathing was too rapid and shallow, her skin far too clammy, and her ground had a bad gray tinge that went hand in hand with grave damage, in his unpleasant experience.

"Well . . . well, find something, then. For in between."

Now was not, definitely *not,* the time to argue with female irrationality. "Right."

He poked up the faint remains of the fire, fed it with some wood chips, and lit two wax stubs, one of which he left on the hearth for her; the other he took with him for a quick exploration. A couple of those chests and wardrobes upstairs had still had things in them, he dimly recalled. A patroller should be resourceful. What did the girl most need? A miscarriage was a natural enough process, even if this one was most unnaturally triggered; women survived them all the time, he was fairly sure. He just wished they had *discussed* them more, or that he had listened more closely. Lie flat, check, they'd got that far. Make her comfortable? Cruel joke . . . *peace.* He supposed she'd be more comfortable cleaned up than filthy; at any rate, he'd always been grateful for that when recovering from a serious injury. *What, you can't fix the real problem, so you'll fix something else instead? And which of you is this supposed to aid?*

Peace. And a bucket and an unfouled well, with luck.

It took more time than he'd have liked, during which to his swallowed aggravation she insisted on lying on the blighted kitchen *floor,* but he eventually assembled a clean gownlike garment, rather too large for her, some old mended sheets, an assortment of rags for pads, actual soap, and water. In a moment of ruthless inspiration, he broke through her reticence by persuading her to wash his hand first, as though he needed help.

She still had the shakes, which she seemed to take for residual fear but which he recognized as one with the chilled skin and grayness in her ground, and which he treated by piling on whatever blanketlike cloths he could find, and building up the fire. The last time he'd seen a woman coiled around her belly that hard, a blade had penetrated almost to her spine. He heated a stone, wrapped it in cloth, and gave it to Fawn to clutch to herself, which to his relief seemed finally to help; the shakes faded and her ground lightened. Eventually, she was arranged all tidy and sweet and patient-like, her curl around the stone relaxing as she warmed, blinking up at him in the candlelight as he sat cross-legged beside the tick.

"Did you find any clothes you could use?" she asked. "Though I suppose you'd be lucky to find a fit."

"Haven't looked, yet. Got spares in my saddlebags. Which are on my horse. Somewhere. If I'm lucky, my patrol will find him and bring him along sometime. They had better be looking for me by now."

"If you could find something else to wear, I bet I could wash those tomorrow. I'm sorry that—"

"Little Spark," he leaned forward, his ragged voice cracking, *"do not apologize to me for this."*

She recoiled.

He regained control. "Because, don't you see, a crying patroller is a very embarrassing sight. M' face gets all snivelly and snotty. Combine that with this blue eye I've got starting, and it'd be like to turn your stomach. And then there'd just be another mess to clean up, and we don't want that now, do we." He tweaked her nose, which was on the whole an insane thing to do to a woman who'd just saved the world, but it worked to break her bleak mood; she smiled wanly.

"All right, we're making great progress here, you know. Food, what about food?"

"I don't think I could, yet. You go ahead."

"Drink, then. And no arguments with me about that one, I know you need to drink when you've lost blood." *Are losing blood. Still.* Too much, too fast. How long was it supposed to go on?

Candlelight explorations in the rather astonishing cellar yielded a box of dried sassafras; uncertain of the unknown well water, he boiled some up for tea and dosed them both. He was thirstier than he'd thought, and set Fawn an example, which she followed as docilely as a naive young patroller. *Why, why do they do whatever you tell them like that?* Except when they didn't, of course.

He sat against the wall facing her, legs stretched out, and sipped some more. "There would be more I could do for you on the inside, patroller tricks with my groundsense, if only . . ."

"Groundsense." She uncurled a little more and regarded him gravely. "You said you'd tell me about that."

He blew out his breath, wondering how to explain it to a farmer girl in a way she wouldn't take wrong. "Groundsense. It's a sense of . . . everything around us. What's alive, where it is, how it's doing. And not just what's alive, though that's brightest. No one quite knows if the world makes ground, or ground makes the world, but ground is what a malice sucks out to sustain itself, the loss of which kills everything around its lair. In the middle of a really bad patch of blight, not only is everything once alive now dead, even rocks don't hold their form. Ground's what groundsense senses."

"Magic?" she said doubtfully.

He shook his head. "Not the way farmers use the term. It's not like getting something for nothing. It's just the way the world *is,* deep down." He forged on against her frankly blank look. "We use words from sight and touch and the other senses to describe it, but it isn't like any of those things, really. It's like how you know . . . Close your eyes."

She raised her brows at him in puzzlement, but did so.

"Now. Which way is down? Point."

Her thumb rotated toward the floor, and the big brown eyes opened again, still puzzled.

"So how did you know? You didn't see down."

"I . . . " She hesitated. "I felt it. With my whole body."

"Groundsense is something more like that. So." He sipped more

tea; the warm spice soothed his throat. "People are the most complicated, brightest things groundsense sees. We see each other, unless we
close it down to block the distraction. Like shutting your eyes, or wrapping a lantern up in a cloak. You can—Lakewalkers can—match our
body's ground to someone else's body's ground. If you get the match up
really close, almost like slipping inside each other, you can lend strength,
rhythm . . . help with wounds, slow bleeding, help with when a hurt body
starts to go all wrong down into that cold gray place. Lead the other back
to balance. Did something like that for a patroller boy last—ye gods, last
night? Saun. I have to stop thinking of him as Saun the Sheep, it's going
to slip out my mouth someday, and he'll never forgive me, but anyway.
Bandit whaled him in the chest with a sledgehammer during the fight,
broke ribs, stunned his heart and lungs. I whacked my ground into a
match with his right quick, persuaded his to dance with mine. It was all
a bit brutal, but I was in a hurry."

"Would he have *died*? But for you?"

"I . . . maybe. If he thinks so, I'm not going to argue; might finally
get him to give up those overblown sword moves of his while he's still
impressed with me." Dag grinned briefly, but the grin faded again. More
tea. "Trouble is . . . " Blight, out of tea. "You've taken a wound to your
womb. I can sense it in you, like a rip in your ground. But I can't match it
to lend you anything helpful through our grounds because, well, I haven't
got one. A womb, that is. Not part of my body *or* its ground. If Mari or
one of the girls were here, they could maybe help. But I don't want to
leave you alone for eight or twelve hours or however long it would take
to find one and bring her back."

"No, don't do that!" Her hand clutched at his leg, then drew back shyly
as she coiled more tightly on her side. How much pain was she in? *Plenty.*

"Right. So, that means we have to ride this thing out the farmer
way. What do farmer women do, do you know?"

"Go to bed. I think."

"Didn't your mother or sisters ever say?"

"Don't have any sisters, and my brothers are all older than me. My mother, she's taught me a lot, but she doesn't do midwifery. She's always so busy with, well, everything. Mostly I think the body just cleans itself out like a bad monthly, though some women seem to get poorly, after. I think it's all right if you bleed some, but bad if you bleed a lot."

"Well, tell me which you're doing, all right?"

"All right . . . " she said doubtfully.

Her expression was so very reserved and inward. As though painfully trying to listen to the marred song of her own body with a ground-sense blighted deaf. Or futilely looking for that other light within her, so bright and busy just this morning, now dark and dead. In all, Dag thought Fawn had been much too quiet ever since they'd left the lair. It made him feel unsettled and desperate.

He wondered if he ought to invent a few sisters for himself, to bolster his authority in the matter. "Look, I am a very experienced patroller," he blathered on into that fraught silence. "I delivered a baby single-handedly on the Great Lake Road, once." Wait, was this a good tale to tell now? Perhaps not, but it was too late to stop. "Well, not single-handedly, I had two hands then, but they were both pretty clumsy. Fortunately, it was the woman's fourth, and she could tell me how to go on. Which she did, pretty tartly. She was not best pleased to be stuck with me for a midwife. She called me *such* names. I stored 'em up to treasure—they came in right useful later on, when *I* was dealing with feckless young patrollers. Twenty-two I was, and so proud of myself after, you'd think I did all the work. Let me tell you, next bandit I faced after that didn't look *nearly* so scary."

This won a watery chuckle, as he'd hoped. Good, because if he'd gone with the fictional sisters, she might have asked their names, and he didn't think his invention would last so far. His eyelids felt as if someone had attached lead weights to them when he wasn't looking. The room was beginning to waver unpleasantly.

"She was one straightforward lady. Set me an example I never forgot."

"I can see that," murmured Fawn. And after a quiet moment added, "Thank you."

"Oh, you're an easy patient. I won't have to shave you in the morning, and you won't throw your boots at my head because you're cranky and hurting. Bored cranky patrollers who hurt, world's worst company. Trust me."

"Do they really throw boots?"

"Yes. I did."

A yawn cracked his face. His bruises and strains were reporting for duty, right enough. Reminded of his boots' existence, he slowly drew up his feet and began to undo his laces. He'd had those boots on for two—no, four days, because he'd slept in them night before last.

"Would you feel more comfortable if I went out to sleep on the porch?" he asked.

Fawn eyed him over her sheets, now pulled up nearly to her lips. Pink, those lips, if much paler than he would have liked to see them, but not gray or bluish, good. "No," she said in a curiously distant tone, "I don't think I would."

"Good . . . " Another yawn split the word, and others crowded after: "Because I don't think . . . I could crawl through all that . . . sticky jam right now. Softer here. You can have the inside, I'll take the outside." He flopped forward facedown in the tick. He really should turn his head so he could breathe, he supposed. He turned toward Fawn, that being the better view, and eyed what he could see of her over the hillock of stuffed cloth. Dark curls, skin petal-fair where it was not bruised. Smelling infinitely better than him. A surprised brown eye.

"Mama," he muttered, "the sheep are safe tonight."

"Sheep?" she said after a moment.

"Patroller joke." About farmers, come to think. He wasn't going to tell it to her. Ever. Fortunately, he was growing too bludgeoned by his fatigue to talk. He roused himself just enough to stretch over, pinch out the candle, and flop again.

"I don't get it."

"Good. 'Night." His rueful consciousness of that short curving body separated from his by only a couple of layers of fabric was intense, but very brief.

Fawn woke in the dark of night on her right side, facing the kitchen wall, with a weight across her chest and a long, lumpy bolster seemingly wrapped around her in back. The weight was Dag's left arm, she realized, and he must be dead asleep indeed to have flung it there, because he always seemed to carry it subtly out of the way, out of sight, when he was awake. His chin was scratching the back of her neck, his nose was buried in her hair, and she could feel her curls flutter with his slow breath. He lay very solidly between her and the door.

And whatever might come through the door. Scary things out there. Bandits, mud-men, blight bogles. And yet . . . wasn't the tall patroller the scariest of all? Because, at the end of the day, bandits, mud-men, and bogles all lay strewn in his path, and he was still walking. Limping, anyhow. How could someone scarier than anything make her feel safer? A riddle, that.

If not precisely trapped by his menace, she did find herself pinned by his exhaustion. Her attempt to slip out without waking him failed. There followed disjointed mumbled arguments in the dark about a trudge to the privy versus a chamber pot (he won), the change and care of blood-soaked dressings (he won again), and where he would go to sleep next (hard to tell who won that one, but he did end up on the tick between her and the door as before). Despite a new hot stone, her gnawing cramps ordained that he was asleep again before her. But the unlikely comfort of that bony body, wrapped like a fort wall around her hurting, assured that it wasn't so very much before.

When next she awoke it was broad day outside, and she was alone. Yesterday's agony in her belly was reduced to a knotting ache, but her dressings were soaked again. Before she had time to panic, boot steps sounded on the porch, accompanied by a tuneless chirping whistle. She had never heard Dag whistle, but it could be no one else. He ducked in through the door and smiled at her, gold eyes bright from the light.

He must have been out bathing by the well, for his hair was wet and his damp skin free of blood and grime, leaving all his scratches looking tidier and less alarming. Also, he smelled quite nice, last night's reek—although it had been reassuring to know exactly where he was even from several feet away in the dark—replaced with the clean sharpness of the lost farmwife's homemade soap, rough brown stuff that she had nonetheless scented with lavender and mint.

He was shirtless, wearing a pair of unbloodied gray trousers clearly not his own cinched around his waist with a stray bit of rope. She suspected they came about a foot short lengthwise, but with the ends tucked into his boots, no one could tell. He had an uneven tan, his coppery skin paler where his shirt usually fell, although not nearly as pale as hers. He favored long sleeves even in summer, it seemed. His collection of bruises was almost as impressive as her own. But he was not so bony underneath as she'd feared; his long, strappy muscles moved easily under his skin. "Morning, Spark," he said cheerily.

The first order of business was the repellent medical necessities, which he took on with such straightforward briskness that he left her almost feeling that blood clots were an achievement rather than a horror. "Clots are good. Red, spurting blood is bad. Thought we'd agreed on that one, Spark. Whatever the malice ripped up inside you is starting to mend, that says to me. Good work. Keep lying down."

She lay dozily as he wandered in and out. Things happened. A ragged white shirt appeared on his back, too tight across the shoulders and with the sleeves rolled up. More tea happened, and food: the remains of the pan bread she made yesterday rolled around some meat stew from the cellar. He had to coax her to eat, but miraculously, it stayed down, and she could feel strength starting to return to her body almost immediately because of it. Her hot stones were swapped out regularly. After a second longish expedition outside, he returned with a cloth full of strawberries from the farmwoman's kitchen garden and sat himself down on the floor beside her, sharing them out in mock exactitude.

She woke from a longer doze to see him sitting at the kitchen table, mulling glumly over his hand contraption laid out atop it.

"Can you fix it?" she asked muzzily.

"Afraid not. Not a one-hand job even if I had the tools here. Stitching's all ripped, and the wrist cap is cracked. This is beyond Dirla. When we get to Glassforge, I'll have to find a harnessmaker and maybe a wood-turner to put it right again."

Glassforge. Was she still going to Glassforge, when the reason for her flight had been so abruptly removed? Her life had been turned upside down one too many times lately, too fast, for her to be sure of much just now. She turned to the wall and clutched her stone—by the heat, he'd renewed it again while she'd slept—tighter to her aching, emptying womb.

In the past weeks, she had experienced her child as fear, desperation, shame, exhaustion, and vomiting. She had not yet felt the fabled quickening, although she had gone to sleep nightly waiting intently for that sign. It was disquieting to think that this chance-met man, with his strange Lakewalker senses, had gained a more direct perception of the brief life of her child than she had. The thought hurt, but pressing the rag-wrapped stone to her forehead didn't help.

She rolled back over and her eye fell on Dag's knife pouch, set aside last night near the head of her feather mattress. The intact knife with the blue hilt was still in its sheath where she'd shoved it. The other—green hilt and bone fragments—seemed to have been rewrapped in a bit of scavenged cloth, ends tied in one of Dag's clumsy one-handed knots. The fine linen, though wrinkled and ripped and probably from the mending basket, had embroidery on it, once-treasured guest-day work.

She looked up to see him watching her examine them, his face gone expressionless again.

"You said you'd tell me about these, too," she said. "I don't guess it was just any bit of bone that killed an immortal malice."

"No. Indeed. The sharing knives are by far the most complex of our . . . tools. Hard and costly to make."

"I suppose you'll tell me they aren't really magic, again."

He sighed, rose, came over, and sat down cross-legged beside her. He took the pouch thoughtfully in his hand.

"They're human bone, aren't they," she added more quietly, watching him.

"Yes," he said a little distantly. His gaze swung back to her. "Understand, patrollers have had trouble with farmers before over sharing knives. Misunderstandings. We've learned not to discuss them. You have earned . . . there are reasons . . . *you* must be told. I can only ask that you don't talk about it with anyone, after."

"Anyone at all?" she puzzled.

He made a little jerk of his fingers. "Lakewalkers all know. I mean outsiders. Farmers. Although in this case . . . well, we'll get to that."

Roundaboutly, it seemed. She frowned at this uncharacteristic loss of straightforwardness on his part. "All right."

He took a breath, straightening his spine a trifle. "Not just any human bones. Our own, Lakewalker bones. Not farmer bones, and most *especially* not kidnapped farmer children's bones, all right? Adult. Have to be, for the length and strength. You'd think people would—well. Thighbones, usually, and sometimes upper arms. It makes our funeral practices something outsiders are not invited to. Some of the most aggravating rumors have been started around stray glimpses . . . we are *not* cannibals, rest assured!"

"I actually hadn't heard that one."

"You might, if you're around long enough."

She had seen hogs and cows butchered; she could imagine. Her mind leaped ahead to picture Dag's long legs—*no.*

"Some mess is unavoidable, but it's all done respectfully, with ceremony, because we all know it could be our turn later. Not everyone donates their bones; it would be more than needed, and some aren't suitable. Too old or young, too thin or fragile. I mean to give mine, if I die young enough."

The thought made an odd knot in her belly that had nothing to do with her cramping. "Oh."

"But that's just the body of the knife, the first half of the making. The other half, the thing that makes it possible to share death with a malice, is the priming." The quick would-be-reassuring smile with this did not reach his eyes. "We prime it with a death. A donated death, one of our own. In the making, the knife is bonded, matched to the intended primer, so they are very personal, d'you see."

Fawn pushed herself up, increasingly riveted and increasingly disturbed. "Go on."

"When you're a Lakewalker who means to give your death to a knife and you're close to dying—wounded in the field beyond hope of recovery, or dying at home of natural causes, you—or more often your comrade or kin—take the sharing knife and insert it into your heart."

Fawn's lips parted. "But . . ."

"Yes, it kills us. That's the whole point."

"Are you saying people's souls go into those knives?"

"*Not* souls, ah! Knew you'd ask that." He swiped his hand through his hair. "That's another farmer rumor. Makes so much trouble . . . Even our groundsense doesn't tell us where people's souls go after their deaths, but I promise you it's not into the knives. Just their dying ground. Their mortality." He started to add, "Lakewalker god-stories say the gods have . . . well, never mind that now."

Now, there was a rumor she *had* heard. "People say you don't believe in the gods."

"No, Little Spark. Somewhat the reverse. But that doesn't enter into this. That knife" —he pointed to the blue hilt—"is my own, grounded to me. I had it made special. The bone for it was willed to me by a woman named Kauneo, who was slain in a bad malice war up northwest of the Dead Lake. Twenty years ago. We were way late spotting it, and it had grown very powerful. The malice hadn't found many people to use out in that wilderness, but it had found wolves, and . . . well. The other knife, which you used yesterday, that was her primed knife, grounded to her. Her heart's death was in it. The bone of it was from an uncle of hers—I never met him, but he was a legendary patroller up that way in his day, fellow named Kaunear. You probably didn't have time to notice it, but his name and his curse on malices were burned on the blade."

Fawn shook her head. "Curse?"

"His choice, what to have written on his bone. You can order the makers to put any personal message you want that will fit. Some people write love notes to their knife-heirs. Or really bad jokes, sometimes. Up to them. Two notes, actually. One side for the donor of the bone, the other for the donor of the heart's death, which is put on after the knife is primed. If there's a chance."

Fawn imagined that bone blade she'd held being slowly shoved into a dying patroller woman's heart, maybe someone like Mari, by . . . who had done it? Dag? Twenty years seemed terribly long ago—could he really be as old as, say, forty?

"The deaths we share with the malices," said Dag quietly, "are our own, and no others'."

"Why?" whispered Fawn, shaken.

"Because that's what works. How it works. Because we can, and no one else can. Because it is our legacy. Because if a malice, every malice, is not killed when it emerges, it just keeps growing. And growing. And getting stronger and smarter and harder to get at. And if there is ever one we can't get, it will grow till the whole world is gray dust, and then it, too, will die. When I said you'd saved the world yesterday, Spark, I was not joking. That malice could have been the one."

Fawn lay back, clutching her sheets to her breast, taking this in. It was a lot to take in. If she had not seen the malice up close—the rock-dust scent of its foul breath still seemed to linger in her nostrils—she was not sure she *could* have understood fully. *I still don't understand. But oh, I do believe.*

"We just have to hope," Dag sighed, "that we run out of malices before we run out of Lakewalkers."

He held the sheath-pouch down on his thigh with his stump and pulled out the blue-hilted knife. He cradled it thoughtfully for a moment, then, with a look of concentration, touched it to his lips, closing his eyes. His face set in disturbed lines. He laid the knife down exactly between himself and Fawn, and drew back his hand.

"This brings us to yesterday."

"I jabbed that knife into the malice's thigh," said Fawn, "but nothing happened."

"No. Something happened, because this knife was not primed, and now it is."

Fawn's face screwed up. "Did it suck out the malice's mortality, then? Or immortality? No, that makes no sense."

"No. What I think"—he looked up from under wary brows—"mind you, I'm not sure yet, I need to talk with some folks—but what I think is, the malice had just stolen your baby's ground, and the knife stole it back. Not soul, don't you go imagining trapped souls again—just her mortality." He added under his breath, "A death without a birth, very strange."

Fawn's lips moved, but no sound came out.

"So here we sit," he went on. "The body of this knife belongs to me, because Kauneo willed me her bones. But by our rules, the priming in this knife, its mortality, belongs to you, because you are its next of kin. Because your unborn child, of course, could not will it herself. Here things get really . . . get even more mixed up, because usually no one is allowed to will and give their priming till they are adult enough to have their groundsense come in fully, about fourteen or fifteen, and older is stronger. And anyway, this was a farmer child. Yet no death but mine should have been able to prime this knife. This is a . . . this is a right mess, is what it is, actually."

Though still shaken by her sudden miscarriage, Fawn had thought all decisions about her personal disaster were behind her, and had been wearily grateful that no more were to be faced. It was a kind of relief, curled within the grief. Not so, it seemed. "Could you use it to kill another malice?" Some redemption, in all this chain of sorrows?

"I would want to take it to my camp's best maker, first. See what he has to say. I'm just a patroller. I am out of my experience and reckoning, here. It's a strange knife, could do something unknown. Maybe unwanted. Or not work at all, and as you have seen, to get right up to a malice and then have your tools fail makes a bit of a problem."

"What should we do? What *can* we do?"

He gave a rough nod. "On the one hand, we could destroy it."

"But won't that waste . . . ?"

"Two sacrifices? Yes. It wouldn't be my first pick. But if you speak it, Spark, I will break it now in front of you, and it will be over." He laid his hand over the hilt, his face a mask but his eyes searching hers.

Her breath caught. "No—no, don't do that. Yet, anyhow." *And on the other hand, there is no other hand.* She wondered if his sense of humor was gruesome enough to have had exactly that thought as well. She suspected so.

She gulped and continued, "But your people—will they care what some farmer girl thinks?"

"In this matter, yes." He rolled his shoulders, as though they ached. "If it's all right with you, then, I'll speak of this first with Mari, my patrol leader, see what notions she has. After that, we'll think again."

"Of course," she said faintly. *He means it, that I should have a say in this.*

"I would take it kindly if you would take charge of it till then."

"Of course."

He nodded and handed her the leather pouch, leaving her to resheathe the knife. The linen bag, however, he picked up to put with his arm contraption. His joints crackled and popped as he stood up and stretched, and he winced. Fawn sank back down on the tick and stole a closer look at the bone blade. The faint, flowing lines burned brown into the bone's pale surface read: *Dag. My heart walks with yours. Till the end, Kauneo.*

The Lakewalker woman must have written this directive some time before she died, Fawn realized. Fawn imagined her sitting in a Lakewalker tent, tall and graceful like the other patroller women she'd glimpsed; writing tablet balanced on the very thigh that she must have known would come to bear the words, if things went ill. Had she pictured this knife, made from her marrow? Pictured Dag using it someday to drink his own heart's blood in turn? But she could not ever, Fawn thought, have pictured a feckless young farmer girl fumbling it into this strange confusion, a lifetime—at any rate, Fawn's lifetime—later.

Brow furrowed, Fawn slipped the sharing knife out of sight again in its sheath.

6

To Dag's approval, Fawn dozed off again after lunch. *Good, let her sleep and make up her blood loss.* He'd had enough practice to translate the gore on the dressings to a guess as to the amount. When he mentally doubled the volume to make up for the fact that she was about half the size of most men he'd nursed, he was very thankful that the bleeding had plainly slowed.

He came in from checking on the bay mare, now idling about in the front pasture he'd repaired by pulling rails from the fence opposite, to find Fawn awake and sitting up against the back kitchen wall. Her face was drawn and quiet, and she pulled bored fingers through her curls, which were abundant, if tangled.

She peered up at him. "Do you own a comb?"

He ran his hand through his hair. "Does it look that bad?"

Her smile was too ghostly for his taste, though the quip was worth no more. "Not for you. For me. I usually keep my hair tied up, or it gets in an awful mess. Like now."

"I have one in my saddlebag," he offered wryly. "I think. It sifts to the bottom. Haven't seen it in about a month."

"That, I do believe." Her eyes crinkled just a little, then sobered again. "Why don't you wear your hair fancy like the other patrollers?"

He shrugged. "There are a lot of things I can do one-handed. Braiding hair isn't one of them."

"Couldn't someone do it for you?"

He twitched. "Doesn't work if no one's there. Besides, I need enough other favors."

She looked puzzled. "Is the supply so limited?"

He blinked at the thought. Was it? Shrewd question. He wondered if his passion for proving himself capable and without need of aid, so earnestly undertaken after his maiming, was something a man might outgrow. *Old habits die hard.* "Maybe not. I'll look around upstairs, see what I can find." He added over his shoulder, "Lie flat, you." She slid back down obediently, though she made a face.

He returned with a wooden comb found behind an upended chest. It was gap-toothed as an old man, but it served, he found by experiment. She was sitting up again, the cloth-wrapped hot stone laid aside, another promising sign.

"Here, Spark; catch." He tossed the comb to her, and studied her as she jerked up her hand in surprise and had it bounce off her fingers.

She looked up at him in sudden curiosity. "Why did you call *Watch!* when you threw the knife pouch at me?"

Quick, she is. "Old patroller training trick. For the girls—and some others—who come in claiming they can't catch things. It's usually because they're trying too hard. The hand follows the eye if the mind doesn't trip it. If I yell at them to catch the ball, or whatever, they fumble, because that's the picture they have in their heads. If I yell at them to count the spins, it goes right to their hand while they're not attending. And they think I'm a marvel." He grinned, and she smiled shyly back. "I didn't know if you had played throwing games with those brothers of yours or not, so I took the safe bet. In case it was the only one we got."

Her smile became a grimace. "Just the throwing game where they tossed me into the pond. Which wasn't so funny in winter." She eyed the comb curiously, then started in on the end of one tangle.

Her hair was springy and silky and the color of midnight, and Dag couldn't help thinking how soft it would feel to his touch. Another reason to wish for two hands. The smell of it, so close last night, returned to his memory. And perhaps he had better go check on that horse again.

In the late afternoon, Fawn complained for the first time of being hot, which Dag seemed to take as a good sign. He claimed he was sweltering, set up a padded seat out on the shaded porch floor, and permitted her up just long enough to walk out to it. She settled down with her back against the house wall, staring out into the bright summer light. The green fields, and the darker greens of the woods, seemed deceptively peaceful; the horse grazed at the far end of the pasture. The burned outbuilding had stopped smoldering. Clothing, hers and his from yesterday, lay damply over the fence rail in the sun, and Fawn wondered when Dag had laundered it. Dag lowered himself to her left, stretched out his legs, leaned his head back, and sighed as the faint breeze caressed them.

"I don't know what's keeping my patrol," he remarked after a time, opening his eyes again to stare down the lane. "It's not like Mari to get lost in the woods. If they don't show soon, I'll have to try and bury those poor dogs myself. They're getting pretty ripe."

"Dogs?"

He made an apologetic gesture. "The farm dogs. Found 'em out behind the barn yesterday. The only animals that weren't carried off, seemingly. I think they died defending their people. Figured they ought to be buried nice, maybe up in the woods where it's shady. Dogs ought to like that."

Fawn bit her lip, wondering why this made her suddenly want to burst into tears when she had not cried for her own child.

He glanced down at her, his expression growing diffident. "Among Lakewalker women, a loss like yours would be a private grief, but she would not be so alone. She'd maybe have her man, closest friends, or kin around her. Instead, you're stuck with me. If you" —he ducked his head nervously—"need to weep, be sure that I wouldn't mistake it for any lack of strength or courage on your part."

Fawn shook her head, lips tight and miserable. "Should I weep?"

"Don't know. I don't know farmer women."

"It's not about being a farmer." She held out her hand, which clenched. "It's about being *stupid*."

After a moment, he said in a very neutral tone, "You use that word a lot. Makes me wonder who used to whip you with it."

"Lots of people. Because I *was*." She lowered her gaze to her lap, where her hands now twisted the loose fabric of her gown. "It's funny I can tell you this. I suppose it's because I never saw you before, or will again." The man was carrying out her revolting blood clots, after all. Before yesterday, the very thought would have slain her with embarrassment. She remembered the fight in the cave, the bear-man . . . the deathly breath of the malice. What was a mere stupid story, compared to that?

His silence this time took on an easy, listening quality. Unhurried. She felt she might fill it in her own good time. Out in the fields, a few early-summer insects sang in the weeds.

In a lower voice she said, "I didn't mean to have a child. I wanted, wanted, something else. And then I was so scared and mad."

Seeming to feel his way as cautiously as a hunter in the woods, he said, "Farmer customs aren't like ours. We hear pretty lurid songs and tales about them. Your family—did they cast you out?" He scowled; Fawn was not sure why.

She shook her head harder. "No. They'd have taken care of me and the child, if they'd been put to it. I didn't tell them. I ran away."

He glanced at her in surprise. "From a place of safety? I don't understand."

"Well, I didn't think the road would be *this* dangerous. That woman from Glassforge made it, after all. It seemed like an even trade, me for her."

He pursed his lips and stared off down the lane to ask, even more quietly, "Were you forced?"

"No!" She blew out her breath. "I can clear Stupid Sunny of that, at least. I wanted—to tell the truth, I asked *him*."

His brows went up a little, although a tension eased out of his shoulders. "Is there a problem with this, among farmers? It seems quite the thing to me. The woman invites the man to her tent. Except I suppose you don't have tents."

"I could have wished for a tent. A bed. Something. It was at his sister's wedding, and we ended up out in the field behind the barn in the dark, hiding in the new wheat, which I thought could have stood to be taller. I hoped it might be romantic and wild. Instead, it was all mosquitoes and hurry and dodging his drunken friends. It hurt, which I expected, but not unbearably. I'd just thought there would be . . . more to it. I got what I asked for but not what I wanted."

He rubbed his lips thoughtfully. "What did you want?"

She took a breath, thinking. As opposed to flailing, which was maybe what she had been doing back home. "I think . . . I wanted to *know*. It— what a man and a woman do—was like some kind of wall between me and being a grown-up woman, even though I was plenty old."

"How old is plenty old?" He cocked his head curiously at her.

"Twenty," she said defiantly.

"Oh," he said, and though he managed to keep the amusement out of his voice, his gold eyes glinted a bit.

She would have been annoyed, but the glint was too pretty to complain about, and then there were the crow's-feet, which framed the glint so perfectly. She waved her hands in defeat and went on, "It was like a big secret everyone knew but me. I was tired of being the youngest, and littlest, and always the child." She sighed. "We were a bit drunk, too."

She added after a morose silence, "He did say a girl couldn't be got with child the first time."

Dag's eyebrows climbed higher. "And you believed this? A country girl?"

"I *said* I was stupid about it. I thought maybe people were different than heifers. I thought maybe Sunny knew more than me. He could hardly know less. It's not as if anyone talked about it. To me, I mean." She added after a moment, "And . . . I'd had such a hard time nerving myself up to it, I didn't want to stop."

He scratched his head. "Well, among my people, we try not to be crude in front of the young ones, but we have to instruct and be instructed. Because of the hazards of tangling our grounds. Which young couples still do. There's nothing so embarrassing as having to be rescued from an unintended groundlock by your friends, or worse, her kin." At Fawn's baffled look, he added, "It's a bit like a trance. You get wound up in each other and forget to get up, go eat, report for duty . . . after a couple of hours—or days—the body's needs break you out. But that's pretty uncomfortable. Dangerous in an unsafe place to be so unaware of your surroundings for that long, too."

It was her turn to say, "Oh," rather blankly. She glanced up at him. "Did you ever . . . ?"

"Once. When I was very young." His lips twitched. "Around twenty.

It's not something most people let happen twice. We look out for each other, try not to let the first learning kill anyone."

A couple of days? I think I had a couple of minutes . . . She shook her head, not sure if she believed this tale. Or understood it, for that matter. "Well, that—what Sunny said then—wasn't what made me so mad. Maybe he didn't know either. Even getting with child didn't make me mad, just scared. So I went to Sunny, because I reckoned he had a right to know. Besides, I thought he liked me, or maybe even loved me."

Dag started to say something, but then at her last statement stopped himself, looking taken aback, and just waved her to continue. "This has to have happened to other farmer women. What do your folk usually do?"

Fawn shrugged. "Usually, people get married. In kind of a hurry. Her folks and his folks get together and put a good face on it, and things just go on. I mean, if no one is married already. If he's already married, or if she is, I guess things get uglier. But I didn't think . . . I mean, I had nerved myself up for the one, I figured I could nerve myself up for the other.

"But when I told Sunny . . . it wasn't what I'd expected. I didn't necessarily think he'd be delighted, but I did expect him to follow through. After all, I had to. But" —she took a deeper breath—"it seems he had other arrangements. His parents had made him a betrothal with the daughter of a man whose land bordered theirs. Did I say Sunny's folks have a big place? And he's the only son, and she was the only child, and it had been understood for years. And I said, why didn't he tell me earlier, and he said, everyone knew and why should he have, if I was giving myself away for free, and I said, that's fine but there's this baby now, and it was all going to have to come out, and both our parents would make us stand up together anyhow, and he said, no, his wouldn't, I was portionless, and he would get three of his friends to say they'd had me that night too, and he'd get out of it." She finished this last in a rush, her face hot. She stole a glance at Dag, who was sitting looking down the lane with a curiously blank face but with his teeth pressed into his lower lip. "And at *that* point, I decided I didn't care if I was pregnant with *twins,* I wouldn't have Stupid Sunny for my husband on a *bet*." She jerked up her chin in defiance.

"Good!" said Dag, startling her. She stared at him.

He added, "I'd been wondering what to make of Stupid Sunny, in all this tale. Now I think maybe a drum skin would be good. I've never tanned a human skin, mind you, but how hard could it be?" He blinked cheerfully at her.

A spontaneous laugh puffed from her lips. "Thank you!"

"Wait, I haven't done it, yet!"

"No, I mean, thank you for saying it." It had been a joke offer. Hadn't it? She remembered the bodies strewn in his wake yesterday and was suddenly less sure. Lakewalkers, after all. "Don't really do it."

"Somebody should." He rubbed his chin, which was stubbled and maybe itchy, and she wondered if shaving was something he didn't do one-handed, either, or if it was just that his razor was in the bottom of his lost saddlebags along with his comb. "It's different for us," he went on. "You can't lie about such things, for one. It shows in your ground. Which is not to say my people don't get tangled up and unhappy in other ways." He hesitated. "I can see why his family might choose to believe his lie, but would yours have? Is that why you ran off?"

She pressed her lips together, but managed a shrug. "Likely not. It wasn't that, exactly. But I'd have been lessened. Forever. I would always be the one who . . . who had been so stupid. And if I got any smaller in their eyes, I was afraid I'd just disappear. I don't suppose this makes any sense to you."

"Well," he said slowly. "No. Or maybe yes, if I broaden the notion from just having babies to living altogether. I am put in mind of a certain not-so-young patroller who once moved the world to get back on patrol, for all that there were plenty of one-handed tasks needing doing back in the camps. His motives weren't too sensible at the time, either."

"Hm." She eyed him sideways. "I figured I could learn to deal with a baby, if I had to. It was dealing with Stupid Sunny and my family that seemed impossible."

In the exact same distant tone that he'd inquired about Sunny and rape, he asked, "Was your family, um . . . cruel to you?"

She stared a moment in some bewilderment, trying to figure out what he was picturing. Beatings with whips? Being locked up on nothing but bread and water? The fancy seemed as slanderous of her poor overworked parents and dear Aunt Nattie as what Sunny had threatened to say of her. She sat up in mortified indignation. "No!" After a reflective moment she revised this to, "Well, my brothers can be a plague. When they notice me at all, that is." Justice served, but it brought her back to the depressing notion that it was all something wrong with her. Well, maybe it was.

"Brothers can be that," he conceded. He added cautiously, "So could you go home now? There no longer being a"—his gesture finished, *baby,* but his mouth managed—"an obstacle."

"I suppose," she said dully.

His brows drew down. "Wait. Did you leave some word, or did you just vanish?"

"Vanished, more or less. I mean, I didn't write anything. But I would think they could see I'd taken some things. If they looked closely."

"Won't your family be frantic? They could think you were hurt. Or dead. Or taken by bandits. Or who knows what—drowned, caught in a snare. Won't Stu—Sunny confess and turn out to help search?"

Fawn's nose wrinkled in doubt. "It's not what I'd pictured." Not of

Sunny, anyway. Now relieved of the driving panic of her pregnancy, she thought anew of the baffling scene she'd likely left behind her at West Blue, and gulped guilt.

"They have to be looking for you, Spark. I sure would be, if I were your"— He bit off the last word, whatever it was, abruptly. Chewed and swallowed it, too, as if uncertain of the taste.

She said uneasily, "I don't know. Maybe if I went back now, Stupid Sunny would think *I* had been lying. To trap him. For his stupid farm."

"Do you care what he thinks? Compared to your kin, anyway?"

Her shoulders hunched. "Once, I cared a lot. He seemed . . . he seemed splendid to me. Handsome . . . " In retrospect, Sunny's face was round and bland, and his eyes far too dull. "Tall . . . " Actually, short, she decided. He was as tall as her brothers, true. Who would come up maybe to Dag's chin. "He had a good horse." Well, so it had appeared, until she'd seen the long-legged beasts the patrollers all rode. Sunny had shown off his horse, making it sidle and step high, making out that it was a restive handful only an expert might dare bestride. Patrollers rode with such quiet efficiency, you didn't even notice how they were doing it. "You know, it's odd. The farther away I get from him, the more he seems to . . . shrink."

Dag smiled quietly. "He's not shrinking. You're growing, Spark. I've seen such spurts in young patrollers. They grow fast, sometimes, in the crush, when they have to get strong or go under. Takes some adjusting after, be warned—like when you put on eight inches of height in a year and nothing fits anymore."

An example not, she suspected, pulled out of the air. "That was what I wanted. To be grown-up, to be real, to matter."

"Worked," he said reflectively. "Roundaboutly."

"Yes," she whispered. And then, somehow, finally, the dam cracked, and it all came loose. "*Hurts.*"

"Yes," he said simply, and put his arm around her shoulders, and snugged her in tight to him, because she had not cried all that night or day, but she was crying now.

Dag studied the top of Fawn's head, all he could see as she pressed her face into his chest and wept. Even now, she choked her sobs half to silence, shuddering with their suppression. His certainty that she needed to release the strain in her ground was confirmed; if he'd been forced to put it into words for her, he might have said that the fissures running through her seemed to grow less impossibly dark as her sorrow was disgorged, but he wasn't sure if that would make sense to her. Sorrow and rage. There was more erosion of spirit here, going back further, than the malice's destruction of her child.

His instinct was to let her weep the grief out, but after a time his worry roused anew as she clutched her belly once more, a sign of physical pain returning. "Sh," he whispered, hugging her one-armed. "Sh. Don't be making yourself sick, now. Would you like your hot stone again?"

Her clutch transferred to his sleeve and tightened. "No," she muttered. She briefly raised her face, mottled white and flushed where it was not dark with bruises. "'M too hot now."

"All right."

She ducked back down, gaining control of her breathing, but the tight stress in her body didn't ease.

He wondered if her abandonment of her family without a word was as appallingly ruthless as it seemed, or if there was more to the tale. But then, he came from a group that watched out for each other systematically, from partnered pairs through linkers to patrols to companies and right on up in a tested web. *I sure would be looking for you, Spark, if I were your*— and then his tongue had tangled between two choices, each differently disturbing: *father* or *lover. Leave it alone. You are neither, old patroller.* But he was the only thing she had for a partner here. So.

He lowered his lips toward her ear, nestled in the black curls, and murmured, "Think of something beautifully useless."

Her face came up, and she sniffed in confusion. "What?"

"There are a lot of senseless things in the world, but not all of them are sorrows. Sometimes—I find—it helps to remember the other kind. Everybody knows some light, even if they forget when they're down in the dark. Something"—he groped for a term that would work for her—"everyone else thinks is stupid, but you know is wonderful."

She lay still against him for a long time, and he started to muster another explanation, or perhaps abandon the attempt as, well, stupid, but then she said, "Milkweed."

"Mm?" He gave her another encouraging hug, lest she mistake his query for objection.

"Milkweed. It's a just a weed, we have to go around and tear it out of the garden and the crops, but I think the smell of its flowers is prettier than my aunt's climbing roses that she works on and babies all the time. Sweeter than lilacs. Nobody else thinks the flower heads are pretty, but they are, if you look at them closely enough. Pink and complicated. Like wild carrot lace gone plump and shy, like a handful of bitty stars. And the smell, I could breathe it in . . . " She uncurled a little more, unlocking from her pain, pursuing the vision. "In the fall it grows pods, all wrinkled and ugly, but if you tear them open, beautiful silk flies out. The milkweed bugs make houses and pantries of them. Milkweed bugs, now, they aren't pests. They don't bite, they don't eat anything else. Bright burnt-orange wings with black bands, and shiny black legs and feet . . . they just tickle, when they crawl on your hand. I kept some in a box for a while. Gathered them milkweed seeds, and let them drink out of a bit of wet cloth." Her lips, which had softened, tightened again. "Till one of my brothers upset the box, and Mama made me throw them out. It was winter by then."

"Mm." Well, that had worked, till she'd reached the tailpiece. But nonetheless her body was relaxing, the lingering shudders tamping out.

Unexpectedly, she said, "Your turn."

"Uh?"

She poked his chest with a suddenly determined finger. "I told you my useless thing, now you have to tell me one."

"Well, that seems fair," he had to allow. "But I can't think of . . . " And then he did. *Oh*. He was silent for a little. "I haven't thought of this in years. There's a place we went—still go—every summer and fall, a gathering camp, at a place called Hickory Lake, maybe a hundred and fifty miles northwest of here. Hickory nuts, elderberries, and a kind of water lily root, which is a staple of ours—harvesting and planting in one operation. Lakewalkers farm too, in our way, Spark. A lot of wet work, but fun, if you're a child who likes to swim. Maybe I can show . . . anyway. I was, oh, maybe eight or nine, and I'd been sent out in a pole-boat to collect elderberries in the margins, around behind the islands. Forget why I was by myself that day. Hickory Lake sits on clay soil and tends to be muddy and brown most of the time, but in the undisturbed back channels, the water is wonderfully clear.

"I could see right to the bottom, bright as Glassforge crystal. The water weeds wound down and around each other like waving green feathers. And floating on the top were these flat lily pads—not the ones whose roots we eat. Not planted, not useful, they just grew there, probably from before there ever were Lakewalkers. Deep green, with red edges, and thin red lines running down the stems in the water. And their lily flowers had just opened up, floating there like sunbursts, white as . . . as nothing I had ever seen, these translucent petals veined like milky dragonfly wings, glowing in the light reflecting off the water. With luminous, powdery gold centers seeming flowers within flowers, spiraling in forever. I should have been gathering, but I just hung over the edge of the boat staring at them, must have been an hour. Watching the light and the water dance around them in celebration. I could not look away." He gulped a suddenly difficult breath. "Later, in some very dry places, the memory of that hour was enough to go on with."

A hesitant hand reached up and touched his face in something like awe. One warm finger traced a cool smear of wet over his cheekbone. "Why are you crying?"

Responses ran though his mind: *I'm not crying,* or, *I'm just picking up reverberations from your ground,* or, *I must be more tired than I thought.* Two of which were somewhat true. Instead, his tongue found the truth entire. "Because I had forgotten water lilies." He dropped his lips to the top of her head, letting the scent of her fill his nose, his mouth. "And you just made me remember."

"Does it hurt?"

"In a way, Spark. But it's a good way."

She cuddled down thoughtfully, her ear pressed to his chest. "Hm."

The smell of her hair reminded him of mown hay and new bread without being quite either, mingled now with the fragrance of her soft warm body. A faint mist of sweat shimmered on her upper lip in the afternoon's heat. The notion of lapping it off, followed up with a lingering exploration of the taste of her mouth, flashed through his mind. He was suddenly keenly aware of how full his arm was of round young woman. And how the heat of the hour seemed to be collecting in his groin.

If you've a brain left in your head, old patroller, let her go. Now. This was not the time or the place. Or the partner. He had let his groundsense grow far too open to her ground, very dangerous. In fact, to list everything wrong with the impulse he would have to sit here wrapped around her for another hour, which would be a mistake. Grievous, grievous mistake. He took a deep breath and reluctantly unwound his arm from her shoulders. His arm protested its cooling emptiness. She emitted a disappointed mew and sat up, blinking sleepily.

"It's getting hotter," he said. "Best I'd see to those dogs." Her hand trailed over his shirt, falling back as he creaked to his feet. "You'll be all right, resting here a while? No, don't get up . . ."

"Bring me that mending basket, then. And your shirt and sleeve off that fence, if they're dry enough. I'm not used to sitting around doing nothing with my hands."

"It's not your mending."

"It's not my house, food, water, or bedding, either." She raked her curls out of her eyes.

"They owe you for the malice, Spark. This farm and everything in it."

She wriggled her fingers and looked stern at him, and he melted.

"All right. Basket. But no bouncing around while my back is turned, you hear?"

"The bleeding's really slowed," she offered. "Maybe, after that first rush, it'll tail off quick, same way."

"Hope so." He gave her an encouraging nod and went inside to retrieve the basket.

Fawn watched Dag trudge off around the barn, then bent to his ripped-up shirt. After that, she sorted through the mending basket for other simple tasks that she could not spoil. It was hazardous to mess with another woman's system, but the more worn and tattered garments seemed safe to attempt. This stained child's dress, for example. She wondered how many people had lived here and where they had got off to. It was unsettling to think that she might be mending clothes for someone no longer alive.

In about an hour, Dag reappeared. He stopped by the well to strip off his ill-fitting scavenged shirt and wash again with the slice of brown soap, by which she concluded that the burial must have been a hot, ugly, and smelly job. She could not picture how he had managed a shovel one-handed, except slowly, apparently. He was pretty smooth at getting the bucket cranked up from the well and poured out into the trough, though. He ended by sticking his whole head in the bucket, then shaking his hair out like a dog. He had no linens to dry himself with, but likely the wetness beading on his skin felt cooling and welcome. She imagined herself drying his back, fingers tracing down those long muscles. Speaking of keeping one's hands busy. He hadn't seemed to mind her washing his hand last night, but that had been by way of medical preparation. She'd liked the shape of his hand, long-fingered, blunt-nailed, and strong.

He sat on the edge of the porch, accepted his own shirt from her with a smile of thanks, rolled up the sleeves, and pulled it back on once more. The sun was angling toward the treetops, west where the lane vanished into the woods. He stretched. "Hungry, Spark? You should eat."

"A little." She set the mending aside. "So should you." Maybe she could sit at the kitchen table and at least help fix the dinner, this time.

He sat up straight suddenly, staring down the lane. After a minute, the horse at the far end of the pasture raised its head too, ears pricking.

In another minute, a motley parade appeared from the trees. Four men, one riding a plow horse and the others afoot; some cows in a reluctant string; half a dozen bleating sheep held in a bunch by desultory threats from a tall boy with a stick.

"Think someone's made it home," said Dag. His eyes narrowed, but no more figures came out of the woods. "No patrollers, though. Blight it."

Wordlessly, still eycing the men and animals in the distance, he rolled down his left sleeve and let it hang over his stump. But not the right sleeve, Fawn noticed with a pinch of breath. All the lively amusement faded out of his bony face, leaving it closed and watchful once more.

7

The farm folk spotted the pair on the porch about the time they exited the lane, Fawn guessed by the way they paused and stared, taking stock. The stringy old man on the horse stayed back. Under his eye, the boy made himself busy taking down some rails and urging the sheep and cows into the pasture. Once the first few animals spread out in a lumbering burst of bawled complaint, quickly converted to hungry grazing, the rest followed willingly. The three adult men advanced cautiously toward the house, gripping tools like weapons: a pitchfork, a mattock, a big skinning knife.

"If those fellows are from here, they've just had some very bad days, by all the signs," Dag said, whether in a tone of warning or mere observation Fawn was not certain. "Stay calm and quiet, till they're sure I'm no threat."

"How could they think that?" said Fawn indignantly. She straightened her spine against the house wall, twitching the white folds of her overabundant gown tighter about her, and frowned.

"Well, there's a bit of history, there. Some bandits have claimed to *be* patrollers, in the past. Usually we leave bandits to their farmer-brethren, but those we string up good, if we catch 'em at it. Farmers can't always tell. I expect these'll be all right, once they get over being jumpy."

Dag stayed seated on the porch edge as the men neared, though he too sat up straighter. He raised his right hand to his temple in what might have been a salute of greeting or just scratching his head, but in either case conveyed no threat. "Evenin'," he rasped.

The men sidled forward, looking ready either to pounce or bolt at the slightest provocation. The oldest, a thickset fellow with a bit of gray in his hair and the pitchfork in his grip, stepped in front. His glance at Fawn was bewildered. She smiled back and waved her fingers.

Provisionally polite, the thickset man returned a "How de'." He grounded the butt of his pitchfork and continued more sternly, "And who might you be, and what are you doing here?"

Dag gave a nod. "I'm from Mari Redwing's Lakewalker patrol. We were called down from the north a couple of days ago to help deal with your blight bogle. This here's Miss Sawfield. She was kidnapped off the road yesterday by the bogle I was hunting, and injured. I'd hoped to find folks here to help her, but you were all gone. Not willingly, by the signs."

He'd left out an awful lot of important complications, Fawn thought. Only one was hers alone to speak to: "Bluefield," she corrected. "M' name's Fawn Bluefield."

Dag glanced over his shoulder, eyebrows rising. "Ah, right."

Fawn tried to lighten the frowns of the farmers by saying brightly, "This your place?"

"Ayup," said the man.

"Glad you made it back. Is everyone all right?"

A look of thankfulness in the midst of adversity came over the faces of all the men. "Ayup," the spokesman said again, in a huff of blown-out breath. "Praise be, *we* didn't suffer no one getting killed by those, those . . . things."

"It was a near chance," muttered a brown-haired fellow, who looked to be a brother or cousin of the thickset man.

A younger man with bright chestnut hair and freckles slid around to Dag's left, staring at his empty shirt cuff. Dag feigned not to notice the stare, but Fawn thought she detected a slight stiffening of his shoulders. The man burst out, "Hey—you wouldn't be that fellow Dag all those other patrollers are looking for, would you? They said you couldn't hardly be mistook—tall drink of water with his hair cropped short, bright goldy eyes, and missing his left hand." He nodded in certainty, taking inventory of the man on the porch.

Dag's voice was suddenly unguarded and eager. "You've seen my patrol? Where are they? Are they all right? I'd expected them to find me before now."

The red-haired fellow made a wry face, and said, "Spread out between Glassforge and that big hole back in the hills those crazy fellows were trying to make us dig, I guess. Looking for you. When you hadn't turned up in Glassforge by this morning, that scary old lady carried on like she was afraid you were dead in a ditch somewheres. I had four different patrollers buttonhole me with your particulars before we got out of town."

Dag's lips lifted at that apt description of what Fawn guessed must be his patrol leader, Mari. The boy and the skinny graybeard on the horse, once the fence rails were replaced, drifted up to the edge of the group to watch and listen.

The thickset man gripped his pitchfork haft tighter again, although not in threat. "Them other patrollers all said you must have killed the bogle. They said that had to be what made all them monsters, mud-men they calls 'em, run off like that yesterday night."

"More or less," said Dag. A twitch of his hand dismissed—or concealed—the details. "You're right to travel cautious. There might still be a few bandits abroad—that'll be for the Glassforge folks to deal with. Any mud-men who escaped my patrol or Chato's will be running mindless through the woods for a while, till they die off. I put down two yesterday, but at least four I know of got away into the brush. They won't attack you now, but they're still dangerous to surprise or corner, like any sick wild animal. The malice's—bogle's—lair was up in the hills not eight miles due east of here. You all were lucky to escape its attentions before this."

"You two look like you collected some attentions yourselves," said the thickset man, frowning at their visible bruises and scrapes. He turned to the lanky boy. "Here, Tad—go fetch your mama." The boy nodded eagerly and pelted back down the lane toward the woods.

"What happened here?" Dag asked in turn.

This released a spate of increasingly eager tale-telling, one man interrupting another with corroboration or argument. Some twenty, or possibly thirty, mud-men had erupted out of the surrounding woods four days ago, brutalizing and terrifying the farm folk, then driving them off in a twenty-mile march southeast into the hills. The mud-men had kept the crowd under control by the simple expedient of carrying the three youngest children and threatening to dash out their brains against the nearest tree if anyone resisted, a detail that made Fawn gasp but Dag merely look more expressionless than ever. They had arrived at length at a crude campsite containing a couple dozen other prisoners, mostly victims of road banditry; some had been held for many weeks. There, the mud-men, uneasily supervised by a few human bandits, seemed intent on making their new slaves excavate a mysterious hole in the ground.

"I don't understand that hole," said the thickset man, eldest son of the graybeard and apparent leader of the farm folk, whose family name was Horse-ford. The stringy old grandfather seemed querulous and addled—traits that seemed to predate the malice attack, Fawn judged from the practiced but not-unkind way everyone fielded his complaints.

"The malice—the blight bogle—was probably starting to try to mine," said Dag thoughtfully. "It was growing fast."

"Yes, but the hole wasn't right for a mine, either," put in the red-haired man, Sassa. He'd turned out to be a brother-in-law of the house, present that day to help with some log-hauling. He seemed less deeply shaken than the rest, possibly because his wife and baby had been safely back in Glassforge and had missed the horrific misadventure altogether. "They didn't have enough tools, for one thing, till those mud men brought in the ones they stole from here. They had folks digging with their hands and hauling dirt in bags made out of their clothes. It was an awful mess."

"Would be, at first, till the bogle caught someone with the know-how to do it right," said Dag. "Later, when it's safe again, you folks should get some real miners to come in and explore the site. There must be something of value under there; the malice would not have been mistaken about that. This part of the country, I'd guess an iron or coal seam, maybe with a forge planned to follow, but it might be anything."

"I'd wondered if they were digging up another bogle," said Sassa. "They're supposed to come out of the ground, they say."

Dag's brows twitched up, and he eyed the man with new appraisal. "Interesting idea. When two bogles chance to emerge nearby, which happily doesn't occur too often, they usually attack each other first thing."

"That would save you Lakewalkers some trouble, wouldn't it?"

"No. Unfortunately. Because the winning bogle ends up stronger. Easier to take them down piecemeal."

Fawn tried to imagine something stronger and more frightening than the creature she had faced yesterday. When you were already as terrified as your body could bear, what difference could it make if something was even worse? She wondered if that explained anything about Dag.

Movement at the end of the lane caught her eye. Another plow horse came out of the woods and trotted ponderously up to the farmyard, a middle-aged woman riding with the lanky boy up behind. They paused on the other side of the well, the woman staring down hard at something, then came up to join the others.

The red-haired Sassa, either more garrulous or more observant than his in-laws, was finishing his account of yesterday's inexplicable uproar at the digging camp: the sudden loss of wits and mad flight of their captor mud-men, followed, not half an hour later, by the arrival from the sunset woods of a very off-balance patrol of Lakewalkers. The Lakewalkers had been trailed in turn by a mob of frantic friends and relatives of the captives from in and around Glassforge. Leaving the local people to each other's care, the patrollers had withdrawn to their own Lakewalkerish concerns, which seemed mainly to revolve around slaying all the mud-men they could catch and looking for their mysterious missing man Dag, who they seemed to think somehow responsible for the bizarre turn of events.

Dag rubbed his stubbled chin. "Huh. I suppose Mari or Chato must have thought this mining camp might be the lair. Following up traces from that bandit hideout we raided night before last, I expect. That explains where they were all day yesterday. And well into the night, sounds like."

"Oh, aye," said the thickset man. "Folks was still trailing into Glassforge all night and into this morning, yours and ours."

The farmwife slid down off the horse and stood listening to this, her eyes searching her house, Dag, and especially Fawn. Fawn guessed from the farm men's talk that she must be the woman they'd called Petti. Judging by the faint gray in her hair, she was of an age with her husband, and as lean as he was thick, tough and strappy, if tired-looking. Now she stepped forward. "What blood is all that in the tub out by the well?"

Dag gave her a polite duck of his head. "Miss S—Bluefield's mostly, ma'am. My apologies for filching your linens. I've been throwing another bucket of water on them each time I go by. I'll try to get them cleaned up better before we leave."

We not *I,* some quick part of Fawn's mind noted at once, with a catch of relief.

"Mostly?" The farmwife cocked her head at him, squinting. "How'd she get hurt?"

"That would be her tale to tell, ma'am."

Her face went still for an instant. Her eye flicked up to Fawn and then back, to take in his empty cuff. "You really kill that bogle that did all this?"

He hesitated only briefly before replying, precisely but unexpansively, "We did."

She inhaled and gave a little snort. "Don't you be troubling about my laundry. The idea."

She turned back to, or upon, her menfolk. "Here, what are you all doing standing about gabbing and gawking like a pack of ninnies? There's work to do before dark. Horse, see to milking those poor cows, if they ain't been frightened dry. Sassa, fetch in the firewood, if those thieves left any in the stack, and if they didn't, make some more. Jay, put away and put right what can be, what needs fixin', start on, what needs tomorrow's tools, set aside. Tad, help your grandpa with the horses, and then come and start picking up inside. Hop to it while there's light left!"

They scattered at her bidding.

Fawn said helpfully, pushing up, "The mud-men didn't find your storage cellar—" And then her head seemed to drain, throbbing unpleasantly. The world did not go black, but patterned shadows swarmed around her, and she was only dimly aware of abrupt movement: a strong hand and truncated arm catching her and half-walking, half-carrying her inside. She blinked her eyes clear to find herself on the feather pallet once more, two faces looming over her, the farmwife's concerned and wary, Dag's concerned and . . . tender? The thought jolted her, and she blinked some more, trying to swim back to reason.

"—*flat,* Spark," he was saying. "Flat was working." He brushed a sweat-dampened curl out of her eyes.

"What happened to you, girl?" demanded Petti.

"'M not a girl," Fawn mumbled. "'M twenty . . ."

"The mud-men knocked her around hard yesterday." Dag's intent gaze on her seemed to be asking permission to continue, and she shrugged assent. "She miscarried of a two-months child. Bled pretty fierce, but it seems to have slowed now. Wish one of my patrolwomen were here. You do much midwifery, ma'am?"

"A little. Keeping her lying down is right if she's been bleeding much."

"How do you know if she . . . if a woman is going to be all right, after that?"

"If the bleeding tails off to nothing within five days, it's a pretty sure bet things are coming back around all right inside, if there's no fever. Ten days at the most. A two-months child, well, that's as chance will happen. Much more than three months, now, that gets more dangerous."

"Five days," he repeated, as if memorizing the number. "Right, we're still all right, then. Fever . . . ?" He shook his head and rose to his feet, wincing as he rubbed his left arm, and followed the farmwife's gaze around her kitchen. With an apologetic nod, he removed his arm contraption from her table, bundled it up, and set it down at the end of the tick.

"And what knocked you around?" asked Petti.

"This and that, over the years," he answered vaguely. "If my patrol doesn't find us by tomorrow, I'd like to take Miss Bluefield to Glassforge. I have to report in. Will there be a wagon?"

The farmwife nodded. "Later on. The girls should bring it tomorrow when they come." The other women and children of the Horseford family were staying in town with Sassa's wife, it seemed, sorting out recovered goods and waiting for their men to report the farm safe again.

"Will they be making another trip, after?"

"Might. Depends." She scrubbed the back of her neck, staring around as if a hundred things cried for her attention and she only had room in her head for ten, which, Fawn guessed, was just about the case.

"What can I do for you, ma'am?" Dag inquired.

She stared at him as if taken by surprise by the offer. "Don't know yet. Everything's been knocked all awhirl. Just . . . just wait here."

She marched off to take a look around her smashed-up house.

Fawn whispered to Dag, "She's not going to get settled in her mind till she has her things back in order."

"I sensed that." He bent over and took up the knife pouch, lying by the head of the pallet. Only then did Fawn realize how careful he'd been not to glance at it while the farmwife was present. "Can you put this somewhere out of sight?"

Fawn nodded, and sat up—slowly—to flip open her bedroll, laid at the pallet's foot. Her spare skirt and shirt and underdrawers lay atop the one good dress she'd packed along to go look for work in, that hasty night she'd fled home. She tucked the knife pouch well away and rolled up the blanket once more.

He nodded approval and thanks. "Best not to mention the knife to these folks, I think. Bothersome. That one worse than most." And, under his breath, "Wish Mari would get here."

They could hear the farmwife's quick footsteps on the wooden floors overhead, and occasional wails of dismay, mostly, "My poor *windows!*"

"I noticed you left a lot out of your story," said Fawn.

"Yes. I'd appreciate it if you would, too."

"I promised, didn't I? I sure don't want to talk about that knife to just anyone, either."

"If they ask too many questions, or too close of ones, just ask them about their troubles in turn. It'll usually divert them, when they have so much to tell as now."

"Ah, so that's what you were doing out there!" In retrospect, she could spot how Dag had turned the talk so that they had learned so much of the Horsefords' woes, but the Horsefords had received so little news in return. "Another old patroller trick?"

One corner of his mouth twitched up. "More or less."

The farmwife came back downstairs about the time her son Tad came in from the barn, and after a moment's thought she sent the boy and Dag off together to clean up broken glass and rubble around the house. She surveyed her kitchen and climbed down into her storage cellar, from which she emerged with a few jars for supper, seeming much reassured. After setting the jars in a row on the table—Fawn could almost see her counting stomachs and planning the upcoming meal in her head—she turned back and frowned down at Fawn.

"We'll have to get you into a proper bed. Birdy's room, I think, once Tad gets the glass out. It wasn't too bad, otherwise." And then, after a pause, in a much lower voice, "That patroller fellow tell the straight story on you?"

"Yes, ma'am," said Fawn.

The woman's face pinched in suspicion. "'Cause he didn't get those scratches on his face from no mud-man, I'll warrant."

Fawn looked back blankly, then said, "Oh! *Those* scratches. I mean, yes, that was me, but it was an accident. I mistook him for another bandit, at first. We got that one straightened out right quick."

"Lakewalkers is strange folk. Black magicians, they say."

Fawn struggled up on one elbow to say hotly, "You should be grateful if they are. Because blight bogles are blacker ones. I *saw* one, yesterday. Closer than you are to me now. Anything patrollers have to do to put them down is all right by me!"

Petti's thoughts seemed to darken. "Was that what—did the blight bogle . . . blight you?"

"Make me miscarry?"

"Aye. Because girls don't usually miscarry just from being knocked around, or falling down stairs, or the like. Though I've seen some try for it. They just end up being bruised mothers, usually."

"Yes," said Fawn shortly, scrunching back down. "It was the bogle." Were these too-close questions? Not yet, she decided. Even Dag had offered some explanations, just enough to satisfy without begging more questions. "It was ugly. Uglier than the mud-men, even. Bogles kill everything they touch, seemingly. You should go look at its lair, later. The woods are all dead for a mile around. I don't know how long it will take for them to grow back."

"Hm." Petti busied herself unsealing jars, sniffing for wholesomeness and fishing out the broken wax to be rinsed and remelted, later. "Them mud-men was ugly enough. The day before we was brought to the digging camp, seems there was a woman had a sick child, who went to them and insisted on being let go to get him help. She tried carrying on, weeping and wailing, to force them. Instead, they killed her little boy. And ate him. She was in a state by the time we got there. Everybody was. Even them bandits, who I don't think was in their right minds either, wasn't too easy about that one."

Fawn shuddered. "Dag said the mud-men ate folks. I wasn't sure I believed him. Till after . . . afterwards." She hitched her shoulders. "Lakewalkers hunt those things. They go *looking* for them."

"Hm." The woman frowned as she kept trying to assemble the meal by her normal routine and coming up short against missing tools and vessels. But she improvised and went on, much as Fawn had. She added from across the room after a while, "They say Lakewalkers can beguile folk's minds."

"Look, you." Fawn lurched back up on her elbow, scowling. "*I* say, *that* Lakewalker saved my life yesterday. At least twice. No, three times, because I'd have bled to death in the woods trying to walk out if he'd died in the fight. He fought off five of those mud-men! He took care of me all last night when I couldn't move for the pain, and carried out my bloody clouts with never a word of complaint, *and* he cleaned up your kitchen *and* he fixed your fence *and* he buried your dogs nice in the shady woods, and he didn't have to do *any* of that." *And his heart breaks for the memory of water lilies.* "I've seen that man do more good with one hand in a day than I've seen any other man do with two in a week. Or ever. If he's beguiled *my* mind, he sure has done it the hard way!"

The farmwife had both her hands raised as if to ward off this hot, pelting defense, half-laughing. "Stop, stop, I surrender, girl!"

"Huh!" Fawn flopped back again. "Just don't you give me any more *they says.*"

"Hm." Petti's smile dwindled to bleakness, but whatever shadowed her thoughts now, she did not confide to Fawn.

Fawn lay quietly on her pallet till dusk drove the men indoors. At that point, Tad was made to carry off the feather tick, and the space was used for a trestle table. Makeshift benches—boards placed across sawed-off logs—were brought in to serve for the missing chairs. Petti allowed to Dag as how she thought it all right for Fawn to sit up long enough to take the meal with the family. Since the alternative appeared to be having Petti bring her something in bed in some lonely nook of the house, Fawn agreed decisively to this.

The meal was abundant, if makeshift and simple, eaten by the limited light of candle stubs and the fire at the end of the long summer day. Everyone would be going to bed right after, not just her, Fawn thought. The room was hot and the conversation, at first, scant and practical. All were exhausted, their minds filled with the recent disruptions in their lives. Since everyone was mostly eating with their hands anyhow, Dag's slight awkwardness did not stick out, Fawn observed with satisfaction. You wouldn't think his missing hand bothered him a bit, unless you noticed how he never raised his left wrist into sight above the table edge. He spoke only to encourage Fawn, next to him, to eat up, though about that he was quite firm.

"Kind o' you to help Tad with all that busted glass," the farmwife said to Dag.

"No trouble, ma'am. You should all be able to step safe now, leastways."

Sassa offered, "I'll help you to get new windows in, Petti, soon as things are settled a bit."

She gave her brother-in-law a grateful look. "Thankee, Sassa."

Grandfather Horseford grumbled, "Oiled cloth stretched on the frames was good enough in *my* day," to which his gray-haired son responded only, "Have some more pan bread, Pa." The land might still be the old man's, in name at least, but it was plain that the house was Petti's.

Inevitably, Fawn supposed, the talk turned to picking over the past days' disasters. Dag, who looked to Fawn's eye as though he was growing tired, and no wonder, was not expansive; she watched him successfully use his diversion trick of answering a question with a question four times running. Until Sassa remarked to him, sighing, "Too bad your patrol didn't get there a day sooner. They might've saved that poor little boy who got et."

Dag did not exactly wince. It was merely a lowering of his eyelids, a slight, unargumentative tilt of his head. A shift of his features from tired to expressionless. And silence.

Fawn sat up, offended for him. "Careful what you wish after. If Dag's patrol had got there anytime before I—we—before the bogle died and the mud-men ran off, there'd have been a big fight. Lots of folks might have gotten killed, and that little boy, too."

Sassa, brow furrowed, turned to her. "Yes, but—*et*? Doesn't it bother you extra? It sure bothers me."

"It's what mud-men do," murmured Dag.

Sassa eyed him, disconcerted. "Used to it, are you?"

Dag shrugged.

"But it was a *child*."

"Everyone's someone's child."

Petti, who'd been staring wearily at her plate, looked up at that.

In a tone of cheery speculation, Jay said, "If they'd have been *five* days faster, *we'd* not have been raided. And our cows and sheep and dogs would still be alive. Wish for that, while you're at it, why don't you?"

With a grimace that failed to quite pass as a smile, Dag pushed himself up from the table. He gave Petti a nod. "'Scuse me, ma'am."

He closed the kitchen door quietly behind him. His booted steps sounded across the porch, then faded into the night.

"What bit him?" asked Jay.

Petti took a breath. "Jay, some days I think your mama must have dropped you on your head when you was a baby, really I do."

He blinked in bewilderment at her scowl, and said less in inquiry than protest, "What?"

For the first time in hours, Fawn found herself chilled again, chilled and shaking. Her wan droop did not escape the observant Petti. "Here, girl, you should be in bed. Horse, help her."

Horse, mercifully, was much quieter than his younger relations; or perhaps his wife had given him some low-down on their outlandish guests in private. He propelled Fawn through the darkening house. The loss of light was not from her going woozy, this time, though her skull was throbbing again. Petti followed with a candle in a cup for a makeshift holder.

The ground floor of one of the add-ons consisted of two small bedrooms opposite each other. Horse steered Fawn inside to where her feather tick had been laid across a wooden bed frame. The slashed rope webbing had been reknotted sometime recently, maybe by Dag and Tad. A moist summer night breeze wafted through the small, glassless windows. Fawn decided this must be a daughter's bedchamber; the girls would likely be arriving home tomorrow with the wagon.

As soon as the transport was safely accomplished, Petti shooed Horse out. Awkwardly, Fawn swapped out her dressings, half-hiding under a light blanket that she scarcely needed. Petti made no comment on them, beyond a "Give over, here," and a "There you go, now." A day ago, Fawn reflected, she would have given anything to trade her strange man helper for a strange woman. Tonight, the desire was oddly reversed.

"Horse 'n' me have the room across," said Petti. "You can call out if you need anything in the night."

"Thank you," said Fawn, trying to feel grateful. She supposed it would not be understood if she asked for the kitchen floor back. The floor and Dag. Where would these graceless farmers try to put the patroller? In the barn? The thought made her glower.

Long, unmistakable footfalls sounded in the hall, followed by a sharp double rap against the door. "Come in, Dag," Fawn called, before Petti could say anything.

He eased inside. A stack of dry garments lay over his left arm, the laundry Fawn had seen draped over the pasture fence earlier, Fawn's blue dress and linen drawers; underneath were his own trousers and drawers that had been so spectacularly bloodied yesterday. He had her bedroll tucked under his armpit.

He laid the bedroll down in a swept corner of the room, with her cleaned clothes atop. "There you go, Spark."

"Thank you, Dag," she said simply. His smile flickered across his face like light on water, gone in the instant. Didn't anyone ever just say *thank you* to patrollers? She was really beginning to wonder.

With a wary nod at the watching Petti, he stepped to Fawn's bedside and laid his palm on her brow. "Warm," he commented. He traded the palm for the inside of his wrist. Fawn tried to feel his pulse through their skins, as she had listened to his heartbeat, without success. "But not feverish," he added under his breath.

He stepped back a little, his lips tightening. Fawn remembered those lips breathing in her hair last night, and suddenly wanted nothing more than to kiss and be kissed good night by them. Was that so wrong? Somehow, Petti's frowning presence made it so.

"What did you find outside?" she asked, instead.

"Not my patrol." He sighed. "Not for a mile in any direction, leastways."

"Do you suppose they're all still looking on the wrong side of Glassforge?"

"Could be. It looks like it's fixing to rain; heat lightning off to the west. If I really were stuck in a ditch, I wouldn't be sorry, but I hate to think of them running around in the woods in the dark and wet, in fear for me, when I'm snug inside and safe. I'm going to hear about that later, I expect."

"Oh, dear."

"Don't worry, Spark; another day it will be the other way around.

And then it will be my turn to be, ah, humorous." His eyes glinted in a way that made her want to laugh.

"Will we really go to Glassforge tomorrow?"

"We'll see. See how you're doing in the morning, for one."

"I'm doing much better tonight. Bleeding's no worse than a monthly, now."

"Do you want your hot stone again?"

"Really, I don't think I need it anymore."

"Good. Sleep hard, then, you."

She smiled shyly. "I'll try."

His hand made a little move toward her, but then fell back to his side. "Good night."

"G'night, Dag. You sleep hard too."

He gave her a last nod, and withdrew; the farmwife carried the candle out with her, closing the door firmly behind. A faint flash of the heat lightning Dag had mentioned came through the window, too far away even to hear the thunder, but otherwise all was darkness and silence. Fawn rolled over and tried to obey Dag's parting admonishment.

"Hold up," murmured the farmwife, and since she carried the only light, the stub melting down to a puddle in the clay cup, Dag did so. She shouldered past and led him to the kitchen. Another candle, and a last dying flicker from the fireplace, showed the trestle table and benches taken down and stowed by the wall, and the plates and vessels from dinner stacked on the drainboard by the sink, along with the bucket of water refilled.

The farmwife looked around the shadows and sighed. "I'll deal with the rest of this in the morning, I guess." Belying her words, she moved to cover and set aside the scant leftover food, including a stack of pan bread she had apparently cooked up with breakfast in mind.

"Where do you want me to sleep, ma'am?" Dag inquired politely. Not with Fawn, obviously. He tried not to remember the scent of her hair, like summer in his mouth, or the warmth of her breathing young body tucked under his arm.

"You can have one of those ticks that little girl mended; put it down where you will."

"The porch, maybe. I can watch out for my people, if any come out of the woods in the night, and not wake the house. I could pull it into the kitchen if it comes on to rain."

"That'd be good," said the farmwife.

Dag peered through the empty window frame into the darkness, letting his groundsense reach out. The animals, scattered in the pasture, were calm, some grazing, some half-asleep. "That mare isn't actually mine. We found it at the bogle's lair and rode it out. Do you recognize it for anyone's?"

Petti shook her head. "Not ours, anyways."

"If I ride it to Glassforge, it would be nice to not be jumped for horse thieving before I can explain."

"I thought you patrollers claimed a fee for killing a bogle. You could claim it."

Dag shrugged. "I already have a horse. Leastways, I hope so. If no one comes forward for this one, I thought I might have it go to Miss Bluefield. It's sweet-tempered, with easy paces. Which is part of what inclines me to think it wasn't a bandit's horse, or not for long."

Petti paused, staring down at her store of food. "Nice girl, that Miss Bluefield."

"Yes."

"You wonder how she got in this fix."

"Not my tale, ma'am."

"Aye, I noticed that about you."

What? That he told no tales?

"Accidents happen, to the young," she went on. "Twenty, eh?"

"So she says."

"*You* ain't twenty." She moved to kneel by the fire and poke it back for the night.

"No. Not for a long time, now."

"You could take that horse and ride back to your patrol tonight, if you're that worried about them. That girl would be all right, here. I'd take her in till she's mended."

That had been precisely his plan, yesterday. It seemed a very long time ago. "Good of you to offer. But I promised to see her safe to Glassforge, which was where she was bound. Also, I want Mari to look her over. My patrol leader—she'll be able to tell if Fawn's healing all right."

"Aye, figured you'd say something like that. I ain't blind." She sighed, stood, turned to face him with her arms crossed. "And then what?"

"Pardon?"

"Do you even know what you're doing to her? Standing there with them cheekbones up in the air? No, I don't suppose you do."

Dag shifted from cautious to confused. That the farmwife was shrewd and observant, he had certainly noticed; but he did not understand her underlying distress in this matter. "I mean her only good."

"Sure you do." She frowned fiercely. "I had a cousin, once."

Dag tilted his head in faint encouragement, torn between curiosity and an entirely unmagical premonition that wherever she was going with this tale, he didn't want to go along.

"Real nice young fellow; handsome, too," Petti continued. "He got a job as a horse boy at that hotel in Glassforge where your patrols always stay, when they're passing through these parts. There was this patroller girl, young one, came there with her patrol. Very pretty, very tall. Very nice. Very nice to *him,* he thought."

"Patrol leaders try to discourage that sort of thing."

"Aye, so I understood. Too bad they don't succeed. Didn't take too long for him to fall mad in love with the girl. He spent the whole next year just waiting for her patrol to come back. Which it did. And she was nice to him again."

Dag waited. Not comfortably.

"Third year, the patrol came again, but she did not. Seems she was only visiting, and had gone back to her own folks way west of here."

"That's usual, for training up young patrollers. We send them to other camps for a season or two, or more. They learn other ways, make friends; if ever we have to combine forces in a hurry, it makes everything easier if some patrollers already know each other's routes and territories. The ones training up to be leaders, we send 'em around to all seven hinterlands. They say of those that they've walked around the lake."

She eyed him. "You ever walk around the lake?"

"Twice," he admitted.

"Hm." She shook her head, and went on, "He got the notion he would go after her, volunteer to join with you Lakewalkers."

"Ah," said Dag. "That would not work. It's not a matter of pride or ill will, you understand; we just have skills and methods that we cannot share."

"You mean to say, not pride or ill will alone, I think," said the woman, her voice going flat.

Dag shrugged. *Not my tale. Let it go, old patroller.*

"He did find her, eventually. As you say, the Lakewalkers wouldn't have him. Came back after about six months, with his tail between his legs. Bleak and pining. Wouldn't look at no other girl. Drank. It was like, if he couldn't be in love with her, he'd be in love with death instead."

"You don't have to be a farmer for that. Ma'am," Dag said coolly.

She spared him a sharp glance. "That's as may be. He never settled, after that. He finally took a job with the keelboat men, down on the Grace River. After a couple of seasons, we heard he'd fallen off his boat and drowned. I don't think it was deliberate; they said he'd been drunk and had gone to piss over the side in the night. Just careless, but a kind of careless that don't happen to other folks."

Maybe that had been the trouble with his own schemes, Dag thought. He had never been careless enough. If Dag had been twenty instead of thirty-five when the darkness had overtaken him, it might have all worked rather differently . . .

"We never heard back from that patroller girl. He was just a bit of passin' fun to her, I guess. She was the end of the world to him, though."

Dag held his silence.

She inhaled, and drove on: "So if you think it's amusin' to make that girl fall in love with you, I say, it won't seem so funny down the road. I don't know what's in it for you, but there's no future for her. Your people will see to that, if hers won't. You and I both know that—but she don't."

"Ma'am, you're seeing things." Very plausible things, maybe, given that she could not know the true matter of the sharing knife that bound Dag and Fawn so tightly to each other, at least for now. He wasn't about to try to explain the knife to this exhausted, edgy woman.

"I know what I'm seeing, thank you kindly. It ain't the first time, neither."

"I've scarcely known the girl a day!"

"Oh, aye? What'll it be after a week, then? The woods'll catch fire, I guess." She snorted derision. "All I know is, in the long haul, when folks tangle hearts with your folks, they end up dead. Or wishing they was."

Dag unclenched his jaw, and gave her a short nod. "Ma'am . . . in the long haul, all folks end up dead. Or wishing they were."

She just shook her head, lips twisting.

"Good *night*." He touched his hand to his temple and went to haul the tick, stuffed into the next room, out onto the porch. If Little Spark was able to travel at all tomorrow, he decided, they would leave this place as soon as might be.

8

To Dag's discontent, no patrollers emerged from the woods that night, either before or after the rain drove him inside. He did not see Fawn again till they met over the breakfast trestle. They were both back in their own clothes, dry and only faintly stained; in the shabby blue dress she looked almost well, except for a lingering paleness. A check of the insides of her eyelids, and of her fingernails, showed them not as rosy as he thought they ought to be, and she still grew dizzy if she attempted to stand too suddenly, but his hand on her brow felt no fever, good.

He was pressing her to eat more bread and drink more milk when the boy Tad burst through the kitchen door, wide-eyed and gasping. "Ma! Pa! Uncle Sassa! There's one of them mud-men in the pasture, worrying the sheep!"

Dag exhaled wearily; the three farm men around the table leaped up in a panic and scattered to find their tool-weapons. Dag loosened his war knife in its belt sheath and stepped out onto the porch. Fawn and the farmwife followed, peering fearfully around him, Petti clutching a formidable kitchen knife.

At the far end of the pasture, a naked man-form had pounced across the back of a bleating sheep, face buried in its woolly neck. The sheep bucked and threw the creature off. The mud-man fell badly, as if its arms were numb and could not properly catch itself. It rose, shook itself, and half loped, half crawled after the intended prey. The rest of the flock, bewildered, trotted a few yards away, then turned to stare.

"Worried?" Dag murmured to the women. "I'd say those sheep are downright appalled. That mud-man must have been made from a dog or a wolf. See, it's trying to move like one, but nothing works. It can't use its hands like a man, and it can't use its jaws like a wolf. It's trying to tear that silly sheep's throat out, but all it's getting is a mouthful of wool. Yech!"

He shook his head in exasperation and pity, stepped off the porch, and strode toward the pasture; behind him, Petti gasped, and Fawn muffled a squeak.

He jogged to the end of the lane, to circle between the mud-man and the woods, then hopped up and swung his legs over the rail fence. He stretched his shoulders and shook out his right arm, trying to work out the soreness and knots, and drew his knife. The morning air was heavy with moisture, gray on the ground, lilac and pale pink rising to turquoise in the sky beyond the tree line. The grass was wet from the rain, beaded droplets glimmering like scattered silver, and the saturated soil squelched under his boots. He weaved around a few sodden cow flops and eased toward the mud-man. Aptly named—the creature was filthy, smeared with dung, hair matted and falling in its eyes, and it whiffed of nascent rot. Its flesh was already starting to lose tone and color, the skin mottled and yellowish. Its lips drew back as it snarled at Dag and froze, undecided between attack and flight.

Jump me, you clumsy suffering nightmare. Spare me the sweat of chasing you down. "Come along," Dag crooned, crouching a little and bringing his arms in. "End this. I'll get you out of there, I promise."

The creature's hips wriggled as it leaned forward, and Dag braced himself as it sprang. He almost missed his move as it stumbled on the lunge, hands pawing the air, neck twisting and straining in a vain attempt to bring its all-too-human jaw to Dag's neck. Dag blocked one black-clawed hand with his left arm, spun sideways, and slashed hard.

He jumped back as hot blood spurted from the creature's neck, trying to save himself more laundry duty. The mud-man managed three steps away, yowling wordlessly, before it fell to the mucky ground. Dag circled in cautiously, but no further mercy cut was required; the mud-man shuddered and grew still, eyes glazed and half-open. A tuft of dirty wool, stuck to its lips, stopped fluttering. *Absent gods, this is an ugly cleanup chore.* But neatly enough done, this time. He wiped his blade on the grass, making plans to beg a dry rag from the farmwife in a moment.

He stood up and turned to see the farm men, huddled in a terrified knot clutching their tools, staring at him openmouthed. Tad came running from the fence and was caught around the waist by his father as he attempted to approach the corpse. "I told you to stay back!"

"It's dead, Pa!" Tad wriggled free and gazed up with a glowing face at Dag. "He just walked right up to it and took it down slick as anything!"

Ah. The last mud-men these folk had encountered had still been bound by the will of their maker, intelligent and lethal. Not like this forsaken, sick, confused animal trapped in its awkward body. Dag didn't feel any overwhelming need to correct the farm men's misperceptions of his daring. Safer if they remained cautious of the mud-men anyway. His lips curled up in grim amusement, but he said only, "It's my job. You can have the burying of it, though." The farm men gathered around the corpse, poking it at tool-handle distance. Dag strolled past them toward the house, not looking back.

Most of the animals had collected in the upper end of the pasture, away from the disturbing intruder. The bay mare raised her head and snuffled at him as he approached. He paused, wiped his knife dry on her warm side, sheathed it, and scratched her poll, which made her flop her ears sideways, droop her lip, and sigh contentedly. The farmwife's tart suggestion of last night that he take the mare and ride off surfaced in his memory. Tempting idea.

Yes. But not alone.

He climbed the fence, crossed the yard, and made his way up onto the porch. Fawn gazed up at him with nearly as worshipful an expression as Tad, only with keener understanding. The farmwife had her arms crossed, torn between gratitude and glowering.

Dag was suddenly mortally tired of mistrustful strangers. He missed his patrol, for all their irritations. He almost missed the irritations, in their comfortable familiarity.

"Hey, Little Spark. I was going to wait for the wagon and take you to Glassforge lying flat, but I got to thinking. We might double up and ride out the way we came in the other day, and you wouldn't be jostled around any worse."

Her face lit. "Better, I should think. That lane would rattle your teeth, in a wagon."

"Even taking it slowly and carefully, we could reach town in about three hours' time. If you think it wouldn't overtire you?"

"Leave now, you mean? I'll pack my bedroll. It'll only take a moment!" She twirled about.

"Put my arm harness in it, will you? Along with the other things." Arm harness, knife pouch, and the linen bag of shattered bone and dreams—everything else that he'd arrived in, he was wearing; everything he'd borrowed was put back.

She paused, lips pursing as if following the same inventory, then nodded vigorously. "Right."

"Don't bounce. Don't *scamper,* either. Gently!" he called after her. The kitchen door shut on her trailing laugh.

He turned to find Petti giving him a measuring look. He raised his brows back at her.

She shrugged, and said on a sigh, "Not my business, I suppose."

He bit back rude agreement, converting the impulse to a more polite nod, and turned to collect the mare.

By the time he'd reaffixed the rope to the halter for reins and led the horse to the porch, murmuring promises of grain and a nice stall in Glassforge into the fuzzy flicking ears, Fawn was back out, breathless, with her bedroll slung over her shoulder, pelting Petti with good-byes and thank-yous. The honest warmth of them drew an answering smile from the farmwife seemingly despite herself.

"You be a lot more careful of yourself, now, girl," Petti admonished.

"Dag will look after me," Fawn assured her cheerily.

"Oh, aye." Petti sighed, after a momentary pause, and Dag wondered what comment she'd just bit back. "That's plain."

From the mounting block of the porch, Dag slid readily aboard the mare's bare back. Happily, the horse had wide-sprung ribs and no bony back ridge, and so was as comfortable to sit as a cushion; he needed to beg neither saddle nor pads from the farm. He stiffened his right ankle to make a stirrup of his foot for Fawn, and she scrambled up and sat across his lap as before. Wriggling into place, she smoothed her skirts and slipped her right arm around him. A little to his surprise, Petti shuffled forward and thrust a wrapped packet into Fawn's hands.

"It's only bread and jam. But it'll keep you on the road."

Dag touched his temple. "Thank you, ma'am. For everything." His hand found the rope reins again.

She nodded stiffly. "You, too." And, after a moment, "You just think about what I said, patroller. Or just think, anyways."

This seemed to call for either no answer at all, or a long defensive argument; Dag prudently chose the first, helped Fawn tuck the packet in her bedroll, nodded again, and turned the horse away. He extended his groundsense to its limit in one last check, but nothing resembling an aggravated patroller beating through the bushes stirred for a mile in any direction, nor more distraught dying mud-men either.

The bay mare's hooves scythed through the wiry chicory, its blossoms looking like bits of blue sky fallen and scattered along the ruts, and the nodding daisies. The farm men were dragging the mud-man's corpse into the woods as they rode down the fence line. They all waved, and Sassa trotted over to the end of the lane in time to say, "Off to Glassforge already? I'll be going in soon. If you see any of our folks, tell them we're all right! See you in town?"

"Sure!" said Fawn, and "Maybe," said Dag. He added, "If any of my people turn up here, would you tell them we're all right and that I'll meet them in town too?"

"'Course!" Sassa promised cheerily.

And then the track curved into the woods, and the farm and all its folk fell out of sight behind. Dag breathed relief as the quiet of the humid summer morning closed in, broken only by the gentle thump of the mare's hooves, the liquid trill of a red-crest, and the rain-refreshed gurgle of the creek that the road followed. A striped ground squirrel flickered across the track ahead of them, disappearing with a faint rustle into the weeds.

Fawn cuddled down, her head resting on his chest, and allowed herself to be rocked along, not speaking for a while. Ambushed again by the deep fatigue of her blood loss after the dawn's spate of excitement, Dag judged; like other injured younglings he'd known, she seemed likely to overestimate her capacity, swinging between imprudent activity and collapse. He hoped her recovery would be as swift. She made a warm and comfortable burden, balanced on his lap. The mare's walk was certainly smoother than a wagon would have been in these muddy ruts, and he had no intention of jostling either of them with a trot. A few mosquitoes whined around them in the damp shade, and he gently bumped them away from her fair skin with a flick of his ground against theirs.

The scent of her skin and hair, the moving curve of her breasts as she breathed, and the pressure of her thighs on his stimulated him, but not nearly so much as the light, the contentment, and the flattering sense of safety swirling through her complex ground. She was not herself aroused, but her air of openness, of sheer physical acceptance of his presence, made him unreasonably happy in turn, like a man warmed by a fire. The deep red note of her inmost injury still lurked underneath, and the violet shadings of her bruises clouded her ground as they did her flesh, but the sharp-edged glints of pain were much reduced.

She could not sense his ground in turn; she was unaware of his lingering inspection. A Lakewalker woman would have felt his keen regard, seeing just as deeply into him if he did not close himself off and keep closed, trading blindness for privacy. Feeling guiltily perverse, he indulged his inner senses upon Fawn without excuse of need—or fear of self-revelation.

It was a little like watching water lilies; rather more like smelling a dinner he was not allowed to eat. Was it possible to be starved for so long as to forget the taste of food, for the pangs of hunger to burn out like ash? It seemed so. But both the pleasure and the pain were his heart's secret, here. He was put in mind, suddenly, of the soil at the edge of a recovering blight; the weedy bedraggled look of it, unlovely yet hopeful. Blight was a numb gray thing, without sensation. Did the return of green life *hurt*? Odd thought.

She stirred, opening her eyes to stare into the shadows of the woods, here mostly beech, elm, and red oak, with an occasional towering cottonwood, or, in more open areas around the stream, stubby dogwood or redbud, long past their blooming. Splashes of the climbing sun spangled the leaves of the upper branches, sparking off lingering water drops.

"How will you find your patrol in Glassforge?" she asked.

"There's this hotel patrols stay at—we make it our headquarters when we're in this area. Nice change from sleeping on the ground. It'll also be our medicine tent. I'm pretty sure that more patrollers than my partner Saun took blows when we jumped those bandits the other night, so that's where they'll be holed up. They're used to our ways, there."

"Will you be there long?"

"Not sure. Chato's patrol was on their way south over the Grace River to trade for horses when they got waylaid by this trouble, and my patrol was riding a pattern up northeast, when we broke off to come here. Depends on the injured, I suspect."

She said thoughtfully, "Lakewalkers don't run the hotel, do they? It's Glassforge folks, right?"

"Right."

"What all jobs do they do in a hotel?"

He raised his brows. "Chambermaid, cook, scullion, horse boy, handyman, laundress . . . lots of things."

"I could do some of that. Maybe I could get work there."

Dag tensed. "Did Petti tell you about her cousin?"

"Cousin?" She peered up at him without guile.

Evidently not. "No—never mind. The couple that run the place have owned it for years; it's built on the site of an old inn, I think, which was his father's before. Mari would know. It's brick, three floors high, very fine. They burn brick as well as glass in Glassforge, you know."

She nodded. "I saw some houses in Lumpton Market once, they say were built from Glassforge brick. Must have been quite a job hauling it."

He shifted a little beneath her. "In any case, there'll be no work for you till you stop fainting when you jump up. Some days yet, I expect. *If you eat up and rest.*"

"I suppose," she said doubtfully. "But I don't have much money."

"My patrol will put you up," he said firmly. "We owe you for a malice, remember." *We owe you for your sacrifice.*

"Yes, all right, but I need to look ahead, now I'm on my own. I'm glad I met all those Horsefords. Nice folks. Maybe they'll introduce me around, help get me a start."

Would she not go home? Neither the picture of her dragging back to the realm of Stupid Sunny nor the notion of her as a Glassforge chambermaid pleased him much. "Best see what Mari has to say about that knife, before making plans."

"Mm." Her eyes darkened, and she huddled down again.

The peace of the woodland descended again, easing Dag's spirit. The light and air and solitude, the placid mare moving warmly beneath him, and Fawn curled against him with her ground slowly releasing its accumulation of anguish, put him wholly in a present that required nothing more of him, nor he of it. Released, for a moment, from an endless chain of duty and task, tautly pulling him into a weary future not chosen, merely accepted.

"How're you doing?" he murmured into Fawn's hair. "Pain?"

"No worse than when I was sitting up at breakfast, anyhow. Better than last night. This is all right."

"Good."

"Dag . . . " She hesitated.

"Mm?"

"What do Lakewalker women do who get in a fix like mine?"

The question baffled him. "Which fix?"

She gave a small snort. "I suppose I have been collecting troubles, lately. A baby and no husband was the one I was thinking of. Grass widowhood."

He could sense the grating of grief and guilt through her with that reminder. "It doesn't exactly work like that, for us."

She frowned. "Are young Lakewalkers all really, really . . . um . . . virtuous?"

He laughed softly. "No, if by virtuous you just mean keeping their trousers buttoned. Other virtues are more in demand. But young is young, farmer or Lakewalker. Pretty much everyone goes through an awkward period of fumbling around finding things out."

"You said a woman invites a man to her tent."

"If he's a lucky man."

"Then how do . . . " She trailed off in confusion.

He finally figured out what she was asking. "Oh. It's our grounds, again. The time of the month when a woman can conceive shows as a beautiful pattern in her ground. If the time and place are wrong for a child, she and her man just pleasure each other in ways that don't lead to children."

Fawn's silence following this extended for a quite a long time. Then she said, "What?"

"Which what?"

"How do people . . . people can do that? How?"

Dag swallowed uneasily. How much *could* this girl not know? By the evidence so far, quite a lot, he reflected ruefully. How far back did he need to begin?

"Well—hands, for one."

"Hands?"

"Touching each other, till they trade release. Tongues and mouths and other things, too."

She blinked. "Release?"

"Touch each other as you'd touch yourself, only with a better angle and company and, well, just better all around. Less . . . lonely."

Her face screwed up. "Oh. Boys do that, I know. I guess girls could do it for them, too. Do they like it?"

"Um . . . generally," he said cautiously. This unexpected turn of the conversation sped his mind, and his body was following fast. *Calm yourself, old patroller.* Fortunately, she could not sense the heated ripple in him. "Girls like it, too. In my experience."

Another long, digestive silence. "Is this some Lakewalker lady thing? Magic?"

"There are tricks you can do with your grounds to make it better, but no. Lakewalker ladies and farmer girls are equally magical in this. Anyway, farmers have grounds too, they just can't sense them." *Absent gods be thanked.*

Her expression now was intensely cogitative, and a stuttering swirl of arousal had started in her as well. It wasn't, he realized suddenly, just her hurts that blocked its flow. Something that half-blood woman at Tripoint had once told him, that he'd scarcely believed, came back to him now: that some farmer women never learned how to pleasure themselves, or to find release. She'd laughed at his expression. *Come, come, Dag. Boys practically trip over their own parts. Women's are all tucked neatly up inside. They can be just as tricky for us as for the farmer boys to find. Many's the farmwife has me to thank for providing her man with the treasure map, scandalized as she'd be to learn it.* Since he'd had much to thank her for as well, he'd set about it, dismissing the ineptness of farm boys from his mind and, in a short time, from hers.

That had been a long time ago . . .

"What other things?" Fawn said.

"Beg pardon?"

"Besides hands and tongues and mouths."

"Just . . . don't . . . not . . . never mind." And now his arousal had grown to serious physical discomfort. Atop a horse, of all things. There were many things not to try on a horse, even one as good-natured as this mare. He couldn't avoid remembering several of them, which *didn't help.*

Spark couldn't sense his ground. He could stand in front of her rigid with mind-numbing lust, and as long as he kept his trousers on, she wouldn't know. And considering all her recent disastrous experiences, she oughtn't to know. Bad if she laughed . . . no, upon reflection, good if she laughed. *Bad* if she was disgusted or horrified or frightened, taking him for another lout like Stupid Sunny or that poor fool he'd shot in the backside. If it grew too excruciating, he could slip off the horse and disappear into the woods for a spell, pretending to be answering a call of nature. Which he would be; no lie there. *Stop it. You did this to yourself. Suffer in silence. Think of something else. You can control your body. She can't tell.*

She sighed, rustled about, and gazed up into his face. "Your eyes change color with the light," she observed in a tone of new interest. "In the sun they're all bright gold like coins. In the shade they go brown like clear spice tea. In the night, they're black like deep pools." She added after a moment, "They're really dark right now."

"Mm," said Dag. Every breath brought her heady scent to his mouth, to his mind. He could not very well stop breathing.

A flash of motion at treetop height caught both their eyes.

"Look, a red-tailed hawk!" she cried. "Isn't he beautiful!" Her head and body turned to follow the pale clean-cut shape, ruddy translucent tail feathers almost glowing against the washed blue of the sky, and her hot small hand came down to support herself. Directly on Dag's aching erection.

His startled recoil was so abrupt, he fell off the horse.

He landed on his back with a breath-stealing thump. Thankfully, she landed atop him and not underneath. Her weight was soft upon him, her breath accelerated by the shock. Her pupils were too wide for this light, and, as she twisted around and thrust out one hand to support herself, her gaze grew fixed upon his mouth.

Yes! Kiss me, do. His hand spasmed, and he laid it out flat and stiff, palm up upon the grass, lest he lunge at her. He moistened his lips. The damp of the grass and the soil began soaking into the back of his shirt and trousers. He could feel every curve of her body, pressed into his, and every curse of her ground. Absent gods, he was halfway to groundlock all by *himself* . . .

"Are you all right?" she gasped.

Terror shot through him, wilting his arousal, that the fall might have torn something loose inside her to start her bleeding again like the first day. It would take the better part of hour to carry her back to the farm, and in her current depleted state, she might not survive another such draining.

She scrambled off him and plunked herself ungracefully on the ground, panting.

"Are *you* all right?" he asked urgently in turn.

"I guess so." She winced a little, but she rubbed her elbow, not her belly.

He sat up and ran his hand through his hair. *Fool, fool, blight you, pay attention . . . ! You might have killed her.*

"What happened?" she asked.

"I . . . thought I saw something out of the corner of my eye, but it was just a trick of the light. I didn't mean to shy like a horse." Which had to be the weakest excuse for an excuse he'd ever uttered.

The mare, in fact, was less shaken than either of them. She had sidestepped as they'd gone over, but now stood peacefully a few yards off, looking at them in mild astonishment. No further excitement seeming forthcoming, she put her head down and nibbled a weed.

"Yes, well, after that mud-man this morning, it's no wonder you're jumpy," Fawn said kindly. She stared around at the woods in renewed worry, then balanced a hand on his shoulder, pushed herself up, and tried to brush the dirt off her sleeve.

Dag took a few deep breaths, letting his pounding heart slow, then rose as well and went to recapture the mare. A fallen tree a few steps into the woods looked like an adequate mounting block; he led the horse up to it, and Fawn dutifully followed. And if they started this all over again, he feared he would disgrace himself before they ever got to Glassforge.

"To tell the truth," Dag lied, "my left arm was getting a bit tired. Do you think you could sit behind and hang on pillion style, for a while?"

"Oh! I'm sorry. I was so comfortable, I didn't think it might be awkward for you!" she apologized earnestly.

You have no idea how awkward. He grinned to hide his guilt, and to reassure her, but he was afraid it just came out looking demented.

Up they climbed once more. Fawn settled herself with both dainty feet to one side, and both dainty hands wrapped around his waist in a firm, warm grip.

And all Dag's stern resolve melted in the unbidden thought: *Lower. Lower!*

He set his teeth and dug his heels into the blameless mare's sides to urge her to a brisker walk.

Fawn balanced herself, wondering if she laid her head to Dag's back if she could hear his heartbeat again. She'd thought she'd been recovering well this morning, but the little accident reminded her of how tired she yet was, how quickly the least exertion stole her breath. Dag was more tired than he looked, too, it seemed, judging by his long silences.

She was embarrassed by how close she'd come to trying to kiss him, after their clumsy fall. She'd probably landed an elbow in his gut, and he'd been too kind to say anything. He'd even grinned at her, helping her up. His teeth were a trifle crooked, but nothing to signify, strong and sound, with a fascinating little chip out of one of the front ones. His smile was too fleeting, but it was probably safer for her tattered dignity that his grin was even rarer. If he'd grinned at her so kissably while they were still flat on the grass, instead of giving her that peculiar look—maybe it had been suppressed pain?—she'd likely have disgraced herself altogether.

The nasty name that Sunny had called her during their argument over the baby stuck in her craw. With one mocking word, Sunny had somehow turned all her love-in-intent, her breathless curiosity, her timid daring, into something ugly and vile. He'd been happy enough to kiss her and fondle her in the wheatfield in the dark, and call her his pretty thing; the slur came later. Dubious therefore, but still . . . was it typical for men to despise the women who gave them the attention they claimed to want? Judging from some of the rude insults she'd heard here and there, maybe so.

She did not want Dag to despise her, to take her for something low. But then, she would never apply the word *typical* to him.

So . . . was Dag lonely? Or lucky?

He didn't seem the lucky sort, somehow.

So how would you know? Her heart felt as if it knew him better than any man, no, any *person* she'd ever met. The feeling did not stand up to inspection. He could be married, for all he'd said to the contrary. He could have children. He could have children almost as old as her. Or who knew what? He hadn't said. There was a lot he hadn't talked of, when she thought about it.

It was just that . . . what little he'd talked about had seemed so important. As though she'd been dying of thirst, and everyone else had wanted to give her piles of dry gimcrackery, and he'd offered her a cup of plain pure water. Straightforward. Welcome beyond desire or deserving. Unsettling . . .

The valley they were riding down opened out, the creek ran away through broad fields, and the farm lane gave onto the straight road at last.

Dag turned the mare left. And whatever opportunity she had just wasted was gone forever.

The straight road was busier today, and grew more so as they neared the town. Either the removal of the bandit threat had brought more people out on the highway, or it was market day. Or both, Fawn decided. They passed sturdy brick-wagons and goods-wagons drawn by teams of big dray horses pulling hard going out, and rode alongside ones returning, not empty, but loaded with firewood or hitchhiking county folk taking produce and handcrafts to sell. She caught snatches of cheerful conversation, the girls flirting with the teamsters when no elders rode with them. Farm carts and haywains and yes, even that manure wagon she'd wished for in vain the other day. The scent of coal smoke and woodsmoke came to Fawn's nose even before they rounded the last curve and the town came into sight.

Nothing about this arrival was like anything she had pictured when she'd started out from home, but at least she'd *got* here. Something that she'd begun, finally finished. It felt like breaking a curse. Glassforge. At last.

9

Fawn leaned precariously around Dag's shoulder and gazed down the main street, lined with older buildings of wood and stone or newer ones of brick. Plank sidewalks kept people's feet out of the churned mud of the road. A block farther on, the mud gave way to cobblestones, and beyond that, brick. A town so rich they paved the street with brick! The road curved away to follow the bend in the river, but she could just glimpse a town square busy with a day market. Most of the smokes that smudged the air seemed to be coming from farther downstream and downwind. Dag turned the mare into a side street, jerking his chin at the brick building rising to their left, blunt and blocky but softened by climbing ivy.

"There's our hotel. Patrols always stay there for free. It was written into the will of the owner's father. Something about the last big malice we took out in these parts, nigh on sixty years ago. Must've been a scary one. Good thinking on someone's part, because it gets the area patrolled more often."

"You looked for sixty years without finding another?"

"Oh, there've been a couple in the interim, I believe. We just got them so small, the farmers never knew. Like, um . . . pulling a weed instead of chopping down a tree. Better for us, better for everyone, except harder to convince folks to chip in some payment. Farsighted man, that old innkeep."

They turned again under a wide brick archway and into the yard between the hotel and its stable. A horse boy polishing harness on a bench glanced up and rose to come forward. He did not reach for the mare's makeshift bridle.

"Sorry, mister, miss." His nod was polite, but his look seemed to sum up the worth of the battered pair riding bareback and find it sadly short. "Hotel's full up. You'll have to find another place." The twist of his lips turned slightly derisive, if not altogether without sympathy. "Doubt you could make the price of a room here anyways."

Only Fawn's hand on Dag's back felt the faint rumble of—anger? no, amusement pass through him. "Doubt I could too. Happily, Miss Bluefield, here, has made the price of all of them."

The boy's face went a little blank, as he tried to work this out to anything that made sense to him. His confusion was interrupted by a pair of Lakewalkers hobbling out of the doorway into the yard, staring hard at Dag.

These two looked more like proper patrollers, neat in leather vests, with their long hair pulled back in decorated braids. One had a face nearly as bruised as Fawn's, with a strip of linen wrapped awkwardly around his head and under his jaw not quite hiding a line of bloody stitches. He leaned on a stick. The other had her left arm, thickened with bandages, supported in a sling. Both were dark-haired and tall, though their eyes were an almost normal sort of clear bright brown.

"Dag Redwing Hickory . . . ?" said the woman cautiously.

Dag swung his right leg over the mare's neck and sat sideways a moment; smiling faintly, he touched his hand to his temple in a gesture of acknowledgment. "Aye. You all from Chato's Log Hollow patrol?"

Both patrollers stood straighter, despite their evident hurts. "Yes, sir!" said the man, while the woman hissed at the hotel servant, "Boy, take the patroller's horse!"

The boy jumped as though goosed and took the halter rope, his stare growing wide-eyed. Dag slid down and turned to help Fawn, who swung her legs over.

"Ah! Don't you dare jump," he said sternly, and she nodded and slid off into his arm, collecting something pleasantly like a hug as he eased her feet to the ground. She stifled her longing to lean her head into his chest and just stand there for, oh, say, about a week. He turned to the other patrollers, but his left arm stayed behind her back, a solid, anchoring weight.

"Where is everyone?" Dag asked.

The man grinned, then winced, his hand going to his jaw. "Out looking for you, mostly."

"Ah, I was afraid of that."

"Yeah," said the woman. "Your patrol all kept swearing you'd turn up like a cat, and then went running out again anyway without hardly stopping to eat or sleep. Looks like the cat fanciers had the right of it. There's a fellow upstairs name of Saun's been fretting his heart out for you. Every time we go in, he badgers for news."

Dag's lips pursed in a breath of relief. "On medicine tent duty, are you?"

"Yep," said the man.

"How many carrying-wounded have we got?"

"Just two—your Saun and our Reela. She got her leg broke when some mud-men spooked her horse over a drop."

"Bad?"

"Not good, but she'll get to keep it."

Dag nodded. "Good enough, then."

The man blinked in belated realization of Dag's stump, but he added nothing more awkward. "I don't know how tired you are, but it would be kindly done if you could step up and put Saun's mind at ease first thing. He really has been fretting something awful. I think he'd rest better for seeing you with his own eyes."

"Of course," said Dag.

"Ah . . . " said the woman, looking at Fawn and then, inquiringly, at Dag.

"This here's Miss Fawn Bluefield," said Dag.

Fawn dipped her knees. "How de' do?"

"And she is . . . ?" said the man dubiously.

"She's with me." Something distinctly firm in Dag's voice discouraged further questions, and the two patrollers, after civil if still curious nods at Fawn, led the way inside.

Fawn had only a glimpse of the entry hall, featuring a tall wooden counter and archways leading off to some big rooms, before she followed the patrollers up a staircase with a time-polished banister, cool and smooth under her hesitant fingertips. One flight up, they turned into a hallway lined with doors on either side and a glass window set in the end for light.

"You partner's mostly lucid today, although he still keeps claiming you brought him back from the dead," said the man over his shoulder.

"He wasn't dead," said Dag.

The man shot a look at the woman. "Told you."

"His heart had stopped and he'd quit breathing, was all."

Fawn blinked in bafflement. And, she was heartened to see, she wasn't the only one.

"Er . . . " The man stopped outside a door with a brass number 6 on it. "Pardon, sir? I'd always been taught it was too risky to match grounds with someone mortally injured, and unworkable to block the pain at speed."

"Likely." Dag shrugged. "I just skipped the extras and went in and out fast."

"*Oh*," said the woman in a voice of enlightenment that Fawn did not share.

The man blurted, "Didn't it hurt?"

Dag gave him a long, slow look. Fawn was very glad it wasn't her at the focus, because that look could surely reduce people to grease spots on the floor. Dag gave the other patroller a moment more to melt—precisely timed, she was suddenly certain—then nodded at the door. The woman hastened to open it.

Dag passed in. If the two patrollers had been respectful before, the look they now exchanged behind his back was downright daunted. The woman glanced at Fawn doubtfully but did not attempt to exclude her as she slipped through the door in Dag's wake.

The room had cutwork linen curtains, pushed open and moving gently in the summer air, and flanking the window two beds with feather ticks atop straw ticks. One was empty, though it had gear and saddlebags piled on the floor at its foot. So did the other, but in it lay an—inevitably—tall young man. His hair was light brown, unbraided, and spread out upon his pillow. A rumpled sheet was pulled up to his chest, where his torso was wrapped around with bandages. He stared listlessly at the ceiling, his pale brow wrinkled. When he turned his head at the sound of steps and recognized his visitor, the pain in his face transformed to joy so fast it looked like a flash flood washing over him.

"Dag! You made it!" He laughed, coughed, grimaced, and moaned. "Ow. Knew you would!"

The patroller woman raised her eyebrows at this broad claim but grinned indulgently.

Dag walked to the bedside and smiled down, adopting a cheerful tone. "Now, I know you had six broken ribs at least. I ask you, *is* this the time for speeches?"

"Only a short one," wheezed the young man. His hand found Dag's and grasped it. "Thank you."

Dag's brows twitched, but he didn't argue. Such sincere gratitude shone in the young man's eyes, Fawn warmed to him at once. Finally, somebody seemed to be taking Dag at his worth. Saun turned his head to peer somewhat blearily at her, and she smiled at him with all her heart. He blinked rapidly and smiled back, looking a bit flummoxed.

Dag gave the hand a little shake from side to side, and asked more softly, "How're you doing, Saun?"

"It only hurts when I laugh."

"Oh? Don't let the patrol know that." The dry light in Dag's eyes was mirth, Fawn realized.

Saun sputtered and coughed. "Ow! Blast you, Dag!"

"See what I mean?" He added more sternly, "They tell me you haven't been sleeping. I said, couldn't be—this is the patroller we have to roll out of his blankets by force in camp in the morning. Feather beds too soft for you now? Shall I bring you a few rocks to make it more homelike?"

Saun held a hand to his bandaged chest and carefully refrained from chuckling. "Naw. All *I* want is your tale. They said" —his face grew grave in memory, and he moistened his lips—"they found your horse yesterday miles from the lair, found the lair, found half your gear and your bow abandoned in a pile. Your *bow*. Didn't think you'd ever leave *that* on purpose. Two rotting mud-men and a pile of something Mari swore was the dead malice, and a trail of blood leading off to nothing. What were we supposed to think?"

"I was rather hoping someone would think I'd found shelter at the nearest farm," Dag said ruefully. "I begin to suspect I'm not exciting enough for you all."

Saun's eyes narrowed. "There's more than that," he said positively.

"Quite a bit, but it's for Mari's ears first." Dag glanced at Fawn.

Saun slumped in apparent acceptance of this. "As long as I get more sometime."

"Sometime." Dag hesitated, then added diffidently, "So . . . did they also find the body I'd left in the tree?"

Three faces turned to stare.

"Evidently not yet," Dag murmured.

"See what I told you? See?" said Saun to his companions in a voice of vindication. He added to Dag through slightly gritted teeth, "Sometime soon, all right?"

"As I can." Dag nodded at the two from the other patrol. "Did Mari say when she'd be back?"

They shook their heads. "She left at dawn," the woman offered.

"Need anything more right now, Saun?" asked the patroller man.

"You just brought me what I wanted most," said Saun. "Take a break, eh?"

"I think I will." With a barely audible grunt of pain, the patroller man sat down on the other bed, evidently his own, shed his boots, and used his hands to swing the stiff leg inboard. "Ah."

Dag nodded in farewell. "Sleep hard, Saun. Try and wake up smarter, eh?"

A faint snort and a muffled *Ow!* followed the three out. Dag's face, turning away, softened like a man finding grace in an unexpected hour. "Yeah, he'll be all right," he muttered in satisfaction.

The patroller woman closed the door quietly behind them.

"So, was that Saun the Sheep?" asked Fawn.

"Aye, the very lamb," said Dag. "If he lives long enough to trade in some of that enthusiasm for brains, he'll be a good patroller. He's made it to twenty, so far. Must be luck." His smile took a twist. "Same as you, Little Spark."

As they started down the hall, a woman's voice called weakly from a room with an open door.

"That's Reela," said the patroller woman quickly. "Do you have all you need, sir?"

"If not, I'll find it." Dag gave a dismissing wave. "I've known this place for years."

"Then if you'll excuse me, I'll go see what she wants." She nodded and stepped away.

As they made their way down the stairs, Fawn heard Dag mutter under his breath, "Stop sir-ing me, you dreadful puppies!" He paused at the bottom, his hand on the rail, and looked back upward, his face going distant.

"Now what are you thinking?" Fawn asked softly.

"I'm thinking . . . that when our walking wounded are set to look after our carrying-wounded, it's a sure sign we're too short-rostered. Mari's patrol is sixteen, four by four. It should be twenty-five, five by five. I wonder how many Chato's patrol is down by? Ah, well." He vented a sigh. "Let's rustle us up some food, Spark."

Dag led her to a rather astonishing little commode chamber, where she was able to swap out her dressings and wash up in the pretty painted tin basin provided. When she emerged, he escorted her in turn to one of the big downstairs rooms, full of tables with benches or chairs but, at this hour, empty of other people. In a few minutes, a serving girl came out of the kitchen in back with a tray of ham, cheese, two kinds of bread, cream-and-rhubarb pie, and strawberries, with a pitcher of beer and a jug of milk, fresh, the girl informed them, from the hotel's own cows kept out back. Fawn mentally added *serving girl* to her list of potential Glassforge jobs, as well as *milkmaid,* and set to under Dag's benign eye. More relaxed than she'd ever seen him, he plowed in heartily, she noted with satisfaction.

They were contesting the last strawberry, each trying to press it on the other, when Dag's head came up, and he said "Ah." In a moment, Fawn could hear through the open windows the clatter of horses and echo of voices in the stable yard. In another minute, the door slammed open and booted footsteps rapped across the floorboards. Mari, trailed by two other patrollers, swept into the dining room, halted by their table, planted her fists on her hips, and glowered at Dag.

"*You,*" she uttered, and never had Fawn heard one syllable carry so much freight.

Deadpan, Dag topped up his beer glass and handed it to her. Not taking her exasperated eyes from him, she raised it to her lips and gulped down half. The other two patrollers were grinning broadly.

"Were you *trying* to give me the fright of my life, boy?" she demanded, plunking the glass back down almost hard enough to crack it.

"No," Dag drawled, rescuing the glass and filling it again, "I suspect that was just a bonus. Sit down and catch your breath, Aunt Mari."

"Don't you *Aunt Mari* me till I'm done reaming you out," she said, but much more mildly. One of the patrollers at her shoulder, catching Dag's eye, pulled out a chair for her, and she sat anyhow. By the time she'd blown out her breath and stretched her back, her posture had grown much less alarming. Except for the underlying exhaustion creeping to the surface; Dag's brows drew down at that.

He reached across the table and gripped her hand. "Sorry for any false scares. Saun told me about you finding my messes yesterday. I kind of had my hand full, though."

"Aye, so I heard."

"Oh, did you find the Horsefords' farm, finally?"

"About two hours ago. Now, there was a garbled tale and a half." She glanced speculatively at Fawn, and her frown at Dag deepened.

Dag said, "Mari, may I present Miss Fawn Bluefield. Spark, this is my patrol leader, Mari Redwing Hickory. Mari's her personal name, Redwing is our tent name, and the Hickory is for Hickory Lake Camp, which is our patrol's home base."

Fawn ducked her head politely. Mari returned an extremely provisional nod.

Gesturing, Dag continued, "Utau and Razi, also of Hickory Camp." The two other patrollers made friendly salutes of greeting to her not unlike Dag's. Utau was older, shorter, and burlier, and wore his thinning hair in a knot like Mari's. Razi was younger, taller, and gawkier; his hair hung down his back in a single plait almost to his waist, with dark red and green cords woven in.

The older one, Utau, said, "Congratulations on the malice, Dag. The youngsters were all hopping mad that they'd missed their first kill, though. I'd suggested we have you take them all out to the lair and walk them through it, for consolation, and to show them how it's done."

Dag shook his head, caught between a low laugh and a wince. "I don't think that would be all that useful to them, really."

"So just how much of a foul-up was it?" Mari inquired tartly.

The residue of amusement drained from Dag's eyes. "Foul enough. The short tale is, Miss Bluefield, here, was kidnapped off the road by the pair I'd trailed from the bandit camp. When I caught up with them all at the lair, I was outmatched by the mud-men, who got a good way into taking me apart. But I noticed that the malice, mud-men, and all, were making the interesting mistake of ignoring Miss Bluefield in the scuffle. So I tossed my sharing knives to her, and she got one into the malice. Took it down. Saved my life. World too, for the usual bonus."

"*She* got that close to a malice?" asked Razi, in a voice somewhere between disbelief and amazement. "How?"

For answer, Dag leaned over and, after a glance at her for permission, gently folded back the collar of her dress. His finger traced over numb spots of flesh around her neck that Fawn realized belatedly must be the bruises from the malice's great hands, and she shuddered involuntarily despite the summer warmth of the room. "Closer than that, Razi."

The two patrollers' lips parted. Mari leaned back in her chair, her hand going to her mouth. Fawn had not seen a mirror for days. Whatever did the marks look like?

"The malice misjudged her," Dag continued. "I trust you all will not. But if you want to repeat those congratulations to the right person, Utau, feel free."

Under Dag's cool eye, Utau unscrewed his face and slowly brought his hand to his temple. After groping a moment for his voice, he managed, "Miss Bluefield."

"Aye," Razi seconded, after a stunned moment.

"Wildly demonstrative bunch, you know, we patrollers," Dag murmured in Fawn's ear, his dry amusement flickering again.

"I can see that," she murmured back, making his lip twitch.

Mari rubbed her forehead. "And the long tale, Dag? Do I even want to hear it?"

The grim look he gave her locked all her attention. "Yes," he said. "As soon as may be. But in private. Then Miss Bluefield needs to rest." He turned to Fawn. "Or do you want to rest up first?"

Fawn shook her head. "Talk first, please."

Mari braced her hands on her trousered knees and rolled her shoulders. "Ah. All right." She peered around, eyes narrowing. "My room?"

"That would do."

She pushed to her feet. "Utau, you were up all night. You're now off duty. Razi, get some food in you, then ride out to Tailor's Point and let them know Dag's been found. Or shown up, anyway." The patrollers nodded and turned away.

Dad murmured to Fawn, "Bring your bedroll."

Mari's room proved to be on the third floor. Fawn found herself dizzy and shaky by the time she'd climbed the second flight of stairs, and she was grateful for Dag's supporting hand. Mari led them into a narrower room than Saun's, with only one bed, though otherwise similar right down to the messy pile of gear and saddlebags at the foot. Dag gestured for Fawn to lay her bedroll across the bed. Fawn untied the bindings and unrolled it; the contents clinked.

Mari's brows rose. She picked up Dag's ruptured hand harness and held it out like the sad carcass of some dead animal. "*That* took some doing. I see now why you didn't bother to take your bow along. You still got your arm?"

"Just barely," said Dag. "I need to get that thing restitched with stronger thread, this time."

"I'd rethink that idea if I were you. Which do you want to have come apart first, you or it?"

Dag paused a moment, then said, "Ah. You have a point, there. Maybe I'll get it fixed just the same."

"Better." Mari set the harness back down and picked up the makeshift linen bag and let it drift through her hand, feeling the contents shift within. Her expression grew sad, almost remote. "Kauneo's heart's knife, wasn't it?"

Dag nodded shortly.

"I know how long you've kept it aside. This fate was worthy."

Dag shook his head. "They're all the same, really, I've come to believe." He took a breath and advanced to the bed, motioning Fawn to sit.

She perched cross-legged on the bed's head, smoothing her skirt over her knees, and watched the two patrollers. Mari had gold eyes much like Dag's, if a shade more bronze, and she wondered if she really was his aunt and his use of the title not, as she'd first thought, just a joke or a respectful endearment.

Mari set the bag back down. "Do you plan to send it up to be buried with the rest of her uncle's bones? Or burn it here?"

"Not sure yet. It will keep with me; it has so far." Dag drew a deeper breath, staring down at the other knife. "Now we come to the long story."

Mari sat down at the bed's foot and crossed her arms, listening closely as Dag began his tale again, this time starting with the night raid on the bandit camp. His descriptions of his actions were succinct but very exact, Fawn noticed, as though certain details might matter more, though she was not sure how he sorted which to leave in or out. Until he came to, "I believe the mud-man lifted Miss Bluefield from the road because she was two months pregnant. And came back and took her from the farm for the same reason."

Mari's lips moved involuntarily, *Was?,* then compressed. "Go on."

Dag's voice stiffened as he described his risky raid on the malice's cave. "I was just too late. When I hit the entrance and the mud-men, the malice was already taking her child."

Mari leaned forward, her brows drawing down. "Separately?"

"So it seems."

"Huh . . . " Mari leaned back, shook her head, and peered at Fawn. "Excuse me. I am so sorry for your loss. But this is new to me. We knew malices took pregnant women, but then, they take anyone they can catch. Rarely, the women's bodies are recovered. I did not know the malice didn't always take both grounds together."

"I don't think," said Fawn distantly, "it would have kept me around very long. It was about to break my neck when I finally got the right knife into it."

Mari blinked, glanced down at the blue-hilted bone knife lying on the bedroll, and stared up again at Dag. "What?"

Carefully, Dag explained Fawn's mix-up with his knives. He was very kind, Fawn thought, to excuse her from any blame in the matter.

"The knife had been unprimed. You know what I was saving it for."

Mari nodded.

"But now it's primed. With the death of Spark's—of Miss Bluefield's daughter, I believe. What I don't know is if that's all it drew from the malice. Or whether it will even work as a sharing knife. Or . . . well, I don't know much, I'm afraid. But with Miss Bluefield's permission, I thought you could examine it too."

"Dag, I'm no more a maker than you are."

"No, but you are more . . . you are less . . . I could use another opinion."

Mari glanced at Fawn. "Miss Bluefield, may I?"

"Please. I want to understand, and . . . and I don't, really."

Mari leaned over and picked up the bone knife. She cradled it, ran her hand along its smooth pale length, and finally, much as Dag had, held it to her lips with her eyes closed. When she set it down again, her mouth stayed tight for a moment.

"Well" —she took a breath—"it's certainly primed."

"That, I could tell," said Dag.

"It feels . . . hm. Oddly pure. It's not that souls go into the knives— you did explain that to her, yes?" she demanded of Dag.

"Yes. She's clear on that part."

"But different people's heart's knives do have different feels to them. Some echo of the donor lingers, though they all seem to work alike. Perhaps it's that the lives are different, but the deaths are all the same, I don't know. I'm a patroller, not a lore-master. I think"—she tapped her lips with a forefinger—"you had better take it to a maker. The most experienced you can find."

"Miss Bluefield and I," said Dag. "The knife is properly hers, now."

"This isn't any business for a farmer to be mixed up in."

Dag scowled. "What would you have me do? Take it from her? *You?*"

"Explain, please?" Fawn said tightly. "Everyone is talking past me again. That's all right mostly, I'm used to it, but not for *this.*"

"Show her your knives, Mari," Dag said, a rasp of challenge in his voice, for all that it was soft.

She looked at him, then slowly unbuttoned her shirt partway down and drew out a dual knife pouch much like Dag's, though of softer leather. She pulled the strap over her head, pushed the bedroll aside, and laid out two bone knives side by side on the quilt. They were nearly identical, except for different-colored dye daubed on the lightly carved hilts, red and brown this time.

"These are a true pair, both bones from the same donor," she said, caressing the red one. "My youngest son, as it happens. It was his third year patrolling, up Sparford way, and I'd just got to thinking he was getting over the riskiest part of the learning . . . well." She touched the brown one. "This one is primed. His father's aunt Palai gave her death to it. Tough, tough old woman—absent gods, we loved her. Preferably from a safe distance, but there's one like that in every family, I think." Her hand drifted again to the red one. "This one is unprimed, bonded to me. I keep it by me in case."

"So what would happen," said Dag dryly, "to anyone who tried to take them from you?"

Mari's smile grew grim. "I'd outstrip the worst wrath of Great-aunt Palai." She sat up and slipped the knives away, then nodded at Fawn. "But I think it's different for her."

"It's all strange to me." Fawn frowned, staring at the blue-hilted knife. "I have no happy memories about this to balance the sorrows. But they're my memories, all the same. I'd rather they weren't . . . wasted."

Mari raised both hands in a gesture of frustrated neutrality.

"So could I have leave from the patrol to travel on this matter?" asked Dag.

Mari grimaced. "You know how short we are, but once this Glassforge business is settled, I can't very well refuse you. Have you ever drawn leave? Ever? You don't even get sick!"

Dag thought a moment. "Death of my father," he said at last. "Eleven years ago."

"Before my time. Eh! Ask again when we're ready to decamp. If there's no new trouble landed in our laps by then."

He nodded. "Miss Bluefield's not fit to travel far yet anyway. You can see by her eyelids and nails she's lost too much blood, even without how her knees give way. No fever yet, though. Please, Mari, I did all I could, but could you look her over?" His hand touched his belly, making his meaning clear.

Mari sighed. "Yes, yes, Dag."

He stood expectantly for a moment; she grimaced and sat up, waving to a set of saddlebags leaning in the corner. "There's your gear, by the by. Luckily your fool horse hadn't got round to scraping it off in the woods. Go on, now."

"But will you . . . can't I . . . I mean, it's not as though you have to undress her."

"Women's business," she said firmly.

Reluctantly, he made for the door, though he did scoop up his arm harness and recovered belongings. "I'll see about getting you a room, Spark."

Fawn smiled gratefully at him.

"Good," said Mari. "Scat."

He bit his lip and nodded farewell. His boot steps faded down the hall.

Fawn tried not to be too unnerved by being left alone with Mari. Scary old lady or not, the patrol leader seemed to share some of Dag's straightforward quality. She had Fawn sit quietly on the bed while she ran her hands over her. She then sat behind Fawn and hugged her in close for several silent minutes, her hands wrapped across Fawn's lower belly. If she was doing something with her groundsense, Fawn could not feel it, and wondered if this was what being deaf among hearing people was like. When she released Fawn, her face was cool but not unkind.

"You'll do," she said. "It's clear you were ripped up unnatural, which accounts for the suddenness of the bleeding, but you're healing about as quick as could be expected for someone so depleted, and your womb's not hot. Fever's a commoner killer in these things than bleeding, though less showy. You'll have some blight-scarring in there, I guess, slow to heal like the ones on your neck, but not enough to stop you having other children, so you be more careful in future, *Miss* Bluefield."

"Oh." Fawn, looking back through clouds of regret, had not even thought ahead to her future fertility. "Does that happen to some women, after a miscarriage?"

"Sometimes. Or after a bad birth. Delicate parts in there. It amazes me the process works at all, when I think about all the things I've seen can go wrong."

Fawn nodded, then reached to put away Dag's blue-hilted knife, still lying on her bedroll atop her spare clothes.

"So," said Mari in a carefully bland tone, "who's the other half owner 'sides you of that knife's priming? Some farm lout?"

Fawn's jaw set. "Just me. The lout made it very clear he was giving it all to me. Which was why I was out on the road in the first place."

"Farmers. I'll never understand 'em."

"There are no Lakewalker louts?"

"Well . . . " Mari's long, embarrassed drawl conceded the point.

Fawn reread the faded brown lettering on the bone blade. "Dag meant to drive this into his own heart someday. Didn't he." This Kauneo had intended that he should.

"Aye."

Now he couldn't. That was something, at least. "You have one, too."

"Someone has to prime. Not everyone, but enough. Patrollers understand the need better."

"Was Kauneo a patroller?"

"Didn't Dag say?"

"He said she was a woman who'd died twenty years ago up northwest someplace."

"That's a bit close-mouthed even for him." Mari sighed. "It's not my place to tell his tales, but if you are to have the holding of that knife, farmer girl, you'd better understand what it is and where it comes from."

"Yes," said Fawn firmly, "please. I'm so tired of making stupid mistakes."

Mari twitched a—provisionally—approving eyebrow at this. "Very well. I'll give you what Dag would call the short tale." Her long inhalation suggested it wasn't going to be as short as all that, and Fawn sat cross-legged again, intent.

"Kauneo was Dag's wife."

A tremor of shock ran through Fawn. Shock, but not surprise, she realized. "I see."

"She died at Wolf Ridge."

"He hadn't mentioned any Wolf Ridge to me. He just called it a bad malice war." Though there could be no such thing as a good malice war, Fawn suspected.

"Farmer girl, Dag doesn't talk about Wolf Ridge to anyone. One of his several little quirks you have to get used to. You have to understand, Luthlia is the biggest, wildest hinterland of the seven, with the thinnest population of Lakewalkers to try to patrol it. Terrible patrolling—cold swamps and trackless woods and killing winters. The other hinterlands lend more young patrollers to Luthlia than to anywhere, but they still can't keep up.

"Kauneo came from a tent of famously fierce patrollers up that way. She was very beautiful I guess—courted by everyone. Then this quiet, unassuming young patrol leader from the east, walking around the lake on his second training tour, stole her heart right out from under all of them." A hint of pride colored her voice, and Fawn thought, *Yes, she's really his aunt.* "He made plans to stay. They were string-bound—you farmers would say, married—and he got promoted to company captain."

"Dag wasn't always a patroller?" said Fawn.

Mari snorted. "That boy should have been a hinterland lieutenant by now, if he hadn't . . . agh, anyway. Most of our patrols are more like hunts, and most turn up nothing. In fact, it's possible to patrol all your life and never be in on a malice kill, by one chance or another. Dag has his ways of improving those odds for himself. But when a malice gets entrenched, when it goes to real war . . . then we're all making it up as we go along."

She rose, stalked across the bedchamber to her washstand, poured a glass of water, and drank it down. She fell to pacing as she continued.

"Big malice slipped through the patrol patterns. It didn't have many people to enslave up that way, no bandits like the malice you slew here. There are no farmers in Luthlia, nor anywhere north of the Dead Lake, save now and then some trapper or trader slips in that we escort out. But the malice did find wolves. It *did* things to wolves. Wolf-men, man-wolves, dire wolves as big as ponies, with man-wits. By the time the thing was found, it had grown itself an army of wolves. The Luthlian patrollers sent out a call-up for help from neighbor hinterlands, but meanwhile, they were on their own.

"Dag's company, fifty patrollers including Kauneo and a couple of her brothers, was sent to hold a ridge to cover the flank of another party trying to strike up the valley at the lair. The scouts led them to expect an attack of maybe fifty dire wolves. What they got was more like five hundred."

Fawn's breath drew in.

"In one hour Dag lost his hand, his wife, his company all but three, and the ridge. What he didn't lose was the war, because in the hour they'd bought, the other group made it all the way through to the lair. When he woke up in the medicine tent, his whole life was burned up like a pyre, I guess. He didn't take it well.

"In due course his dead wife's tent folk despaired of him and sent him home. Where he didn't take it well some more. Then Fairbolt Crow, bless his bones—our camp captain, though he was just a company captain back then—got smart, or desperate, or furious, and dragged him off to Tripoint. Got some clever farmer artificer he knew there to make up the arm harness, and they went round and round on it till they hit on devices that worked. Dag practiced with his new bow till his fingers bled, pulled himself together to meet Fairbolt's terms, and let me tell you Fairbolt didn't cut him any slack, and was let back on patrol. Where he has been ever since.

"Some ten or twelve sharing knives have passed through Dag's hand since—people keep giving them to him because they're pretty sure to get used—but he always kept that pair aside. The only mementos of Kauneo I know of that he didn't shove away like they scorched him. So that's the knife now in your keeping, farmer girl."

Fawn held it up and drew it through her fingers. "You'd think it would be heavier." *Did I really want to know all this?*

"Aye." Mari sighed.

Fawn glanced curiously at Mari's gray head. "Will you ever be a company captain? You must have been patrolling for a long time."

"I've had far less time in the field than Dag, actually, for all I'm twenty years older. I walked the woman's path. I spent four or five years training as a girl—we *must* train up the girls, for all that fellows like Dag disapprove, because if ever our camps are attacked, it'll be us and the old men defending them. I got string-bound, got blood-bound—had my children, that is—and then went back to patrolling. I expect to keep walking till my luck or my legs give out, five more years or ten, but I don't care to deal with anything more fractious than a patrol, thank you. Then back to camp and play with my grandchildren and their children till it's time to share. It will do, as a life."

Fawn's brow wrinkled. "Did you ever imagine another?" Or being thrown into another, as Fawn had been?

Mari cocked her head. "Can't say as I ever did. Though I'd have my boy back first if I were given wishes."

"How many children did you have?"

"Five," Mari replied, with distinct maternal pride that sounded plenty farmerish to Fawn, for all she suspected Mari would deny any such thing.

A rap on the door was followed by Dag's plaintive voice: "Mari, can I please come back in now?"

Mari rolled her eyes. "All right."

Dag eased himself around the door. "How is she doing? Is she healing at all? Could you match grounds? Or do a little reinforcement, even?"

"She's healing as well as could be expected. I did nothing with my ground, because time and rest will do the job every bit as well."

Dag took this in, seeming a bit disappointed, but resigned. "I have you a room, Spark, down one floor. Tired?"

Exhausted, she realized. She nodded.

"Well, I'll take you down and you can start in on the resting part, leastways."

Mari rubbed her lips and studied her nephew through narrowed eyes. Groundsense. Fawn wondered what the patrol leader had seen with hers that she wasn't saying. Did closed mouths run in the Redwing family like golden eyes? Fawn rolled up her bedroll and let Dag shoo her out.

"Don't let Mari scare you," Dag said, letting his left arm drift along at her back, whether protectively or for subtle concealment Fawn could not tell, as they descended the stairs. They turned into the adjoining corridor.

"She didn't, much. I liked her." Fawn took a breath. Some secrets took up too much space to keep tiptoeing around. "She told me a little more about your wife, and Wolf Ridge. She thought I needed to know."

Silence stretched for three long footfalls. "She's right."

And that, evidently, was all Fawn was going to get for now.

Fawn's new room was narrow like Mari's, except this one overlooked the main street instead of the stable yard. A washstand with ewer already filled, piecework curtains and a quilt in a matching pattern, and rag rugs on the floor made it fine and homey to Fawn's eyes. A door in the side wall apparently led into the next chamber. Dag swung the bar across and shoved it down into its brackets.

"Where is your room?" Fawn asked.

Dag gestured at the closed door. "Through there."

"Oh, good. Will you take a rest? Don't tell me you aren't owed some healing too. I saw your bruises."

He shook his head. "I'm going out to find a harnessmaker. I'll come back and take you down to dinner later, if you'd like."

"I'd like that fine."

He smiled a little at that and backed himself out. "Seems all I do in this place is tell folks to go to sleep."

"Yes, but I'm actually going to do it."

He grinned—*that grin should be illegal*—and shut the door softly.

On the wall beside the washstand hung a shaving mirror, fine flat Glassforge glass. Reminded, Fawn slid up to it and turned down the collar of her blue dress.

The bruise masking most of the left side of her face was purple going greenish around the edges, with four dark scabs from the mudman's claws mounting to her cheekbone, still tender but not hot with infection. The pattern of the malice's hand on her neck, four blots on one side and one on the other, stood out in sharp contrast to her fair skin. The marks had a peculiar black tint and an ugly raised texture unlike any other contusion Fawn had ever seen. Well, if there was any special trick to their healing, Dag would know it. Or might have experienced it himself, if he had got close enough to as many malices as Mari's inventory of his past knives suggested.

Fawn went to the window and just caught a glimpse of Dag's tall form passing below, arm harness tossed over his shoulder, striding up the street toward the town square. She gazed out at Glassforge after he'd made his way out of sight along the boardwalk, but not for long; yawning uncontrollably, she slipped off her dress and shoes and crawled into the bed.

10

Dag returned at dinnertime as promised. Fawn had put on her good dress, the green cotton that her aunt Nattie had spun and woven; she followed him downstairs. The raucous noises coming out of the room where they'd eaten their quiet lunch gave her pause.

Seeing her hesitate, Dag smiled and bent his head to murmur, "Patrollers can be a rowdy bunch when we all get together, but you'll be all right. You don't have to answer any questions you don't want. We can make out you're still too shaken by our fight with the malice and don't want to talk about it. They'll accept that." His hand drifted to her collar as if to arrange it more tidily, and Fawn realized he was not covering up the strange marks on her neck, but rather, making sure they showed. "I think we don't need to mention what happened with the second knife to anyone besides Mari."

"Good," said Fawn, relieved, and allowed him to take her in, his arm protective at her back.

The tables this evening were indeed full of tall, alarming patrollers, twenty-five or so, variously layered with road dirt. Given Dag's warning, Fawn managed not to jump when their entrance was greeted with whoops, cheers, table pounding, and flying jibes about Dag's three-day vanishing. The roughness of some of the jests was undercut by the real joy in the voices, and Dag, smiling crookedly, gave back: "Some trackers! I swear you lot couldn't find a drink in a rain barrel!"

"Beer barrel, Dag!" someone hooted in return. "What's wrong with you?"

Dag surveyed the room and guided Fawn toward a square table on the far side where only two patrollers sat, the Utau and Razi she'd met earlier. The two waved encouragement as they approached, and Razi shoved out a spare chair invitingly with his boot.

Fawn was not sure which patrollers were Mari's and which were Chato's; the two patrols seemed to be mingled, not quite at random. Any sorting seemed to be more by age, as there was one table with half a dozen gray heads at it, including Mari; also two other older women Fawn had not seen at the well-house, so presumably from the Log Hollow patrol. The young woman with her arm in the sling was at a table with three young men, all vying to cut her meat for her; she was presently holding them off with jabs of her fork and laughing. The men patrollers seemed all ages, but the women were only young or much older, Fawn noticed, and remembered Mari's account of her life's course. In the home camps would the proportions be reversed?

Breathless serving maids and boys weaved among the tables lugging trays laden with platters and pitchers, rapidly relieved by reaching hands. The patrollers seemed more interested in speed and quantity than in decorum, an attitude shared with farmhouse kitchens that made Fawn feel nearly comfortable.

They sat and exchanged greetings with Razi and Utau; Razi leaped up and acquired more plates, cutlery, and glasses, and both united to snag passing food and drink to fill them. They did ply Dag with questions about his adventures although, with cautious glances, spared Fawn. His answers were either unexcitingly factual, vague, or took the form that Fawn recognized from the Horsefords' table of effectively diverting counterquestions. They finally desisted and let Dag catch up with his chewing.

Utau glanced around the room, and remarked, "Everyone's a lot happier tonight. Especially Mari. Fortunately for all of us downstream of her."

Razi said wistfully, "Do you suppose she and Chato will let us all have a bow-down before we go back out?"

"Chato looks pretty cheerful," said Utau, nodding across the room at another table of patrollers, although which was the leader Fawn could not tell. "We might get lucky."

"What's a bow-down?" asked Fawn.

Razi smiled eagerly. "It's a party, patroller-style. They happen sometimes, to celebrate a kill, or when two or more patrols chance to get together. Having another patrol to talk to is a treat. Not that we don't all love one another"—Utau rolled his eyes at this—"but weeks on end of our own company can get pretty old. A bow-down has music. Dancing. Beer if we can get it . . ."

"We could get lots of beer, here," Utau observed distantly.

"Lingerrrring in dark corners—" Razi trilled, catching up the tail of his braid and twirling it.

"Enough—she gets the idea," said Dag, but he smiled. Fawn wondered if it was in memory. "Could happen, but I guarantee it won't be till Mari thinks the cleanup is all done. Or as done as it ever gets." His eye was caught by something over Fawn's shoulder. "I feel prophetic. I predict chores before cheer."

"Dag, you're such a morbid crow—" Razi began.

"Well, gentlemen," said Mari's voice. "Do your feet hurt?"

Fawn turned her head and smiled diffidently at the patrol leader, who had drifted up to their table.

Razi opened his mouth, but Dag cut in, "Don't answer that, Razi. It's a trick question. The safe response is, 'I can't say, Mari, but why do you ask?'"

Mari's lips twitched, and she returned in a sugary voice, "I'm *so* glad you asked that question, Dag!"

"Maybe not so safe," murmured Utau, grinning.

"How's the arm-harness repair coming?" Mari continued to Dag.

Dag grimaced. "Done tomorrow afternoon, maybe. I had to stop at two places before I found one that would do it for free. Or rather, in exchange for us saving his life, family, town, territory, and everyone in it."

Utau said dryly, "Naturally, you forgot to mention it was you personally who took their malice down."

Dag shrugged this off in irritation. "Firstly, that wasn't so. Secondly, none of us could do the job without the rest of us, so all are owed. I shouldn't . . . none of us should have to *beg.*"

"It so happens," said Mari, letting this slide by, "that I have a sitting-down job for a one-handed man tomorrow morning. In the storeroom here is a trunkful of patrol logs and maps for this region that need a good going-over. The usual. I want someone with an eye for it to see if we can figure how this malice slipped through, and stop up the crack in future. Also, I want a listing of the nearby sectors that have been especially neglected. We're going to stay here a few extra days while the injured recover, and to repair gear and furbish up."

Utau and Razi both brightened at this news.

"We'll do some local search-pattern catch-up at the same time," Mari continued. "And let the Glassforge folk see us doing so," she added, with dour emphasis and a nod at Dag. "Give 'em a show."

Dag snorted. "Better we should offer them double their blight bogles back if they're not happy with our work."

Razi choked on the beer he was just swallowing, and Utau kindly if unhelpfully thumped his back. "Oh, how I wish we could!" Razi wheezed when he'd caught his breath again. "Love to see the looks on their stupid farmer faces, just once!"

Fawn congealed, her beginning ease and enjoyment of the patrollers' banter abruptly quenched. Dag stiffened.

Mari cast them both an enigmatic look, but moved off without comment, and Fawn remembered their exchange earlier on the universal nature of loutishness. *So.*

Razi burbled on obliviously, "Patrolling out of Glassforge is like a holiday. Sure, you ride all day, but when you come back there are real beds. Real baths! Food you don't have to fix, not burned over a campfire. Little comforts to bargain for up in the town."

"And yet farmers built this place," Fawn murmured, and she was sure by his wince that Dag heard clearly the missing *stupid* she'd clipped out.

Razi shrugged. "Farmers plant crops, but who planted farmers? We did."

What? Fawn thought.

Utau, perhaps not quite as oblivious as his comrade, glanced at her, and countered, "You mean our ancestors did. Pretty broad claim of credit, there."

"Why shouldn't we get the credit?" said Razi.

"And the blame as well?" said Dag.

Razi made a face. "I thought we did. Fair's fair."

Dag smiled tightly, drew a breath, and pushed himself up. "Well. If I'm to spend tomorrow peering at a bunch of ill-penned, misspelled, and undoubtedly incomplete patrol logs, I'd better get my eyes some rest now. If everyone else is as short on sleep as I am, it'll be a good quiet night for catching up."

"Find us lots of local patrols, Dag," urged Razi. "*Weeks'* worth."

"I'll see what I can do."

Fawn rose too, and Dag shepherded her out. He made no attempt to apologize for Razi, but an odd look darkened his eyes, and Fawn did not like her sense of his thoughts receding to someplace barred to her. Outside, the late-summer dusk was closing in. He bade her good night at her door with studied courtesy.

The next morning Dag woke at dawn, but Fawn, to his approval, still slept. He went quietly downstairs and nabbed two patrollers from their breakfast to lug the records trunk upstairs to his room. In a short time he had logs, maps, and charts spread out on the room's writing table, bed, and, soon after, the floor.

He heard the muffled creak of the bed and Fawn's footsteps through the adjoining wall as she finally arose and rattled around her room getting dressed. At length, she poked her head cautiously around the frame of his door open to the hall, and he jumped up to escort her down to a breakfast much quieter than last night's dinner, as a last few sleepy patrollers drifted out singly or in pairs.

After the meal, she followed him back upstairs to stare with interest at the paper and parchment drifting across his room. "Can I help?"

He remembered her susceptibility to boredom and itchy hands, but mostly he heard the underlying, *Can I stay?* He obligingly set her to mending pens, or fetching a paper or logbook from across the room from time to time—make-work, but it kept her quietly occupied and pleasantly near. She grew fascinated with the maps, charts, and logs, and fell to reading them, or trying to. It was not just the faded and often questionable handwriting that made this a slow process for her. Her claim to be able to read proved true, but it was plain from her moving finger and lips and the tension in her body that she was not fluent, probably due to never having had enough text to practice on. But when he scratched out a grid on a fresh sheet to turn the muddled log entries into a record visible at a glance, she followed the logic swiftly enough.

Around noon, Mari appeared in the open doorway. She raised an eyebrow at Fawn, perched on the bed poring over a contour map annotated with hand corrections, but said only, "How goes it?"

"Almost done," said Dag. "There is no point going back more than ten years, I think. Quiet around here this morning. What are folks up to?"

"Mending, cleaning gear, gone uptown. Working with the horses. We found a blacksmith whose sister was among those we rescued from the mine, who's been very willing to help out in the stable." She wandered in and peered over his shoulder, then leaned back against the wall with her arms folded. "So. How did this malice slip past us?"

Dag tapped his grid, laid out on the table before him. "That section was last walked three years ago by a patrol from Hope Lake Camp. They were trying to run a sixteen-man pattern with just thirteen. Three short. Because if they'd dropped it down to a twelve-pattern, they'd have had to make two more passes to clear the area, and they were already three weeks behind schedule for the season. Even so, there's no telling they missed anything; that malice might well not have been hatched out yet."

"I'm not looking to lay blame," said Mari mildly.

"I know." Dag sighed. "Now, as for neglected sections . . . " His lips peeled back in a dry smile. "That was more revealing. Turns out all sections within a day's ride of Glassforge that can be patrolled from horseback are up-to-date, or as up-to-date as anything, meaning no more than a year overdue. What's left are some swampy areas to the west and rocky ravines to the east that you can't take a horse through." He added reflectively, "Lazy whelps."

Mari smiled sourly. "I see." She scratched her nose. "Chato and I figured he'd lend me two men, and we'd both send out sixteen-groups, dividing up the neglected sections between us. He and I are both going to be stuck here arguing with Glassforgers about what we're due for our recent work on their behalf, so I'd thought to put you in charge of our patrol. Give you first pick of sections, though."

"You're so sweet, Mari. Waist-deep wading through smelly muck, with leeches, or sudden falls onto sharp rocks? They both sound so charming, I don't know how I can decide."

"Alternatively, you can roll up your sleeves and come help me arm wrestle with Glassforgers. That works exceptionally well, I've noticed."

Fawn, who had set down the map and was following the talk closely, blinked at this.

Dag grimaced in distaste. In his list of personal joys, parading their wounded to shame farmers into pitching in ranked well below frolicking with leeches and barely above lancing oozing saddle boils. "I swore the last time I put on that show for you, it would be the last." He added after a reflective moment, "And the time before. You have no shame, Mari."

"I have no *resources*," she returned, her face twisting in frustration. "Fairbolt once figured it takes at least ten folks back in the camps, not counting the children, to support one patroller in the field. Every bit of help we fail to pull in from outside puts us that bit more behind."

"Then why don't we pull in more? Isn't that why farmers were planted in the first place?" The argument was an old one, and Dag still didn't know the right answer.

"Shall we become lords again?" said Mari softly. "I think not."

"What's the alternative? Let the world drift to destruction because we're too ashamed to call for help?"

"Keep the balance," said Mari firmly. "As we always have. We cannot ever let ourselves become dependent upon outsiders." Her glance slid over Fawn. "Not us."

A little silence fell, and Dag finally said, "I'll take swamps."

Her nod was a bit too satisfied, and Dag wondered if he'd just made a mistake. He added after a moment, "But if you let us take along a few horse boys from the stables here to watch the mounts, we won't have to leave a patroller with the horse lines while we slog."

Mari frowned, but said at last, reluctantly, "All right. Makes sense for the day-trips, anyway. You'll start tomorrow."

Fawn's brown eyes widened in mild alarm, and Dag realized the source of Mari's muffled triumph. "Wait," he said. "Who will look after Miss Bluefield while I'm gone?"

"I can. She won't be alone. We have four other injured recovering here, and Chato and I will be in and out."

"I'm sure I'll be fine, Dag," Fawn offered, although a faint doubt colored her voice.

"But can you keep her from trying to overdo?" Dag said gruffly. "What if she starts bleeding again? Or gets chilled and throws a fever?"

Even Fawn's brow wrinkled at that last one. Her lips moved on a voiceless protest, *But it's midsummer.*

"Then I'll be better fit to deal with that than you would," said Mari, watching him.

Watching him flail, he suspected glumly. He drew back from making more of a show of himself than he already had. He'd had his ground-sense closed down tight since they'd hit the outskirts of Glassforge yesterday, but Mari clearly didn't need to read his ground to draw her own shrewd conclusions, even without the way Fawn glowed like a rock-oil lamp in his presence.

He rolled up his chart and handed it to Mari. "You can have that to tack on the wall downstairs, and we can mark it off as we go. For whatever amusement it will provide folks. If you hint there could be a bowdown when we reach the end, it might go more briskly."

She nodded affably and withdrew, and Dag put Fawn to work helping him restack the contents of the trunk in rather better order than he'd found it.

As she brought him an armload of stained and tattered logbooks, she asked, "That's twice now you've talked about *planting farmers*. What do you mean?"

He sat back on his heels, surprised. "Don't you know where your family comes from?"

"Sure I do. It's written down in the family book that goes with the farm accounts. My great-great-great-grandfather"—she paused to check the generations on her fingers, and nodded—"came north to the river ridge from Lumpton with his brother almost two hundred years ago to clear land. A few years later, Great-great-great got married and crossed the western river branch to start our place. Bluefields have been there ever since. That's why the nearest village is named West Blue."

"And where were they before Lumpton Market?"

She hesitated. "I'm not sure. Except that it was just Lumpton back then, because Lumpton Crossroads and Upper Lumpton weren't around yet."

"Six hundred years ago," said Dag, "this whole region from the Dead Lake to nearly the southern seacoast was all unpeopled wilderness. Some Lakewalkers from this hinterland went down to the coasts, east and south, where there were some enclaves of folks—your ancestors—surviving. They persuaded several groups to come up here and carve out homes for themselves. The idea was that this area, south of a certain line, had been cleared enough of malices to be safe again. Which proved to be not quite the case, although it was still much better than it had once been. Promises were exchanged . . . fortunately, my people still remember what they were. There were two more main plantations, one east at Tripoint and one west around Farmer's Flats, besides the one south of the Grace at Silver Shoals that most folks around here eventually came from. The homesteaders' descendants have been slowly spreading out ever since.

"There were two notions about this scheme among the Lakewalkers—

still are, in fact. One faction figured that the more eyes we had looking for malice outbreaks, the better. The other figured we were just setting out malice food. I've seen malices develop in both peopled and unpeopled places, and I don't see much to choose between the horrors, so I don't get too excited about that argument anymore."

"So Lakewalkers were here before farmers," said Fawn slowly.

"Yes."

"What was here before Lakewalkers?"

"What, you know nothing?"

"You don't have to sound so shocked," she said, obviously stung, and he made a gesture of apology. "I know plenty, I just don't know what's true and what's tall tales and bedtime stories. Once upon a time, there was supposed to have been a chain of lakes, not just the big dead one. With a league of seven beautiful cities around them, commanded by great sorcerer-lords, and a sorcerer king, and princesses and bold warriors and sailors and captains and who knows what all. With tall towers and beautiful gardens and jeweled singing birds and magical animals and holy whatnot, and the gods' blessings flowing like the fountains, and gods popping in and out of people's lives in a way that I would find downright unnerving, I'm pretty sure. Oh, and ships on the lakes with silver sails. I think maybe they were plain white cloth sails, and just looked silver in the moonlight, because it stands to reason that much metal would capsize a boat. What I *know* is the tall tale is where they say some of the cities were five miles across, which is impossible."

"Actually"—Dag cleared his throat—"that part I know to be true. The ruins of Ogachi Strand are only a few miles out from shore. When I was a young patroller up that way, some friends and I took an outrigger to look at them. On a clear, quiet day you can see down to the tops of stone wreckage along the old shoreline, in places. Ogachi really was five miles across, and more. These were the people who built the straight roads, after all. Which were thousands of miles long, some of them, before they got so broken up."

Fawn stood up and dusted her skirt, and sat on the edge of his bed, her face tight with thought. "So—where'd they all go? Those builders."

"Most died. A remnant survived. Their descendants are still here."

"Where?"

"Here. In this room. You and me."

She stared at him in real surprise, then looked down at her hands in doubt. "Me?"

"Lakewalker tales say . . . " He paused, sorting and suppressing. "That Lakewalkers are descended from some of those sorcerer-lords who got away from the wreck of everything. And farmers are descended from ordinary folks on the far edges of the hinterlands, who somehow survived the original malice wars, the first great one, and the two that came after, that killed the lakes and left the Western Levels." Also dubbed the Dead Levels, by those who'd skirted them, and Dag could understand why.

"There was more than one war? I never heard that," she said.

He nodded. "In a sense. Or maybe there's always only been one. The question you didn't ask is, where do the malices come from?"

"Out of the ground. They always have. Only"— she hesitated, then went on in a rush—"I suppose you're going to say, not always, and tell me how they got into the ground in the first place, right?"

"I'm actually a little vague on that myself. What we do know is that all malices are descendants of the first great one. Except not descended like we are, with marriage and birth and the passing of generations. More like some monstrous insect that laid ten thousand eggs that hatch up out of the ground at intervals."

"I saw that thing," said Fawn lowly. "I don't know what it was, but it sure wasn't a bug."

He shrugged. "It's just a way of trying to think about them. I've seen a few dozen of them in my life, so far. I could as well say the first was like a mirror that shattered into ten thousand splinters to make ten thousand little mirrors. Malices aren't material at all, in their inner nature. They just pull matter in from around them to make themselves a house, a shell. They seem to feed on ground itself, really."

"How did it shatter?"

"It lost the first war. They say."

"Did the gods help?"

Dag snorted. "Lakewalker legends say the gods abandoned the world when the first malice came. And that they will return when the earth is entirely cleansed of its spawn. If you believe in gods."

"Do you?"

"I believe they are not here, yes. It's a faith of sorts."

"Huh." She rolled up the last maps and tied their strings before handing them to him. He settled them in place and closed the trunk.

He sat with his hand on the latch a moment. "Whatever their part really was," he said finally, "I don't think it was just the sorcerer-lords who built all those towers and laid those roads and sailed those ships. Your ancestors did, too."

She blinked at this, but what she was thinking, he could not guess.

"And the lords didn't come from nowhere, or elsewhere, either," Dag continued tenaciously. "One line of thought says there was just one people, once, and that the sorcerers rose out of them. Except that then they bred up for their skills and senses, and then used their magic to make themselves more magical, and lordly, and powerful, and so grew away from their kin. Which may have been the first mistake."

She tilted her head, and her lips parted as if to speak, but at that point a pair of footsteps echoed from the hall. Razi stuck his head through the doorframe.

"Ah, Dag, there you are. You should smell this." He thrust out a small glass bottle and pulled off the leather stopper plugging its neck. "Dirla found this medicine shop up in town that sells the stuff."

Dirla smiled proudly over his shoulder.

"What is it?" asked Fawn, leaning in and sniffing as the patroller waved the bottle past her. "Oh, pretty! It smells like chamomile and clover flowers."

"Scented oil," he answered. "They have seven or eight kinds."

"What do you use it for?" Fawn asked innocently.

Dag mentally consigned his comrade to the middle of the Dead Levels. "Sore muscles," he said repressively.

"Well, I suppose you could," said Razi thoughtfully.

"Scented back rubs," breathed Dirla in a warm voice. "Mm, nice idea."

"How *useful* of you two to stop by," Dag overrode this before it could grow more interesting still, either to himself, who didn't hanker after a repeat of the discomforts of his ride from the Horsefords', or to Fawn, who would undoubtedly *ask more questions*. "Happens I need this trunk taken back downstairs to the storeroom." He stood up and pointed. "Lug."

They grumbled, if lightheartedly, and lugged.

Dag closed the door behind them, shooed Fawn to her own room, and followed. Wondering if he dared ask just where that shop was located, and if it might be on the way to the harnessmaker's.

Walking the patterns in the marshes west of Glassforge took six days.

Dag chose the closest section first, and so was able to bring the patrol back to the hotel's comforts that night, and to check on Fawn.

After an increasingly worried search of the premises, he found her shelling peas in the kitchen and making friends with the cooks and scullions. With some relief, he gave over his vision of her as distressed and lonely among condescending Lakewalker strangers although not his fear of her imprudently overtaxing her strength.

For the next section he chose the most distant, of necessity a three-day outing, to get it out of the way. Dag met the complaints of the younger patrollers with a few choice tales of swamp sweeps north of Farmer's Flats in late winter, icily gruesome enough to silence all but the most determined grumblers. The patrol was able to leave most of their gear with the horses, but the need for skin protection meant that boots, shirts, and trousers took the brunt of the muck and mire. When they draggled back to Glassforge late the following night, they were greeted by the attendants of the hotel's pleasant bathhouse, conveniently sited with its own well between the stable and the main building, with a marked lack of joy; the laundresses were growing downright surly at the sight of them. This time Dag found Fawn waiting up for him, filling the time and her hands by helping to mend hotel linens and coaxing stories from a pair of seamstresses.

He returned the next night to exchange tales with her over a late supper. He held her fascinated with his account of a roughly circular and distinctively flat stretch of marsh some six miles across that he was certain was a former patch of blight, recovering and again supporting life—most of it noxious, not to mention ravenous, but without question thriving. He thought the slaying of that malice must have predated the arrival of farmer settlers in this region by well over a century. She entertained him in turn with a long, involved account of her day's adventures in the town. Sassa the Horseford brother-in-law, now home again, had stopped by and made good on his promise to show her his glassworks. They had capped the tour with a visit to his brother's papermaking shop, and for extras, the back premises of the ink maker's next door.

"There are more kinds of work to do here than I ever dreamed," she confided in a tone of thoughtful speculation.

She had also, clearly, overdone; when he escorted her to her door, she was drooping and yawning so hard she could scarcely say good night. He spent a little time persuading her ground against an incipient cold, then checked the healing flesh beneath the ugly malice scabs for necrosis or infection and made her promise to rest on the morrow.

The next day's pattern walk was truncated for Dag in the early afternoon when one patroller managed to trade up from mere muck and leeches to a willow root tangle, water over his head, and a nest of cottonmouths. Leaving the patrol to Utau, Dag rode back to town supporting the very sick and shaken man in front of him. Dag was not, happily, called upon to do anything unadvised and perilous with their grounds on the way, though he was grimly aware Utau had urged the escort upon him against just that chance. But the snakebit man survived not only the ride, but also being dipped briskly in the bathhouse, dried, and carried up and slung into bed. By that time, Chato and Mari had been found, allowing Dag to turn the responsibility for further remedies over to them.

Some news Mari imparted sent Dag in search of Fawn even before a visit to the bathhouse on his own behalf. The sound of Fawn's voice raised in, what else, a question, tugged his ear as he was passing down the end stairs, and he about-faced into the second-floor corridor. A door stood open—Saun's—and he paused outside it as Saun's voice returned:

"My *first* impression of him was as one of those grumpy old fellows who never talks except to criticize you. You know the sort?"

"Oh, yes."

"He rode or walked in the back and never spoke much. The light began to dawn for me when Mari set him at the cap—that's the patroller in the end or edge position of a grid with no one beyond. We don't spread out to the limits of our vision, d'you see, but to the limits of our groundsenses. If you and the patrollers to your sides can just sense each other, you know you aren't missing any malice sign between you. Mari sent him out a *mile*. That's more than double the best range of my groundsense."

Fawn made an encouraging noise.

Saun, suitably rewarded, continued, "Then I got to noticing that whenever Mari wanted something done out of the ordinary way, she'd send him. Or that it was his idea. He didn't tell tales often, but when he did, they were from all over, I mean everywhere. I'd start to add up all the people and places in my head, and think, *How?* I'd thought he had no humor, but finally figured out it was just maddening-dry. He didn't seem like much at first, but he sure accumulated. And you?"

"Different than yours, I'll say. He just *arrived*. All at once. Very . . . definitely there. I feel like I've been unpacking him ever since and am nowhere near the bottom yet."

"Huh. He's like that on patrol, in a way."

"Is he good?"

"It's like he's more there than anyone . . . no, that's not right. It's like he's so nowhere-else. If you see?"

"Mm, maybe. How old is he really? I've had trouble figuring that out—"

Suppressed ground or no, someone was bound to notice the swamp reek wafting from the hall on the humid summer air pretty soon. Dag unquirked his lips, knocked on the doorframe, and stepped inside.

Saun lay abed wearing, above, only his bandages; the rest, however clothed, was covered by a sheet. Fawn, in her blue dress, sat leaning back in a chair with her bare feet up on the bed edge, catching, presumably with her wriggling toes, whatever faint breeze might carry from the window. For once, her hands were empty, but Saun's brown hair showed signs of being recently combed and rebraided into two neat, workman-like plaits.

Dag was greeted with broad smiles on two faces equally fresh with youth and pale with recent injury. Both hurt near-fatally on his watch—now, there was a thought to cringe from—but their expressions showed only trust and affection. He tried to muster a twinge of generational jealousy, but their beauty just made him want to weep. Not good. Six days on patrol with nary a malice sign shouldn't leave him this tired and strange.

"How de', Spark. Lookin' for you. Hello, Saun. How're the ribs?"

"Better." Saun sat up eagerly, his flinch belying his words. "They have me walking up and down the hall now. Fawn here's been keeping me company."

"Good!" said Dag genially. "And what have you two found to talk about?"

Saun looked embarrassed. "Oh, this and that."

Fawn returned more nimbly, "Why were you looking for me?"

"I have something to show you. In the stable, so find your shoes."

"All right," she said agreeably, and rose.

Her bare feet thumped away up the hallway, and he called after her, "Slow down!" He did not consider himself a wit, but this fetched her usual floating laugh. In her natural state, did she ever travel at any pace other than a scamper?

He studied Saun, wondering if any warning-off might be in order here. That the broad-shouldered youth was attractive to women, he'd had occasion to note, if never before with concern. But in Saun's current bashed state, he was no menace to curious farmer girls, Dag decided. And cautions might draw counterquestions Dag was ill equipped to answer, such as, *What business is it of yours?* He settled on a friendly wave farewell and started to withdraw into the hall again.

"Oh, Dag?" called Saun. "Old patroller?" He grinned from his propping pillows.

"Yes?" Blight it, when had the boy picked up on that catchphrase? Saun must have paid closer attention to Dag's occasional mutters than he would have guessed.

"No need for the fishy glower. All your pet Spark wants to hear are Dag tales." He settled back with a snicker, no, a snigger.

Dag shook his head and retreated. At least he managed to stop wincing before he exited the stairs.

Dag arrived in the stable, its stalls crowded with the horses of the two patrols, barely before Fawn did. He led her to the straight stall housing the placid bay mare, and pointed.

"Congratulations, Spark. Mari's made it official. You now own this nice horse. Your share of our pay from the Glassforge town fathers. I found you that saddle and bridle on the peg, too; should be about the right size for you. Not new, but they're in real good condition." He saw no need to mention that the tack had been part of a private deal with the willing harnessmaker who had done such a fine job repairing his arm-harness.

Fawn's face lit with delight, and she slid into the stall to run her hands over the horse's neck and scratch her star and her ears, which made the mare round her nostrils and drop her poll in pleasure. "Oh, Dag, she's wonderful, but" —Fawn's nose wrinkled in suspicion—"are you sure this isn't your share of the pay? I mean, Mari's been nice to me and all, but I didn't think she'd promoted me to patroller."

A little too shrewd, that. "If it had been left to me, there would be a lot more, Spark."

Fawn did not look entirely convinced, but the horse nudged her for more scratches, and she turned back to the task. "She needs a name. She can't go on being *that mare*." Fawn bit her lip in thought. "I'll name her Grace, after the river. Because it's a pretty name and she's a pretty horse, and because she carried us so smoothly. Do you want to be Grace, sweet lady, hm?" She carried on with the petting and making-much; the mare signified her acceptance of the affection, the name, or both by cocking her hips, easing one hind hoof, and blowing out her breath, which made Fawn laugh. Dag leaned on the stall partition and smiled.

At length, Fawn's face sobered in some new thought. She wandered back out of the stall and stood with her arms folded a moment. "Except . . . I'm not sure if I'll be able to keep her on a milkmaid's pay, or whatever."

"She's yours absolutely; you could sell her," Dag said neutrally.

Fawn shook her head, but her expression did not lighten.

"In any case," Dag continued, "it's too early for you to be thinking of taking on work. You're going to need this mare to ride, first."

"I'm feeling much better. The bleeding stopped two days ago, if I were going to get a fever I think I would have by now, and I don't get dizzy anymore."

"Yes, but . . . Mari has given me leave to take the sharing knife back to camp and have it looked at by a maker. I know the best. I was thinking, since Lumpton Market and West Blue are more or less on the way to Hickory Lake from here, we ought to stop in at your farm on the way and put your folks out of their cruel suspense."

Her eyes flashed up at him with an unreadable look. "I don't want to go back." Her voice wavered. "I don't want my whole stupid story to come out." And firmed: "I don't want to be within a hundred miles of Stupid Sunny."

Dag took a breath. "You don't have to stay. Well, you can't stay;

your testimony will be needed on the matter of the knife. Once that's done, the choice of where to go next is yours."

She sucked on her lower lip, eyes downcast. "They'll try to make me stay. I know them. They won't believe I can be a grown . . . " Her voice grew more urgent. "Only if you promise to go with me, *promise* not to leave me there!"

His hand found its way to her shoulder in attempted reassurance of this odd distress. "And yet I might with your goodwill leave you here?"

"Mm . . ."

"Just trying to figure out if it's the here or the there or the me leaving that's being objected to."

Her eyes were wide and dark, and her moist lips parted as her face rose at these words. Dag felt his head dipping, his spine bending, as his hand slipped around her back, as if he were falling from some great height, falling soft . . .

A throat cleared dryly behind him, and he straightened abruptly.

"There you are," said Mari. "Thought I might find you here." Her voice was cordial but her eyes were narrowed.

"Oh, Mari!" said Fawn, a bit breathlessly. "Thank you for getting me this nice horse. I wasn't expecting it." She made her little knee-dip.

Mari smiled at her, managing to give Dag an ironic eyebrow-cock at the same time. "You've earned much more, but it was what I could do. I am not *entirely* without a sense of obligation."

This crushed conversation briefly. Mari continued blandly, "Fawn, would you excuse us for a while? I have some patrol business to discuss with Dag, here."

"Oh. Of course." Fawn brightened. "I'll go tell Saun about Grace." And she was off again at a scamper, flashing a grin over her shoulder at Dag.

Mari leaned against the end post of the stall and crossed her arms, staring up at Dag, till Fawn had vanished through the stable door and out of earshot. The aisle was cool and shady compared to the white afternoon outside, redolent with horses, quiet but for the occasional champing and shifting of the heat-lazy animals and the faint humming of the flies. Dag raised his chin and clasped his hand and hand replacement behind his back, winding his thumb around the hook-with-spring-clamp presently seated in the wooden cuff, and waited. Not hopefully.

It wasn't long in coming. "What are you about, boy?" Mari growled.

Any sort of response that came to, *Whatever do you mean, Mari?* seemed a waste of time and breath. Dag lowered his eyelids and waited some more.

"Do I need to list everything that's wrong with this infatuation?" she said, exasperation plain in her voice. "I daresay you could give the blighted lecture yourself. I daresay you have."

"A time or two," he granted.

"So what are you thinking? Or are you thinking?"

He inhaled. "I know you want to tell me to back away from Fawn, but I can't. Not yet anyway. The knife binds us, till I get it up to camp. We're going to have to travel together for a time yet; you can't argue with that."

"It's not the traveling that worries me. It's what's going to happen when you stop."

"I'm not sleeping with her."

"Aye, yet. You've had your groundsense locked down tight in my presence ever since you got in. Well, that's partly just you—it's such a habit with you, you stay veiled in your *sleep*. But this—you're like a cat who thinks it's hiding because it's got its head stuck in a sack."

"Ah, mental privacy. Now, there's a farmer concept that could stand to catch on."

She snorted. "Fine chance."

"I'm taking her up to camp," Dag said mulishly. "That's a given."

In a sweetly cordial voice, Mari murmured, "Going to show her off to your mother? Oh, how lovely."

Dag's shoulders hunched. "We'll go by her farm, first."

"Oh, and you'll meet *her* mother. Wonderful. That'll be a success. Can't you two just hold hands and jump off a cliff together? It'd be faster and less painful."

His lips twitched at this, involuntarily. "Likely. But it has to be done."

"Does it?" Mari pushed off the post and stalked back and forth across the stable aisle. "Now, if you were a young patroller lout looking to dip his wick in the strange, I'd just thump him on the side of the head and end this thing here and now. I can't tell if you're trying to fool me, or yourself!"

Dag set his teeth and went on saying nothing. It seemed wisest.

She fetched up at her post again, leaned back, scuffed her boot, and sighed. "Look, Dag. I've been watching you for a long time, now. Out on patrol, you'd never neglect your gear or your food or your sleep or your feet. Not like the youngsters who get heroic delusions about their stamina, till they crash into a rock wall. You pace your body for the long haul."

Dag tilted his head in acknowledgment, not certain where she was going with this.

"But though you'd never starve your body to wasting and still expect to go on, you starve your heart, yet act as though you can still draw on it forever without the debt ever coming due. If you fall—*when* you fall, you're going to fall like a starving man. I'm standing here watching you start to topple now, and I don't know if any words of mine are strong enough to catch you. I don't know why, blast and blight it"—her voice shifted in renewed aggravation—"you haven't let yourself get string-bound with any one of the nice widows that your mother—well, all right, not your mother—that one of your friends or other kin used to introduce you to, till they gave up in despair. If you had, I daresay you'd be immune to this foolishness now, knife or no."

Dag hunched tighter. "It would not have been fair to the woman. I can't have what I had with Kauneo over again. Not because of any lack on the woman's part. It's me. I can't *give* what I gave to Kauneo." *Used up, emptied out, dry.*

"Nobody expected that, except maybe you. Most people don't have what you had with Kauneo, if half of what I've heard is true. Yet they contrive to rub along tolerably well just the same."

"She'd die of thirst, trying to draw from that well."

Mari shook her head, mouth flat with disapproval. "Dramatic, Dag."

He shrugged. "Don't push for answers you don't want to hear, then."

She looked away, pursed her lips, stared up at the rafters stuck about with dusty cobwebs and wisps of hay, and tried another tack. "Now, all things considered, I can't object to your indulging yourself. Not you. And after all, this farmer girl has no relatives here to kick up a fuss for me."

Dag's eyes narrowed, and a fool's hope rose in his heart. Was Mari about to say she wouldn't interfere? Surely not . . .

"If you can't be turned or reasoned with, well, these things happen, eh?" The sarcasm tingeing her voice quenched the hope. "But if you are so bound and determined to get in, you'd better have a plan for how you're going to get out, and I want to hear it."

I don't want to get out. I don't want an end. Unsettling realization, and Dag wasn't sure where to put it. Blight it, he hadn't even *begun* . . .

anything. This argument was moving too fast for him, no doubt Mari's intent. "All the great plans I ever made for my life ended in horrible surprises, Mari. I swore off plans sometime back."

She shook her head in scorn. "I halfway wish you were some lout I could just thump. Well . . . no, I don't. But you're you. If she's cut up at the end—and I don't see how this can be anything other than a real short ride—so will you be. Double disaster. I can see it coming, and so can you. So what *are* you going to do?"

Dag said tightly, "What do you suggest, seeress?"

"That there's no way you can end this well. So *don't start.*"

I haven't started, Dag wanted to point out. A truth on his lips and a lie in his ground, perhaps? Endurance had been his last remaining virtue for a long, long time, now; he hugged his patience to him and stood, just stood.

In the face of his stubborn silence, Mari shifted her stance and her attack once more. "There are two great duties given to those born of our blood. The first is to carry on the long war, with resolute fortitude, in living and in dying, in hope or out of it. In that duty you have not ever failed."

"Once."

"Not ever," she contradicted this. "Overwhelming defeat is not failure; it's just defeat. It happens sometimes. I never heard that you ran from that ridge, Dag."

"No," he admitted. "I didn't have the chance. *Surrounded* makes running away a bit of a puzzle, which I did not get time to solve."

"Aye, well. But then there's the other great duty, the second duty, without which the first is futile, dross and delusion. The duty you have so far failed altogether."

His head came up, stung and wary. "I've given blood and sweat and all the years of my life so far. I still owe my bones and my heart's death, which I mean to give, which I *will* give in their due time if chance permits, but suicide is a self-indulgence and a desertion of duty no one will ever accuse me of, I decided that years ago, so I don't know what else you want."

Her lips compressed; her gaze went intent with conviction. "The *other* duty is to create the next generation to hand on the war *to*. Because all we do, the miles and years we walk, all that we bleed and sweat and sacrifice, will come to nothing if we do not also pass on our bodies' legacy. And that's a task on which you have turned your back for the past twenty years."

Behind his back, his right hand gripped the arm cuff till he could hear the wood creak, and he forced his clench to loosen lest he break what had been so recently mended. He tried clamping his teeth down just as tight on any response, but one leaked out nonetheless: "Borrow my mother's jawbone, did you?"

"I expect I could do her whole speech by rote, I've had to listen to her complaints often enough, but no. This is my own, hard-won with my life's blood. Look, I know your mother pushed you too soon and too hard after Kauneo and set your back up good and stiff, I know you needed more time to get over it all. But time's gone by, Dag, time and past time. That little farmer girl's the proof of it, if you needed any. And I don't want to be caught underneath when you come crashing down."

"You won't be; we're leaving."

"Not good enough. I want your word."

You can't have it. And was that, itself, some decision? He knew he wavered, but had he already gone beyond some point of no return? *And what would that point be?* He scarcely knew, but his head was pounding with the heat, and a bone-deep exhaustion gripped him. His drying clothing itched and stank. He longed for a cold bath. If he held his head under for long enough, would the pain stop? Ten or fifteen minutes ought to do it.

"If I had died at Wolf Ridge, I would be childless now just the same," he snarled at Mari. *And not even my kin could complain. Or leastways, I wouldn't have to listen.* "I have a plan. Why don't you just pretend that I'm dead?"

He turned on his heel and marched out.

Which would have made a grander exit if she hadn't shouted so furiously and so accurately after him, "Oh, certainly—why not? You do!"

11

$\mathcal{D}$ag thought he'd had his groundsense strapped down tight, but whatever of his vile mood still leaked through the cracks was enough to clear the bathhouse of the three convalescent patrollers idling there within five minutes of his entry. Still, at length both his body and his wits cooled, and he went off to find some useful task to occupy himself, preferably away from his comrades. He found it in taking a saddle with a broken tree uptown to the harnessmaker's to trade in for a replacement, and retrieving some other mended gear there, which filled the time till dinner and the arrival of the anxious Utau and the rest of his swamp-slimed patrol.

Mari's arguments were not, any of them, wrong, exactly. *Or at all,* Dag admitted glumly to himself. Ashamed, he dutifully set his mind to the upholding of a self-restraint that had once been more routine than breathing . . . which had somehow grown as heavy as a stone cairn upon his chest. *Dead men don't need air, eh?*

At dinner that night he behaved toward Fawn with meticulous courtesy, no more. Her eyes watched him curiously, wary. But there were enough other patrollers at the table for her to pelt with her questions, tonight mostly about how patrol patterns were arranged and walked, that his silence passed unremarked.

Never had rectitude seemed less rewarding.

The next day was officially devoted to rest and the preparations for the bow-down, and Dag allowed himself to be made mule to help carry in supplies from uptown gathered by the more eager. He crossed paths with Mari only long enough to volunteer for evening watch and door duty, and be briskly refused.

"I can't put the patroller who slew the malice onto guard duty during the celebration of his own deed," she said shortly. "I'd have a revolt on my hands—and rightly, too." She added after a reluctant moment, stopping his protest, "Make sure that little farmer girl knows she's invited, too."

Shortly after, he ran into the enthusiast from Log Hollow who was nabbing the volunteer musicians from the combined patrols for *practice,* a novelty in the experience of most involved, and did not escape till almost time to collect Fawn.

Fawn peered at her hair in the shaving mirror and decided that the green ribbons, loaned by Reela of the broken leg, matched her good dress very well. Reela had been teaching her how to do Lakewalker hair braids, which had turned out to have various meanings; the knot at the nape, Fawn had found out, was a sign of mourning, except when it was a prudent arrangement for going into a fight. Knowing this made the mob of patrollers look different to Fawn's eyes, and gave her a strange feeling, as though the world had shifted under her feet, if only a little, and could never shift back. In any case she could be certain that tonight's style, with her hair tied up high on the back of her head by a jaunty bow and allowed to swing like a horsetail, curls bouncing, didn't say anything she didn't intend in patroller.

Dag came to her door, seeming more relaxed this evening; Fawn wondered if Mari had imparted some bad news to him in the stable yesterday, to so depress his spirits last night. But now his eyes were bright. His simple white shirt made his coppery skin seem to glow. Yesterday's reek of swamp and horse and emergency was replaced with lavender soap and something warm underneath that was just Dag. His hair was clean and soft and already escaping whatever order a stern combing had imposed upon it, looking very touchable, if only she could reach that high. Tiptoes. A stepladder. Something . . .

The atmosphere in the dining room was not too different from other nights, ravenous and raucous, except more crowded because for once everyone was there at the same time. They were all notably cleaned up, and many seemed to have obtained, or shared, scent water. Party clothes seemed to be everyone's same clothes, except laundered. Fawn supposed saddlebags didn't really have room for many changes; the women were all still wearing trousers. Did they ever wear skirts? Hairstyles seemed more elaborate, though. Some of the younger patrollers even wore bells in their braids.

Food and drink, especially drink, overflowed through the entry hall into the next room, where chairs were pushed to the walls and rugs rolled up to make a space to dance. Fawn found herself a seat with the rest of the convalescents, Saun and Reela and the man from Chato's patrol with the game knee and stitches in his jaw, and that poor subdued fellow who'd managed to get snakebit yesterday and was now good-naturedly enduring some pretty merciless ribbing about it. The teasers also distributed fresh beer to all the chair-bound, however, and seemed dedicated to keeping it coming. Fawn sipped hers and smiled shy thanks.

Dag had vanished briefly, but now he returned, screwing something into his wrist cap. Fawn blinked in astonishment to recognize a tambourine, fitted with a wooden peg so he might hold it securely.

"My goodness! I didn't know you played anything."

He grinned at her, giving the frame a last adjustment and drumming his fingers over the stretched skin. The staccato sound made her sit up.

"How clever. What did you play before you lost your hand?"

"Tambourine," he replied cheerily. "I tried the flute, but it tangled my fingers up even when I had twice as many, and when I tackled the fiddle, I was accused of tormenting cats. With this, I can never strike a wrong note. Besides"—he lowered his voice conspiratorially—"it gets me off the hook for the dancing." He winked at her and drifted up to the head of the room, where some other patrollers were collecting.

Their array of instruments seemed a bit random, but mostly small, as would fit in a spare corner of a saddlebag. There were several flutes, of wood, clay, or bone, two fiddles, and a makeshift collection of over-turned tubs for thumping on, obviously filched from around the hotel. The room filled and quieted.

A gray-haired man with a bone flute stepped forward into the hush and began a melody Fawn found haunting; it made the hairs stir on her arms. Disturbed, she studied that pale length of bone, its surface burned about with writing, and was suddenly certain it was someone's relative. Because thighbones came in pairs, but hearts came one by one, so what *did* Lakewalker makers do with the leftovers, in all honor? The tune was so elegiac, it had be some prayer or hymn or memorial; Fawn could see a few people's lips moving on words they obviously knew by heart. A hush followed for a full minute, with everyone's eyes downcast.

A rattle like a snake from the tambourine, and a sudden spatter of drumming, broke the sorrow to bits as if trying to blow it out the windows. The fiddlers and flute players and tub-thumpers struck up a lively dance tune, and patrollers swung out onto the floor. They did not dance in couples but in groups, weaving complex patterns around one another. Except for the shifting about of partners in blithe disregard of anyone's sex, it reminded Fawn a lot of farmer barn dances, although the patrollers seemed to do without a caller. She wondered if they were doing something with their groundsenses to take the place of that outside coordination. Intensely complex as the patterns seemed, the dancers seldom missed a step, although when someone did, it was greeted with much hooting and laughter as the whole bunch rearranged themselves, picked up the pulse, and started again. The bells rang merrily. Dag stood at the back of the musicians, keeping steady time, punctuating his rhythms with well-placed spurts of jingling, watching it all and looking unusually happy; he didn't talk or sing, but he smiled a bit as the jokes flew by.

The younger patrollers' appetites for fast dances seemed insatiable, but at length the wheezing musicians traded out for a couple of singers. Outside, the long summer sun had gone down, and the room was hot with candles and lamps and sweaty bodies. Dag unscrewed his tambourine and came to sit at Fawn's feet, catching up on his beer-drinking with the aid of what seemed a bucket brigade of well-wishers.

One song was new to Fawn, another to a known tune but with different words, and a third she'd heard her aunt Nattie croon as she spun thread, and she wondered if it had originated with farmers or Lakewalkers. The singers were a man and a woman from Chato's patrol, and their voices blended beguilingly, hers pure and fair, his low and resonant. By this time, Fawn wasn't sure if the song about a lost patroller dancing in the woods with magical bears was fantasy or not.

The man with the bone flute joined them, making a trio; when he sent a preamble of notes into the air for the next song, Dag set his half-full glass rather abruptly on the floor. His smile over his shoulder at Fawn more resembled a grimace. "Privy run. Beer, eh," he excused himself, and levered to his feet.

Three sets of eyes marked his movement in concern: Mari's, Utau's, and one other older comrade's; Mari made a gesture of query, *Should I . . . ?* to which Dag returned a small headshake. He trod out without looking back.

"Fifty folk walked out that day," the song began, and Fawn quickly

twigged to Dag's sudden retreat, because it turned out to be a long, involved ballad about the battle of Wolf Ridge. It named no names in its weaving of poetry and tune, of woe, gallantry, sacrifice, and victory, subtly inviting all to identify with its various heroes, and under any other circumstances Fawn would have found it thrilling. Most of the patrollers, truly, seemed variously thrilled or moved; Reela swiped away a tear, and Saun hung openmouthed in the intensity of his listening.

They do not know, Fawn realized. Saun, who had patrolled with Dag for a year and claimed to know him well, did not know. Utau did, listening with his hand over his mouth, eyes dark; Mari, of course, did, with her glances at the archway out which Dag had quietly vanished, and through which he did not return. The song finished at last, and another, more cheerful one started.

When Dag still did not return, Fawn slipped out herself. Someone else was exiting the commode chamber, so she tried outside. It was blessedly cooler out here, the blue shadows relieved by yellow light from the cheery windows, from the lanterns flanking the porch door, and, across the yard, from above the stable doors. Dag was sitting on the bench outside the stable, head back against the wall, staring up at the summer stars.

She sat down beside him and just let the silence hang for a time, for it was not uncomfortable, cloaking them like the night. The stars burned bright and seeming-close despite the lanterns; the sky was cloudless. "You all right?" she asked at last.

"Oh, yeah." He ran his hand through his hair, and added reflectively, "When I was a boy, I used to just love all those heroic ballads. I memorized dozens. I wonder if all those other old battle songs would have seemed as obscene to their survivors?"

Yet he claims not to sing. Unable to answer this, Fawn offered, "At least it helps people remember."

"Yes. Alas."

"It wasn't a *bad* song. In fact, I thought it was awfully good. As a song, I mean."

"I don't deny it. Not the fault of the song-maker—whoever it was did a fine job. If it were less effective, it wouldn't make me want to weep or rage so bad, I suppose. Which was why I left the room. My ground-sense was a little open, in aid of the music-making. I didn't want to blight the mood. Pack thirty-eight tired, battle-nervy patrollers into one building for a week, and moods start to get around fast."

"Do you often make music, when you're out on patrol?" She tried to picture patroller song and dance around a campfire; the weather likely didn't always cooperate.

"Only sometimes. Camps can be pretty busy in the evenings. Curing hides and meat, preserving medicinal plants we pick up while patrolling, keeping logs and maps up to date. If it's a mounted patrol, a lot of horse care. Weapons training for the youngsters and practice for everyone. Mending, of clothes and boots and gear. Cooking, washing. All simple tasks, but they do go on."

His voice slowed in reminiscence. "Patrols vary in size—in the north they send out companies of a hundred and fifty or two hundred for the great seasonal wilderness sweeps—but south of the lake, patrols are usually smaller and shorter. Even so, you're like to be in each other's hair for weeks on end with no entertainment *but* each other. After a while, everyone knows all the songs. So there's gossip. And factions. And jokes. And practical jokes. And revenge for practical jokes. And fistfights over revenge for practical jokes. And knife fights over—well, you get the idea. Although if the emotions are allowed to melt down into that sour a soup, you can bet the patrol leader will be having a very memorable talk with Fairbolt Crow about it, later."

"Have you ever?"

"Not about that. Although all talks with Fairbolt tend to be memorable." In the shadows, he scratched his nose and smiled, then leaned his head back and let his eyes rest on the mellow windows across the yard. The singing had stopped, and dance tunes had begun again; feet thumping on the floor made the whole building pulse like a drum.

"Let's see, what else? On warm summer nights, gathering firewood is always a popular activity."

Fawn considered this, and the amusement underlying his voice. "Should think that would be wanted on cold nights, more."

"Mm, but you see, on warm nights, no one complains if folks are gone for two hours and come back having forgotten the firewood. Bathing in the river, that's another good one."

"In the dark?" said Fawn doubtfully.

"In the river is even more the question. Especially when the season's turned frosty. Walks, oh sure, that's believable, when everyone's been out slogging since dawn. Scouting around, too—that draws many selfless volunteers. Some dangerous squirrels out in those woods, they could mount an attack at any time. You can't be too prepared." A rumbling chuckle escaped his chest.

"Oh," said Fawn, finally understanding. Her lips curled up, if only for the rare sight of the laugh lines at the corners of his eyes.

"Followed by the breakups and the makeups and the people not talking to each other, or worse, going over it all *again* till you're ready to stuff your head in your blanket and scream for the listening to it. Ah, well." He vented a tolerant sigh. "The older patrollers generally have things worked out smooth, but the younger ones can be downright restive. It's not as though folks' lives stop for patrol. Walking the patterns isn't some emergency where you can drop everything, deal heroically, and then go home for good and all. It all starts again tomorrow at dawn. And you'll have to get up and walk your share just the same." He stretched, joints creaking a bit, as if in contemplation of such an early start.

"It's not that we're all mad, you know, although sometimes it seems like it," he went on in a lower voice. "Groundsense makes our moods very contagious. Not just by speech and gestures; it's like it gets in the air." His hand traced an upward spiral. "Now, for instance. Once a certain number of people open their grounds to each other, there starts to be . . . leakage. Bow-downs are really good for that. That building over there's downright awash, right now. All *sorts* of things can start to seem like a good idea. Absent gods be thanked for the beer."

"The beer?"

"Beer, I have concluded"—he held up an edifying finger, and Fawn began to realize that he was slightly drunk; people had kept the musicians well supplied with encouraging refreshment, earlier—"*exists* for the purpose of being blamed the next day. Very regrettable beverage, beer."

"Farmers use it for that, too," Fawn observed.

"A universal need." He blinked. "I think I need some more."

"Are you thirsty?"

"No." He slumped down, staring at her sidelong. His eyes were dark pools in this light, like night condensed. The lanternlight made glimmering orange halos around his hair, and slid across his faintly sweat-sheened features like a caress. "Just considering the potential of regret . . ."

He leaned toward her, and Fawn froze in hope so strong it felt like terror. Did he mean to kiss her? His breath was tinged with beer and exertion and Dag. Hers stopped altogether.

Stillness. Heartbeats.

"No," he sighed. "No. Mari was right." He sat up again. Fawn nearly burst into unfathomable tears. Nearly reached for him.

No, you can't. Daren't. He'll think you're that . . . that awful word Sunny used. It burned in her memory like an infected gash, *Slut.* It was an ugly word that had somehow turned her into an ugly thing, like a splash of ink or blood or poison discoloring water. *For Dag, I would be only beautiful.* And tall. She wished herself taller. If she were taller, no one could call her names just for, for *wanting* so much.

He sighed, smiled, rose. Gave her a hand up. They went back inside.

In the entry hall Dag's head turned, listening. "Good, someone's using the tambourine. They can get along without me for what's left of this." Truly, the music coming through the archway seemed slower and sleepier. He made for the staircase.

Fawn found her voice. "You going up?"

"Yeah. It was good, but it's been enough for one night. You?"

"I'm a little tired, too." She followed after him. What had happened, or not happened, out on the bench felt a lot like that moment on the road, some turn she had somehow missed.

As they exited the staircase on the second floor, bumping and laughter echoed up behind them. Dirla and two young patrollers from Chato's group burst out giggling, saluted Dag with cheerful hellos, and swung down the adjoining hallway. Fawn stopped and stared as they paused at Dirla's door, for one fellow looped his arm around her neck and kissed her, but she was still holding the other's hand to her . . . chest. Dirla— tall Dirla—extended one booted foot and pushed the door open, and they all fell through; it closed, cutting off some jest.

"Dag," Fawn said hesitantly, "what was that?"

He cocked an amused eyebrow at her. "What did it look like to you?"

"Is Dirla taking that . . . I mean, them . . . is she going to *bed* with those fellows?"

"Seems likely."

Likely? If his groundsense did half what he said, he *likely* knew very well. "*Both* of them?"

"Well, numbers are generally uneven, out on patrol. People make adjustments. Dirla is very . . . um . . . generous."

Fawn swallowed. "Oh."

She followed him up their hallway. Razi and Utau were just unlocking the door to their room; Utau looked, and smelled, distinctly the worse for beer, and Razi's hair, escaping his long braid, hung plastered in sweaty strands across his forehead from the dancing. They both bade Dag a civil good night and disappeared within.

"Well," said Fawn, determined to be fair, "it's too bad they weren't lucky enough to find ladies, too. They're too nice to be lonely." She added after a suspicious glance upward, "Dag, why are you biting your wrist?"

He cleared his throat. "Sometime when I am either a lot more sober or a lot more drunk, Spark, I shall attempt to explain the exceedingly complicated story of how those two came to both be married to the same accommodating woman back at Hickory Lake Camp. Let's just say, they look out for each other."

"Lakewalker ladies can marry more than one fellow? At a time? You're gulling me!"

"Not normally, and no, I'm not. I said it was complicated."

They fetched up before his door. He gave her a slightly strained smile.

"Well, *I* think Dirla is greedy," Fawn decided. "Or else those fellows are awfully pushy."

"Ah, no. Among Lakewalkers of the civil sort, which you know we all are, the woman invites. The man accepts, or not, and let me tell you, saying no gracefully without giving offense is a burden. I guarantee, whatever is going on back there was her idea."

"Among farmers, that would be thought too forward. Only bad

girls, or, or" *stupid* "foolish ones would, well. Good girls wait to be asked." *And even then they're supposed to say no unless he comes with land in hand.*

He stretched his right arm out, supporting himself on the wall, half sheltering her. He stared down at her. After a long, long, thoughtful pause, he breathed, "Do they, now?" He scraped his teeth over his lower lip, the chip catching briefly. His eyes were lakes of darkness to fall into, going down for fathoms. "So, um, Spark . . . how many nights would you say we have wasted, here?"

She turned her face upward, swallowed, and said tremulously, "Way too many?"

They did not exactly fall into each other's arms. It was more of a mutual lunge.

He kicked his door open and kicked it closed again after them, because his arms were too full of her. Her feet did not touch the floor, but that was not the only reason she felt as though she was flying. Half his kisses missed her mouth, but that was all right, almost any part of his skin sliding beneath her lips was joy. He set her down, reached for the door bar, and stopped himself, wheezing slightly. *No, don't stop now . . .*

His voice recaptured seriousness. "If you mean this, Spark, bar the door."

Not taking her eyes from his dear, bony, faintly frenzied face, she did so. The oak board fell into place in its brackets with a solid, satisfying *clunk*. It seemed a sufficient compromise of customs.

His hand, reluctantly, slid from her shoulder and let her go just long enough for him to stride over and turn up the oil lamp on the table beside his bed. Dull orange glow became yellow flare within the glass chimney, filling the room with light and shadow. He sat rather abruptly on the edge of his bed, as if his knees had given way, and stared at her, holding out his hand. It was shaking. She climbed up into the circle of his arm, then folded her knees under her to raise her face to his again. His kisses slowed, as if tasting her lips, then, startlingly, tasting in truth, his tongue slipping inside her mouth. Odd, but nice, she decided, and earnestly tried to do it back. His hand wound in her hair, undid her ribbon, and let her curls fall down to her shoulders.

How did people get rid of their clothes, at times like these? Sunny had merely lifted her skirts and shoved down her drawers; so had the malice, come to think.

"Sh, now, what dark thought went past just now?" Dag chided. "Be here. With me."

"How did you know what I thought?" she said, trying not to be unnerved.

"I don't. I read grounds, not minds, Spark. Sometimes, all groundsense does is give you more to be confused about." His hand hesitated on the top button of her dress. "May I?"

"Please," she said, relieved of a procedural worry. Of course Dag would know how to do this. She had only to watch and copy.

He undid a few more fastenings, gently pulled down one sleeve, and kissed her bared shoulder. She gathered her courage and went after the buttons of his shirt. Mutual confidence established, things went faster after that, cloth tumbling to the floor over the side of the bed. The last thing he undid, after a hesitation and a glance at her from under his lashes, was his arm harness, unbuckling the straps around his lower arm and above his elbow, and setting it on the table. His hand rubbed the red marks left by the leather. For him, she realized dimly, it was a greater gesture of vulnerability and trust than removing his trousers had just been.

"Light," Dag muttered, hesitating. "Light? Farmers are supposed to like it dark, I've heard."

"Leave it on," Fawn whispered, and he smiled and lay back. When all that height was laid out flat, it stretched a long way. His bed was not as narrow as hers in the next room, but still he filled it from corner to corner. She felt like an explorer facing a mountain range that crossed her whole horizon. "I want to look at you."

"I'm no rose, Spark."

"Maybe not. But you make my eyes happy."

The corners of his eyes crinkled up enchantingly at that, and she had to stretch up and kiss them. Skin slid on skin for the length of her body. His muscles were long and tapering, and the skin of his torso was unevenly tanned where his shirts had been on or off, paler still below his waist along his lean flank. A faint dusting of dark hair across his chest narrowed and thickened, going down in a vee below his belly. Her fingers twined in it, brushing with and against the grain. So, with his odd Lakewalker senses, what more of her did he touch?

She swallowed, and dared to say, "You said you could tell."

"Hm?" His hand spiraled around her breast, and how could such a soft caress make it suddenly ache so sweetly?

"The time of the month a woman can get a child, you said you could tell." Or wait, no, was that only Lakewalker ladies? "A beautiful pattern in her ground, you said." Yes, and she'd believed Sunny, hadn't she, on a piece of bed lore that, if not a mean lie, had turned out to be a costly untruth, and Sunny's tale had seemed a lot less unlikely than this. A shiver of unease, *Am I being stupid again . . . ?* was interrupted when Dag propped himself up on his left elbow and looked at her with a serious smile.

His hand traced her belly, crossing the malice marks there that had turned to thin black scabs. "You're not at risk tonight, Spark. But I should be right terrified to try to make love to you that way so soon after your injuries. You're so dainty, and I'm, um, well, there are other things I'd very much like to show you."

She risked a peek down, but her eye caught on the parallel black lines beneath his beautiful hand, and a flash of sorrow and guilt shook her. Would she ever be able to lie down with anyone without these cascades of unwelcome memory washing through her? And then she wondered if Dag—with, it seemed, so many more accumulated memories—had a similar problem.

"Sh," he soothed, and his thumb crossed her lips, though she had not spoken. "Reach for lightness, bright Spark. You do not betray your sorrow to set it aside for an hour. It'll be waiting patiently for you to pick it up again on the other side."

"How long?"

"Time wears grief smooth like a river stone. The weight will always be there, but it'll stop scraping you raw at the slightest touch. But you have to let the time flow by; you can't rush it. We wear our hair knotted for a year for our losses, and it is not too long a while."

She reached up and ran her hand through his dark tousle, petting and winding it through her fingers. Gratified fingers. She gave a lock a little tug. "So what was this supposed to mean?"

"Shaved for head lice?" he offered, breaking the bleakness as she giggled, no doubt his intent.

"Go on, you did not either have head lice!"

"Not lately. They're another story, but I have better things to do with my lips right now . . . " He began kissing his way down her body, and she wondered what magic was in his tongue, not just for his kisses and how they seemed to lay trails of cool fire across her skin, but for how, with his words, he seemed to lift stones from her heart.

Her breath caught as his tongue reached the tip of her breast and did exhilarating things there. Sunny had merely pinched her through her dress, and, and *blight* Sunny for haunting her head like this, *now*. Dag's hand drifted up, his thumb caressing her forehead, then he sat up.

"Roll over," he murmured. "Let give you a back rub. Think I can bring your body and ground into better tune."

"Do you—if you want—"

"I won't say, *trust me*. I will say, *try me,*" he whispered into her curls. "Try me."

For a one-handed man, he did this *awfully* well, she thought muzzily a few minutes later, her face pressed into the pillow. Memory seemed to melt out of her brain altogether. The bed creaked as he moved off it briefly, and she opened one eye, *don't let him get away,* but he returned in a moment. A slight gurgle, a cool splash pooling on the inward curve of her back, the scent of chamomile and clover . . .

"Oh, you got some of that nice oil." She thought a moment. "When?"

"Seven days ago."

She muffled a snicker.

"Hey, a patroller should be prepared for any emergency."

"Is this an emergency?"

"Just give me a bit more time, Spark, and we'll see . . . Besides, it's good for my hand, which tends to get rough. You don't want hangnails catching in tender places, trust me on that."

The oil did change the texture of his touch as he worked his way smoothly down to her toes, turned her over, and started back up.

Hand. Soon supplemented with tongue, in very tender and surprising places indeed. His touch was like silk, there, there, *there?* ah! She jerked in surprise, but eased back. So, this was *making love*. It was all very nice, but it seemed a bit one-sided.

"Shouldn't it be your turn?" she asked anxiously.

"Not yet," he said, rather muffled. "'M pretty happy where I am. And your ground is flowing almost right, now. Let me, let me just . . ."

Minutes flew. *Something* was swirling through her, like some astonishingly sweet emergency. His touch grew firmer, swifter, surer. Her eyes closed, her breath came faster, and her spine began to arch. Then her breath caught, and she went rigid, silent, openmouthed, as the sensation burst from her, climbing up to white out her brain, to rush like a tide to her fingers and toes, and ebb.

Her back eased, and she lay shaking and amazed. *"Oh."* When she could, she raised her head and stared down over her body, strange new landscape that it had become. Dag was up on one elbow, watching her in return, eyes black and bright, with a grin on his face bordering on smug.

"Better?" he inquired, as if he didn't know.

"Was that some . . . some Lakewalker magic?" No wonder folks tried to follow these people to the ends of the world.

"Nope. That was Little Spark magic. All your own."

A hundred mysteries seemed to fly up and away like a flock of startled birds into the night. "No *wonder* people want to do this. It all makes much more sense now . . ."

"Indeed." He crawled up the bed to kiss her again. The taste of herself on his lips, mixed with the scent of chamomile and clover, was a little disturbing, but she valiantly kissed him back. Then brushed her lips across his enthralling cheekbones, his eyelids, definite chin, and back to his mouth, as she giggled helplessly. She could feel an answering rumble from deep in his chest as she lay across him.

She had brushed against him, but she had not yet *touched* him. It was surely his turn now. Hands should work two ways. She sat up, blinking against dizziness.

He stretched out straight and smiled up, his crinkling eyes now resting inquiringly on her, downright inviting, in an unhurried sort of way. He lay open to her, to her gaze, in a way that astonished her anew. All but his mysterious ground, of course. That was beginning to seem an unfair advantage. Where to begin, *how* to begin? She recalled how he had started.

"May I . . . touch you too?"

"Please," he breathed.

It might be mere mimicry, but it was a start, and once started, acquired its own momentum. She kissed her way down and up his body, and arrived back at the middle.

Her first tentative touch made him jerk and catch his breath, and she shied back.

"No, it's all right, go on," he huffed. "I'm a little, um, sensitized just at the moment. It's good. Almost anything you can do is good."

"Sensitized. Is that what you call it?" Her lips curled up.

"I'm trying to be *polite,* Spark."

She tried various touches, strokes, and grips, wondering if she was doing this right. Her hands felt clumsy and rather too small. The occasional catches of his breath were not very informative, she thought, though once in a while his hand covered hers to squeeze some silent suggestion. Was that gasp pleasure or pain? His apparent endurance for pain was a bit frightening, when she thought about it. "Can I try your oil on *my* hands?"

"Certainly! Although . . . this may be over rather quickly if you do."

She hesitated. "Couldn't we . . . do it again? Sometime?"

"*Oh* yes. I'm very renewable. Just not very fast. Not"—he sighed—"as quick as when I was younger, anyway. Though that's mostly been to my advantage, tonight."

And mine. His patience humbled her. "Well, then . . ."

The oil made her hands slip and slide in ways that intrigued her and seemed to please him, too. She grew more daring. *That,* for example, made him jerk, no, convulse, much as he'd done to her a while ago.

"Brave Spark!" he gasped.

"Is that good?"

"*Yes . . .*"

"Figured if you thought it would please me, it might be something that pleased you, too."

"Clever girl," he crooned, his eyes closing again.

She chilled. "Please don't make fun of me."

His eyes opened, and his brows drew in; he raised his head from the pillow and frowned down over his torso at her. "Wasn't. You have one of the hungriest minds it's ever been my pleasure to meet. You may have been starved of information, but your wits are as sharp as a blade."

She caught her breath, lest it escape as a sudden surprised sob. His words could not be true, but *oh* they sounded so nice to hear!

At her shocked look, he added a little impatiently, "Come, child, you can't be that bright and not know it."

"Papa said I must be a fool to ask so many questions all the time."

"Never that." His head tilted, and his eyes took on that uncanny inward look. "There's a deep, dark place in your ground just there. Major fissure and blockage. I . . . it's not going to be the work of an hour to find the bottom of that one, I'm afraid."

She gulped. "Then let's set it aside with the rest of the stones, for now. It'll wait." She bent her head. "I'm neglecting you."

"I won't argue with that . . ."

Tongues, she discovered, worked like fingers on fellows quite as well, if differently, as they worked on ladies. Well, then. What would happen if she did *this* and also *this* and *that* at the same time . . .

She found out. It was fascinating to watch. Even from the oblique angle of view down here she could see his expression grow so inward it might have been a trance. For a moment, she wondered if levitation were a Lakewalker magical skill, for he seemed about to rise off the bed.

"Are you all right?" she asked anxiously, when his body stopped shuddering. "Your forehead got all wrinkled up funny there for a minute, when your, um, back curved up like that."

His hand waved while he regained his breath; his eyes stayed squeezed shut, but finally opened again. "Sorry, what? Sorry. Was waiting for all those white sparks on the insides of my eyelids to finish exploding. *That* wasn't something to miss."

"Does that often happen?"

"No. No, indeed."

"Are you all right?" she repeated.

His grin lit his face like a streak of fire. "All right? I think I'm down-right *astounding*." From an angle of attack that would seem to allow, at best, a wallow, he lunged up and wrapped both arms around her, and dragged her back down to his chest, heedless of the mess they'd made. It was his turn to kiss her face all over. Laughter turned to accidental touching, to—

"Dag, you're *ticklish*."

"No, I'm not. Or only in certain *aiee!*" When he got his breath back, he added, "You're fiendish, Spark. I like that in a woman. Gods. I haven't laughed this much in . . . I can't remember."

"I like how you giggle."

"I was not *giggling*. That would be undignified in a man of my years."

"What was that noise, then?"

"Chortling. Yes, definitely. Chortling."

"Well," she decided, "it looks good on you. Everything looks good on you." She sat up on her elbow and let her gaze travel the long route down his body and back. "*Nothing* looks good on you, too. It's most un-fair."

"Oh, as if *you* aren't sitting there looking, looking . . ."

"What?" she breathed, sinking back into his grip.

"Naked. Edible. Beautiful. Like spring rain and star fire."

He drew her in again; their kisses grew longer, lazier. Sleepier. He made a great effort, and reached out and turned off the lamp. Soft summer-night air stirred the curtains. He flung the sheet up and let it settle over them. She cuddled into his arm, pressing her ear to his chest, and closed her eyes.

To the ends of the world, she thought, melting into deeper darkness.

12

Dag spent the radiant summer dawn proving beyond doubt to Fawn that her last night's first-in-a-lifetime experience needn't be a once-in-a-lifetime experience. When they woke from the ensuing sated nap, it was midmorning. Dag seriously considered the merits of lying low till the patrols had taken their planned departure, but unexpectedly sharp hunger drove both him and Fawn to rise, wash, dress, and go see if breakfast was still to be had downstairs.

Fawn entered the staircase ahead of Dag and turned sideways to let Utau, clumping up to collect more gear to load, pass her by. Dag smiled brightly at his sometime-linker. Utau's head cranked over his shoulder in astonishment, and he walked into the far wall with a muffled thud, righted himself, and wheeled to stare. Prudently deciding to ignore that, Dag followed Fawn before Utau could speak. Dag suspected he needed to get better control of his stretching mouth, as well as of his sparking ground. A responsible, mature, respected patroller should not walk about grinning and glowing like some dementedly carved pumpkin. It was like to frighten the horses.

Mari's patrol was slated to ride north and pick up their pattern again where it had been broken off almost two weeks ago by the call for aid. With his patrol's purse newly topped off by the Glassforgers, Chato planned to continue on his mission to purchase horses from the limestone country south of the Grace. He would be slowed on the first leg by a wagon to carry Saun and Reela, neither quite ready to ride yet;

the pair were to finish convalescing at a Lakewalker camp that controlled a ferry crossing down on the river, and be picked up again on the return journey. Both patrols had planned their removals for the crack of noon, a merciful hour. Dag sensed Chato's moderating influence at work. Mari was perfectly capable of ordering a dawn departure after a bow-down, then concealing her evil hilarity behind a rod-straight face as her bleary troop stumbled out. Mari was far and away Dag's favorite relative, but that was a pretty low fence to get over, and he prayed to the absent gods that he might avoid her altogether this morning.

After breakfast Dag helped lug the last of Saun's gear to the wagon, and turned to find his prayers, as usual, unanswered. Mari stood holding the reins of her horse, staring at him in mute exasperation.

He let his eyebrows rise, trying desperately not to smile. Or worse, chortle. "What?"

She drew a long breath, but then just let it out. "Besotted fool. There's no more use trying to talk to you this morning than to those twittering wrens in that elm across the yard. I said my piece. I'll see you back in camp in a few weeks. Maybe the novelty will have worn off by then, and you'll have your wits back, I don't know. You can do your own blighted explaining to Fairbolt, is all I can say."

Dag's back straightened. "That I will."

"Eh!" She turned to gather her reins, but then turned back, seriousness replacing the aggravation in her eyes. "Be careful of yourself in farmer country, Dag."

He would have preferred a tart dressing-down to this true concern, against which he had no defense. "I'm always careful."

"Not so's I ever noticed," she said dryly. Silently, Dag offered her a leg up, which she accepted with a nod, settling in her saddle with a tired sigh. She was growing thinner, he thought, these last couple of years. He gave her a smile of farewell, but it only made her lean on her pommel and lower her voice to him. "I've seen you in a score of moods, including foul. I've never before seen you so plain happy. Enough to make an old woman weep, you are . . . Take care of that little girl, too, then."

"I plan to."

"Huh. Do you, now." She shook her head and clucked her horse forward, and Dag belatedly recalled his last statement to her on the subject of plans.

But he could almost watch himself being displaced in her head with the hundred details a patrol leader on duty must track—as well he remembered. Her gaze turned to sweep over the rest of her charges, checking their gear, their horses, their faces; judging their readiness, finding it enough to go on with. This day. Again.

Fawn had been helping Reela, apparently one of the several dozen people, or so it seemed to Dag, that Fawn had managed to make friends of in this past week. The two young women bade each other cheery good-byes, and Fawn popped down off the wagon to come stand with him as he watched his patrol form up and trot out through the gateway. At least as many riders gave a parting wave to her as to him. In a few minutes, Chato's patrol too mounted up and wheeled out, at a slower pace for the rumbling wagon. Saun waved as enthusiastic a farewell as his injuries permitted. Silence settled in the stable yard.

Dag sighed, caught as usual between relief to be rid of the whole maddening lot of them, and the disconcerting loneliness that always set in when he was parted from his people. He told himself that it made no sense to be shaken by both feelings simultaneously. Anyway, there were more practical reasons to be wary when one was the only Lakewalker in a townful of farmers, and he struggled to wrap his usual guarded courtesy back about himself. Except now with Fawn also inside.

The horse boys disbanded toward the tack room or the back door to the kitchen, walking slowly in the humidity and chatting with each other.

"Your patrollers weren't so bad," said Fawn, staring thoughtfully out the gate. "I didn't think they'd accept me, but they did."

"This is patrol. Camp is different," said Dag absently.

"How?"

"Eh . . . " Weak platitudes rose to his mind, *Time will tell, Don't borrow trouble.* "You'll see." He felt curiously loath to explain to her, on this bright morning, why his personal war on malices wasn't the sole reason that he volunteered for more extra duty than any other patroller in Hickory Lake Camp. His record had been seventeen straight months in the field without returning there, though he'd had to switch patrols several times to do it.

"Must we leave today, too?" asked Fawn.

Dag came to himself with a start and wrapped his arm around her, snugging her to his hip. "No, in fact. It's a two-day hard ride to Lumpton from here, but we've no need to ride hard. We can make an easy start tomorrow, take it in gentle stages." Or even later, the seductive thought occurred.

"I was wondering if I ought to give my room back to the hotel. Since I'm not really a patroller and all."

"What? No! That room is yours for as long as you want it, Spark!" Dag said indignantly.

"Um, well, that's sort of the point, I thought." She bit her lip, but her eyes, he realized, were sparkling. "I was wondering if I could sleep in with you? For . . . frugality."

"Of course, frugality! Yes, that's the thing. You are a thoughtful girl, Spark."

She cast him a merry smirk. She flashed an entrancing dimple when she smirked, which made his heart melt like a block of butter left in the summer sun. She said, "I'll go move my things."

He followed, feeling as utterly scatter-witted as Mari had accused him of being. He could not, could *not* run up and down the streets of Glassforge, leaping and shouting to the blue sky and the entire population, *She says I make her eyes happy!*

He really wanted to, though.

They did not leave the next day, for it was raining. Nor the next either, for rain threatened then, too. On the following morning, Dag declared Fawn too sore from the previous night's successfully concluded bed experiments to ride comfortably, although by midafternoon she was hopping around as happily as a flea and *he* was limping as the pulled muscle in his back seized up. Which provided the next day's excuse for lingering, as well. He pictured the conversation with Fairbolt, *Why are you late, Dag? Sorry, sir, I crippled myself making passionate love to a farmer girl.* Yeah, that'd go over well.

Watching Fawn discover the delights that her own body could provide her was an enchantment to Dag as endlessly beguiling as water lilies. He had to cast his mind far back for comparisons, as he'd made those discoveries at a much younger age. He could indeed remember being a little crazed with it all for a while. He found he really didn't need to rack his brains to provide variety in his lovemaking, for she was still overwhelmed by the marvel of repeatability. So he probably hadn't created anything he couldn't handle, quite.

Dag also discovered in himself a previously unsuspected weakness for foot rubs. If ever Fawn wanted to fix him in one place, she didn't need to hog-tie him with ropes; when her small firm hands worked their way down past his ankles, he slumped like a man poleaxed and just lay there paralyzed, trying not to drool too unattractively into his pillow. In those moments, never getting out of bed again for the rest of his life seemed the very definition of paradise. As long as Spark was in the bed with him.

The short summer nights filled themselves, but Dag was unsettled by how swiftly the long days also slipped by. A gentle ride out for Fawn to try her new mare and riding trousers, with a picnic by the river, turned into an afternoon under a curtaining willow tree that lasted till sundown. Sassa the Horseford kinsman popped up again, and Dag found in Fawn an apparently bottomless appetite for tours of Glassforge crafters. Her endless curiosity and passion for questions was by no means limited to patrollers and sex, flattering as that had been, but seemed to extend to the whole wide world. Sassa's willing, nay, proud escort and array of family connections guided them through the complex back premises of a brick burner, a silversmith, a saddler, three kinds of mills, a potter—Fawn cast a simple pot under the woman's enthusiastic tutelage, becoming cheerfully muddied—and a repeat of the visit to Sassa's own glassworks, because Dag had missed it before on account of being up to his waist in swamp.

Dag at first mustered a mere polite interest—he seldom paid close attention anymore to the details of anything he wasn't being asked to track and slay—but found himself drawn in along the trail of Fawn's fascination. With studied and sweating intensity, the glass workers brought together sand and fire and meticulous timing to effect transformations of the very ground of their materials into fragile, frozen brilliance. *This is farmer magic, and they don't even realize it,* Dag thought, completely taken by their system of blowing glass into molds to make rapid, reliable replicas. Sassa gave to Fawn a bowl that she had seen being made the other day, now annealed, and she determined to take it home to her mother. Dag was doubtful about getting it to West Blue intact in a saddlebag, but Sassa provided a slat box padded with straw and hope. Which was going to be bulky and awkward; Dag steeled himself to deal with it.

Later, Fawn unpacked the bowl to set on the table beside their bed to catch the evening light. Dag sat on the bed and stared with nearly equal interest at the way the patterns pressed into it made wavering rainbows.

"All things have grounds, except where a malice has drained them," he commented. "The grounds of living things are always moving and changing, but even rocks have a sort of low, steady hum. When Sassa made that batch of glass and cast it, it was almost as if its ground came alive, it transformed so. Now it's become still again, but changed. It's like it" —his hand reached out as if grasping for the right word—"sings a brighter tune."

Fawn stood back with her hands on her hips and gave him a slightly frustrated look; as if, for all her questions, he walked in a place she could not follow.

"So," she said slowly, "if things move their grounds, can pushing on grounds move things?"

Dag blinked in faint shock. Was it chance or keen logic that brought her question so close to the heart of Lakewalker secrets? He hesitated. "That's the theory," he said at last. "But would you like to see how a Lakewalker would move the ground in that bowl from one side of the table to the other?"

Her eyes widened. "Show me!"

Gravely, he leaned over, reached out with his hand, and shoved the bowl about six inches.

"Dag!" Fawn wailed in exasperation. "I thought you were going to show me magic."

He grinned briefly, although mostly because he could scarcely look at her and *not* smile. "Trying to move anything through its ground is like pushing on the short end of a long lever. It's always easier to do it by hand. Although it's said . . . " He hesitated again. "It's said the old sorcerer-lords linked together in groups to do their greater magics. Like matching grounds for healing, or a lovers' groundlock, only with some lost difference."

"Don't you do that now?"

"No. We are too reduced—maybe our bloodlines were adulterated in the dark times, no one knows. Anyway, it's forbidden."

"I mean for your pattern walking."

"That's just simple perception. Like the difference between feeling with your hand and pushing with your hand, perhaps."

"Why is pushing forbidden? Or was that linking up in bunches to push that's not allowed?"

He should have known that the last remark would elicit more questions. Throwing one fact to Fawn was like throwing one piece of meat to a pack of starving dogs; it just caused a riot. "Bad experiences," he replied in a quelling tone. All right, by the pursing of her lips and wrinkling of her brow, quelling wasn't going to work; try for distraction. "Let me tell you, though, not a patroller up Luthlia way survives the lake country without learning how to bounce mosquitoes through their grounds. Ferocious little pests—they'll drain you dry, they will."

"You use magic to repel *mosquitoes*?" she said, sounding as though she couldn't decide whether to be impressed or offended. "We just have recipes for horrible stuff to rub on our skins. Once you know what's in them, you'd almost rather be bit."

He snickered, then sighed. "They say we are a fallen folk, and I for one believe it. The ancient lords built great cities, ships, and roads, transformed their bodies, sought longevity, and brought the whole world crashing down at the last. Though I suspect it was a really good run for a while, till then. Me—I bounce mosquitoes. Oh, and I can summon and dismiss my horse, once I get him trained up to it. And help settle another's hurting body, if I'm lucky. And see the world double, down to the ground. That's about it for Dag magic, I'm afraid."

Her eyes lifted to his face. "And kill malices," she said slowly.

"Aye. That mainly."

He reached for her, swallowing her next question with a kiss.

It took the better part of a week for Dag's boat anchor of a conscience to drag him out of the clouds and back onto the road. He wished he could just jettison the blighted deadweight. But one morning he turned back from shaving to find Fawn, half-dressed and with her bedroll open on the bed, frowning down at the sharing knife that lay there.

He came and wrapped her in his arms, her bare back to his bare torso.

"It's time, I guess," she said.

"I guess so, too." He sighed. "Not that you couldn't count my unused camp-time by years, but Mari gave me leave to solve the mystery of that thing, not to linger here in this brick-and-clapboard paradise. The hirelings have been giving me squinty looks for days."

"They've been real nice to *me*," she observed accurately.

"You're good at finding friends." In fact, everyone from the cooks, scullions, chambermaids, and horse boys up to the owner and his wife had grown downright defensive of Fawn, farmer heroine as she was. To the point where Dag suspected that if she demanded, *Throw this lanky fellow into the street!* he'd shortly find himself sitting in the dust clutching his saddlebags. The Glassforgers who worked here were used to patrollers and their odd ways with each other, but it was clear enough to Dag that they just barely tolerated this mismatch, and that only for the sake of Fawn's obvious delight. Other patrons now drifting in, drovers and drivers and traveling families and boatmen up from the river to secure cargoes, looked askance at the odd pair, and even more askance after collecting whatever garbled gossip was circulating about them.

Dag wondered how askance he would be looked at in West Blue. Fawn had gradually grown reconciled to the planned stop at her home, partly from guilt at his word picture of her parents' probable anxiety, and partly by his pledge not to abandon her there. It was the only promise she'd ever asked him to repeat.

He dropped a kiss on the top of her head, letting his finger snake around and drift over the healing wounds on her left cheek. "Your bruises are fading now. I figure if I bring you back to your family claiming to be your protector, it'll be more convincing if you don't look like you just lost a drunken brawl."

Her lips twitched up as she caught his hand and kissed it, but then her fingers drifted to the malice marks on her neck. "Except for these."

"Don't pick."

"They itch. Are they ever going to drop off? The other scabs did already."

"Soon enough, I judge. It'll leave these deep bitter-red dents underneath for a time, but they'll fade almost like other scars. They'll turn silvery when they're old."

"Oh—that long shiny groove on your leg that starts behind your knee and goes around up your thigh—was that a malice-clawing, then?" She had mapped every mark upon him as assiduously as a pattern-grid surveyor, these past days and nights, and demanded annotations for most of them, too.

"Just a touch. I got away, and my linker put his knife in a moment later."

She turned to hug him around the waist. "I'm glad it didn't grab any higher," she said seriously.

Dag choked a laugh. "Me too, Spark!"

They were on the straight road north by noon.

They rode slowly, in part for their dual disinclination for their destinations, but mostly because of the dog-breath humidity that had set in after the last rain. The horses plodded beneath a brassy sun. Their riders talked or fell silent with, it seemed to Dag, equal ease. They spent the next afternoon—rainy again—in the loft of the barn at the well-house where they'd first glimpsed each other, picnicking on farm fare and listening to the soothing sounds of the drops on the roof and the horses champing hay below, didn't notice when the storm stopped, and lingered there overnight.

The next day was brighter and clearer, the hot white haze blown away east, and they reluctantly rode on. On the fifth night of the two-day ride they stopped a short leg from Lumpton Market to camp one last time. Fawn had figured an early start from Lumpton would bring them to West Blue before dark. It was hard for Dag to guess what would happen then, though her slowly unfolding tales of her family had at least given him a better sense of who he would encounter.

They found a campsite by a winding creek, out of view of the road, beneath a scattered stand of leatherpod trees. Later in the fall, the seedpods would hang down beneath the big spade-shaped leaves like hundreds of leather straps, but now the trees were in full bloom. Spikes stood up from crowns of leaves with dozens of linen-white blossoms the size of egg cups clustered on them, breathing sweet perfume into the evening air. As the moonless night fell, fireflies rose up along the creek and from the meadow beyond it, twinkling in the mist. Beneath the leatherpod tree, the shadows grew black.

"Wish I could see you better," Fawn murmured, as they lay down across their combined blankets and commenced a desultory fiddling with each other's buttons. No one wanted a blanket atop, in this heat.

"Hm." Dag sat up on one elbow and smiled in the dark. "Give me a minute, Spark, and I might be able to do something about that."

"No, don't put more wood on the fire. 'S too hot now."

"Wasn't going to. Just wait and see. In fact, close your eyes."

He extended his groundsense to its full range and found no menace for a mile, just the small nesting life of the grass: mice and shrews and rabbits and sleepy meadowlarks; above, a few fluttering bats, and the silent ghostly passage of an owl. He drew his net finer still, filling it with tinier life. Not a bounce, but a persuasion . . . yes. This still worked. The tree began to throng with his invited visitors, more and more. Beside him, Fawn's face slowly emerged from the gloom as though rising from deep water.

"Can I open them yet?" she asked, her eyes dutifully scrunched up.

"Just a moment more . . . yes. Now."

He kept his eyes on her face as she looked up, so as not to miss the best wonder of all. Her eyes opened, then shot wide; her lips parted in a gasp.

Above them, the leatherpod tree was filled with hundreds, perhaps thousands, of—in Dag's wide-open perception, slightly bewildered—fireflies, so dense the lighter branches bent with their load. Many of them crawled inside the white blossoms, and when they lit, the clusters of petal cups glowed like pale lanterns. The cool, shadowless radiance bathed them both. Her breath drew in. "Oh," she said, rising on one elbow and staring upward. "Oh . . ."

"Wait. I can do more." He concentrated, and drew down a lambent swirl of insects to spiral around and land in her dark hair, lighting it like a coronet of candles.

"Dag . . . !" She gave a wild laugh, half delight, half indignation, her hands rising to gently prod her curls. "You put bugs in my hair!"

"I happen to know you like bugs."

"I do," she admitted fairly. "Some kinds, anyhow. But how . . . ? Did you learn to do this up in the woods of Luthlia, too?"

"No, actually. I learned it in camp, back when my groundsense first came in—I was about twelve, I guess. The children learn it from each other; no adult ever teaches it, but I think most everyone knows how to catch fireflies this way. We just forget. Grow up and get busy and all. Though I admit, I never collected more than a handful at one time before."

She was smiling helplessly. "It's a bit eerie. But I like it. Not sure about the hair—eh! Dag, they're tickling my ears!"

"Lucky bugs." He leaned in and blew off the wanderers from the curve of her ear, kissing the tickle away. "You should be crowned with light like the rising moon."

"Well," she said, in a gruff little voice, and sniffed. Her gaze traced the bending lantern-flowers above, and returned to his face. "What do you want to go and do a thing like that for anyhow? I'm already as full of joy for you as my body can hold, and there you go and put *more* in. Downright wasteful, I say. It's just going to spill over . . . " The light shimmered in her swimming eyes.

He pulled her up and across him, and let the warm drops spatter across his chest like summer rain. "Spill on me," he whispered.

He released her twinkling tiara and let the tiny creatures fly up into the tree again. In the scintillant glow, they made slow love till midnight brought silence and sleep.

Lumpton Market was a smaller town than Glassforge, but lively nonetheless. It lay at the confluence of two rocky rivers, which flanked a long shale-and-limestone ridge running northward. Two old straight roads crossed there, and it had surely been the site of a hinterland city when the lords ruled. As it was, much of the new town was made of ancient building blocks mined out of the encroaching woods, and dry-stone walls of both ordinary fieldstone and much less identifiable rubble abounded around both outlying fields and house yards. Now that Dag's eye was alerted to it, however, he noticed a few newer, finer houses on the outskirts built of brick. The bridges were timber, recent, and wide and sturdy enough for big wagons.

The hostelry familiar and friendly to patrollers for which Dag was aiming lay on the north side of Lumpton, so he and Fawn found themselves in early afternoon riding through the town square, where the day market was in full swing. Fawn turned in her saddle, looking over the booths and carts and tarps as they passed around the edge of the busy scene.

"I have that glass bowl for Mama," she said. "I wish I had something to bring Aunt Nattie. She hardly ever gets taken along when my parents come down here." A yearly ritual, Dag had been given to understand.

Aunt Nattie was Fawn's mother's much older sister, blind since a childhood infection had stolen her sight at age ten. She had come along with Fawn's mother when she'd married years ago, in some sort of dowry deal. Semi-invalid but not idle, she did all the spinning and weaving for the farm, with extra to sell for cash money sometimes. And was the only member of her family Fawn spoke of without hidden strain in her voice and ground.

Obligingly, now that he understood her purpose, Dag followed Fawn's gaze. One would not, presumably, carry food to a farm. The cloth and clothing for sale, new and used, likewise would seem foolish. His eye ran over the more permanent shops lining the square. "Tools? Scissors, needles? Something for her weaving or sewing?"

"She has a lot of those." Fawn sighed.

"Something that gets used up, then. Dyes?" His voice faded in doubt. "Ah. Likely not."

"Mama did most of the coloring, though I do it nowadays. Wish I could get her something just for her." Her gaze narrowed. "Furs . . . ?"

"Well, let's look." They dismounted, and Fawn looked over the tarp where a farmwoman offered some, in Dag's expert view, rather inferior pelts; all common local beasts, raccoon and possum and deerhide.

"I can get her something much better, later," Dag murmured, and with a grimace of agreement Fawn gave over poking through the sad piles. They strolled onward side by side, leading their horses.

Fawn stopped and wheeled, lips pursing, as they passed a narrow medicine shop tucked between a shoemaker and a barber-toothdrawer-scribe—it was unclear if the latter was all one man. The medicine shop had a broad window, with small square glass panes set in a bowed-out wooden frame to make a larger view. "I wonder if they sell scent water like what your patroller girls found in Glassforge?"

Or oil, Dag could not help wondering. They could stand to re-stock for future use, although the likelihood of immediate future use at the Bluefield homestead seemed remote. Whatever gratitude her family might feel for his bringing their only daughter back alive was unlikely to extend to letting them sleep together there. In any case, they tied their horses to one of the hitching rails conveniently lining the cobblestone sidewalk and went inside.

The shop had four kinds of scent water but only plain oil, which made Dag's selection immediate. He occupied himself looking over the shop's actually impressive stock of herbals, several of which he recognized as of high quality and coming from Lakewalker sources, while Fawn made herself redolent with happy indecision. Her choice finally made, they waited while their small purchases were wrapped. Or not so small in proportion to Fawn's thin purse, Dag noted as she braced herself to trade out some of her few coins for the little luxury.

Outside, Dag tucked the packets away in his saddlebags and turned to give Fawn a leg up on the bay mare. She was standing staring at her saddle in dismay.

"My bedroll's gone!" Her hand went to the dangling rawhide strings behind her cantle. "Did it drop on the road? I know I tied it on better than . . ."

His hand followed hers, and his voice tightened. "These are cut. See, the knots are still tied. Sneak thief."

"Dag, the knife was in my bedroll!" she gasped.

He snapped open his groundsense, flinching as it was battered by the uproar pouring from all the people nearby. He searched through the noise for a faint, familiar chime. Just . . . there. His head came up, and he looked along the square to where a slight figure was disappearing between two buildings, the roll cast casually over his shoulder as though he owned it.

"I see it," he said thickly. "Wait here!" His legs stretched as he followed after, not quite running. Behind him, he could hear Fawn demanding of passersby, *Did you see anyone fooling around by our horses?*

Dag tamped outrage down to annoyance, mostly at himself. If he'd been traveling through here with a group of patrollers, someone would always have been left with the horses as a routine precaution. So what had made him drop his guard? Some misplaced sense of anonymity? The fact that if only he'd bothered to glance out the window, he could have kept an eye on the horses himself? If he'd left his groundsense more open, he might have picked up some restive response from Copperhead as a stranger came too near. Too late, never mind.

In an alley in back of the buildings he closed with his quarry. The boy was crouched behind a woodpile, and not alone; a much larger and older companion—brother, friend, thief-boss?—knelt with him as they spread open the bedroll to examine their prize.

The big man was saying disgustedly, "This is just some girl's clothes. Why didn't you pinch those saddlebags, you fool?"

"That red brute of a horse tried to kick me, and people were looking," the boy replied in a surly tone. "Wait, what's that?"

The big man lifted the sharing knife sheath by its broken strap; the pouch swung, and his hand went toward the bone hilt.

"Your death, if you touch it," Dag snarled, coming up on them. "I'll see to that."

The boy took one look at him, yelped, and sprang away, casting a panicked glance over his shoulder as he ran. The big man, his eyes widening, shoved to his feet, hand closing on a stout log from the pile. It was plain that they were far past the point of lame explanations and apologies, sir, about mistaken ownership, even if the burly thief had possessed the wits and nerve to try to escape that way. He came around already swinging.

Dag flung up his arm to protect his face from a blow that would have caved it in. As it was, the oak log connected with his forearm with a sickening thud, and he was bashed by his own arm-plus-log so hard as to be knocked half off his feet. Hot agony burst in his forearm. No chance to go for his knife, but the hook-and-spring presently attached to his left arm cuff doubled as a weapon of no small menace; the big man ducked back in fright as Dag's return swing grazed his throat. Rapidly revising his chances against this unexpected unhanded reprisal—brighter than he looked?—the would-be thief dropped both knife pouch and log and galloped after his smaller partner.

Fawn and a party of three or four Lumpton locals rounded the corner as Dag staggered upright again. Quietly, he flipped a corner of the blanket over the leather pouch with a booted toe.

"Dag, are you all right?" Fawn cried in alarm. "Your nose is bleeding!"

Dag could feel a wet trickle over his lip, and licked at it, unmistakable iron tang. He tried to raise his hand to touch his throbbing face but found it would not work properly. Drawing breath through his teeth in a long hiss at the flaring pain, he searched his mind for curses and found none strong enough. His groundsense, turned in upon himself, left him in no doubt. He wheeled away, bent over, and spat blood and fury on the ground before turning back to her. "Nose is all right," he mumbled in frustrated wrath. "Right arm's broken. *Blight* it!"

13

Their hostelry in Lumpton Market turned out to be an elderly inn just off the straight road north from town. Fawn thought it a sad comedown from the fine hotel in Glassforge, for it was small and grubby, if not without a certain air of shabby comfort. Further, it demanded cash money even from patrollers. In summer, however, patrons were sent out back of the kitchen to eat their dinners on plank tables and benches under some graceful old black walnut trees overlooking the side road, much better than the dank common room. Looking around curiously, Fawn saw no other Lakewalkers here tonight, just a quartet of teamsters at one table intent on their beer and, beyond them, a farm couple busy with a pack of noisy young children. Even with his height, striking looks, and splinted arm in a sling, Dag drew only brief stares, and Fawn felt reassuringly unnoticed in his shadow.

Dag slumped onto his bench with an understandably tired grunt, and Fawn slid in at his right. She plucked loose the ties of the lumpy leather wrap he'd directed she bring from his saddlebag, unrolling it to find it contained an array of extra devices for his wrist cuff. "Goodness, what are all these?"

"This and that. Experiments, or things I don't use every day." As she stared in bewilderment and held up a wooden bolt anchoring a curved and edged metal piece looking like a small stirrup, he added, "That's a scraper. I spend a lot of time in the evening scraping hides, out on patrol. Boring as all get out, but one of the first jobs I took on after I got the arm harness. Forced me to strengthen the arm, which was good when I took up the bow."

The scullion who doubled as servingwoman plunked down mugs of beer and trotted back inside. With hook and splinted hand, Dag clumsily reached, winced, and fell back, and Fawn said, "Ah! The bonesetter *told* you not to try and use your hand. Five times when I was listening, and I don't know how many more while I was out of the room. I thought he was going to slap you at one point." The man had hardly needed Fawn's encouragement to bind Dag's arm with quelling thoroughness, having taken the measure of his aggravated patient very quickly. The barest tips of Dag's fingers stuck out beyond the cotton wrappings. "You just keep it down in that sling there. We need to figure out how we're to get along with all this."

Hurriedly, she held the mug to his lips; he grimaced, but drank thirstily. She managed not to splash him too badly when he nodded he was done, and whisked her handkerchief from her pocket to overtake his right arm up to mop his lips. "And if you use your bandages for a napkin they're going to stink long before six weeks are up, so don't."

He scowled sideways at her, ferociously.

"*And* if you keep looking at me like that, you're going to make me break out in giggles, and then you'll be throwing your boots at my head, and then where will we be?"

"No, I won't," he growled. "I need you to get the blasted boots off in the first place."

But the corner of his mouth curled up nonetheless. Fawn was so relieved she got up on one knee and kissed the curl, which made it curve up more.

He vented a long, apologetic sigh for his touchiness. "Third from the left, there" —he nodded to the leather wrap—"should be a sort of fork-spoon thing."

She pulled it out and examined it, an iron spoon with four short tines on the tip. "Ah, clever."

"I don't use it too often. A knife's usually better, if I have anything at the table but my hook or the social hand." That last was Dag's name for the wooden hand-in-glove, which seemed to have little use but disguise among strangers, and not a very effective one at that.

With a slight *clunk,* Dag set his wooden cuff against the table edge. "Try swapping it out."

Dag's most commonly used device, the hook with the clever little spring strip, was set in tight. Fawn, leaning in, had to take a better grip before she was able to twist it out. The eating tool replaced it more readily. "Oh, that's not too hard."

Their plates arrived, piled with carrots and mashed potatoes with cream gravy and a generous portion of pork chops. After an exchange of silent looks—Fawn could see Dag working to keep his frayed temper—she leaned over and efficiently cut his meat, leaving the rest to him. The fork-spoon worked tolerably well, although it did involve his extending his elbow awkwardly. Thoughtfully, she kept the beer coming. It might just have been getting a good hot meal into him after a too-long day, but he slowly relaxed. The stout scullion then brought thick wedges of cherry pie, which threatened to push relaxation into sleep right there on the benches.

Fawn said, "So . . . should we stay here and rest up tomorrow, or push on and rest at West Blue? Will you be able to ride so far?" He had ridden from the bonesetter's, his reins wrapped around his hook, but that had only been a mile.

"I've done more with worse. The powder will help." He'd prudently picked up what he said was a Lakewalker remedy for pain from the medicine shop before they'd left the town square. Fawn wasn't sure if the faint glaze in his eyes was from the drug or the ache in his arm; but on reflection, it was just as well the medicine didn't work better, or there would be no slowing him down at all. Confirming this, he stretched, and said, "I wouldn't mind pushing on. There's folks at Hickory Lake who can do things to help this heal faster."

"Is it set all right?" she asked anxiously.

"Oh, yes. That bonesetter might have been a ham-handed torturer, but he knew his trade. It'll heal straight."

Dag had called him much worse things than that during the setting, but the fellow had just grinned, evidently used to colorful invective from his patients. Possibly, Fawn thought, he collected the choice bits.

"If you don't knock it around." Fawn felt a little sick with anticipation of her homecoming. But if she had to do it at all, better to get it over with. Dag clearly thought it her duty, the right thing to do; and not even for Stupid Sunny and all her brothers put together would she risk Dag thinking her craven. *Even if I am.* "All right. We'll ride on."

Dag rubbed his chin with his left sleeve. "In that case, we'd best get our tales straight. I want to leave out the primed knife in front of your family, just as we did for my patrol all but Mari."

That seemed both fair and prudent. Fawn nodded.

"Anything else is up to you, but you have to tell me what you want."

She stared down at the red streaks and crumbs on her empty plate. "They don't know about me and Sunny. So they're going to be mad that I scared them for seemingly nothing, running off like that."

He leaned over and touched his lips to a red dent in her neck where one of the malice scabs had finally flaked off. "Not for nothing, Spark."

"Yeah, but they don't know much about malices, either."

"So," he said slowly, as if feeling his way, "if your Sunny has 'fessed up, you will have one situation, and if he hasn't, you'll have another."

"He's not my Sunny," Fawn said grumpily. "We were both real clear on that."

"Hm. Well, if you don't tell your folks why you really left, you'll have to make up some lie. This creates a tension and darkness in your ground that weakens a person, in my experience. I really don't see why you feel any need to protect Sunny. Seems to me he benefits more from you keeping this secret than you do."

Fawn's eyebrows rose. "The shame of the thing goes on the girl. *Used goods,* they call you. You can't get another suitor with good land, if word gets around you're no virgin. Though . . . I think a lot of girls do anyhow, so you really have to wonder."

"Farmers, eh." Dag pursed his lips. "Does the same apply to widows, then? Real ones, not grass ones."

Fawn colored at this reminder, though she had to smile a little. "Oh, no. Widows are a whole different matter. Widows, now . . . well, nobody can do as they please, really, there might be children, there might be no money, but widows hold their heads up fine and make their own way. Better if they're not poor, to be sure."

"So, ah . . . do you hanker after a suitor with good land, Spark?"

She sat up, startled. "Of course not! I want you."

He cocked an eyebrow at her. "So why are you worrying about this, again? Habit?"

"No!" She hesitated; her heart and voice fell. "I suppose . . . I thought we were a midsummer dream. I just keep trying real hard not to wake up. Stupid, I guess. Somewhere, sometime . . . someone will come along who won't let me keep you. Not for always."

He looked away, through the deep shade of the walnut trees and down the side road where dust from the recent passage of a pony cart still hung golden in the westering sun. "However difficult your family is, mine is going to be worse, and I expect to stand up to them. I won't lie, Spark; there are things that can take me from you, things I can't control. Death is always one." He paused. "Can't think of anything else right at the moment, though."

She gave a short, shaken nod, turning her face into his shoulder till she got her breath back.

He sighed. "Well, what you'll say to your people is not my choice. It's yours. But my recommendation is to tell as much truth as you can, save for the knife priming."

"How will we explain my going to your camp?"

"Your testimony to my captain is required in the death of the malice. Which is true. If they ask for more, I'll get up on my tall horse and say it's Lakewalker business."

Fawn shook her head. "They won't want to let me go off with you."

"We'll see. You can't plan other people's actions; only your own. If you try, you just end up facing the wrong way for the trouble you actually get. Hey." He bent down and kissed her hair. "If they chain you to the wall with iron bolts, I undertake to break you out."

"With no hands?"

"I'm very ingenious. And if they don't chain you, then you can walk away. All it takes is courage, and I know you have that."

She smiled, comforted, but admitted, "Not in my heart, not really. They . . . I don't know how to explain this. They have ways of making me smaller."

"I don't know how they'll be, but you are not the same as you were. One way or another, things will be different than you expect."

Truly.

Exhausted, hurting, and uneasy, they did not make love that night, but held each other close in the stuffy inn chamber. Sleep was slow in coming.

The summer sun was again slanting west when Fawn halted her mare and sat staring up the hill where a descending farm lane intersected the road. It had been a twenty-mile ride from Lumpton Market, and Dag had to admit, if only to himself, that his right arm was swollen and aching more than he cared for, and that his left, picking up an unaccustomed load, was not at its best either. They had taken the straight road north along the spreading ridge between the rivers for almost fifteen miles before turning west. Descending into the valley of the western branch, they'd crossed at a stony ford before turning north once more along the winding river road. A shortcut, Fawn claimed, to avoid doubling back a mile to the village of West Blue with its wagon bridge and mill.

And now she was home. Her ground was a complicated swirl at the moment, but it hardly took groundsense to see that her foremost emotion was not joy.

He kneed his horse up next to hers. "I think I'd like my social hand, to start," he murmured.

She nodded, and leaned over to open his belt pouch and swap out his hook for the less useful but less startling false hand. She paused to recomb her own hair and retie it in the curly horsetail with the bright ribbon, then stood up in her stirrups to take the comb to him as well; he lowered his head for the, in his unvoiced opinion, useless attempt to make him look his best. He perfectly understood her determination to walk back into her home looking proud and fine, not beaten and bedraggled. He just wished for her sake that he could look more the part of a valiant protector instead of something the cat had dragged in. *You've looked worse, old patroller. Go on.*

Fawn swallowed and turned Grace into the lane, which wound up the slope for almost a quarter mile, lined on both sides with the ubiquitous drystone walls. Past a grove of sugar maple, walnut, and hickory trees, a dilapidated old barn appeared on the right, and a larger, newer barn on the left. Above the new barn lay a couple of outbuildings, including a smokehouse; faint gray curls of smoke leaked from its eaves, and Dag's nose caught the pleasant tang of smoldering hickory. A covered well sat at the top of the yard, and, on around to the right, the large old farmhouse loomed.

The central core of it was a two-story rectangle of blocky yellowish stone, with a porch and front door in the middle overlooking the river valley. On the far north end, a single-story add-on looked as though it contained two rooms. On the near end, an excavation was in progress, with piles of new stone waiting, evidently an addition planned to match the other. On the west, another add-on girdled with a long, covered porch ran the length of the house, clearly the kitchen. No one was in sight.

"Suppertime," said Fawn. "They must all be in the kitchen."

"Eight people," said Dag, whose groundsense left him in no doubt.

Fawn took a long, long breath, and dismounted. She tied both their horses to the back porch rail and led Dag around to the steps. Her lighter and his heavier tread echoed briefly on the porch floor. Top and bottom halves of a double door were open wide and hooked to bolts in the wall, but beyond them was another, lighter doorframe with a gauze screen. Fawn pushed the screen door open and slipped in, holding it for him. He let his wooden hand rest briefly on her shoulder before dropping it to his side.

At a long table filling most of the right-hand half of the room, eight people turned and stared. Dag swiftly tried to match faces with the names and stories he'd been given. Aunt Nattie could be instantly identified, a very short, stout woman with disordered curly gray locks and eyes as milky as pearls, her head now cocked with listening. The four brothers were harder to sort, but he thought he could determine Fletch, bulky and oldest, Reed and Rush, the nonidentical twins, brown-haired and brown-eyed, and ash-haired and blue-eyed respectively, and Whit, black-haired like Fawn, skinny, and youngest but for her. A plump young woman seated next to Fletch defeated his tutorial. Fawn's parents, Sorrel and Tril Bluefield, were no hardship to identify, a graying man at the table's head who'd stood up so fast his chair had banged over, and on the near end a short, middle-aged woman stumbling out of her seat shrieking.

Fawn's parents descended upon her in such a whirl of joy, relief, and rage that Dag had to close off his groundsense lest he be overwhelmed. The brothers, behind, were mostly grinning with relief, and Aunt Nattie was asking urgently, "What? Is that Fawn, you say? Told you she wasn't dead! About time!"

Fawn, her face nearly unreadable, endured being hugged, kissed, and shaken in equal measure; the dampness in her blinking eyes was not, Dag thought, caught only from the emotions around her. Dag stiffened a little when her father, after hugging her off her feet, put her down and then threatened to beat her; but while his paternal relief was very real, it seemed his threats were not, for Fawn didn't flinch in the least from them.

"Where have you *been,* girl?" her mother's voice finally rose over the babble to demand.

Fawn backed up a trifle, raised her chin, and said in a rush, "I went to Glassforge to look for work, and I may have found some too, but first I have to go with Dag, here, to Hickory Lake to help make his report to his captain about the blight bogle we killed."

Her family gazed at Fawn as though she'd started raving in a fever; Dag suspected the only part they'd really caught was *Glassforge*.

Fawn went on a bit breathlessly, before they could start up again, "Mama, Papa, this here is my friend, Dag Redwing Hickory." She gave her characteristic little knee-dip, and pulled Dag forward. He nodded, trying to find some pleasantly neutral expression for his face. "He's a Lakewalker patroller."

"How de' do," said Dag politely and generally.

A silence greeted this, and a lot more staring, necks cranked back. Short stature ran in Fawn's family, evidently.

Confirming Dag's guess, Fawn's mother, Tril, said, "Glassforge? Why would you want to go there to look for work? There's plenty of work right here!"

"*Which* you left on all of us," Fletch put in unhelpfully.

"And wouldn't Lumpton Market have been a lot closer?" said Whit in a tone of judicious critique.

"Do you *know* how much trouble you caused, girl?" said Papa Bluefield.

"Yeah," said Reed, or maybe Rush—no, Rush, ash-headed, check— "when you didn't show for dinner market-day night, we figured you were out dawdling and daydreaming in the woods as usual, but when you didn't show by bedtime, Papa made us all go out with torches and look and call. The barn, the privy, the woods, down by the river—it would have saved a deal of stumbling around in the dark and yelling if Mama had counted your clothes a day sooner!"

Fawn's lip had given an odd twitch at something in this, which Dag determined to ask about later. "I am sorry you were troubled," she said, in a carefully formal tone. "I should have written a note, so's you needn't have worried I'd met with an accident."

"How would *that* have helped for worrying, fool girl!" Fawn's mother wept a bit more. "Thoughtless, selfish . . ."

"Papa made *me* ride all the way to Aunt Wren's, in the idea you might have gone there, and he made Rush ride to Lumpton asking after you," Reed said.

A spate more of complaint and venting from all parties followed this. Fawn endured without argument, and Dag held his tongue. The ill words were not ill meant, and Fawn, apparently a native speaker of this strange family dialect, seemed to take them in their spirit and let the barbs roll off, mostly. Her eyes flashed resentment only once, when the plump girl beside Fletch chimed in with some support of one of his more snappish comments. But Fawn said only, "Hello, Clover. Nice to see you, too," which reduced the girl to nonplussed silence.

Notably missing was any word about Sunny Sawman. So Fawn's judgment on that score was proven shrewd. Too early to guess at the consequences . . .

Dag was not sure how long the uproar would have continued in this vein, except that Aunt Nattie levered herself up, grasped a walking stick, and stumped around the table to Fawn's side. "Let me see you, girl," she said quietly, and Fawn hugged her—the first hug Dag had seen going the other way—and let the blind woman run her hands over her face. "Huh," said Aunt Nattie. "Huh. Now introduce me to your patroller friend. It's been a long time since I've met a Lakewalker."

"Dag," said Fawn, reverting to her breathless, anxious formality, "This is my aunt Nattie that I've told you about. She'd like to touch you, if that's all right."

"Of course," said Dag.

The little woman stumped nearer, reached up, and bounced her fingers uncertainly off his collarbone. "Goodness, boy, where *are* you?"

"Say something," Fawn whispered urgently.

"Um . . . up here, Aunt Nattie."

Her hand went higher, to touch his chin; he obligingly bent his head. "Way up there!" she marveled. The knobby, dry fingers brushed firmly over his features, pausing at the slight heat of the bruises on his face from yesterday, circling his cheekbones and chin in inexplicable approval, tracing his lips and eyelids. Dag realized with a slight shock that this woman possessed a rudimentary groundsense, possibly developed in the shadow of her lifelong blindness, and he let his reach out to touch hers.

Her breath drew in. "Ah, Lakewalker, right enough."

"Ma'am," Dag responded, not knowing what else to say.

"Good voice, too," Nattie observed, Dag wasn't sure who to. She stopped short of checking his teeth like a horse's, although by this time Dag would scarcely have blinked at it. She felt down his body, her touch hesitating briefly at the splints and sling; her eyebrows went up as she felt his arm harness through his shirt and briefly gripped his wooden hand. But she added only, "Nice deep voice."

"Have you eaten?" asked Tril Bluefield, and when Fawn explained no, they'd ridden all day from Lumpton, shifted to what Dag guessed was her more normal motherly mode, driving a couple of her sons to set chairs and places. She put Fawn next to herself, and Fawn insisted Dag be placed on her own right, "On account of I promised to help him out with his broken arm." They settled at last. Clover, finally introduced as Fletch's betrothed, was also drafted to help, plopping plates and cups of what smelled like cider down in front of them. Dag, by this time very thirsty, was most interested in the drink. The food was a well-cooked stew, and Dag silently rejoiced at being confronted with something he could handle by himself, though he wondered who in the household had bad teeth.

"The fork-spoon, I think," he murmured in Fawn's ear, and she nodded and rummaged it out of his belt pouch.

"What happened to your arm?" asked Rush, across from them.

"Which one?" asked Dag. And endured the inevitable moment of rustling, craning, and stunned stares as Fawn calmly unscrewed his hand and replaced it with the more useful tool. "Thank you, Spark. Drink?" He smiled down at her as she lifted the cup to his lips. It was fresh cider, very tart from new summer apples. "And thanks again."

"You're welcome, Dag."

He licked the spare drop off his lower lip, so she didn't have to chase it with her napkin, yet.

Rush finally found his voice, more or less. "Er . . . I was going to ask about the, er, sling . . ."

Fawn answered briskly, "A sneak thief at Lumpton Market lifted my bedroll yesterday. Dag got it back, but his arm was broken in the fight before the thieves got scared and ran off. Dag gave a real good description to the Lumpton folks, though, so they might catch the fellows." Her jaw set just a trifle. "So I kind of owe him for the arm."

"Oh," said Rush. Reed and Whit stared across the table with renewed, if daunted, interest.

Tril Bluefield, looking hungrily and now more carefully at her restored daughter, frowned and let her hand drift to Fawn's cheek where the four parallel gouges were now paling pink scars. "What are those marks?"

She glanced sidelong at Dag; he shrugged, *Go on.* She said, "That's where the mud-man hit me."

"The what?" said her mother, face screwing up.

"A . . . sort of bandit," Fawn revised this. "Two bandits grabbed me off the road near Glassforge."

"What? What happened?" her mother gasped. The assorted brothers, too, sat up; on Dag's right, he could feel Fletch tense.

"Not too much," said Fawn. "They roughed me up, but Dag, who was tracking them, came up just then and, um. Ran them off." She glanced at him again, and he lowered his eyelids in thanks. He did not especially wish to begin his acquaintance with her family with a listing of all the dead bodies he'd left around Glassforge, the human ones at least. Far too many human ones, this last round. "That's how we first met. His patrol had been called to Glassforge to deal with the bandits and the blight bogle."

Rush asked, "What happened to the bandits after that?"

Fawn turned to Dag, who answered simply, "They were dealt with." He applied himself to his stew, good plain farm food, in the hope of avoiding further expansion on this subject.

Fawn's mother bent her head, eyes narrowing; her hand went out again, this time to the left side of Fawn's neck and the deep red dent and three ugly black scabs. "Then what are those nasty-looking things?"

"Um . . . well, that was later."

"*What* was later?"

In a desperately bright voice, Fawn replied, "That's where the blight bogle lifted me up. They make those sorts of marks—their touch is deadly. It was big. How big, would you say, Dag? Eight feet tall, maybe?"

"Seven and a half, I'd guess," he said blandly. "About four hundred pounds. Though I didn't have the best vantage. Or light."

Reed said, in a tone of growing disbelief, "So what happened to this supposed blight bogle, if it was so deadly?"

Fawn's look begged help, so Dag replied, "It was dealt with, too."

"Go on, Fawn," said Fletch scornfully. "You can't expect *us* to swallow your tall tales!"

Dag let his voice go very soft. "Are you calling your sister a liar . . . sir?" He let the *and me?* hang in implication.

Fletch's thick brows wrinkled in honest bewilderment; he was not a man sensitive to implication, either, Dag guessed. "She's my sister. I can call her anything I want!"

Dag drew breath, but Fawn whispered, "Dag, let it go. It doesn't matter."

He did not yet speak this family dialect, he reminded himself. He had worried about how to conceal the strange accident with the sharing knife; he'd not imagined such feeble curiosity or outright disbelief. It was not in his present interest—or capacity—to bang Bluefield heads together and bellow, *Your sister's courage saved my life, and dozens, maybe thousands, more. Honor her!* He let it go and nodded for more cider.

Blatantly changing the subject, Fawn asked Clover after the progress of her wedding plans, listening to the lengthy reply with well-feigned interest. The addition in progress on the south end of the house, it appeared, was intended for the soon to be newlyweds. The true purpose of the question—camouflage—was revealed to Dag when Fawn added casually, "Anyone hear from the Sawmans since Saree's wedding?"

"Not too much," said Reed. "Sunny's spent a lot of time at his brother-in-law's place, helping clear stumps from the new field."

Fawn's mother gave her a narrow-eyed look. "His mama tells me Sunny's betrothed to Violet Stonecrop as of midsummer. Hope you're not disappointed. I thought you might be getting kind of sweet on him at one point."

Whit piped up, in a whiny, practiced brotherly chant, "Fawn is sweet on Suh-nee, Fawn is sweet on Suh-nee . . ."

Dag cringed at the spate of deathly blackness that ran through Fawn's ground. *He does not know,* he reminded himself. *None of them do.* Although he would not have cast bets on Tril Bluefield's unvoiced suspicions, because she now said in a flat voice unlike any he'd yet heard from her, brooking no argument, "Stop that, Whit. You'd think you were twelve."

Dag could see the little ripple in Fawn's jaw as she unset her teeth. "Not sweet in the least. I think Violet deserves better."

Whit looked disappointed at not having drawn a more spectacular rise out of his sister from his expert lure but, glancing at his mother, did not resume his heckling.

"Perhaps," Dag suggested gently, "we should go see to Grace and Copperhead."

"Who?" asked Rush.

"Miss Bluefield's horse, and mine. They've been waiting patiently out there."

"What?" said Reed. "Fawn doesn't have a horse!"

"Hey, Fawn, where'd *you* get a horse?"

"Can I ride your horse?"

"*No.*" Fawn thrust back her chair. Dag rose more quietly with her.

"Where *did* you get a horse, Fawn?" asked Papa Bluefield curiously, staring anew at Dag.

Fawn stood very straight. "She was my share for helping deal with the blight bogle. Which Fletch here doesn't believe in. I must have ridden all the way from Glassforge on a wish horse, huh?"

She tossed her head and marched out. Dag cast a polite nod of farewell in the general direction of the table, thought to add a spoken, "Good evening, Aunt Nattie," and followed. Behind him, he could hear her father's growl, "Reed, go help your sister and that fellow with their horses." Which in fact launched a general migration of Bluefields onto the porch to examine the new horse.

Grace was exhaustively discussed. At last Dag swapped back for his hook and led his own horse in an escape to the old barn, where spare stalls were to be found. He lingered looking over the stall partition, keeping a light contact with his groundsense so the gelding wouldn't snake around and attempt to savage Reed, his unfamiliar groom. Copperhead was not named for his chestnut color, despite appearances. When both horses were at last safely rubbed down, watered, and fed, Dag walked back to the house through the sunset light with Fawn, temporarily out of ear shot of the rest of her relations.

"Well," she said under her breath, "that could have gone worse."

"Really?" said Dag.

"Really."

"I'll take your word. Truth to tell, I'm finding your family a bit strange. My nearest kin don't often like what I have to say, but they certainly *hear* what I have to say, and not something else altogether."

"They're better one at a time than in a bunch like that."

"Hm. So . . . what was that about market-day night?"

"What?"

"When Rush said they'd missed you market-day night."

"Oh. Nothing much. Except that I left market-day morning while it was still dark. Wonder where they thought I was all day?"

A number of Bluefields had collected in the front parlor, including Aunt Nattie, now plying a drop spindle, and Fawn's mother. Dag set down his saddlebags and let Fawn unpack her gifts. Fletch, about to escort his betrothed home to her nearby farm, paused to watch as well.

Tril held the sparkling glass bowl up to the light of an oil lamp in astonishment. "You really did go to Glassforge!"

Fawn, who had wobbled all evening between trying to put on a good show and what seemed to Dag a most unfamiliar silent shrinking, said only, "That's what I told you, Mama."

Fawn pressed the corked scent bottle into her aunt's hands and urged her to splash some on her wrists, which, smiling agreeably, she did. "Very pretty, lovie, but this sort of foolery is for courtin' girls to entice their boys, not for lumpy old women like me. Better you should give it to Clover."

"That's Fletcher's job," said Fawn, with a more Spark-like edged grin at her brother. "Anyhow, all sorts of folks wear it in Glassforge— patroller men and women both, for some."

Reed, hovering, snorted at the idea of men wearing scent, but Nattie showed willing and eased Dag's heart by splashing a bit more on both herself and her younger sister Tril, and some on Fawn as well. "There! Sweet of you to think of me, lovie."

It was growing dark outside. The boys dispersed to various evening chores, and Clover made farewells to her prospective in-laws. The two young women, Fawn and Clover, eyed each other a little stiffly as Clover made more congratulations on Fawn's safe return, and Dag wondered anew at the strangeness of farmer customs. A Lakewalker only-girlchild would have been the chief inheritor of her family's tent, but that position here was apparently held by Fletch; and not Fawn but Clover would take Tril Bluefield's place as female head of this household in due time. Leaving Fawn to go . . . where?

"I suppose," said Papa Bluefield a trifle grudgingly, "if your friend here has a bedroll, he could lay it in the loft. Keep an eye on his horse."

"Don't be daft, Sorrel," Aunt Nattie spoke up unexpectedly. "The man can't climb the loft ladder with that broken arm."

"He needs to be close by me, so's I can help him," said Fawn firmly. "Dag can lay his bedroll in Nattie's weaving room."

"Good idea, Fawn," said Nattie cheerily.

Fawn slept in with her aunt; the boys shared rooms upstairs, as did their parents. Papa Bluefield looked as though he was thinking hard, suddenly, about the implications of leaving Fawn and Dag downstairs with a blind chaperone. And then—inevitably—of the implications of how long Dag and Fawn had been on the road together. Did he know anything about his aging sister-in-law's groundsense?

"I'll try harder not to cut your throat with your razor tomorrow, Dag," Fawn said.

"I've lost more blood for less," he assured her.

"We should likely try to get on the road early."

"What?" said Papa Bluefield, coming out of his frowning cogitation. "You're not going anywhere, girl!"

She turned to him, stiffening up tight. "I told you first thing, Papa. I have an obligation to give witness."

"Are you stupid, Fawn!"

Dag caught his breath at the hard black rip through Fawn's ground; his eyes went to Nattie, but she gave no visible reaction, though her face was turned toward the pair.

Papa Bluefield went on, "Your obligations are here, for all you've run off and turned your back on them this past month! You've had enough gallivanting for a while, believe you me!"

Dag interposed quietly and quite truthfully, "Actually, Spark, my arm's not doing all that well tonight. I wouldn't mind a day or two to rest up."

She turned anxious eyes up at him, as if not sure whether she was hearing support or betrayal. He gave her a small, reassuring nod.

Papa Bluefield gave Dag a sideways look. "You'd be welcome to go on, if you've a need."

"*Papa!*" snapped Fawn, gyrating back to something not strained show, but blazingly sincere. "The idea! Dag saved my life *three* times, twice at great risk to his own, once from the bandits, once from the malice—the bogle—and once again the night after the bogle . . . hurt me, because I would have bled to death right there in the woods if he hadn't helped me. I will *not* have him turned out on the road by himself with two bad arms! For shame! Shame on this house if you dare!" She actually stamped her foot; the parlor floor sounded like a drum.

Papa Bluefield had stepped backward. His wife was staring at Dag with eyes wide, holding the glass bowl tightly. Nattie . . . was amazingly hard to read, but she had a strange little smile on her lips.

"Oh." Papa Bluefield cleared his throat. "You hadn't exactly made that plain, Fawn."

Fawn said wearily, "How could I? No one would let me finish a story without telling me I must be making things up."

Her father glanced at Dag. "*He's* a quiet one."

Dag could not touch his temple; he had to settle for a short nod. "Thinking. Sir."

"Are you, now?"

It was not, in the Bluefield household, apparently possible to *finish* a debate. But when the squabbling finally died into assorted mumblings, drifting away up stairs or down halls in the dark, Dag ended up with his bedroll set down beside Aunt Nattie's loom, with an impressive pile of quilts and pillows arranged for his ease. He could hear the shortest two women of the family rustling around in the bedroom beyond in low-voiced preparation for bed, and then the creak of the bed frames as they settled down.

Dag disposed his throbbing arm awkwardly, grateful for the pillows. Save for the night on the Horsefords' kitchen floor, he had never slept inside a farmer's house, certainly not as an invited guest, though his patrols had sometimes been put up, by arrangement, in farmers' barns. This beat a drafty hayloft with snow sifting in all hollow. Before he'd met Fawn's family, he would scarcely have understood why she would want to leave such comforts.

He wasn't sure if it was worse to be loved yet not valued than valued but not loved, but surely it was better to be both. For the first time, he began to think a farm's brightest treasure need not be furtively stolen; it might be honestly won. But the hopes forming in his mind would have to wait on tomorrow for their testing.

14

The next morning passed quietly. To Fawn's eye Dag looked tired, moved slowly, and said little, and she thought his arm was probably troubling him more than he let on. She found herself caught up, will or nil, in the never-ending rhythm of farm chores; cows took no holidays even for homecomings. She and Dag did take a walk around the place in the midmorning, and she pointed out the scenes and sites from her tales of childhood. But her guess about his arm was confirmed when, after lunch, he took some more of the pain powder that had helped him through yesterday's long ride. He slipped out—wordlessly—to the front porch overlooking the river valley and sat leaning against the house wall, nursing the arm and thinking . . . whatever he was thinking about all this. Fawn found herself assigned to stirring apple butter in the kitchen, and while you are about it, dear, why don't you make up some pies for supper?

She was fluting the edge of the second one and reluctantly contemplating building up the fire under the hearth oven, which would make the hot room hotter still, when Dag came in.

"Drink?" she guessed.

"Please . . ."

She held the water ladle to his lips; when he'd drained it, he added, "There's a young fellow who's tethered his horse in your front woods. I believe he imagines he's sneaking up the hill in secret. His ground seems pretty unsettled, but I don't think he's a house robber."

"Did you see him?" she asked, then halted, considering what an absurd question that sounded if you didn't know Dag. And then how well she *had* come to know Dag, that it should fall so readily from her lips.

"Just a glimpse."

"Was he bright blond?"

"Yes."

She sighed. "Sunny Sawman. I'll bet Clover told folks that I'm back, and he's come to see for himself if it's true."

"Why not ride openly up the lane?"

She flushed a little, not that he'd likely notice in this heat, and admitted, "He used to sneak up to steal kisses from me that way, from time to time. He was afraid of my brothers finding out, I think."

"Well, he's afraid of something." He hesitated. "Do you want me to stay?"

She tilted her head, frowning. "I better talk to him alone. He won't be truthful if he's in front of anyone." She glanced up uneasily at him. "Maybe . . . don't go far?"

He nodded; she didn't seem to need to explain further. He stepped into Aunt Nattie's weaving room, flanking the kitchen, and set the door open. She heard him dragging a chair behind it, and the creak of wood and possibly of Dag as he settled into it.

A few moments later, footsteps sounded on the porch, attempted tiptoe; they paused outside the kitchen window above the drainboard. She stepped up and stared without pleasure at Sunny's face, craning around and peering in. He jerked back as he saw her, then whispered, "Are you alone?"

"For now."

He nodded and nipped in through the back door. She regarded him, testing her feelings. Straw-gold hair still curled around his head in soft locks, his eyes were still bright blue, his skin fair and fine and summer-flushed, his shoulders broad, his muscular arms, tanned where his sleeves were rolled up, coated with a shimmer of gold hairs that had always seemed to make him gleam in sunlight. His physical charm was unchanged, and she wondered how it was that she was now so wholly unmoved by it, who had once trembled beneath it in a wheatfield in such wild, flattered elation.

His daughter would have been a pretty girl. The thought twisted in her like a knife, and she fought to set it aside.

"Where is everyone?" he asked cautiously, looking around again.

"Papa and the boys are up cutting hay, Mama is out giving the chickens a dusting with that antilice powder she got from your uncle, and Aunt Nattie's bad knee hurt so she went to lie down after lunch."

"Nattie's blind, she won't see me anyhow. Good." He loomed nearer, staring hard at her. No—just at her belly. She resisted an impulse to slump and push it out.

His head cocked. "As little as you are, I'd have thought you'd be popping out by now. Clover sure would have bleated about it if she'd noticed."

"You talk to her?"

"Saw her at noon, down in the village." He shifted restlessly. "It's all the talk there, you turning up again." He turned again, scowling. "So, did you come back to fuss at me some more? It won't do you any good. I'm betrothed to Violet now."

"So I heard," said Fawn, in a flat voice. "I actually hadn't planned to see you at all. We wouldn't have stayed on today except for Dag's broken arm."

"Yeah, Clover said you had some Lakewalker fellow trailing you. Tall as a flagpole, with one arm wooden and the other broke, who didn't hardly say boo. Sounds about useless. You been running around alone with him for three or four weeks, seemingly." He wet his lips. "So, what's your plan? Switching horses in the middle of the river? Going to tell him the baby is his and hope he can't count too good?"

A cast-iron frying pan was sitting on the drainboard. Swung in an appropriate arc, it would just fit Sunny's round face, Fawn thought through a red haze. "No."

"I'm not playing your little game, Fawn," said Sunny tightly. "You won't pin this on me. I meant what I said." His hands were trembling slightly. But then, so were hers.

Her voice went, if possible, even flatter. "Well, you can put your mind and your nasty tongue to rest. I miscarried down near Glassforge the day the blight bogle nearly killed me. So there's nothing left to pin on anyone, except bad memories."

His breath of relief was visible and audible; he squeezed his eyes shut with it. The tension in the room seemed to drop by half. She thought Sunny must have gone into a flying panic when he'd heard of her return, watching his comfortable little world teeter, and felt grimly recompensed. *Her* world had been turned upside down. But if she could now turn it back upright, make all her misery not have been, at the cost of losing all she'd learned on the road to Glassforge—would she?

She could not, she thought, in all fairness judge Sunny for acting as though his daughter weren't real to him; she'd scarcely seemed real to Fawn a deal of the time either, after all. She asked instead, "So where did you think I'd gone?"

He shrugged. "I thought at first you might have thrown yourself in the river. Gave me a turn, for a while."

She tossed her head. "But not enough of one to do anything about it, seemingly."

"What would there have been to do at that point? It seemed like the sort of stupid thing you'd do when you get a mad on. You always did have a temper. I remember how your brothers'd get you so wound up you could scarcely breathe for screaming, sometimes, till your pa'd tear his hair and come beat you for making such awful noise. Then the word got around that some of your clothes had gone missing, which made it seem you'd run off, since not even you would take three changes to go drowning. Your folks all looked, but I guess not far enough."

"You didn't help look then, either, I take it."

"Do *I* look stupid? I didn't want to find you! You got yourself into this fix, you could get yourself out."

"Yeah, that's what I figured." Fawn bit her lip.

Silence. More staring.

Just go away, you awful lout. "I haven't forgotten what you said to me that night, Sunny Sawman. You aren't welcome in my sight. In case you'd any doubt."

He shrugged irritably. His golden brows drew together over his snub nose. "I figured the blight bogle was a tall tale. What really happened?"

"Bogles are real enough. One touched me. Here and there." She fingered her neck where the dents glowed an angry red, and, reluctantly, laid her palm over her belly. "Lakewalkers make special knives to kill malices—that's their name for blight bogles. Dag had one. Between us, we did for the bogle, but it was too late for the child. It was almost too late for the two of us, but not quite."

"Oh, magic knives, now, as well as magic monsters? Sure, I believe that. Or maybe some of those secret Lakewalker medicines did the job, and the rest is a nice tale to cover it, make you look good in front of your family, eh?" He moved closer to her. She moved back.

"They don't even know I was pregnant. I didn't tell them that part." She drew a long breath. "Do you really care which, so long as it's not on you? Feh!" She gripped her hair, then drew her hands down hard over her face. "You know, I really don't give two pennies what you think as long as you go think it somewhere else." Aunt Nattie had once remarked that the opposite of love was not hate, but indifference. Fawn felt she was beginning to see the point of that.

Sunny edged closer again; she could feel his breath stir the sweat-dampened hairs on her neck. "So . . . have you been letting that patroller fellow poke you? Does your family know *that*?"

Fawn's breath clogged in rage. She would *not* scream . . . "After a *miscarriage*? You got no brains at all, Sunny Sawman!"

He did hesitate at that, doubt flickering in his blue eyes.

"Besides," she went on, "you're marrying Violet Stonecrop. Are you poking her yet?"

His lips drew back in something like a smile, except that it was devoid of humor. He stepped closer still. "I was right. You *are* a little slut." And grinned in countertriumph at the fury she knew was reddening her face. "Don't give me that scowl," he added, lifting a hand to squeeze her breast. "I *know* how easy you are."

Her fingers groped for the frying-pan handle.

Long footsteps sounded from the weaving room; Sunny jumped back hurriedly.

"Hello, Spark," said Dag. "Any more of that cider around?"

"Sure, Dag," she said, backing away from Sunny and escaping across the room to the crock on the shelf. She shifted the lid and drew a cup, willing her hands to stop shaking.

Somehow, Dag was now standing between her and Sunny. "Caller?" he inquired, with a nod at Sunny. Sunny looked as though he was furiously wondering whether Dag had just come in, if they had been overheard, and if the latter, how incriminatingly much.

"This here's Sunny Sawman," said Fawn. "He's leaving. Dag Redwing Hickory, a Lakewalker patroller. He's staying."

Sunny, looking unaccustomedly up, gave a wary nod. Dag looked back down without a whole lot of expression one way or another.

"Interestin' to meet you at last, Sunny," said Dag. "I've heard a lot about you. All true, seemingly."

Sunny's mouth opened and closed—shocked that his slanderous threats had failed to silence Fawn? Well, he had only his own mouth to blame now. He looked toward the weaving room, which had no other exit except into Nattie and Fawn's bedroom, and did not come up with a reply.

Dag continued coolly, "So . . . Sunny . . . has anyone ever offered to cut out your tongue and feed it to you?"

Sunny swallowed. "No." He might have been trying for a bold tone, but it came out rather a croak.

"I'm surprised," said Dag. He gently scratched the side of his nose with his hook, a quiet warning, Fawn thought, if both unobserved and unheeded by Sunny.

"Are you trying to start something?" asked Sunny, recovering his belligerence.

"Alas." Dag indicated his broken arm with a slight movement of the sling. "I'll have to take you up later."

Sunny's eyes brightened as the apparent helplessness of the patroller dawned on him. "Then maybe you'd better keep a still tongue in *your* head till then, Lakewalker. Ha! Only Fawn would be fool enough to pick a cripple for a bullyboy!"

Dag's eyes thinned to gold slits as Fawn cringed. In that same level, affable tone, he murmured, "Changed my mind. I'll take you up now. Spark, you said this fellow was leaving. Open the door for him, would you?"

Plainly unable to imagine what Dag could possibly do to him,

Sunny set his teeth, planted his legs, and glowered. Dag stood quite still. Confused, Fawn hastily set down the cup, slopping cider on the table; she swung the screen door inward and held it.

When Dag moved, his speed was shocking. She caught only a glimpse of him swerving half-around Sunny, his leg coming up hard behind Sunny's knees, and his left arm whipping around with a wicked whir and glint of his hook. Suddenly Sunny was flailing forward, mouth agape, lifted by Dag's hook through the seat of his trousers. His feet churned but barely touched the floor; he looked like someone tumbling on ice. Three long Dag-strides, a loud ripping noise, and Sunny was sailing through the air in truth, headfirst all the way over the porch boards to land beyond the steps in an awkward heap, haunches up, face scraping the dirt.

It was partly terrorized relief that Dag hadn't just torn Sunny's throat out with his hook as calmly as he'd slain that mud-man, but Fawn burst into a shriek of laughter. She clapped her hand across her mouth and stared at the ridiculously cheering sight of Sunny's drawers flapping through the new vent in his britches.

Sunny twisted around and glared up, his face flushing a dull, mottled red, then scrambled to his feet, fists clenching. Between the dirt and the curses filling his mouth his spluttering was nearly incoherent, but the general sense of *I'll get you, Lakewalker! I'll get you both!* came through clearly enough, and Fawn's breath caught in new alarm.

"Best bring a few friends," Dag recommended dryly. "If you have any." Aside from the flaring of his nostrils, he seemed barely winded.

Sunny took two steps up onto the porch, but then veered back uncertainly as that hook came quietly to the fore. Fawn darted for the frying pan. As Sunny hovered in doubt, his head jerked up at a thumping and shuffling sounding from the weaving room—blind Aunt Nattie with her cane. She had risen from her nap at last. Sunny stared wildly around, tripped backward down the steps, turned, and fled around the side of the house.

"You're right, Spark," Dag said, closing the screen door again. "He doesn't much care for witnesses. You can sort of see why."

Nattie wandered into the kitchen. "Hello, Fawn, lovie. Hello, Dag. My, that apple butter smells good." Her face turned, following the retreating footsteps rounding the house and fading. "Young fool," she added reflectively. "Sunny always thinks if I can't see him, I can't hear him. You have to wonder, really you do."

Fawn gulped, dropped the pan on the table, and flew into Dag's embrace. He wrapped his left arm around her in a reassuring hug. Aunt Nattie's head tilted toward them, a smile touching her lips. "Thank you kindly for that bit o' housecleaning, patroller."

"My pleasure, Aunt Nattie. Here, now." Dag folded Fawn closer. "For what it's worth, Spark, he was more afraid of you than you were of him." He added reflectively, "Sort of like a snake, that way."

She gave a shaken giggle, and his grip eased. "I was about to hit him with the frying pan, just before you came in."

"Thought something like that might be up. I was having a few daydreams along that line myself."

"Too bad you couldn't really have cut his tongue out . . . " She paused. "Was that a joke or not? I'm not too sure sometimes about patroller humor."

"Eh," he said, sounding faintly wistful. "Not, in any case, currently practical. Though I suppose I'm right glad to see Sunny doesn't believe any of those ugly rumors about Lakewalkers being black sorcerers."

Her trembling diminished, but her brows pinched as she thought back. "I'm so glad you were there. Though I wish your arm wasn't broken. Is it all right?" She touched the sling in worry.

"That wasn't especially good for it, but I haven't unset it. We're lucky for your aunt Nattie and Sunny's, ah, sudden shyness."

She drew back to stare up at his serious face, her eyes questioning, and he went on, "See, despite whatever hog butchering he's done, Sunny's never been in a lethal fight. I've been in no other kind since I was younger than him. He's used to puppy scraps, the sort you have with brothers or cousins or friends or, in any case, folks you're going to have to go on living with. Age, weight, youth, muscle, would all count against me in that sort of scuffle, even without a broken arm. If you truly want him dead, I'm your man; if you want less, it's trickier."

She sighed and leaned her head against his chest. "I don't want him dead. I just want him behind me. Miles and years. I suppose I just have to wait for the years. I still think of him every day, and I don't *want* to. Dead would be even worse, for that."

"Wise Spark," he murmured.

Her nose wrinkled in doubt. How seriously had he *meant* that lethal offer, to be so relieved that she hadn't taken him up on it? Remembering, she fetched him his drink, which he accepted with a smile of thanks.

Nattie had drifted to the hearth to stir the apple butter which, by the smell, was on the verge of scorching. Now she tapped the wooden spoon on the pot rim to shake off the excess, set it aside, turned back, and said, "You're a smart man, patroller."

"Oh, Nattie," said Fawn dolefully. "How much of that awfulness did you hear?"

"Pretty much all, lovie." She sighed. "Is Sunny gone yet?"

That funny look Dag got when consulting his groundsense flitted over his face. "Long gone, Aunt Nattie."

Fawn breathed relief.

"Dag, you're a good fellow, but I need to talk with my niece. Why don't you take a walk?"

He looked down to Fawn, who nodded reluctantly. He said, "I expect I could stand to go check on Copperhead, make sure he hasn't bitten anybody yet."

"I 'spect so," Nattie agreed.

He gave Fawn a last hug, bent down to touch his cider-scented lips to hers, smiled in encouragement, and left. She heard his steps wend through the house to the front door, and out.

Fawn wanted to put her head down in Nattie's lap and bawl; instead, she busied herself raking the coals under the oven for the pies. Nattie sat on a kitchen chair and rested her hands on her cane. Haltingly at first, then less so, the story came out, from Fawn's foolish tumble at the spring wedding to her growing realization and fear of the consequences to the initial horrid talk with Sunny.

"Tch." Nattie sighed in regret. "I knew you were troubled, lovie. I tried to get you to talk to me, but you wouldn't."

"I know. I don't know if I'm sorry now or not. I figured it was a problem I'd bought all on my own, so it was a problem to pay for all on my own. And then I thought my nerve would fail if I didn't plunge in."

For Nattie today, Fawn resolved to leave out nothing of her journey except the uncanny accident with Dag's sharing knife—partly because she was daunted by the complicated explanations that would have to go with, partly because it made no difference to the fate of her pregnancy, but mostly because Lakewalker secrets were so clearly not hers to give away. No, not just Lakewalker secrets—Dag's privacy. She grasped, now, what an intimate and personal possession his dead wife's bone had been. It was the only confidence he'd asked her to keep.

Taking a breath, Fawn plunged in anew. She described her lonely trudge to Glassforge, her terrifying encounter with the young bandit and the strange mud-man. Her first flying view of the startled Dag, even more frightening, but in retrospect almost funny. The Horsefords' eerie abandoned farm, the second abduction. The whole new measure for terror she'd learned at the malice's hands. Dag at the cave, Dag that night at the farm.

She did end up with her head in Nattie's lap then, though she managed to keep her tears down to a choked sniffling. Nattie petted her hair in the old way she hadn't done since Fawn had been small and weeping in pain for some minor hurt to her body, or in fury for some greater wound to her spirit. "Sh. Sh, lovie."

Fawn inhaled, wiped her eyes and nose on her apron, and sat up again on the floor next to Nattie's chair. "Please don't tell Mama and Papa any of this. They're going to have to go on living with the Sawmans. There's no point in making bad blood between the families now."

"Eh, lovie. But it gars me to see Sunny get off free of all this."

"Yes, but I couldn't stand for my brothers to know. They'd either try to do something to Sunny and cause trouble, or they'd make a mock of me for being so stupid, and I don't think I could bear that about this." She added after a moment of consideration, "Or both."

"I'm not sure even your brothers are thoughtless enough to make mock of *this*." Nattie hesitated, then conceded reluctantly, "Well, perhaps half-Whit."

Fawn managed a watery smile at the old jibe. "Poor Whit, maybe it's that old joke on his name that drives him to be such an awful thorn to everyone. Maybe I should start calling him Whitesmith instead, see if it helps."

"There's a thought." Nattie sat up, staring into her personal dark. "I think maybe you're right about the bad blood, though. Oh my, yes. All right. This story will stop with me unless some other problem comes from it."

Fawn breathed relief at this promise. "Thank you. Talking with you eases me, more than I expected." She thought over Nattie's last words, then said more firmly, "You have to understand, I'm going away with Dag. One way or another."

Nattie did not immediately burst into objections and dire warnings, but said only, "Huh." And then, after a moment, "Curious fellow, that Lakewalker. Tell me more."

Fawn, busying herself once more about the kitchen, was only too glad to expand on her new favorite subject to an unexpectedly sympathetic, or at least not immediately outraged, ear. "I met his patrol in Glassforge . . . " She described Mari and Saun and Reela—if touching only lightly on Dirla and Razi and Utau—and Sassa's proud tours to show off his town, and all the fascinating things folks found for work there that did not involve cows, sheep, or pigs. The bow-down, and Dag's unexpected talents with a tambourine—a word picture that made Nattie laugh along with Fawn. At that point, Fawn came to a sudden stop.

"You're heels-up in love with him, then," Nattie said calmly. And, at Fawn's gasp, "Come, girl, I'm not *that* blind."

In love. It seemed too weak a term. She'd imagined herself *in love* back when she was mooning over Sunny. "More than that. I trust him . . . right down to the ground."

"Oh, aye? After all that tale, I think I'm half in love with him myself." Nattie added after a thoughtful moment, "Haven't heard such joy in your voice for a long, long time, lovie. Years."

Fawn's heart sprang up as though weights had been shifted from it, and she laughed aloud and gave Nattie a hug and a kiss that made the old woman smile foolishly. "Now, now. There's still some provin' to be done, you know."

But then the pies were baked, and Fawn's mother returned to start the rest of supper, sending Fawn to milk the cows so the boys could keep cutting hay while the light lasted. She went by the front porch on the way, but Dag had not yet returned to his thinking seat there.

Dag made his way back to the house after a stroll around the lower perimeter of the farm, in part to stretch his legs and mind and in part to be certain Sunny had indeed packed off. Resentful and ripe for trouble, that boy, and his abrupt and satisfying removal from Fawn's presence had likely been dangerously self-indulgent for a Lakewalker alone in farmer country, but Dag could not regret the act, despite the renewed throbbing of his jostled arm. Dag's last veiled fear that, once back in the safety of her home, Fawn might repent her patroller and double back to her first love, faded altogether.

Once upon a time, Sunny had held star fire in his hand, and thrown it away in the mud of the road. He wouldn't be getting that fortune back, ever. There seemed nothing in the wide green world Dag could do to him worse than what he had already done to himself. Smiling crookedly, Dag dismissed Sunny from his thoughts in favor of more urgent personal concerns.

In the kitchen, he found Fawn gone but her mother, Tril, buzzing about putting together supper for eight. A clicking and whirring from the next chamber proved to be Nattie at her spinning wheel, within sight and call of her sister, and he made sure to say *how de'*; she returned a friendly but unenlightening, "Evening, patroller," and carried on. Evidently the incident with Sunny was not to be discussed. On the whole, Dag was relieved.

He greeted Tril amiably and attempted to make himself useful hooking pots on and off the fire for her, while trying to think his way to other possibilities for a half-handed man to show his worth to the female who was, in Lakewalker terms, the head of Tent Bluefield. Tril watched him in such deep alarm, he began to fear he was looming, too tall for the room, and he finally just sat down and watched, which seemed to ease her. His comment about the weather fell flat, as did a leading question about her chickens; alas, Dag knew little about farm animals beyond horses. But a few questions about Fletch's upcoming wedding led by a short route to West Blue marriage customs generally, which was exactly where Dag wanted her to go. The best way to keep her going, he quickly discovered, was to respond with comments on Lakewalker customs on the same head.

Tril paused in kneading biscuit dough to sigh. "I was afraid last spring Fawn was yearning after the Sawman boy, but that was never a hope. His papa and Jas Stonecrop had had it fixed between them for years that Sunny would marry Violet and the two farms would come together in the next generation. It's going to be a rich spread, that one. If Violet has more than one boy, there may be enough to divide among them without the younger ones having to go off homesteading the way Reed and Rush keep talking of."

The twins spoke of going to the edge of the cultivated zone, twenty miles or so west, and breaking new land between them, after Fletch married. It was a plan much discussed but so far little acted upon, Dag was given to understand. "Fathers arrange marriages, among farmers?"

"Sometimes." Tril smiled. "Sometimes they just think they do. Sometimes the fathers have to be arranged. The land, though, or the family due-share for children who aren't getting land—that has to be understood and written out and kept by the village clerk, or you risk bad blood later."

Land again; farmers were all about land. Other wealth was thought of as land's equivalent, it seemed. He offered, "Lakewalker couples usually choose each other, but the man is expected to bring bride-gifts to her family, which he is considered to be joining. Horses and furs, traditionally, though it depends on what he has accumulated." Dag added, as if casually, "I have eight horses at the moment. The other geldings are on loan to the camp pool, except for Copperhead, who is too evil-tempered to foist on anyone else. The three mares I keep in foal. My brother's wife looks after them along with her mares."

"Camp pool?" Tril said, after a puzzled moment.

"If a man has more than he needs, he can't just sit on it and let it rot. So it goes to the camp pool, usually to outfit a young patroller, and the camp scribe keeps a record of it. It's very handy if you go to switch camps, because you can carry a letter of record and draw for your needs when you get there, instead of carrying all that burden along. At the hinterland meetings every two years, one of the jobs for the camp scribes is to meet and settle up any lingering differences. I have a long credit at Stores." How to translate that into acreage temporarily defeated him, but he hoped she understood he was not by any measure destitute, despite his present road-worn appearance. He rubbed his nose reflectively with the side of his hook. "They tried me as a camp scribe for a while after I lost my hand, but I didn't take to the fiddly work and all the writing. I wanted to be moving, out in the field."

"You can read and write?" Tril looked as though this was a point in Dag's favor—good.

"Pretty much all Lakewalkers can."

"Hm. Are you the oldest in your family, or what?"

"Youngest by ten years, but I've only the one brother living. It was a great sorrow to my mother that she had no daughter to carry on her tent, but my brother married a younger sister of the Waterstriders—they had six—and she took our tent name so's it wouldn't be lost, and moved in so's my mother wouldn't be alone." *See, I'm a nice tame fellow, I have a family too. Of a sort.* "My brother is a very gifted maker at our camp." He decided not to say of what. The production of sharing knives was the most demanding of Lakewalker makings, and Dar was highly respected, but it seemed premature to introduce this to the Bluefields.

"Doesn't he patrol?"

"He did when he was younger—nearly everyone does—but his making skills are too valuable to waste on patrolling." Dag's, needless to say, weren't.

"So what of your father? Was he a maker or a patroller?"

"Patroller. He died on patrol, actually."

"Killed by one of those bogles Fawn talks of?" It was not entirely clear to Dag if Tril had believed in bogles before, but on the whole he thought she'd come to now, and was rendered very uncomfortable thereby.

"No. He went in after a younger patroller who was swept away in a bad river crossing, late in the winter. I wasn't there—I was patrolling in a different sector of the hinterland, and didn't hear for some days."

"Drowned? Seems an odd fate for a Lakewalker."

"No. Or not just then. He took a fever of the lungs and died about four nights later. Drowned in a sense, I suppose." Actually, he'd died of sharing; the two comrades who were trying to fetch him home in his dire illness had entered the tent to find him rolled over on his knife. Whether he'd chosen that end in shrewd judgment or delirium or despair or just plain exhaustion from the struggle, Dag would never know. The knife had come to him, anyway, and he'd used it three years later on a malice up near Cat Lick.

"Oh, aye, lung fever is nasty," Tril said sympathetically. "One of Sorrel's aunts was carried off by that just last winter. I'm so sorry."

Dag shrugged. "It was eleven years ago."

"Were you close?"

"Not really. He was away when I was smaller, and then I was away. I knew his father well, though; Grandfather had a bad knee by then, like

Nattie" —Nattie, listening through the doorway as she spun, lifted up her head and smiled at her name—"and he stayed in camp and helped look after me, among other things. If I'd lost a foot instead of a hand, I might have ended like that, Uncle Dag to my brother's pack." *Or I might have shared early.* "So, um . . . are there any one-handed farmers?"

"Oh, yes, accidents happen on farms. Folks deal with it, I expect. I knew a man with a wooden leg, once. I've never heard tell of anything like that rig of yours, though."

Fawn's mother was relaxing nicely in his presence now and didn't jump at all anymore when he moved. On the whole, Dag suspected that it was easier to coax wild animals to take food from his hand than to lull Bluefields. But he was clearly making progress. He wondered if his Lake-walker habits were betraying him, and if he ought to have started with Fawn's papa instead of with the women. Well, it hardly mattered where he started; he was eventually going to have to beguile the whole lot of them in order to get his way.

And in they clumped, sweaty and ravenous. Fawn followed, smelling of cows, with two covered buckets slung on a yoke, which she set aside to deal with later. The crowd, minus Clover tonight, settled down happily to heaping portions of ham, beans, corn bread, summer squash, assorted pickled things, biscuits, butter, jams, fresh apple butter, cider, and milk. Conversation lagged for a little. Dag ignored the covert glances as he dealt with biscuits by stabbing them whole with his fork-spoon; Tril, if he read her aright, was simply pleased that he seemed to like them. Happily, he did not need to feign this flattery although he would have if necessary.

"Where did you go while I was milking?" Fawn finally asked him.

"Took a walk down to the river and back around. I am pleased to say there's no malice sign within a mile of here, although I wouldn't expect any. This area gets patrolled regularly."

"Really?" said Fawn. "I've never seen patrollers around here."

"We cross settled land at night, mostly, to avoid disturbing folks. You wouldn't notice us."

Papa Bluefield looked up curiously at this. It was quite possible, over the years, that not all patrols had passed as invisibly to him as all that.

"Did you ever patrol West Blue?" Fawn asked.

"Not lately. When I was a boy just starting, from about age fifteen, I walked a lot in this area, so I might have. Don't remember now."

"We might have passed each other all unknowing." She looked thoughtful at this notion.

"Um . . . no. Not then." He added, "When I was twenty I was sent on exchange to a camp north of Farmer's Flats, and started my first walk around the lake. I didn't get back for eighteen years."

"Oh," she said.

"I've been all over this hinterland since, but not just here. It's a big territory."

Papa Bluefield sat back at the table's head and eyed Dag narrowly. "Just how old are you, Lakewalker? A deal older than Fawn, I daresay."

"I daresay," Dag agreed.

Papa Bluefield continued to stare expectantly. The sound of forks scraping plate was suddenly obtrusive.

Cornered. Must this come out here? Perhaps it was better to get it on the table sooner than later. Dag cleared his throat, so that his voice would come out neither squeaking like a mouse's nor too loud, and said, "Fifty-five."

Fawn choked on her cider. He probably should have glanced aside first to see she wasn't trying to swallow anything. His fork-spoon hand was no good for patting her on the back, but she recovered her breath in a moment. "Sorry," she wheezed. "Down the wrong pipe." She looked up sideways at him in muffled, possibly, alarm. Or dismay. He hoped it wasn't horror.

"Papa," she muttered, "is fifty-three."

All right, a little horror. They would deal with it.

Tril was staring. "You look forty, if that."

Dag lowered his eyelids in nonargument.

"Fawn," Papa Bluefield announced grimly, "is eighteen."

Beside him, Fawn's breath drew in, sharply aggravated.

Dag tried, almost successfully, to keep his lips from curling up. It was hard, when she was clearly boiling so much inside she was ready to pop. "Really?" He eyed her blandly. "She told me she was twenty. Although from my vantage, it scarcely makes a difference."

She hunched her shoulders sheepishly. But their eyes connected, and then she had trouble not laughing too, and all was well.

Papa Bluefield said in an aggravated tone, "Fawn had an old bad habit of telling tall tales. I tried to beat it out of her. I should have beat her more, maybe."

Or less, Dag did not say aloud.

"As it happens, I come from a very long-lived kin," Dag said, by way of attempted repair. "My grandfather I told you of was still spry till his death at well over a hundred." One hundred twenty-six, but there was more than enough mental arithmetic going on around the table right now. The brothers, particularly, seemed to be floundering, staring at him in renewed wariness.

"It all works out," Dag went on into the too-long pause. "If, for example, Fawn and I were to marry, we would actually arrive at old age tolerably close together. Barring accidents."

All right, he'd said the magic word, *marry.* It wasn't as if he hadn't done something like this before, long ago. Well, all right, it had been nothing at all like this. Kauneo's kin had been overpowering in an entirely different manner. The terror rippling through him felt the same, though.

Papa Bluefield growled, "Lakewalkers don't marry farmer girls."

He couldn't grip Fawn's hand below the table for reassurance; all he could do was dig his fork into her thigh, with unpredictable but probably unhelpful results at the moment. He did glance down at her. Was he about to jump off this cliff alone or with her? Her eyes were wide. And lovely. And terrified. And . . . thrilled. He drew a long breath.

"I would. I will. I wish to. Marry Fawn. Please?"

Seven stunned Bluefields created the loudest silence Dag had ever heard.

15

In the airless moment while everyone else around the table was still inhaling, Fawn said quickly, "I'd like that fine, Dag. I would and will and wish, too. Yes. Thank you kindly." *Then* she drew breath.

And then the storm broke, of course.

As the babble rose, Fawn thought Dag should have tackled her family one at a time instead of all together like this. But then she noticed that neither Mama nor Aunt Nattie was adding to the rain of objections, and truly, whenever Papa turned to Mama for support he received instead a solemn silent stare that seemed to unnerve him. Aunt Nattie said nothing at all, but she was smiling dryly. So maybe Dag had been doing more than just thinking, all this day.

Fletch, possibly in imitation of Papa's earlier and successful attempt to embarrass Dag about his age, came up with, "We don't take kindly to cradle robbing around these parts, Lakewalker."

Whit, his tone mock-thoughtful but his eyes bright with the excitement of battle, put in, "Actually, I'm not sure if *he's* robbing cradles, or *she's* robbing graves!"

Which made Dag wince, but also offer a wry headshake and a low murmur of, "Good one, Whit."

It also made Fawn so furious that she threatened to serve Whit's pie on his head instead of his plate, or better still his head on his plate instead of his pie, which drew Mama into the side fray to chide Fawn, so Whit won twice, and smirked fit to make Fawn explode. She hated how easily they all could make her feel and act twelve, then treat her so and feel justified about it; if they kept this up much longer, she was afraid they'd succeed in dropping her back to age two and screaming tantrums right on the floor. Which would do just about nothing for her cause. She caught her breath and sat again, simmering.

"I hear Lakewalker men are landless, and do no work 'cept maybe hunting," said Fletch, determinedly returning to the attack. "If it's Fawn's portion you're after, let me tell you, she gets no land."

"Do you think I could carry farm fields away in my saddlebags, Fletch?" said Dag mildly.

"You could stuff in a couple o' chickens, maybe," Whit put in so helpfully.

Dag's eyes crinkled. "Be a bit noisy, don't you think? Copperhead would take such offense. And picture the mess of eggs breaking in my gear."

Which made Whit snicker unwillingly in turn. Whit, Fawn decided, didn't care which side he argued for, as long as he could stir the pot and keep it boiling. And he preened when folks laughed at his jokes. Dag had him half-wrapped around his thumb already.

"So what *do* you want, eh?" asked Reed aggressively, frowning.

Dag leaned back, face growing serious; and somehow, she was not sure how, commanding attention all around the table. It was as if he suddenly grew taller just sitting there. "Fletch brings up some very real concerns," Dag said, with a nod of approval at Fawn's eldest brother that puffed him up a bit despite himself. "As I understand it, if Fawn married a local lad, she would be due clothing, some furniture, animals, seed, tools, and a deal of labor to help set up her new house. Except for her personal gear, it's not Lakewalker custom or expectation that I should have any of that. Nor could I use it. But neither should I like to see her deprived of her rights and due-share. I have an alternate plan for the puzzle."

Papa and Mama were both listening seriously too, as if they were all three speaking the same language of a sudden. "And what would that be, patroller?" said Papa, brows now pinched more in thought than in antagonism and not nearly as red in the face as he'd been at first.

Dag tilted his head as if in thanks, incidentally emphasizing his permission to speak without interruptions from juniors. "I *of course* undertake to care for and protect Fawn for as long as I live. But it's a plain fact that I don't lead a safe life." A slight, emphatic tick of his wrist cuff on the table edge was no accident, Fawn thought. "For now, I would have her leave her marriage portion here, intact, but defined—written out square in the family book and in the clerk's record, witnessed just as is right. No man knows the hour of his shari—of his end. But if ever Fawn has to come back here, I would have it be as a real widow, not a grass one." He tilted his head just enough toward Fawn that only she saw his slight wink, and she was as cheered by the wink as chilled by the words, so that her heart seemed to spin unanchored. "She—and her children, if any—would then have something to fall back on wholly separate from my fate."

Mama, face scrunched up in concentration, nodded thoughtfully at this.

"In the hope that such a day would be long from now or never, it would have to be attested by Fletch and Clover as well. Can't help thinking that Clover would be just as glad to put off paying out that due-share, with all the work she'll have here starting up."

Fletch, opening his mouth, shut it abruptly, as it finally dawned that not only would he not be required to disgorge any family resources right away, but also that Fawn would be out of the house when he brought his new bride home. And only by the slightest brightening of Dag's eyes did Fawn realize that Dag had hit Fletch precisely where he was aiming, and knew it.

A blessed silence fell just long enough to finish consuming pie. Fawn was reattaching Dag's hook before Whit wiped his lips, and said in brotherly bewilderment, "But why ever would you want to marry Fawn in the first place?"

The tone of his voice alone threw Fawn back into a pit of unwelcome memories of youthful mockery. As if she were the most unlikely candidate for courtship in the whole of West Blue and for a hundred miles beyond in any direction, as if she were a cross between a village idiot and a freak of nature. What was that stupid phrase that had worked so well, *repeatedly,* to rile her up? *Hey, Runt! You must have been drinking ugly juice this morning!* And how those words had made her feel like it.

"Need I say?" asked Dag calmly.

"Yes!" said Fletch, in his stern I-am-so-paternal voice that made Fawn long to kick him even more than she longed to kick Whit, and even made Papa cock a bemused eyebrow at him.

"Yeah, old man," said Rush, scowling. Of all at the table but Nattie, the twins had said the least so far, but none of it had been favorable. "Give us three good reasons!"

Dag's eyelids lowered briefly in a cool yet strangely dangerous assent; but his side glance at Fawn felt like a caress after a beating. "Only that? Very well." He held their attention while he appeared to think, deliberately clearing a silence in which to speak. "For the courage of her heart, which I saw face down the greatest horrors I know without breaking. For the high and hungry intelligence of her mind, which never stops asking questions, nor thinking about the answers. For the spark of her spirit, which could teach bonfires how to burn. That's three. Enough for going on with."

He rose from the table, his hook hand briefly touching her shoulder. "All this is set beside me, and you ask me instead if I want *dirt*? I do not understand farmers." He excused himself with a polite nod all around, and a murmured, "Evening, Aunt Nattie," and strode out.

Fawn wasn't sure if she was more thrilled with his words or with his *timing*. He had indeed figured out the only way to get in the last word in a bunch of Bluefields—shoot it into the target and run.

And whatever comment, mockery, or insult might have risen in his wake was undercut to shamed silence by the sound of Mama, weeping quietly into the apron clutched up to her face.

The debate didn't end there, naturally. It mostly broke up into smaller parts, as they took on family members in ones or twos, although Fawn gave Dag credit for trying for efficiency, that first night. The twins cornered her the next afternoon in the old barn, where she had gone to give Grace and Copperhead some treats and a good brushing.

Rush leaned on the stall partition and spoke in a voice of disgust. "Fawn, that fellow is *way* too old for you. He's older than Papa, and Papa's older than rocks. And he's all so banged up. If you were married, you'd have to look at that stump he hides, I bet. Or touch it, *ew*."

"I've seen it," she said shortly, brushing bay hairs into the air in a cloud. "I help him with his arm harness, now his other arm's broke." And a great deal of other assistance that she was not inclined to bring to the twins' attention. "You should see his poor gnarly feet if you want to see banged up."

Reed sat on a barrel of oats across the aisle with his knees drawn up and his arms wrapped around them, rocking uneasily. He said in a thin tone, "He's a Lakewalker. He's *evil*."

This brought Fawn's irritated and vigorous brushing to an abrupt halt; Grace twitched her ears in protest. Fawn turned to stare. "No, he's not. What are you going on about?"

"They say Lakewalkers eat their own dead to make their sorcery. What if he makes you have to eat corpses? Or worse? What does he really want you for?"

"His wife, Reed," said Fawn with grim patience. "Is that so very hard to believe?"

Reed's voice hushed. "What if it's to make magic?"

He already does that would likely not be a useful answer. "What, are you afraid I'll be made a human sacrifice? How sweet of you, Reed. Sort of."

Reed unfolded indignantly. "Don't you laugh. It's true. I saw a Lakewalker once who'd stopped to eat in the alehouse in West Blue. Sunny Sawman dared me to peek in her saddlebags. She had bones in them—human bones!"

"Tell me, was she wearing her hair in a knot at the nape of her neck?"

Reed stared. "How'd you know?"

"You're lucky you weren't caught."

"I was. She took me and shook me and told me I'd be cursed if I ever touched anything of a Lakewalker's again. She scowled so—she told me she'd catch and eat me!"

Fawn's brows drew down. "How old were you, again?"

"Ten."

"Reed, for pity's sake!" said Fawn in utter exasperation. "What would you tell a little boy you caught rifling your bags so as to scare him enough never to do it again? You're just lucky you didn't run into Dag's aunt Mari—I bet she could have come up with a tall tale that would have made you pee yourself into the next week." She was suddenly glad the sharing knife was stored with her own things, and wondered if she ought to warn Dag to watch his saddlebags.

Reed looked a bit taken aback, as if this point had never before occurred to him, but he went on anyhow. "Fawn, those bones were real. They were *fresh*."

Fawn had no doubt of it. She also had no desire to start down some slippery slope of explanation with the twins, who would only ask her how she knew and badger her endlessly when her answers didn't fit their notions. She finished brushing Grace's flanks and turned her attention to her mane and forelock.

Rush was still mired in the age difference. "It's sickening to think of a fellow that old pawing you. What if he got you pregnant?"

She was definitely not ready for that again so soon, but it was hardly a prospect that filled her with horror. Perhaps her and Dag's future children, if any, wouldn't be saddled with being so blasted short—now, there was a heartening thought. She smiled softly to herself as Grace nudged her velvety nose into her hand and whuffled.

Rush went on, "He as much as said it was his plan to keep you till you were and then send you back to batten on us."

"Only if he *dies*, Rush!"

"Yeah, well, how much longer can that be?"

"And what does it matter to you anyhow? You and Reed are going to go west and break land. You won't even be here." She let herself out of the stall and latched the door.

"On Fletch and Clover, then."

"You two are so, so, so"—she groped for a sufficient word—"howling *stupid*."

"Oh, yeah?" Rush shot back. "He claimed he wanted to marry you because you were smart, and how dumb do you have to be to believe that? You know it's just so's he can get his old hands on your young . . . self."

"Hand," she corrected coldly. And how she missed its touch on her young . . . everything. Escape from West Blue, with or without a wedding, could not happen soon enough.

Rush imitated upchucking, with realistic noises. Fawn supposed stabbing him with the pitchfork was out, but maybe she could at least whack him over the head with it . . . ? He added, "And how d'you think we'll feel in front of *our* friends, stuck with that fellow in the family?"

"Considering your friends, I can't say as I'm real moved by that plea."

"I can't see as you've much considered anybody but yourself, lately!"

Reed said, more urgently and with a peculiar fearful tinge in his voice, "I see what it is. He's magicked you up some way already, hasn't he?"

"I don't want to hear another word out of you two."

"Or what?" said Rush. "You'll never speak to us again?"

"I'm working on that one," snarled Fawn, and stalked out of the barn.

Not all of the encounters were so aggravating. Fawn found an unexpected ally in Clover, with whom she'd never before much gotten along, and Clover brought Fletch right into line. The two girls were now in great charity with each other, feeling they could have been best friends forever and mistaken in all their prior judgments; Fletch was a bit dizzied. Dag made undaunted use of the news about his age to put himself rather above it all, and he mainly talked privately with Mama and Papa or Nattie. Whit continued to fire off barbs in blithe disregard for their aim, with the result that *everybody* grew furious with him except for Dag, who continued patient and determined.

"I've dealt with dissolving patrols down to and including breaking up knife fights," he assured Fawn at one especially distraught moment. "No one here's tried to stab each other yet."

"It's been a near thing," Fawn growled.

By supper of the second night after Dag's proposal, Fawn's parents had gone so far as to forbid discussion of the topic at the table, somewhat to Dag's relief. It did render the meal uncharacteristically quiet. Dag thought his plan to extract Fawn gracefully from the clutches of her kin was not going as well as he'd hoped. Whether it took two days or twenty or two hundred, he was determined to persevere, but it was plain Fawn was close to melting in this family crucible, and her strain communicated itself to him, open to her ground as he could not help being.

They'd taken too long on this journey already. Much more tarrying in West Blue, and he'd risk not beating Mari's patrol back to Hickory Lake, and they would panic and think him missing again. And this time, he wouldn't be dragging back in with another malice kill in his bag to buy forgiveness.

Bluefields were falling to him, slowly. Fletch and Clover were openly agreeable, Nattie quietly agreeable, and Tril mainly just quiet. Whit didn't greatly care, and Papa Bluefield still sat on the fence.

Sorrel and Tril Bluefield reminded Dag a bit of patrol leaders, their heads stuffed with too many duties and details, too many people's conflicting desires and needs. An unsolvable dilemma had a good chance of being invited to go away; he thought they might break simply because they could not afford to spend all their time and energy on one problem when so many more crowded upon them. Dag felt almost cruelly ruthless, but he steeled himself to keep up the blandishments and subtle pressure. Fawn took care of the unsubtle pressure.

Reed and Rush remained a stubborn reservoir of resistance. Dag was not sure why, as neither would talk to him despite several friendly lures. Separately, he thought he might have gotten somewhere, but together they stayed locked in a knot of disapproval. Fawn, when he asked her for guidance into their objections, just went tight-lipped. But their more hotheaded remarks at least served to drive their papa further and faster toward conciliation than he would have gone on his own, if only from sheer embarrassment. Some opposition was its own worst enemy.

Still . . . I should have liked to have made some real tent-brothers. Now, *there* was an unreasonable hope to flush from hiding. Dag frowned at himself. The gift of comradeship he'd once found with Kauneo's brothers in Luthlia, so fine in the having, was all the more painful in the loss. Maybe it was better this way.

After the postsupper chores the family usually gathered in the parlor, cooler than the kitchen, to share the lamplight. Dag had walked out with Fawn to feed scraps to the chickens; as they came through the kitchen door and into the central hall, he heard raised voices from the parlor. By this time Dag cringed at opening his groundsense in this raucous company, not a one of them capable of a decent veiling; but he did prick his ears to hear Reed's voice, rumbling, hostile, and indistinct, and then Tril's, raised in sharp fear: "Reed! Put that down! Fawn brought me that all the way from Glassforge!"

Beside him, Fawn drew in her breath and hurried forward. Dag strode after, bracing himself.

In the parlor, Reed and Rush had more or less cornered their parents. Tril was sitting beside the table that held the bright oil lamp, some sewing in her lap; Nattie sat across the room in the shadows with the drop spindle that was rarely out of her hands, now stilled. Whit crouched by Nattie, a spectator on the fringe, for once not heckling. Sorrel stood facing Reed, with Rush pacing nervously around them.

Reed was holding up the glass bowl and declaiming, overdramatically in Dag's view, "—sell your daughter to some bloody-handed corpse-eater for the sake of a piece of glass?"

"Reed!" Fawn cried furiously, dashing forward. "You give that back! It's not yours!"

Dag thought it was sheer force of habit; when confronted with that familiar sisterly rise, Reed quite unthinkingly raised the bowl high out of Fawn's hopping reach. At her enraged squeal, he tossed it to Rush, who just as unthinkingly caught it.

Tears of fury sprang in Fawn's eyes. "You two are just a pair of yard dogs—"

"If you hadn't dragged Useless here home with you—" Rush began defensively.

Ah, yet another new nickname for himself, Dag realized. He was collecting quite a set of them here. But his own fraying temper was not nearly such a grating goad to him as Fawn's humiliated helplessness.

Sorrel glanced at his distraught wife, whose hands had flown to her mouth, and barked angrily, "Boys, that's enough!" He strode forward and started to pull the bowl out of Rush's grasp. Sorrel, unwilling to snatch, let go just as Rush, afraid to resist, did likewise.

It was no one's fault, exactly, or at least no one's intention. Dag saw it coming as did Fawn, and a desolate little wail broke from her lips even before the bowl hit the wooden floor edge on and burst, falling into three large pieces and a sparkling spray of splinters.

Everyone froze in equal horror. Whit opened his lips, looked around, and then closed them flat.

Sorrel recovered his voice first, hoarse and low. "Whit, don't move. You got no shoes on."

Tril cried, "Reed! Rush! How *could* you!" And began sobbing into her sewing.

Their mother's anger might have rolled right off the pair, Dag thought, but the genuine heartbreak in her voice seemed to cut them off at the knees. They both began incoherent apologies.

"Sorry does no mending!" she cried, tossing the scrap of cloth aside. It was flecked with blood where she had inadvertently driven her needle into her palm in the shock of the crash. "I've had it with the whole pack of you—!"

The Bluefield uproar was so painful in Dag's ground, which he tried to close but could not for the strength of his link to Fawn, that he found himself dropping to his knees. He stared at the pieces of glass on the floor in front of him as the angry and anguished voices continued overhead. He could not shut them out, but he could redirect his attention; it was an old, old method of dealing with the unbearable.

He slipped his splinted right arm from its sling, and with it and his hook he clumsily pushed the large pieces of the bowl as close together as he could. Those splinters, now—most of those glass splinters were no bigger than mosquitoes. If he could bounce a mosquito, he could move one splinter, and if he could move one, he could move two and four and more . . . He remembered the sweet song of this bowl's ground as it had rested in the sunset light of their refuge in Glassforge, gifting rainbows, and he began a low humming, searching up and down for the right note, just . . . there.

The glass splinters began to wink, then shift, then rise and flow over the boards of the parlor floor. He shifted them not with his hand, but with the ground of his hand. The ground of his left hand, the hand that was not there, and the very thought was so terrifying he shied from it.

But even that terror did not break his concentration. The splinters flew up, circling and swirling like fireflies around the bowl to find their places once more. The bowl glowed golden along all the spider-lines of its fractures, like kiln fire, like star fire, like nothing earthly Dag had ever seen. It scintillated, reflecting off his draining, chilling skin. He held the pure note faintly through his rounded lips. The lines of light seemed to melt into rivulets, streams, rivers of pale gold running all through the glass, then spread out like a still lake under a winter sunrise.

The light faded. And was gone.

Dag came back to himself bent over on his knees, his hair hanging around his face like a curtaining fringe, mouth slack, staring down at the intact glass bowl. His skin felt as cold and clammy as lard on a winter morning, and he was shivering, shuddering so hard his stomach hurt. He pressed his teeth together so that they would not chatter.

The only sounds in the room were of eight people breathing: some heavily, some rapidly, some choked with tears, some wheezing with shock. He thought he could pick out each one's pattern with his ears alone. He could not force himself to look up.

Someone—Fawn—thumped down on her knees before him. "Dag . . . ?" she said uncertainly. Her small hand reached out to touch his chin, to tilt his face upward to meet her wide, wide eyes.

He pushed the bowl forward with his left arm. It was hot to the touch but not dangerously so. It did not melt or disappear or explode or fall apart again into a thousand pieces. It just sang slightly as it scraped across the floor, the ordinary song of ordinary glass that had never been slain or resurrected. He found his voice, or at least a close imitation of his voice; it sounded utterly unfamiliar in his own ears, as though it was coming from underwater or underground. "Give that back to your mama."

He pressed his wrist cuff to her shoulder and levered himself upright. The room wavered around him, and he was suddenly afraid he was going to vomit, making a mess right there on the middle of the parlor floor in front of everyone. Fawn clutched the bowl to her breast and rose after him, her eyes never leaving his face.

"Are you all right?" she asked.

He gave her a short headshake, wet his cold lips, and stumbled for the parlor door to the central hall. He hoped he could make it out onto the front porch before his stomach heaved. Tril, on her feet, was hovering nearby, and she stepped back as he passed. Fawn followed, pausing only long enough to thrust the bowl into her mother's hands.

Dag heard Fawn's voice behind him, low and fierce: "He does that for hearts, too, you know."

And she marched forthrightly after him.

16

awn followed Dag onto the front porch and watched in worry as he sat heavily on the step, his left elbow on his knee and his head down. In the west behind the house, the sky was draining of sunset colors; to the east, above the river valley, the first stars were pricking through the darkening turquoise vault. The air grew soft as the day's heat eased. Fawn settled down to Dag's right and raised her hand uncertainly to his face. His skin was icy, and she could feel the shudders coursing through his body.

"You've gone all cold."

He shook his head, swallowing. "Give me a little . . . " In a few moments he straightened up, taking a deep breath. "Thought I was going to spew my nice dinner on my feet, but now I think not."

"Is that usual? For after doing things like that?"

"No—I don't know. I'm not a maker. We'd determined that by the time I was sixteen. Hadn't the concentration for it. I needed to be moving all the time. I am *not* a maker, but *that* . . . "

"Was?" she prompted when he stayed stopped.

"That was a *making*. Absent gods." He raised his left arm and rubbed his forehead on his sleeve.

She tucked her arm around him, trying to share warmth; she wasn't sure how much good it did, but he smiled shakily for the attempt. His body was chilled all down his side. "We should go into the kitchen by the hearth. I could fix you a hot drink."

"When I can stand up." He added, "Maybe go around the outside of the house."

Where they would not have to hazard her family. She nodded understanding.

"Groundwork," he began, and trailed off. "You have to understand. Lakewalker groundwork—magic, you might say—involves taking something and making it more so, more itself, through reinforcing its ground. There's a woman at Hickory Lake who works with leather, makes it repel rain. She has a sister who can make leather that turns arrows. She can make maybe two coats a month. I had one once."

"Did it work?"

"Never had occasion to find out while I had it. I saw another turn a mud-man's spear, though. Iron tip left nothing but a scratch in the hide. Of the coat, not of the patroller," he clarified.

"Had? What happened to it?"

"Lent it to my oldest nephew when he began patrolling. He handed it on to his sister when she started. Last I knew my brother's youngest took it with him when he went out of the hinterland. I'm not sure the coats are all that useful, for they're like to make you careless, and they don't protect the face and legs. But, you know . . . you worry for the youngsters." His shudders were easing, but his expression remained strained and distant. "That bowl just now, though . . . I pushed its ground back to purest bowl-ness, and the glass just followed. I felt it so clear. Except that, except that . . . " He leaned his forehead down against hers, and whispered fearfully, "I pushed with the ground of my left hand, and I have no left hand and it *has* no ground. Whatever was there, for that minute, is gone again now. I've never heard of anything like that. But the best makers don't speak of their craft much except to their own. So I don't know. Don't . . . know."

The door swung open; Whit edged out into the shadows of the porch. "Um . . . Fawn . . . ?"

"What, Whit?" she said impatiently.

"Um. Aunt Nattie says. Um. Aunt Nattie says she's had enough of this nonsense and she'll see you and the patroller in her rooms and be having the end of it one way or another as soon as the patroller is up to it. Um. Sir."

Behind the fringe of his hair, Dag's lips twitched slightly. He raised his face. "Thank you, Whit," he said gravely. "Tell Aunt Nattie we'll be along soon."

Whit gulped, ducked his head, and fled back indoors.

They rose and went around the north side of the house to the kitchen, Dag resting his left arm heavily across Fawn's shoulders. He stumbled twice. She made him sit by the hearth while she fixed him a cup of hot water with some peppermint leaves crushed in, holding it to his lips while he drank it down. By then he'd stopped shivering, and his clammy skin had dried and warmed again. She saw her parents and Fletch peeking timidly from the darkness of the hall, but they said nothing and did not venture in.

Aunt Nattie appeared at the door to her shadowed weaving room. "Well, patroller. You were flyin' there for a bit, I guess."

"Yes, ma'am, I was," Dag agreed wryly.

"Fawn, you fetch in the patroller and what lights you want." She turned back into the dark, scuffing feet and cane over the floorboards, not wearily, but just for the company of the sound, as she sometimes did.

Fawn looked anxiously at Dag. The firelight she'd poked up glimmered red-orange over his skin, yellow on his coarse white shirt and the sling, and his eyes were dark and wide. He looked tired, and confused, and as if his arm was hurting, but he smiled reassuringly at her, and she smiled back. "You ready?" she asked.

"Not sure, but I'm too curious to care. Possibly not a trait helpful to longevity in a patroller, but there you go."

She took down the candle lamp with the chipped glass sleeve from the mantel and lit it, grabbing the unlit iron holder with the three stubs while she was at it, and led off. With a muffled *eh,* he levered himself up out of his chair and paced after her.

Nattie called from their bedroom, "Close both doors, lovie. It will keep the noise out."

And in, Fawn reflected. She pushed the door to the kitchen closed with her foot and picked her way around the loom and the piles of Dag's gear. In the bedroom, Nattie seated herself on the side of her narrow bed and motioned to the one across from it. Fawn set the lamp and the iron ring on the table between and lit the other candles, and went back and closed the bedroom door. Dag glanced at her and sat down facing Nattie, the bed ropes creaking under his weight, and Fawn eased down at his left. "Here we are, Aunt Nattie," she announced, to which Dag added, "Ma'am."

Nattie stretched her back and grimaced, then leaned forward on her cane, her pearly eyes seeming to stare at them in a disturbingly penetrating fashion. "Well, patroller. I'm going to tell you a story. And then I'm going to ask you a question. And then we'll see where we're goin' on to."

"I'm at your disposal," Dag said, with that studied courtesy Fawn had learned concealed caution.

"That's to be seen." She sniffed. "You know, you're not the first Lakewalker I've met."

"I sensed that."

"I lead a dull life, mostly. Lived in this house since Tril married Sorrel nigh on thirty years ago. I hardly get off this farm 'cept down to West Blue for the market day or a little sewing bee now and then."

Actually, Nattie did both regularly, being a chief supplier of fine cloth and having a deep ear for village gossip, but Fawn forbore to intrude on the stream of . . . whatever this was going to be. Reminiscence?

Apparently so, for Nattie went on, "Now, the summer before Fawn was born was a tough time. Her mama was sick, and the boys were rambunctious, and her papa was overworked as usual. I wasn't sleeping so good myself, so I did my gathering in the north woods at night after they'd all gone to bed. The boys being less help than more in the woods at that stage of their lives."

Ages three to ten, roughly; Fawn could picture it, and shuddered.

"Roots and herbs and plants for remedies and dyes, you know. Night's not only more peaceful, the scents are sharper. I especially wanted some wild ginger for Tril, thought I might make a tea to settle her poor stomach. Anyhow, I was sorry for the peaceful that night, because I fell and twisted my ankle something fierce. I tried callin' for a bit, but I was too far from the house to be heard."

Truly, the woods on the steep valley slope to the north of their place extended for three miles before the next farm. Fawn made an encouraging noise in lieu of a nod.

"I figured I was doomed to lie in the dew till morning when I'd be missed, but then I heard a sound in the leaves—I was afraid it was a wolf or bear come to eat me, but instead it was a Lakewalker patroller. I was thinking at first I'd rather a bear, but he turned out to be a nice young fellow.

"He laid hands on my foot and eased me amazingly, and picked me up and carried me back to the house. I was skinnier back then, mind, bit of a dab, really. He was not near so tall as you" —she nodded in Dag's general direction—"but right stout. Nice voice, almost as deep as yours.

He explained all about how he was on exchange from some camp way out east, and this was his first patrol in these parts—lonely and homesick, I was thinking. Anyhow, I fed him quiet in the kitchen, and he did a real fine job bandaging my ankle up nice and firm.

"I don't know if he decided I was his adopted aunt, or if he was more like a boy picking up a bird with an injured wing and making a pet of it, but late the next night there came a tapping on my window. He was back with some medicine, some for my foot and some for Tril's tummy, which he handed in—he wouldn't stay that time, though. The powders worked wonderful well, I must say." She sighed in fond recollection.

"Off he went and I thought no more of it, but next summer, about the same time of year, there came that tapping at my window again. We had a bit of a picnic on the back porch in the dark, and talked. He was glad to hear Tril had delivered you safe, Fawn. He gave me some little presents and I gave him some food and cloth. The next summer the same; I got to looking out for him.

"The next year he came back one more time, but not alone. He brought his new bride, just to show her off to me I think, he was that proud of her. He showed me their Lakewalker marriage-bracelets, string-bindings they called 'em, knowin' I had a maker's interest in all things to do with the craft, thread and cords and braids as well as the weaving and knitting. They let me hold them in my hands and feel them. Gave me a turn, they did. They weren't just fancy cord. They were *magical*."

"Yes," said Dag cautiously, and at Fawn's curious look expanded, "Each betrothed puts a tiny bit of their ground into their own cord. The string-binding ceremony tangles the two grounds, then they exchange, his for hers."

"Really?" said Fawn, fascinated, trying to remember if she'd noticed such bracelets on the patrollers at Glassforge. Yes, for Mari'd had one, and so had a couple of other older patrollers. She had thought them merely decorative. "Do they do anything? Can you send messages?"

"No. Well, only that if one spouse dies, the other can feel it, for the ground drains out of their binding cord. They're often put safe away to save wear, although they can be remade if they're damaged. But if one spouse is out on patrol, the other back in camp usually wears theirs. Just . . . to know. To the one out on patrol, it comes as more of a shock, because you don't expect . . . I've seen that happen twice. It's not good. The patroller is dismissed at once to ride home if it's at all possible. There's a special terror to knowing what but not how, except that you are *too late,* and a thought that, you know, *maybe* the string just got burned up in a tent fire or some freak thing—enough hope for agony but not enough for ease. When I woke up in the medicine tent after . . ."

The room grew so quiet, Fawn thought she could hear the candles burning.

She lifted her face to his and said a little wryly, "You know, you've either got to finish those sorts of sentences or not start them."

He sighed and nodded. "I think I can say this to you. If I can't I've no business . . . anyway. I was about to say, when I woke up in the medicine tent after Wolf Ridge with my hand gone, so was Kauneo's binding string, which I wore on that side. Lost on the ridge. I guess I made some difficulties trying to find it, being fairly mixed up in the head right about then. They hadn't wanted to tell me she was gone till I was stronger, but they pretty much had to, and then I wouldn't believe them. It was like, if I could just find that binding string, I could prove them wrong. I got over it in due course."

He was looking away from her as he said this. Fawn drew her breath in and let it out gently between her teeth. He looked back down at her and smiled, sort of, and tried to move his hand to grasp hers in reassurance, wincing as the sling brought him up short in painful reminder. "It was a long time ago," he murmured.

"Before I was born."

"Indeed." He added after a moment, "I don't know why I find that an easing thought, but I do."

Nattie had her head cocked to one side with the intensity of her listening; when he did not go on, she put in, "Now, I do know this, patroller. Without those binding strings, you aren't married in Lakewalker eyes."

He nodded cautiously, then remembered to say aloud, "Yes. That is to say, they are a visible proof of a valid marriage, like your village clerk's record and writing your name in the family book with all the witnesses' signatures below. The string-binding is the heart and center of a wedding. The food and the music and the dancing and the arguments among the relatives are all extra."

"Uh-huh," said Nattie. "And there's the problem, patroller. Because if Fawn and you stand up in the parlor before the family and all like you say you want, and sign your names and make your promises, seems to me *she'd* be getting married, but *you* wouldn't. I said I had a question, and this is it. I want to know exactly what you are about, that you think this won't twist around somehow and leave her cryin'."

Fawn wondered for a moment why he was being held responsible for her future tears but not her for his. She supposed it was the, the *blighted* age thing again. It seemed unfairly unbalanced, somehow.

Dag was silent for several long breaths. He finally raised his chin, and said, "When I first rode in here, I had no thought of a farmer wedding. But it didn't take long to see how little her family valued Spark. Present company excepted," he added hastily. Nattie nodded grimly, not disagreeing. "Not that they don't love her and try to look out for her, in a sort of backhanded, absentminded way. But they don't seem to see her, not as she is. Not as I see her. Of course, they don't have groundsense, but still. Maybe the past fogs the present, maybe they just haven't looked lately, maybe they never have looked, I don't know. But marriage seems to raise a woman's standing in a farmer family. I thought I could give her that, in an easy way. Well, it seemed easy at the time. Not so sure now." He sighed. "I was real clear about the widowhood business, though."

"Seems like a hollow gift, patroller."

"Yes, but I can't do a string-binding here. I can't make the string, for one; it takes two hands and I've got none, and I'm not sure Fawn can make one at all, and we've no one to do the blessing and the tying. I was thinking that when we reached Hickory Lake I might try for a string-binding there, despite the difficulties."

"Think your family will favor this idea?"

"No," he said frankly. "I expect trouble about it. But I've outstubborned everything my life has thrown at me so far."

"He's got a point there, Aunt Nattie," Fawn dared to say.

"Mm," said Aunt Nattie. "So what happens if they pitch her out on her ear? Which Lakewalkers have done to farmer suitors before, I do believe."

Dag fell very quiet for a little, then said, "I'd walk with her."

Nattie's brows went up. "You'd break with your people? *Can* you?"

"Not by choice." His shrug failed to conceal deep unease. "But if they chose to break with me, I couldn't very well stop them."

Fawn blinked, suddenly disquieted. She'd dreamed only of what joy they might bring to each other. But that keelboat seemed to be towing a whole string of barges she hadn't yet peeked into. Dag had, it seemed.

"Huh-huh-hm," said Nattie. She tapped her cane gently on the floorboards. "I'm thinkin' too, patroller. I got two hands. So does Fawn, actually."

Dag seemed to freeze, staring at Nattie sharply. "I'm . . . not at all sure that would work." He added after a longer moment, "I'm not at all sure it wouldn't. I have some know-how. Fawn knows this land, she can help gather the necessaries. Hair from each of us, other things. Mine's a bit short."

"I have tricks for dealing with short fibers," said Nattie equitably.

"You have more than that, I think. Spark . . . " He turned to her. "Give me a piece your aunt has made. I want to hold something of her making. Something especially fine, you know?"

"I think I know what he's wanting. Look in that trunk at the foot of my bed, lovie," said Nattie. "Fletch's wedding shirt."

Fawn hopped up, went around to the wooden trunk, and lifted the lid. The shirt was right on top. She picked it up by the shoulders, letting the white fabric fall open. It was almost finished, except for the cuffs. The smocking around the tops of the sleeves and across the yoke in back was soft under her touch, and the buttons, already sewn down the front placket, were carved of iridescent mussel shell, cool and smooth.

She brought it to Dag, who laid it out in his lap, touching it clumsily and gingerly with his right fingertips and, more hesitantly, letting his hook hand drift above it, careful not to snag. "This isn't just one fiber, is it?"

"Linen for strength, cotton for softness, a bit of nettle flax for the shimmer," Nattie said. "I spun the thread special."

"Lakewalker women never spin or weave thread so fine. It takes too much time, and we never have enough of that."

Fawn glanced at his coarse shirt, which she had thought shoddy, with a new eye. "I remember helping Nattie and Mama set up the loom for that cloth, last winter. It took three days, and was so tedious and finicky I thought I'd scream."

"Lakewalker looms are little hanging things, which can be taken down and carried easy when we move camp. We could never shift that big wooden frame of your aunt's. That's a farmer tool. Sessile, as bad as barns and houses. Targets . . . " He lowered his gaze to the cloth again. "This is good ground, in this. It used to be plants, and . . . and creatures. Now its ground is wholly transformed. All shirt, whole. That's a good making, that is." He raised his face and stared at Nattie with a new and keen curiosity. "There's a blessing worked in."

Fawn would have sworn Nattie's lips twitched in a proud smirk, but the expression fleeted away too fast to be sure. "I tried," Nattie said modestly. "It's a wedding shirt, after all."

"Huh." Dag sat up, indicating with a nod that Fawn should take the shirt back. She folded it away again carefully and sat on the trunk. A tension hung between Nattie and Dag, and she hesitated to walk between them, lest something delicate tear and snap like a spiderweb.

Dag said, "I'm willing to try for the binding strings if you are, Aunt Nattie. It sure would change the argument, up home. If it doesn't work, we're no worse off than we were, except for the disappointment, and if it does . . . we're that much farther along."

"Farther along to where?" asked Nattie.

Dag gave a wry snort. "We'll all find out when we arrive, I expect."

"That's a fair saying," allowed Nattie amiably. "All right, patroller. You got yourself a bargain."

"You mean you'll speak for us to Mama and Papa?" Fawn wanted to jump up and squeal. She stopped it down to a more demure squeak, and leaped to the bed to give Nattie a hug and a kiss.

Nattie fought her off, unconvincingly. "Now, now, lovie, don't carry on so. You'll be giving me the heebie-jeebies." She sat up straight and turned her face once more toward the man across from her. "One other thing . . . Dag. If you'd be willing to hear me out."

His brows twitched up at the unaccustomed use of his name. "I'm a good listener."

"Yeah, I noticed that about you." But then Nattie fell silent. She shifted a little, as if embarrassed, or . . . or shy? Surely not . . . "Before that young Lakewalker fellow left, he gave me one last present. Because I said I was sorry to part never having seen his face. Well, actually, his lady gave it me, I suppose. She was something of a hand at Lakewalker healings, it seemed, of the sort he did for my poor ankle when first we met."

"Matching grounds," Dag interpreted this. "Yes? It's a bit intimate. Actually, it's a lot intimate."

Nattie's voice fell to almost a whisper, as if confiding dark secrets. "It was like she lent me her eyes for a spell. Now, he wasn't too different from what I'd pictured, sort of homely-handsome. Hadn't expected the red hair and the shiny suntan, though, on a fellow who'd been sleeping all day and running around all night. Touch of a shock, that." She went quiet for a long stretch. "I've never seen Fawn's face, you know." The offhand tone of her voice would have fooled no one present, Fawn thought, even without the little quaver at the end.

Dag sat back, blinking.

In the silence, Nattie said uncertainly, "Maybe you're too tired. Maybe it's . . . too hard. Too much."

"Um . . . " Dag swallowed, then cleared his throat. "I am mightily tired this night, I admit. But I'm willing to try for you. Not sure it'll work, is all. Wouldn't want to disappoint."

"If it don't work, we're no worse off than we were. As you say."

"I did," he agreed. He shot a bleak smile at Fawn. "Change places with me, Spark?"

She scrambled off Nattie's bed and took his spot on her own, as he sat down beside Nattie. He hitched his shoulders and slipped his arm out of his sling.

"You be careful with that arm," warned Fawn anxiously.

"I think I can lift it from the shoulder all right now, if I don't try to wriggle my fingers too much or put any pressure on it. Nattie, I'm going to try to touch your temples, here. I can use my fingers for the right side, but I'm afraid I'll have to touch you with the backside of my hook on the left, if only for the balance. Don't jump around, eh?"

"Whatever you say, patroller." Nattie sat bolt upright, very still. She nervously wet her lips. Her pearl eyes were wide, staring hard into space. Dag eased up close to her, lifting his hands to either side of her head. Except for a somewhat inward expression on his face, there was nothing whatsoever to see.

Fawn caught the moment only because Nattie blinked and gasped, shifting her eyes sideways to Dag. "Oh." And then, more impatiently, "No, don't look at that dumpy old woman. I don't want to see her anyhow, and besides, it isn't true. Look over *there*."

Obligingly, Dag turned his head, parallel with Nattie's if rather above it. He smiled at Fawn. She grinned back, her breath coming faster with the thrill shivering about the room.

"My word," breathed Nattie. "My word." The timeless moment stretched. Then she said, "Come on, patroller. There isn't hardly nothing human in the wide green world could be as pretty as that."

"That's what I thought," said Dag. "You're seeing her ground as well as her face, you know. Seeing her as I do."

"Do you, now," whispered Nattie. "Do you. That explains a lot." Her eyes locked hungrily on Fawn, as if seeking to memorize the sightless vision. Her lids welled with water, which glimmered in the candlelight.

"Nattie," said Dag, his voice a mix of strain and amusement and regret, "I can't keep this up much longer. I'm sorry."

"It's all right, patroller. It's enough. Well, not that. But you know."

"Yes." Dag sighed and sat back, slumping. Awkwardly, he slipped his splinted arm back in its sling, then bent over, staring at the floor.

"Are you sick again?" asked Fawn, wondering if she should dash for a basin.

"No. Bit of a headache, though. There are things floating in my vision. There, they're fading now." He blinked rapidly and straightened again. "Ow. You people do take it out of me. I feel as though I'd just come off walking patterns for ten days straight. In the worst weather. Over crags."

Nattie sat up, her tears smearing in tracks like water trickling down a cliff face. She scrubbed at her cheeks and glared around the room that she could no longer see. "My word, this is a grubby hole we've been stuffed in all this time, Fawn, lovie. Why didn't you ever say? I'm going to make the boys whitewash the walls, I am."

"Sounds like a good idea to me," said Fawn. "But I won't be here."

"No, but *I* will." Nattie sniffed resolutely.

After a few more minutes to recover her stability, Nattie planted her cane and hoisted herself up. "Well, come on, you two. Let's get this started."

Fawn and Dag followed her out past the weaving room; once through the door to the kitchen, Fawn cuddled in close to Dag's left side, and he let his arm drift around behind her back and anchor her there, and maybe himself as well. The whole family was seated around the lamplit table, Papa and Mama and Fletch on the near end, Reed and Rush and Whit beyond. They looked up warily. Whatever conference they were having, they'd kept their voices remarkably low; or else they hadn't been daring to talk to one another at all.

"Are they all there?" muttered Nattie.

"Yes, Aunt Nattie."

Nattie stepped up to the center of the kitchen and thumped the floor with her cane, drawing herself up in full Pronouncement Mode such as Fawn had very seldom seen, not since the time Nattie had so-finally settled the argument for damages with the irate Bowyers over the twins' and Whit's cow-racing episode, years ago. Nattie drew a long breath; everyone else held theirs.

"*I'm* satisfied," Nattie announced loudly. "Fawn shall have her patroller. Dag shall have his Spark. See to it, Tril and Sorrel. The rest of you lot" —she glared to remarkable effect, when she put her mind to it, the focused blankness making her eyes seem quite uncanny—"behave yourselves, for once!"

And she turned and walked, very briskly, back into her weaving room. Just in case anyone was foolish enough to try to challenge that last word, she gave her cane a jaunty twirl and knocked the door closed behind her.

17

Dag woke late from a sodden sleep to find that his next duty in this dance was to ride with Fawn and her parents to West Blue to register their intentions with the village clerk, and to beg his official attendance on the wedding. Fawn was fussed and nervous getting Dag shaved, washed up, and dressed, which confused him at first, because she'd had the help down to a fairly straightforward routine, and despite his fatigue he wasn't being gracelessly cranky this morning. He finally realized that at last they would be seeing people outside of her family—ones she'd known all her life. And vice versa. It would be the first view most of West Blue would have of Dag the Lakewalker, *that lanky fellow Fawn Bluefield dragged home* or however he was now known to local gossip.

He tried not to let his imagination descend too far into the disagreeable possibilities, but he couldn't help reflecting that the only resident of West Blue who had met him so far was Stupid Sunny. It seemed too much to hope that Sunny was not given to gossip, and it was already proven he'd a habit of altering the facts to his own favor. His humiliation was more likely to make him sly than contrite. The Bluefields could well be Dag's only allies in the farmer community; it seemed a thin thread to hang from. So he let Fawn carry on in her efforts to turn him out presentably, futile as they seemed.

The hamlet, three miles south via the shade-dappled river road, appeared peaceful and serene as Sorrel drove the family horse cart down the main, and seemingly only, street. It was a day for fluffy white clouds against a bright blue sky utterly innocent of any intent to rain, which added to the illusion of good cheer. The principal reasons for the village's existence seemed to be a grain mill, a small sawmill, and the timber wagon bridge, which showed signs of having been recently widened. Around the little market square, presently largely idle, were a smithy, an alehouse, and a number of other houses, mostly built of the native river stone. Sorrel brought the cart to a halt before one such and led the way inside. Dag ducked his head under an excessively low stone lintel, just missing braining himself.

He straightened cautiously and found the ceiling sufficient. The front room seemed a cross between a farmhouse parlor and a camp lore-tent, with benches, a table, and shelves stuffed with papers, rolled parchments, and bound record books. The litter of records flooded on into the rooms beyond. In through the back hall bustled the clerk himself, who seemed, by the way he dusted the knees of his trousers, to have been interrupted in the midst of gardening. He was on the high side of middle age, sharp-nosed, potbellied, and perky, and was introduced to Dag by the very farmerly name of Shep Sower.

He greeted the Bluefields as old friends and neighbors, but he was clearly taken aback by Dag. "Well, well, well!" he said, when Sorrel, with determined help from Fawn, explained the reason for the visit. "So it's true!" His stout but equally perky wife arrived, gaped at Dag, dipped her knees rather like Fawn upon introduction, smiled a bit frantically, and dragged Tril away out of earshot.

The registry process was not complex. It consisted of the clerk's first finding the right record book, tall and thick and bound in leather, dumping it open on the table, thumbing through to the most recent page, and affixing the date and penning a few lines under some similar entries. He required the place and date of birth and parents' names of both members of the couple—he didn't even ask before jotting down Fawn's, although his hand hesitated and the pen sputtered when Dag recited his own birth date; after a doubtful stare upward, he blotted hastily and asked Dag to repeat it. Sorrel handed him the rough notes of the marriage agreement, to be written out properly in a fair hand, and Sower read it quickly and asked a few clarifying questions.

It was only at this point that Dag discovered there was a fee for this service, and it was customary for the would-be husband to pay it. Fortunately, he had not left his purse with his other things at the farm, and doubly fortunately, because they had been far longer about this journey than he'd planned, he still had some Silver Shoals copper crays, which sufficed. He had Fawn fish the little leather bag from his pocket and pay up. Apparently, arrangements could also be made for payment in kind, for the coinless.

"There always come some here who can't sign their own names," Sower informed Dag, with a nod at his sling. "I sign for them, and they make their X, and the witnesses sign to confirm it."

"It's been six days since I busted the arm," said Dag a little tightly. "For this, I think I can manage." He did let Fawn go first, watching her closely. He then had her dip the quill again and help push it into his fingers. The grip was painful but not impossible. The signature was not his best, but at least it was clearly legible. The clerk's brows went up at this proof of literacy.

The clerk's wife and Fawn's mother returned. Missus Sower's gaze on Dag had become rather wide-eyed. Craning her neck curiously, she read out, "Dag Redwing Hickory Oleana."

"Oleana?" said Fawn. "First I heard of that part."

"So you'll be Missus Fawn Oleana, eh?" said Sower.

"Actually, that's my hinterland name," Dag put in. "Redwing is what you would call my family name."

"Fawn Redwing," Fawn muttered experimentally, brows drawing down in concentration. "Huh."

Dag scratched his forehead with the side of his hook. "It's more confusing than that. Lakewalker custom has the fellow taking the name of his bride's tent, by which I would become, er . . . Dag Bluefield West Blue Oleana, I suppose."

Sorrel looked horrified.

"What do we do, then, swap names?" asked Fawn in a tone of great puzzlement. "Or take both? Redwing-Bluefield. Er. Redfield? Bluewing?"

"You two could be purple-something," Sower suggested genially, with a wheezing laugh.

"I can't think of anything purple that doesn't sound stupid!" Fawn protested. "Well . . . Elderberry, I suppose. That's lake-ish."

"Already taken," Dag informed her blandly.

"Well . . . well, we have a few days to think it over," said Fawn valiantly.

Sorrel and Tril glanced at each other, seemed to inhale for strength, and bent to sign below. The day and time for the wedding was set for the earliest moment after the customary three days at which the clerk would be available to lend his official presence, which to Fawn's obvious relief was the afternoon of the third day hence.

"In a hurry, are you?" Sower inquired mildly, and while Dag did not at first catch his covert glance at Fawn's belly, she did, and stiffened.

"Unfortunately, I have duties waiting at home," Dag put in quellingly, letting his wrist cuff rest on her shoulder. Actually, aside from averting panic by beating Mari back to camp, till this blighted arm healed he was going to be just as useless at Hickory Lake as he was here at West Blue. It hardly mattered at which spot he sat around grinding his teeth in frustration, although West Blue at least had more novelty. But the disturbing mystery of the sharing knife was an itch at the back of his mind, well buried under the new distractions yet never fading altogether.

Three people jerked away from the Sowers' front window and pretended to have been walking up the street when Dag, Fawn, and her parents made their way out the front door. Across the street, a couple of young women clutched each other and bent their heads together, giggling. A group of young men loitering in front of the alehouse undraped themselves from the wall and went back inside, two of them hastily.

"Wasn't that Sunny Sawman just went into Millerson's?" Sorrel said, squinting.

"Wasn't that Reed with him?" said Fawn, in a more curious tone.

"So that's where Reed got off to this morning!" said Tril indignantly. "I'll skin that boy."

"Sawman's place is the second farm south of the village," Fawn informed Dag in an undervoice.

He nodded understanding. It would make the West Blue alehouse a convenient haunt, not that it wasn't a gathering place for the whole community, by the descriptions Dag had garnered. Sunny must realize that his secrets had been kept, or his standing with the Bluefield twins would be very different by now; if not grateful, the relief might at least render him circumspect. So, were any of those loiterers the friends Sunny had threatened to persuade to help slander Fawn? Or had that been an empty threat, and Fawn had merely fallen for the lie? No telling now. The boys were unlikely to cast slurs on her in her brother's presence, surely.

They all climbed back into the cart, and Sorrel, clucking, backed his horse and turned the vehicle around. He slapped the reins against the horse's rump, and it obligingly broke into a trot. West Blue fell behind.

Three days. There was no particular reason that simple phrase should make his stomach feel as though it wanted to flip over, Dag thought, but . . . *three days.*

After the noon dinner, Dag dismissed the obscurities of farmer customs from his mind for a time in favor of his own. He and Fawn went out together on a gathering trip around the farm.

"What are we looking for, really?" she asked him, as he led off first toward the old barn below the house.

"There's no set recipe. Spinnable things with some personal meaning to help catch our grounds upon. A person's own hair is always good, but mine's not long enough to use pure, and a few more hooks never hurt. The horsehair will give length and strength, I figure. It's often used, and not just for wedding cords."

In the cool shade of the barn, Fawn culled two collections of long sturdy hairs from the tails and manes of Grace and Copperhead. Dag hung on the stall partition, eyes half-shut, gently reminding Copperhead of their agreement that the gelding would treat Fawn with the tender concern of a mare for her foal or become wolf-bait. Horses did not reason by consequences so much as by associations, and the rangy chestnut had fewer wits than many, but by dint of repeated groundwork Dag had at length put this idea across. Copperhead nickered and nuzzled and lipped at Fawn, endured having hairs pulled out while scarcely flinching, ate apple slices from her hand without nipping, and eyed Dag warily.

There were no water lilies to be had on the Bluefield acres, and Dag was uncertain that their stems would yield up flax the way the ones at Hickory Lake did anyway, but to his delight they discovered a cattail-crowded drainage ditch up beyond the high fields that sheltered some red-winged blackbird nests. He held Fawn's shoes on his hook and murmured encouragement, grinning at her expression of revulsion and determination, as she waded out in the muck and gathered some goodly handfuls of both cattail fluff and feathers. After that, they tramped all around the margins and crossed and recrossed the fallow fields. It was not the season for milkweed silk, as the redolent flowers were just blooming, and the stems were useless, but at length they discovered a few dried brown sticks lingering from last fall whose pods hadn't broken open, and Dag pronounced the catch sufficient.

They took it all back to Nattie's weaving room, where Fawn stripped feathers and picked out milkweed seeds, and Nattie set out her own chosen mix of fibers: linen for strength, a bit of precious purchased cotton brought from south of the Grace River for softness and something she called *catch,* nettle flax for shine, all dyed dark with walnut stain. Fawn bit her lip and undertook the hair trimming, taking special care with Dag, not so much to avoid stabbing him with the scissors, he eventually realized, as to be sure his head wouldn't look like a scarecrow's on the day after tomorrow. She set up a small mirror to cautiously clip out some of her own curly strands. Dag sat quietly, enjoying watching her contort, counting the hours backward to when they'd last been able to lie together, and forward to the next chance. *Three days . . .*

Under her aunt's close supervision Fawn then mixed the ingredients in two baskets until Nattie, plunging her arms in and feeling while frowning judiciously in a way that had Fawn holding her breath, pronounced them ready for the next step. Shaping such a disparate mass of fibers into the long rolls for spinning could only be done by the gentlest carding and a lot of handwork, and even Fawn's willing fingers looked to be tiring by the end.

They went on to the spinning itself after supper. The male members of the family had some dim idea that the three were up to some outlandish Lakewalker project to please Dag, but they were well trained not to intrude upon Nattie's domain, and Dag doubted they suspected magic, so subtle and invisible a one as this was. They went off about their own usual pursuits. Tril drifted in and out from labors in the kitchen, watching but saying little.

After some debate, it was decided Fawn would be the spinner after all; she was certain Nattie would do it better, but Dag was certain that the more making she put into the task with her own hands, the better the faint chance of tangling her ground in the cord would be. She chose to spin on the wheel, a device Dag had never seen in operation before coming here, saying she was better at it than at the drop spindle. Once she'd finally settled and gathered up her materials and her confidence, the task went much more quickly than Dag had expected. At length she triumphantly handed over for Nattie's inspection two hanks of sturdy if rather hirsute two-ply thread something between yarn and string in texture.

"Nattie could have spun it smoother and more even." Fawn sighed.

"Mm," said Nattie, feeling the bundles. She didn't disagree, but she did say, "This'll do."

"Shall we go on now?" Fawn asked eagerly. Full night had fallen, and they had been working by candlelight for the past hour.

"We'll be more rested in the morning," said Dag.

"I'm all right."

"*I'll* be more rested in the morning, Spark. Have some pity on an old patroller, eh?"

"Oh. That's right. Groundwork drains you pretty dry." She added after a cautious moment, "Will this be as bad as the bowl?"

"No. This is a lot more natural. Besides, I've done this before. Well . . . Kauneo's mother actually did the spinning that time, because neither of us had the skill. Each of us had to do our own braiding, though, to catch our grounds."

Fawn sighed. "I'm never going to be able to sleep tonight."

In fact, she did, although not before Dag had heard through the closed door Nattie telling her to settle, it was worse than sleeping with a bedbug. Fawn's soft giggle was his last memory of the night.

They met again in the weaving room right after breakfast, as soon as the rest of the family had cleared off. This time, Dag closed the door firmly. They'd set up a backless bench, filched from the porch, so that Fawn could sit astride it with Dag directly behind her. Nattie took a seat in a chair just beyond Fawn's knee, listening with her head cocked, her weak groundsense trying to strain beyond its normal limit of the reach of her skin. Dag watched while Fawn practiced on some spare string; it was a four-stranded braiding that produced an extremely strong cord, a pattern called by Lakewalkers *mint-stem* for its square cross section, and by farmers, Dag was bemused to learn, the same.

"We'll start with my cord," he told her. "The main thing is, once I catch my ground in the braiding, don't stop, or the ground-casting will break, and we'll have to undo it all and start again from the beginning. Which, actually, we can do right enough, but it's a bit frustrating to get almost to the end and then sneeze."

She nodded earnestly and finished setting up, knotting the four strands to a simple nail driven into the bench in front of her. She spread out the wound-up balls that kept the loose ends under control, gulped, and said, "All right. Tell me when to start."

Dag straightened and slipped his right arm from its sling, scooting up behind her close enough to touch, kissing her ear for encouragement and to make her smile, succeeding perhaps in the first but not the second. He looked over her head and brought both arms around and over hers, letting his hand and hook touch first the fiber, then her fingers, then hover over her hands. His ground, flowing out through his right hand, caught at once in the thick threads. "Good. Got it anchored. Begin."

Her nimble hands began to pull, flip, twist, repeat. The tug as the thin stream from his ground threaded beneath her touch was palpable to him, and he recalled anew how very strange it had felt the first time, in a quiet tent in wooded Luthlia. It was still very strange, if not unpleasant. The room became exceedingly still, and he thought he could almost mark the shift of the light and shadows beyond the windows as the morning sun crept up the eastern sky.

His right arm was shaking and his shoulders aching by the time she had produced a bit over two feet of cord. "Good," he whispered in her ear. "Enough. Tie off."

She nodded, tied the locking end knot, and held the strands tight. "Nattie? Ready?"

Nattie leaned over with the scissors and, guided by Fawn's touch, cut below the knot. Dag felt the snap-back in his ground, and controlled a gasp.

Fawn straightened and jumped up from the bench. Anxiously, she turned and held out the cord to Dag.

He nodded for her to run it through his fingertips below the increasingly grubby splint wrappings. The sensation was bizarre, like looking at a bit of himself in a distorted mirror, but the anchoring was sound and sweet. "Good! Done! We did it, Spark, Aunt Nattie!"

Fawn smiled like a burst of sunlight and pressed the cord into her aunt's hands. Nattie fingered it and smiled too. "My word. Yes. Even I can feel that. Takes me back, it does. Well done, child!"

"And the next?" she said eagerly.

"Catch your breath," Dag advised. "Walk around, shake out the kinks. The next will be a bit trickier." The next might well be impossible, he admitted bleakly to himself, but he wasn't going to tell Spark that; confidence mattered in these subtle things.

"Oh, yes, your poor shoulders must hurt after all that!" she exclaimed, and ran around to climb up on the bench behind him and knead them with her small strong hands, an exercise he could not bring himself to object to, although he did manage not to fall forward onto the bench and melt. He remembered what else those hands could do, then tried not to. He would need his concentration. Two days, now . . .

"That's enough, rest your fingers," he heroically choked out after a bit. He stood up and walked around the room himself, wondering what else he could do, or should do, or hadn't done, to make the next and most critical task succeed. He was about to step into the unaccustomed and worrisome territory of things he'd never done before—of things no one had ever done before, to his knowledge. Not even in ballads.

They sat on the bench again, and Fawn secured the four strands of her own string on the nail. "Ready when you are."

Dag lowered his face and breathed the scent of her hair, trying to calm himself. He ran his stiff hand and hook gently down and up her arms a couple of times, trying to pick up some fragment, some opening on the ground he could sense swirling, so alive, beneath her skin. Wait, there was something coming . . . "Begin."

Her hands started moving. After only about three turns, he said, "Wait, no. Stop. That isn't your ground, that's mine again. Sorry, sorry."

She blew out her breath, straightened her back, wriggled, and undid her work back to the beginning.

Dag sat for a moment with his head bent, eyes closed. His mind picked at the uncomfortable memory of the left-handed groundwork he'd done on the bowl two nights ago. The break in his right arm did weaken his very dominant ground on that side; maybe the left now tried to compensate for the right as the right had long done for the maimed left. This time, he concentrated hard on trying to snag Fawn's ground from her left hand. He stroked the back of her hand with his hook, pinched with ghostly fingers that were not there, just . . . there! He had something fastened in, fragile and fine, and it wasn't him this time. "Go."

Again, her hands began flying. They were a dozen turns into the braid when he felt the delicate link snap. "Stop." He sighed. "It's gone again."

"Ngh!" Fawn cried in frustration.

"Sh, now. We almost had something, there."

She unknotted, and hitched her shoulders, and rubbed the back of her head against his chest; he could almost feel her scowl, although from this angle of view he could only see her hair and nose. And then he could feel it when her scowl turned thoughtful.

"What?" he said.

"You said. You said, people put their hair in the cords because it was once part of their ground, and so it was easy to pick up again, to hitch on to. Because it was once part of their body, right? Your living body makes its ground."

"Right . . ."

"You also once said, one night when I was asking you all about ground, that people's blood stays alive for a little while even after it leaves their bodies, right?"

"What are you," he began uneasily, but was cut off when she abruptly seized his hook hand and drew it around close in front of her. He felt pressure and a jerk, then another, through his arm harness. "Wait, stop, Spark, what are you—" He leaned forward and saw to his horror that she'd gouged open the pads of both of her index fingers on the not especially sharp point of the hook. She squeezed each hand with the other in turn to make the blood drip, and took up the strands again.

"Try again," she said in an utterly determined little growl. "Come on, quick, before the bleeding stops. *Try.*"

He could not spurn a demand so astonishing. With a fierceness that almost matched hers, he ran his hands, real and ghostly, down her arms once more. This time, her ground fairly leaped out into the blood-smeared string, anchoring firmly. "Go," he whispered. And her hands began to twist and flip and pull.

"You are scaring the piss out of me, Spark, but it's working. Don't stop."

She nodded. And didn't stop. She finished her cord, of about the length of the one they'd done for him, just about the time her fingers ceased bleeding. "Nattie, I'm ready for you."

Nattie leaned in and snipped below the end knot. Dag felt it as Fawn's ground snapped back the way his had.

"Perfect," he assured her. "Absent gods, it's fine."

"Was it?" She twisted around to look up at him, her face tight. "I couldn't feel anything. I couldn't feel anything any of the times. Really?"

"It was . . . you were . . . " He groped for the right words. "That was *smart,* Spark. That was beyond smart. That was brilliant."

The tightness turned to a blaze of glory, shining in her eyes. *"Really?"*

"I would not have made that mental leap."

"Well, of course *you* wouldn't have." She sniffed. "You'd have gone all protective or tried to argue with me."

He gave her a hug, and a shake, and felt a strange new sympathy for her parents and their mixed reaction to her homecoming that first night. "You're probably right."

"I am certainly right." She gave a more Spark-like giggle.

He sat back, releasing her, and slipped his aching splinted arm back into its sling. "For pity's sake, go wash your fingers at once. With strong soap and plenty of it. You don't know where that hook has been."

"Everywhere, hasn't it?" She shot a merry grin over her shoulder, stroked her cord once more, and danced out to the kitchen.

Nattie leaned over and picked up the new cord from the bench, running it thoughtfully through her fingers.

"I didn't know she was going to do that," Dag apologized weakly.

"You never do, with her," Nattie said. "She'll be keeping you alert, I expect, patroller. Maybe more than you bargained for. Funny thing is, *you* think you know what you're doing."

"I used to." He sighed. "Though that may have been because I was only doing the same things over and over."

Spark returned from the kitchen, towing her mother to see their finished work. Dag trusted Fawn wouldn't mention the last wrinkle about the blood. Tril and Nattie handed the cords back and forth; Tril gave one a tug, nodding thoughtfully at its strength. She squared her shoulders and dug in her apron pocket.

"Nattie, do you remember that necklace Mama had with the six real gold beads, one for every child, that broke that time the cart went over in the snow, and she never found all the bits and never had it fixed?"

"Oh, yes," said her sister.

"The piece came to me, and I never did anything with it either. It's been in the back of a drawer for years and years. I thought you might could use the beads to finish off the end knots of these cords of Fawn's."

Fawn, excited, looked into her mother's palm and picked up one of the four oblong gold beads, peering through the hole. "Nattie, can we? Dag, would it work all right?"

"I think it would be a fine gift," Dag said, taking one that Fawn pressed upon him to examine. Actually, he wasn't altogether certain it wasn't a prayer. He glanced at Tril, who gave him a short, nearly expressionless nod. "Very beautiful. They would look really good against that dark braid and make the ends hang better, too. I'd be honored to accept."

Beads and cords were put into Nattie's clever hands, and she made short work of affixing the old gold to the ends, trimming the last bit of cord below the anchoring knots into neat fringes. When she finished, the two lengths—one a little darker, one with a coppery glint—lay glimmering in her lap like live things. Which they were, in a sense.

"That'll look well, when Fawn goes up to your country," said Tril. "They'll know we're . . . we're respectable folks. Don't you think, patroller?"

"Yes," he said, hearing the plea in her voice and hoping he didn't lie.

"Good." She nodded again.

Nattie took charge of the cords, putting them away until the day after tomorrow when she undertook to bind them about the unlikely pair. Tangled and blessed, the cords would complete the ground link, if both hearts willed it, sign and signifier of a valid union that any Lakewalker with groundsense must witness. Faithfully made. Dag was certain he would remember this hour of making as long as he lived, as long as he wore the cord curled around his arm, and how Spark had poured her heart's blood so furiously into it. *And if her true heart stops, I'll know.*

18

One day was Dag's first thought upon awakening the next morning.

He'd expected this wedding-eve day to be one of quiet preparation for the small family ceremony, with perhaps time to meditate with proper seriousness on the step he was about to take—also to calm the tiny voice screeching in the back of his mind, *What are you doing? How did you end up here? This wasn't in your plans! Do you have any idea what's going to happen when you get home?* To the last question a simple *No* seemed to Dag a sufficient answer. More complicated questions, such as, *How are you going to protect Spark when you can't even protect yourself?* or *What about half-blood children?* he tried to ignore, although the last thought led directly to, *Would they be sawed-off and fiery?* and kept on going from there.

But after breakfast there descended upon the Bluefield farm not the one or two neighbor girlfriends of Fawn's he'd been led dimly to expect, but two girlfriends, five of their sisters, four sisters-in-law, a few mutual cousins, and an indeterminate number of mothers and grandmothers. They were like a plague of locusts in reverse, bringing quantities of food with hands that produced and put in order instead of consuming and laying waste. They talked, they laughed, they sang, they—or at least the younger ones—giggled, and they filled the house to bursting. The male Bluefields promptly fled to the far corners of the farm. Dag, fascinated, lingered. For a time.

Being introduced to the young women wasn't too bad, even though he mainly garnered either intimidated silences or nervous titters in return. The bolder ones, however, observing Fawn's aid to him, wanted to try their hands at it too, and he was shortly ducking being fed and watered like some strange new pet. *Fattened for the slaughter,* he tried not to think. An even more giggly troop, albeit led by a sterner matron, along with Fawn, who refused to explain anything, cornered him with strings and proceeded to measure various parts of his body—happily for his shredding equanimity, not *that* one—and floated away again in gales of laughter. Nattie's weaving room, ordinarily a quiet refuge, was jammed, and the kitchen was not only crowded but intolerably overheated from the busy hearth. By noon, Dag followed the men into self-imposed exile, although he lurked close enough to listen to the singing floating out through the open windows. With all the males gone, some of the songs grew unsurprisingly rowdy; this was to be a wedding party, after all. He was glad Fawn was not to be deprived of these flourishes due to her strange choice of partner.

The female help left before supper, although with plans to return again in the morning for the final push, but it wasn't till afterward that Dag found his thinking time. He settled by himself on the front porch, dangling his legs over the edge and watching the quiet river valley turn from gold-green to muted gray as the sun set. In the eaves of the old barn, the soft, tawny mourning doves called in their soft, tawny voices. It was Dag's favorite view on the whole farm, and he thought whoever had originally sited this house must have shared the pleasure. He felt strangely unanchored, all his old certainties falling behind, and no new ones to replace them. Except for Spark. And she made an unlikely fixed point in his spinning world, because she moved so fast he feared he'd miss her if he blinked.

He caught sight of Rush walking down the lane in the gathering shadows. After the bowl episode, the twins had stopped aiming barbs at him, but only because they now avoided talking to him at all. If he couldn't make friends, perhaps intimidation would do instead? Whit by contrast had become rather fascinated with Dag, following him about as though afraid he'd miss another magic show. Dag tried treating him as a particularly feckless young patroller, which seemed to work. If only his arm hadn't been broken he might have offered to teach Whit archery, which would have made a good way to move them along amiably. As it was, his idle comment about it made Whit say, showing willing to a degree that surprised him, "When you come back, maybe?"

Which made him wonder: were they ever coming back? Half of Dag's original intent for the marriage proposal had been to repair Fawn's bridges here in case of some dire need—in case of his death, bluntly. A Lakewalker would be trying to join his bride's family, to fit in as a new tent-brother; and the family in turn would expect to receive him as one. Farmer kin took in new sisters, not new brothers, and they weren't trained up to the reverse. It had taken Dag some time to realize that the only members of the family he really needed to please in order to carry off Fawn were the elders, and they had quite expected her to be carried off sometime by someone in any case. Dag was a stretch of custom, but not a reversal. The questions this begged for Dag's own homecoming niggled hard, the more so since Fawn could not anticipate most of them.

And here came Rush again, walking back up the lane. He spied Dag on the porch and angled toward him between the house and the old barn, a grassy area the sheep were sometimes turned out to crop. What the sheep refused to eat was scythed once a year to keep the space from turning back to woods and blocking the view. Rush, Dag realized as he approached, was tense, and Dag considered opening his groundsense wider, unpleasant as it was likely to prove.

"Hey, patroller," said Rush. "Fawn wants you. Down by the road at the end of the lane."

Dag blinked once, slowly, to cover the fact that he'd just snapped open his groundsense to its full range. Fawn, he determined first, was not down by the end of the lane, but nearly out of his perceptions to the west, up over the ridge. Not alone—with Reed?—she seemed not to be in any special distress, however. So why was Rush lying? Ah. The woods below were not unpeopled. Concealed among the trees near the road were the smudges of four horses, standing still—tied? Four persons accompanied them. Three blurred grounds he did not know, but the fourth he recognized as Stupid Sunny. Was it so wild a guess to think that the other three were also husky young farm boys? Dag thought not.

"Did she say why?" Dag asked, to buy a moment more to think.

Rush took a couple of breaths to invent an answer, apparently having expected Dag to leap up without delay. "Some wedding thing or other," he replied. "She didn't say, but she wants you right now."

Dag scratched his temple gently with his hook, glad that he had mostly stuck to the deeply ingrained habit of not discussing Lakewalker abilities with anyone here, Fawn and Nattie excepted. He was now one move ahead in this game; he tried to figure how not to squander that advantage, because he suspected it was the only one he had. It would be amusing to just sit here and watch Rush dig himself deeper concocting more desperate reasons for Dag to walk down the hill into what was shaping up to be a neat little ambush. But that would leave the whole pack of them running around loose all night to evolve other plans. As little as Dag wanted to deal with this tonight, still less did he want to deal with it in the morning. And most especially did he not want it to impinge on Spark in any way. His brotherly enemies, it seemed, were looking after that angle for him just now. So.

He let his groundsense play lightly over the lower woods, which he had crossed several times on foot in the past days, looking for . . . yes. Just exactly that. A flush, not of excitement, but of that very peculiar calm that came over him when facing a bandit camp or a malice lair jerked his mind up to another level. Targets, eh. He knew what to do with targets. But would targets know what to do with him? His lips drew back. If not, he would teach them.

"Um . . . Dag?" said Rush uncertainly.

He wasn't wearing his war knife. That was fine; he had no hand to wield it. He stood up and shook out his left arm. "Sure, Rush. Where did you say, again?"

"Down by the road," said Rush, both relieved and the reverse. Absent gods, but the boy was a poor liar. On the whole, that was a point in his favor.

"You coming with me, Rush?"

"In a minute. You go along. I have to get something in the house."

"All right," said Dag amiably, and trod off down the hill to the lane. He descended it for a few hundred paces, then cut over to the wooded hillside, plotting his routes. He needed to surprise his ambushers on the correct side for his purpose. He wondered how fast they could run. His legs were long; theirs were young. Best not to cut it too close.

Mari would beat me for trying this fool stunt. It was an oddly comforting thought. Familiar.

Dag ghosted down the hill at an angle until he was about fifteen feet behind the four young men hiding in the shadows of the trees and keeping watch on the lane. *Looks like Sunny took my advice.* It was still early twilight; Dag's groundsense would give him considerable advantage in the dark, but he wanted his quarry to be able to see him. "Evening, boys," he said. "Looking for me?"

They jumped and whirled. Sunny's gold head was bright even in the shadows. The others were more nondescript: one stout, one as muscular as Sunny, and one skinny; young enough to be foolish and big enough to be dangerous. It was an unpleasant combination. Three were armed with cudgels, for which Dag had a new respect. Sunny had both a stick and a big hunting knife, the latter still in the sheath at his belt. For now.

Sunny got his breath back and growled, "Hello, patroller. Let me tell you how it's going to be."

Dag tilted his head as if in curiosity.

"You're not wanted here. In a few minutes Rush is going to bring down your horse and your gear, and you're going to get on and ride north. And you don't come back."

"Amazing!" Dag marveled. "How do you figure you're going to make that happen, son?"

"If you don't, you get the beating of your life. And we'll tie you on your horse and you'll still ride north. Only without your teeth." Sunny's grin showed white in the shadows, to emphasize this threat. His friends shifted, a little too tense and worried to quite share the amusement, although one tried a huffy sort of laugh to show support.

"Not to find fault, but I see a few problems with your plan. First would be a notable absence of horse. I 'spect Rush is going to have a trifle of difficulty handling Copperhead." Dag let his groundsense spread briefly as far as the old barn. Rush's troubles were indeed beginning. He decided he did not have the attention to spare on managing his horse at this distance, and withdrew the link. The entire family had been told, at the dinner table in front of Sorrel and Tril, to leave Copperhead alone unless Dag was there. Rush was on his own. Dag tried not to smile too much.

"Patroller, *Fawn* can handle your horse."

"Indeed she can. But, you know, you sent Rush. Unfortunate, that."

"Then you can start walking."

"After a beating? You have a high opinion of my stamina." He let his voice go softer. "Think the four of you can take me?"

They glanced at his sling, at his handless left arm, at each other. Dag was flattered that they didn't all burst into laughter at this point. He thought they should have, but he wasn't about to say so. The stout one, in fact, looked just a shade ashamed. Sunny, granted, was more guarded. That hunting knife was a new ornament.

"Just to make it clear, I decline your invitation to the road. I don't care to miss my wedding. Now, it does look as if you have the numbers on your side. Are you prepared to kill me tonight? How many of you are ready to die to make that happen? Have you thought how your parents and families will feel about it tomorrow? How the survivors are going to explain to them what happened? Killing gets a lot messier than you'd think, and the mess doesn't end with burying the corpses. I speak from long experience."

He had to stop this; by their uncertain expressions, his words were getting through to at least two of them, and that hadn't exactly been his intent when he'd started babbling, here. Run and chase, that was the game plan. Fortunately, Sunny and the other muscular one were starting to try to stalk him, moving apart and around to get into position for a rush. To encourage them, he started to back up. And called, "No wonder Fawn calls you Stupid Sunny."

Sunny's head jerked up. From the side, one of his friends muffled a guffaw; Sunny shot a glare at him and snapped to Dag, "Fawn's a slut. But you know that. Don't you, patroller."

Right, that's done it. "You'll have to catch me first, boys. If you're as slow-footed as you are slow-witted, I shouldn't have a problem—"

Sunny lunged, his stick whistling through the air. Dag was not there.

Dag stretched his legs, driving up the hill, dodging around trees, boots slipping on old leaves and damp limestone lumps and green-black rolling round hickory husks. By the thump and pained grunt, at least one of his pursuers was finding the footing equally foul. He didn't actually want to lose the boys in the woods, but he wanted a good head start by the time he arrived . . .

Here.

Ah. Hm.

His chosen tree turned out to be a shagbark hickory with a trunk a bit less than a foot and a half wide. And no side branches for twenty feet straight up. This was a mixed blessing. It would certainly be a challenge for the boys to follow him up it. If he could get up it. He pulled his right arm from the sling and let it swing out of his way, reached up with his left, jammed in his hook, clapped his knees around the trunk, and began shinnying. Yanked the hook out again, reached, jammed, shinnied. Again. Again. He was about fifteen feet in the air when the pursuit arrived, winded and swearing and waving their cudgels. It occurred to him, in a meditative sort of way as he dragged his body skyward, that even without the unpleasant searing feeling in his left shoulder muscles, he was putting an awful lot of trust in a small wooden bolt and some stitching *designed* to pull out. The rough bark strips crackled and split beneath his gripping knees, small bits raining down in an aromatic shower. If his hook gave way and he slid down, the bark would have an interesting serrated effect between his legs, too.

He made it to the first sturdy side branch, put an arm and a leg over, winched himself up, and stood. He searched for his objective. Absent gods, another fifteen feet to go. Up, then.

A dry branch gave way under one foot, which was partly useful, for he was then able to kick it free and drop it on the upturned face of the skinny fellow who was being urged up the tree in Dag's wake by his friends. He yelped and fell back, discouraged for a moment. Dag didn't need too many more moments.

To his delight, a rock whistled up past him, then another. "Ow!"

he cried realistically, to lure more of them. A couple more missiles rose and fell, followed by a meaty *clunk* and an entirely authentic "*OW!*" from below. Dag made sure they could hear his evil laugh, even though he was wheezing like a smithy's bellows by now.

Almost to goal. Absent gods, the blighted thing was well out on that side branch. He extended himself, gripping the branch he was half-lying across under his right armpit, feet sliding along the wobbly bough below it, wishing for almost the first time in his life for more height and reach. Overbalance at this elevation, and he could swiftly prove himself stupider than Stupid Sunny. A little more, a little more, get his hook around that attachment . . . and a good yank.

Dag clung hard as the rough gray paper-wasp nest the size of a watermelon parted from the branch and began its thirty-five foot-drop. Most of the nest's residents were home for the evening, his groundsense told him, settling down for the night. *Wake up! You're under attack!* His feeble effort to stir up the wasps with his ground seemed redundant when the plummeting object hit the dirt and ruptured with a loud and satisfying *thwack*. Followed by a deep angry whine he could hear all the way up here.

The first screams were a deal more satisfying, though.

He cuddled back against the trunk of the tree, feet braced on some less flexible side branches, gasping for breath and applying himself to a few refinements. Persuading the furious wasps to advance up trouser legs and down collars proved not as difficult as he'd feared, although he could not simply bounce them like mosquitoes, and they were much less tractable than fireflies. A matter of practice, Dag decided. He set to it with a will.

"Ah! Ah! They're in my hair, they're in my hair, they're *stinging meee!*" came a wail from below, voice too high-pitched to identify.

"Augh, my *ears!* Ow, my hands! Get them off, *get them off!*"

"Run for the river, Sunny!"

The shuffling sounds of retreat filtered up through the leaves; the pell-mell flight wouldn't help them much, for Dag made sure they left under full guard. Even without groundsense, though, he could tell when his trouser-explorers made it all the way to target by the earsplitting shrieks that went up and up until breath was gone.

"*Limp* for the river, Sunny," Dag muttered savagely, as the frantic cries trailed away to the east.

Then came the matter of getting down.

Dag took it slowly, at least till the last ten feet when his hook slipped free and scored a long slash down the trunk in the wake of the flying bark bits from under his knees. But he did manage to land on his feet and avoid banging his splint very much on anything on the way. He staggered upright, gasping. "It was easier . . . when I could just . . . gut them . . ."

No. Not really.

He sighed, and did his best to tidy himself up a trifle, brushing bark and sticks and wide papery leaves from his clothing and hair with the back of his hook, and gratefully slipping his throbbing right arm back into its sling. A few stray wasps buzzed near in investigative menace; he sent them off after their nest mates and slithered back down the slope to where the horses were tied.

He picked apart their ties and did his best to loop up their reins so they wouldn't step on them, led them out onto the road, and pointed them south, trying to plant horsey suggestions about barns and grain and home into their limited minds. They would either find their way, or Sunny and his friends could have a fine time over the next few days looking for them. Once the boys could get their swollen selves out of bed, that is. A couple of the would-be bullies, including Sunny—Dag had made quite sure of Sunny on that score—would *definitely* not be wishing to ride home tonight. Or for many nights to come.

As he was wearily climbing back up the lane, he met Sorrel hastening down. Sorrel gripped a pitchfork and looked thoroughly alarmed.

"What in thunder was that awful screeching, patroller?" he demanded.

"Some fool young fellows trespassing in your woods thought it would be a grand idea to chuck rocks at a wasp nest. It didn't work out the way they'd pictured."

Sorrel snorted in half-amused vexation, the tension draining out of his body, then paused. "Really?"

"I think that would be the best story all around, yes."

Sorrel gave a little growl that reminded Dag suddenly of Fawn. "Plain enough there's more to it. Have it in hand, do you?" He turned again to walk up the lane side by side with Dag.

"That part, yes." Dag extended his groundsense again, this time toward the old barn. His future brother-in-law was still alive, though his ground was decidedly agitated at the moment. "There's another part. Which I think is your place and not mine to deal with." It was not one patrol leader's job to correct another patrol leader's people. On the other hand, teaming up could sometimes be remarkably effective. "But I think we might get forward faster if you'd be willing to take some direction from me."

"About what?"

"In this case, Reed and Rush."

Sorrel muttered something about, ". . . ready to knock their fool heads together." Then added, "What about them?"

"I think we ought to let Rush tell us. Then see."

"Huh," said Sorrel dubiously, but he followed as Dag turned aside from the lane at the old barn.

The sliding door onto the lane was open, and a soft yellow light spilled out from an oil lantern hung on a nail in a rafter. Grace, in a box stall by the door, snorted uneasily as they entered. The packed-dirt aisle smelled not unpleasantly of horses and straw and manure and dove droppings and dry rot. From Copperhead's box sounded an angry squeal. Dag held out a restraining hand as Sorrel started to surge forward. *Wait,* Dag mouthed.

It was hard for Dag not to laugh out loud as the scene revealed itself, although the sight of half his gear strewn across the stall floor being well trampled by Copperhead did quite a lot to help him keep a straight face. On the far wall of the stall, some wooden slats were nailed to make a crude manger, and above it a square was cut in the ceiling to allow hay to be tossed down directly from the loft above. Although the hole was big enough to stuff down an armload of hay, it wasn't quite big enough for Rush's broad shoulders to make the reverse trip. At the moment, having scrambled off the top of the manger as a partial ladder, Rush had one leg and both arms awkwardly jammed through the hole, and was attempting to twist the rest of his body out of range of Copperhead's snapping yellow teeth. Copperhead, ears flat back and neck snaking, squealed and snapped again, apparently for the pure evil pleasure of watching Rush squirm harder.

"Patroller!" Rush cried as he saw them come up to the stall partition. "Help me! Call off your horse!"

Sorrel shot Dag a worried look; Dag returned a small headshake and draped his arms over the partition, leaning comfortably.

"Now, Rush," said Dag in a conversational voice, "I distinctly remember telling you and your brothers that Copperhead was a warhorse, and to leave him alone. Do you remember that, Sorrel?"

"Yes, I do, patroller," said Sorrel, matching his tone, also resting his elbows on the boards.

"I know you magic him in some way! Get him off me!"

"Well, we'll have to see about that. Now, what I'm mightily curious about is just how you happened to be in his stall, without my leave, but with my saddlebags and bedroll and all my gear, which I had left in Aunt Nattie's weaving room. I think your pa would like to hear that story, too." And then Dag fell silent.

The silence stretched. Rush made a tentative move to swing down. Copperhead, excited, stamped and snapped and made a most peculiar noise, halfway between whipsaw menace and a horselaugh, Dag thought. Rush swung up again hastily.

"Your brute of a horse savaged me!" Rush complained. His shirt was ripped on one shoulder, and some blood leaked through, but it was clear to Dag's eye by the way Rush moved that there was nothing broken.

"Now, now," said Dag in a mock-soothing tone. "That was just a love bite, that was. If Copper'd really savaged you, you'd be over there, and your arm would be over here. Speaking from experience and all."

Rush's eyes widened as it dawned on him that if he'd wanted sympathy, he'd gone to the wrong store with the wrong coin.

Dag didn't say anything some more.

"What do you want to know?" Rush finally asked, in a surly tone.

"I'm sure you'll think of something," Dag drawled.

"Pa, make him let me down!"

Sorrel vented an exasperated sigh. "You know, Rush, I've drawn you and your brother out of wells of your own digging more than once when you were younger, because every boy's got to survive his share of foolishness. But as you're both so fond of telling me, you're not youngsters anymore. Seems to me you got yourself up there. You can get yourself down."

Rush looked appalled at this unexpected parental betrayal. He started blurting a somewhat garbled account for his predicament involving an imaginary request relayed from Fawn.

Dag gave Sorrel another small headshake. Sorrel looked increasingly grim.

"No," Dag interrupted in a bored voice, "That's not it. Think harder, Rush." After a moment, he said, "I should also mention, I suppose, that Sunny Sawman and his three strapping friends are now on their way downriver to West Blue. Under escort. Underwater, mostly. I don't think they'll be back for some several days."

"How did you—I don't know what you're talking about!"

More silence.

Rush added in a smaller voice, "Are they all right?"

"They'll live," said Dag indifferently. "You can remember to thank me kindly for that, later." And fell silent again.

After a couple more false starts, Rush at last began to 'fess up. It was more or less the story Dag expected, of alehouse conspiracy and youthful bravado. In Rush's version, Reed was the ringleader, valiantly horrified at the thought of his only sister marrying a Lakewalker corpse-eater and thus making him brother-in-law to one, and Rush's motivations were lost in a mumble; Dag wasn't sure whether this was strict truth or blame-casting, nor did he greatly care, as it was clear enough both boys were in it together. They had found a strangely enthusiastic helper in Sunny, fresh from a summer of stump-pulling and happy to show off his muscle. Unsurprisingly, it appeared Sunny had not seen fit to mention to the twins his prior encounter with Dag. Dag chose not to either. Sorrel looked grimmer and grimmer.

Rush at last stuttered to a halt. A cool silence fell in the warm barn. Rush began to sag down; Copperhead lunged again. Rush tightened up once more, clinging like a possum to a branch. Dag could see that his arms were shaking.

"Now, Rush," said Dag. "I'm going to tell *you* how it's going to be. I am actually prepared to forgive and forget your brotherly plan to beat me crippled or dead and buried in your pa's woods on the night before my wedding. The fact that you also seriously endangered the lives of your friends—because I would not, facing that death, have held back in defending myself I leave to your pa to take up with you two. I'll even forgive your lies to me." Dag's voice dropped to a deadly register that made Sorrel glance aside in alarm. "What I do not forgive is the *malice* of your lies to Fawn. You'd planned for her to wake up joyful on her wedding morning and then tell her I'd scunnered out in the night, make her believe herself shamed and betrayed, humiliate her before her friends and kin, set her to weeping—although I think her real response might have surprised you." He glanced aside. "You like that picture, Sorrel? No? Good." Dag took a long breath. "Whatever reasons your parents tolerated your torment of your sister in the past, it stops tomorrow. You claim Reed was afraid of me? He wasn't near afraid enough. Either of you so much as look cross-eyed at Fawn tomorrow, or anytime thereafter, I will give you reason to regret it every day for the rest of your lives. You hear me, Rush? *Look at me.*" Dag hadn't used that voice since he was a company captain. He was pleased to note it still worked; Rush nearly fell from his perch. Copperhead shied. Even Sorrel stepped backward. Dag hissed, "You hear me?"

Rush nodded frantically.

"All right. I will halter Copperhead, and you will climb down from there. Then you will pick up every bit of my gear and put it back where you found it. What's broken, you and your brother can fix, what's been rolled through the manure you can scrub—which will keep you two out of further mischief for the rest of the evening, I think—what can't be fixed, you'll replace, what can't be replaced, I leave you to work out with your pa."

"You heard the patroller, Rush," said Sorrel, in a deeply paternal snarl. Really, it was almost as good as the company-captain voice.

Dag extended his ground to his horse, a familiar reach long practiced; he'd been saddled with this chestnut idiot for about eight years, now. Disappointed at the loss of his toy, Copperhead lowered his head to the stall floor and began lipping straw, pretending that it all never happened. Dag thought he had a lot in common with Rush, that way. "You can get down," said Dag.

"He isn't haltered," said Rush nervously.

"Yes, he is," said Dag, "now." Sorrel's eyebrows climbed, but he didn't say anything. Cautiously, Rush climbed down. Red-faced, his eyes wary on Copperhead, he began collecting Dag's strewn possessions: clothing and saddlebags and ripped bedroll, knocked-about saddle and pummeled saddle blanket. The adapted bow, though kicked into a corner, was undamaged; Dag was glad. Only the reasonably benign outcome was keeping him from utter fury right now—that, plus not thinking too hard about Spark. But he had to think about Spark.

"Now," Dag said, as Rush made his way out of the stall with his arms loaded, and Dag closed the stall door after him. Rush set the tangled gear down very carefully. "We come to the other question. What of all this would you have me tell Fawn?"

The place had been quiet like a barn; for a moment, it grew quiet like a tomb.

Sorrel's face screwed up. He said cautiously, "Seems to me she'd be near as distressed for the word of this as for the thing itself. I mean, with respect to Reed and Rush," he added, visions of Fawn weeping over Dag's battered corpse evidently presenting themselves to his mind's eye, as indeed they did to Dag's. Rush, who had been rather red, turned rather white.

"Seems that way to me, too," said Dag. "But, you know, there's eight people who know the truth about what happened tonight. Granted, four of them will be telling lies when they drag home tonight, though I doubt even those will all be the same lies. Some kind of word's going to get around."

Dag let them both dwell on this ugly vision for a little, then said, "I'm not Reed's and Rush's linker, though I should have been. I will not lie to *her* for *them*. But I'll give you this much, and no more: I'll not speak first."

Sorrel took this in almost without expression for a moment, clearly thinking through the deeply unpleasant family ramifications. Then he nodded shortly. "Fair enough, patroller."

Dag extended his groundsense briefly, for all that the proximity of the two shaken Bluefields made it painful. He said, "Reed is coming back to the house with Fawn, now. I'd prefer to leave him to you, Sorrel."

"Send him down here to the barn," said Sorrel, somewhat through his teeth.

"That I will, sir." Dag gave a nod in place of his usual salute.

"Thank you—sir." Sorrel nodded back.

Fawn returned to the kitchen with Reed in some annoyance with him for dragging her out in the dark. She lit a few candle stubs on the mantel to lighten both the room and her mood. Better still for the latter was the sound of Dag's long footfalls coming through from the front hall. Reed, who had ducked into Nattie's weaving room for some reason, came out with an inexplicable triumphant smile on his face. She was about to ask why he was so happy all of a sudden when the look was wiped clean at the sight of Dag entering the kitchen. Fawn bit back yet more irritation with her brother. She had better things to do than fuss at Reed; hugging Dag hello was on the top of that list.

He gave her a quick return embrace with his left arm and turned to Reed. "Ah, Reed. Your papa wants to see you in the old barn. Now."

Reed looked at Dag as though he were a poisonous snake surprised in some place he'd been about to put his hand. "Why?" he asked in a suspicious voice.

"I believe he and Rush have quite a lot to say to you." Dag tilted his head and gave Reed a little smile, which had to be one of the least friendly expressions to go by that name Fawn had ever seen. Reed's mouth flattened in return, but he didn't argue; to Fawn's relief, he took himself off. She heard the front door slam behind him.

Fawn pushed back her unruly curls. "Well, *that* was a fool's errand."

"Where did you two go off to?" Dag asked.

"He dragged me all the way to the back pasture to help rescue a calf stuck in a fence. If the brainless thing had got itself in, it had got itself out by the time we made it there. And then he wanted to walk the fence line while we were out there. I didn't mind the walk, but I have things to do." She stood back and looked Dag over. He was often not especially tidy, but at the moment he looked downright rumpled. "Did you have your quiet think?"

"Yes, I just spent a very enlightening hour. Useful, too, I hope."

"Oh, you. I bet you never sat still." She brushed at a few stray bits of bark and leaf stuck to his shirt, and observed with disfavor a new rip in his trouser knee stained with blood from a scrape. "Walking in the woods, I think. I swear, you been walking so long you don't know how to stop. What, were you climbing trees?"

"Just one."

"Well, that was a fool thing to try with that arm!" she scolded fondly. "Did you fall down?"

"No, not quite."

"That's a blessing. You be more careful. Climbing trees, indeed! I thought I was joking. I don't want my bridegroom broken, I'll have you know."

"I know." He smiled, glancing around. Fawn realized that, miraculously, they were actually alone for a moment. He seemed to realize this at the same time, for he sat in the big wooden chair by the hearth and pulled her toward him. She climbed happily into his lap and raised her face for a kiss. The kiss went urgent, and they were both out of breath when their lips parted again.

She said gruffly, "They won't be able to keep us apart much longer."

"Not even with ropes and wild horses," he agreed, his eyes glinting. His smile grew more serious. "Have you decided yet where you want us to be tomorrow night? Ride or bide?"

She sighed and sat up. "Do you have a partiality?"

He brushed her hair from her forehead with his lips, likely because he had a notable reluctance for touching her about the face with his hook. It turned into a small trail of kisses along the arches of her eyebrows before he, too, sat back thoughtfully. "Here would be physically easier. We won't get to Hickory Lake in a day, still less in a couple of hours tomorrow evening. If we camped, you'd have to do most everything."

"I don't mind the work." She tossed her head.

"There is this. We won't just be making love, we'll be making memories. It's the sort of day you remember all your life, when other days fade. Real question, then, the only really important one, is what memories of this do you want to bear away into your future?"

Now, there was a voice of experience, she thought. Best listen to it. "It's farmer custom for the couple to go off to their new house, sleep under the new roof. The party goes on. If we stay, I swear I'll end up washing dishes at midnight, which is not what I want to be doing at midnight."

"I have no house for you. I don't even have a tent with me. It'll be a roof of stars, if it's not a roof of rain."

"It doesn't look like rain. This high blue weather this time of year usually holds for three or four days. I admit I prefer inn chambers to wheatfields, but at least with you there's no mosquitoes."

"I think we might do better than a wheatfield."

She added more seriously, thinking about his words, "This place is chock-full of memories for me. Some are good, but a lot of them hurt, and the hurtful ones have this way of jostling into first place. And this house'll be full of my family. Tomorrow night, I'd like to be someplace with no memories at all." *And no family.*

He ducked his head in understanding. "That's what we'll do, then."

Her spine straightened. "Besides, I'm marrying a patroller. We should go patroller-style. Bedroll under the stars, right." She grinned and nuzzled his neck, and said seductively, "We could bathe in the river . . ."

He was looking immensely seduceable, eyes crinkling in the way she so loved to see. "Bathing in the river is always good. A clean patroller is, um . . ."

"Unusual?" she suggested.

And she also loved the way his chest rumbled under her when he laughed deep down in it. Like a quiet earthquake. "A happy patroller," he finished firmly.

"We could gather firewood," she went on, her lips working upward.

His worked downward. He murmured around his kiss, "Big, big bonfire."

"Scout for rowdy squirrels . . ."

"Those squirrels are a right menace." He looked down over his nose at her, though she didn't see how he could focus his eyes at this distance. "All three? Optimistic, Spark!"

She giggled, joyful to see his eyes so alight. He'd seemed so moody when he'd first come in.

To her aggravation, she could hear heavy footsteps coming down the stairs, Fletch or Whit, heading this way. She sighed and sat up. "Ride, then."

"Unless we have a barker of a thunderstorm."

"Thunder and lightning couldn't keep me in this house one more day," she said fervently. "It's time for me to go on. Do you see?"

He nodded. "I'm beginning to, farmer girl. This is right for you."

She stole one last kiss before sliding off his lap, thinking, *Tomorrow we'll be buying these kisses fair and square.* Her heart melted in the tenderness of the look he gave her as, reluctantly, he let her slip out of his arm. All storms might be weathered in the safe harbor of that smile.

19

Fawn flew through the irreducible farm chores the next morning. The milking fell to her; afterwards, waving a stick with resolute vigor, she sent the bewildered cows off to pasture at a brisk and unaccustomed trot. For practical reasons the rule about the marrying couple's not seeing each other before the wedding was put aside till after the family breakfast, when Aunt Rose Bluefield arrived to help Mama with the food and the house, along with Fawn's closest cousins and girlfriends Filly Bluefield and Ginger Roper to start the primping.

First came proper baths. The women went off to the well; the men were dispatched to the river. Fawn had grave doubts about leaving Dag to the mercies of her father, Fletch, and Whit for such a vulnerable enterprise, although at least the twins weren't to follow till a long list of dirty chores had been completed. Filly and Ginger dragged her away as she was still yelling strict orders down the hill after the men about not letting Dag's splints get wet. There followed a naked, wet, silly, and sudsy half hour by the well; Mama brought out her best scented soap for the task. Once they were back in the bedroom with Ginger and Filly starting on her hair, Fawn was relieved to hear footsteps and men's voices through the closed door to the weaving room, Dag giving some calm instruction to Whit.

Filly and Ginger did their best, from Fawn's dimly remembered description of what Reela had told her, to imitate Lakewalker wedding braids, although Fawn was glumly aware that her own hair was too curly and unruly to cooperate the way Lakewalkers' long locks no doubt did. The result was creditable, anyhow, with the hair drawn up in neat thick ropes from her temples to meet at her crown, and from there allowed to spin down loose behind after its own turbulent fashion. In the little hand mirror, held out at arm's length, Fawn's face looked startlingly refined and grown-up, and she blinked at the strangeness. Ginger's brother had ridden all the way to Mirror Pond this morning, four miles upriver, to get the flowers Fawn had begged of him: three not-too-crumpled white water lilies, which Ginger now bound into the knot of hair on the crown of her head.

"Mama said you could have had all of her roses you wanted," Filly observed, tilting her head to examine the effect.

"These are more lake-ish," said Fawn. "Dag will like them. The poor man doesn't have any family or friends here, and is pretty much having to borrow everything farmer. I know he was pining that he couldn't send down his Lakewalker bride-gifts till after the wedding; they're supposed to be given beforehand, I guess."

Filly said, "Mama wondered if no women of his own people would marry him because of his hand being maimed like that."

Fawn, choosing to ignore the implied reflection upon herself, said only, "I shouldn't think so. A lot of patrollers seem to get banged up, over time. Anyhow, he's a widower."

Ginger said, "My brother said the twins said his horse talks human to him when there's no one around."

Fawn snorted. "If no one's around, how do they know?"

Ginger, considering this, conceded reluctantly, "That's a point."

"Besides, it's the *twins*."

Filly granted, "That's another." She added in regret, "So I guess they made up that story about him magicking together that glass bowl they broke, too?"

"Um. No. That one's true," Fawn admitted. "Mama put it away up-stairs for today, so it wouldn't risk getting knocked down again."

A thoughtful silence followed this, while Filly poked at the curls in back to fluff them, and pushed away Fawn's hands trying to smooth them.

"He's so tall," said Ginger in a newly speculative tone, "and you're *so* short. I'd think he'd squash you flatter than a bug. Plus both his arms bein' hurt. However are you two going to manage, tonight?"

"Dag's very ingenious," said Fawn firmly.

Filly poked her and giggled. "How would you know, eh?"

Ginger snickered. "Someone's been samplin', I think. What *were* you two doin', out on the road together for a month like that?"

Fawn tossed her head and sniffed. "None of your business." She couldn't help adding smugly after a moment, "I will say, there's no going back to farmer boys, after." Which won some hoots, quickly muted as Nattie bustled back in.

Ginger set her a chair by Fawn's bench, and Nattie laid out the cloth in which she'd wrapped the braided cords; she'd just delivered Dag's to him, together with the other, surprise present.

"Did he like his wedding shirt?" Fawn asked, a bit wistful because she couldn't very well ask Nattie *How did it look on him?*

"Oh, yes, lovie, he was very pleased. I'd say, even moved. He said he'd never had anything so fine in his life, and was in a wonder that we got it together so quick and secret. Though he said he was relieved for the explanation of you girls with your measurin' strings yesterday, which had evidently been worryin' him a bit." She unrolled the wrap; the dark cord lay coiled in her lap, the gold beads firm and rich-looking upon the ends.

"Where is he wearing his cord? Where should I wear mine?"

"He says folks mostly wear them on the left wrist if they're right-handed. T'other way around if not, naturally. He's put his around his left arm above the harness, for now. He says when the time comes for the binding, he can sit down and you can stand facing him, left side to left side, and I should be able to do the tyin' between you without too much trouble."

"All right," said Fawn doubtfully, trying to picture this. She stuck out her left arm and let Nattie wrap the cord several times around her wrist like a bracelet, tying the ends in a bow knot for now. The beads dangled prettily, and she twisted her hand to make them bounce on her skin. A little of her most secret self was in it, Dag said, bound in with her blood; she had to take his word.

Then it was time to get her dress on, the good green cotton, washed and carefully ironed for this; her other good dress being warm wool for winter. That Dag would remember this dress from that night in Glassforge when he had so gently and urgently removed it, unwrapping her like a gift, must be a secret between them; but she hoped he would find it a heartening sight. Ginger and Filly together lowered the fabric carefully over her head so as not to muss her hair or crush the lilies.

A knock sounded at the door, from someone who did not wait for permission to enter; Whit, who looked at Fawn and blinked. He opened his mouth as if to fire off one of his usual quip-insults, then appeared to think better of it and just smiled uneasily.

"Dag says, what about the weapons?" he recited, revealing himself as a messenger sent. "He seems to want to put them all on. He means, *all* of them, at once. He says it's to show off what a patroller is bringing to his bride's tent. Fletch says, no one wears weapons to a wedding, it just ain't done. Papa says, he don't know what should be done. So Dag says, ask Spark, and he'll abide."

Fawn started to answer *Yes, it's his wedding too, he should have some of his own customs,* then instead said more cautiously, "Just how many weapons are we talking about, here?"

"Well, there's that great pigsticker that he calls his war knife, for starters. Then there's one he slips down in his boot, and another he straps on his thigh sometimes, evidently. What he wants with three knives when he only has one hand, I don't know. Then there's that funny bow of his, and the quiver of arrows, which also has some little knives stuck in it. He seemed a bit put out that he didn't have a sword by him—seems there's one he inherited from his pa back at his camp, and some ash spear or another for fighting from horseback, which he also doesn't have here. Fortunately."

Ginger and Filly listened to this lengthening catalog with their faces screwing up.

Whit, nodding silent agreement at them, finished, "You'd think the man would clank when he walked. You wouldn't want a patroller to fall into water over his head on his way to his wedding, I'll say." His own brows rose in gruesome enthusiasm. "You suppose he's killed anybody with that arsenal? 'Spect he must have, sometime or another. That's a right sobering collection of scars he has, I saw when we were down washing up. Though I suppose he's had a long time to accumulate 'em." He added after another contemplative moment, "Do you think he's getting nervous 'bout the wedding? He don't hardly show it, but with him, how would you tell?"

With Whit as a helper, it was a wonder Dag wasn't frenzied by now, Fawn thought tartly. "Tell him"—Fawn's tongue hovered between *yes* and *no*, remembering just what all she *had* seen Dag kill with those weapons—"tell him just the war knife." In case it *was* nerves and the weapons a consolation. "Tell him it can *stand for* the rest of them, all right? We'll know."

"All right." Whit did not take himself off at once, but stood scratching his head.

"Did the shirt fit him good?" Fawn asked.

"Oh, yeah, I guess."

"You guess? Didn't you look? Agh! Useless to ask *you,* I suppose."

"He liked it fine. Kept touchin' it with his fingertips peekin' out of those bandages, anyhow, like he liked the feel. But what *I* want explained is—you know, I had to help him button and unbutton his trousers. So how in the green world has he been managing them for the past week? 'Cause I haven't never seen him going around undone. And I don't care how much of a sorcerer he is, he has to have been doin' the necessary *some* time . . ."

"Whit," said Fawn, "go *away.*"

Ginger and Filly, thinking this through, looked at Fawn's flushing face and began to giggle like steam kettles.

"Because," Whit, never one to take a hint, forged on, "I know it wasn't me or Fletch or Pa, and it couldn't have been the twins, who didn't warm to him a bit. Suppose it could have been Nattie, but really, I think it must have been you, and how—ow!" He ended in a yelp as Nattie smacked him firmly and accurately across the knees with her cane.

"Whit, if you don't go find yourself a chore, I'll find you one," she told him. "Don't you go embarrassin' Fawn's patroller with all your supposin', or you'll have me to answer to, and I *will* be here tomorrow."

Whit, daunted at last, took himself out, saying placatingly, "I'll say *just the knife,* right."

Outside, Fawn could hear the sounds of hoofbeats and creaking carts coming up the lane, and calls of greeting, more folks arriving. It felt very peculiar to sit still in this room waiting, instead of being out bustling around doing.

Mama came in, wiping her hands on a towel, to say, "Shep Sower and his wife just got here. They were the last. The sun's as close to noon as makes no never mind. We could start most any time."

"Is Dag ready? Is he all right?"

"He's clean, and dressed neat and plain. He looks very calm and above it all, except that he's had Whit switch out his wooden hand for his hook and back again twice now."

Fawn considered this. "Which did he end up with?"

"Hook, last I seen."

"Hm." So did that mean he was getting more relaxed, to let himself be seen so by strangers, or less, to have the most useful tool and maybe-weapon ready, as it were, to hand? "Well, it'll be over soon. I didn't mean to put him through such an ordeal when I agreed to stop back here."

Mama nodded to Fawn's cousins. "You girls give us a minute."

Nattie rose to her feet, endorsing this. "Come along, chickies, give the bride a breather with her mama." She shepherded Fawn's helpers out to her weaving room and closed the door quietly behind them.

Mama said, "In a few minutes, you'll be a married woman." Her voice was stretched somewhere between anxious and bewildered. "Sooner than I expected. Well, I *never* expected anything like this. We always meant to do right by you, for your wedding. This is all so quick. We've done more preparing for *Fletch*." She frowned at this felt injustice.

"I'm glad it's no more. This is making me nervous enough."

"You sure about this, Fawn?"

"Today, no. All my tomorrows, yes."

"Nattie's kept your confidences. But, you know, if you want to change your mind, we can stop this right now. Whatever trouble you think you're in, we could manage it somehow."

"Mama, we've had this conversation. Twice. I'm not pregnant. Really and truly."

"There are other kinds of troubles."

"For girls, that's the only one folks seem to care about." She sighed. "So how many out there are saying I must be, for you to let this go forward?"

"A few," Mama admitted.

A bunch, I'll bet. Fawn growled. "Well, time'll prove 'em wrong, and I hope you'll make them eat their words when it does, 'cause I won't be here to."

Mama went around behind her and fussed with her hair, which needed nothing. "I admit Dag seems a fine fellow, no, I'll go farther, a good man, but what about his kin? Even he doesn't vouch for your welcome where you're going. What if they treat you bad?"

I'll feel right at home. Fawn bit down on that one before it escaped. "I'll deal. I dealt with bandits and mud-men and blight bogles. I can deal with relatives." *As long as they're not my relatives.*

"Is this *sensible*?"

"If folks were sensible, would anyone ever get married?"

Mama snorted. "I suppose not." She added in a lower voice, "But if you start down a road you can't see the end of, there's a chance you'll find some dark things along it."

About to defend her choice for the hundredth time, Fawn paused, and said simply, "That's true." She stood up. "But it's my road. Our road. I can't stand still and keep breathin'. I'm ready." She kissed her mama on the cheek. "Let's go."

Mama got in one last, inarguable maternal sigh, but followed Fawn out. They collected Nattie and Ginger and Filly along the way. Mama made a quick circuit of the kitchen, finally set aside her towel, straightened her dress, and led the way into the parlor.

The parlor was jammed, the crowd spilling over into the hall. Papa's brother Uncle Hawk Bluefield and Aunt Rose and their son still at home; Uncle and Aunt Roper and their two youngest boys, including the successful water-lily finder; Shep Sower and his cheery wife, always up for a free feed; Fletch and Clover and Clover's folks and sisters and the twins, inexplicably well behaved, and Whit and Papa.

And Dag, a head above everyone but still looking very surrounded. The white shirt fit him well. There hadn't been time for smocking or embroidery, but Nattie and Aunt Roper had come up with some dark green piping to set off the collar and cuffs and button placket. The sleeves were made generous enough to fit over his splints, and over his arm harness on the other side, with second buttons set over to tighten the cuffs later. There had been just enough of the shell buttons left to do the job. Fawn had whisked his sling away from him yesterday long enough to wash and iron it, so it didn't look so grubby even though it was growing a bit tattered. He was wearing the tan trousers with fewer old stains and mends, also forcibly washed yesterday. His worn knife sheath, riding on his left hip, looked so much a part of him as to be almost unnoticeable despite its wicked size.

A bit of spontaneous applause broke out when Fawn appeared, which made her blush. And then Dag wasn't looking at anything else but her, and it all made sense again. She went and stood beside him. His right arm twitched in its sling, as though he desperately wanted to hold her hand but could not. Fawn settled for sliding her foot and hip over, so that they touched along the side, a reassuring pressure. The sense of strain in the room, of everyone trying to pretend this was all right and be nice for Fawn's sake, almost made her want them all to revert back to their normal relaxed horribleness, but not quite.

Shep Sower stepped forth, smiled, cleared his throat, and called them all to attention with a few brief, practiced words. To Fawn's relief, he glanced at Dag and skipped over his usual dire wedding jokes, which everyone else here had likely heard often enough to recite themselves anyhow. He then read out the marriage contract; the older generation listened with attention, nodding judiciously or raising eyebrows and exchanging glances now and then. Dag, Fawn, her parents, the three adult couples, and Fletch and Clover all signed it, Nattie made her mark, and Shep signed and sealed it all.

Then Papa brought out the family book and laid it open on the table, and much the same exercise was repeated. Dag stared curiously over Fawn's shoulder at the pages, and she thumbed back a bit through the entries of births, deaths, and marriages and land swaps, purchases, or inheritances to silently point out her own birth note and, several pages earlier, the note of her own parents' wedding, with the names and countersigned marks of the witnesses—many long dead, a few still right here in this same room doing this same task.

Then Dag and Fawn, coached by Shep, said their promises. There had been a bit of a debate about them, yesterday. Dag had shied at the wording, all the farmer pledges to plow and plant and harvest in due season, since he said he wasn't likely to be doing any of those things and for a wedding vow he ought to be speaking strict truth if ever he did. And as for guarding the land for his children, he'd been doing that all his life for everybody's children. But Nattie had explained the declarations as a poetical way of talking about a couple taking care of each other and having babies and growing old together, and he'd calmed right down. The words did sound odd in his mouth, here in this hot, crowded parlor, but his deep, careful voice somehow gave them such weight it felt as if they might be used to anchor ships in a thunderstorm. They seemed to linger in the air, and all the married adults looked queerly introspective, as if hearing them resonating in their own memories. Fawn's own voice seemed faint and gruff in her ears by comparison, as though she were a silly little girl playing at being a grown-up, convincing no one.

At this point in the usual ceremony it would be time to kiss each other and go eat, but now came the string-binding, about which most everyone had been warned in carefully casual terms. *Something to please Fawn's patroller,* and in case that seemed too alarming, *Nattie will be doing it for them.* Papa brought out a chair and set it in the middle of the room, and Dag sat in it with a nod of thanks. Fawn rolled up Dag's left sleeve; she wondered what was going through his head that he chose to so expose his arm harness to view. But the dark cord with the copper glints was revealed, circling his biceps, Fawn's own cord having been out in plain sight all along.

Papa then escorted Nattie up, and she felt along and found everything, cords and arm and wrist. She pulled loose the bow knots and collected both cords in her hands, winding them about one another, murmuring half-voiced blessings of her own devising. She then rewrapped the combined cords in a figure eight around Dag's arm and Fawn's, and tied them with a single bow. She held her hand on it, and chanted:

"Side by side or far apart,
intertwined may these hearts
walk together."

Which were the words Dag had given Nattie to say, and reminded Fawn disturbingly of the words on Kauneo's thighbone-knife that Dag had carried for so long aimed at his own heart. Possibly the burned script had been meant to recall just such a wedding chant, or charm.

The words, the cords, and the two hearts willing: all had to be present to make a valid marriage in Lakewalker . . . not eyes, but ground-sense, that subtle, invisible, powerful perceiving. Fawn wondered desperately how it was people made their assent work the strings' grounds that way. Thinking really hard about it seemed, for her, about as effective as being a five-year-old wishing hard for a pony, eyes scrunched up in futile effort, because a child had no other power by which to move the world.

Doing has no need of wishing.

She would *do* her marriage then, hour by hour and day by day with the work of her hands, and let the wishing fall where it would.

Dag had his head cocked as though he were listening to something Fawn could not hear; his eyelids lowered in satisfaction, and he smiled. With some difficulty, he lifted his right arm and positioned the fingers of his hand about one end of the knot, gathering up the two gold beads from the two different cords; Fawn, at his nod, grasped the other pair. Together, they pulled the knot apart, and Fawn let the cords unwind from around each other. Fawn then tied her cord on Dag's arm, and Dag, with Nattie's help, or rather Nattie with Dag's hindrance, tied his cord around Fawn's wrist, this time with square knots. Dag glanced up under his lids at her with a muted expression, joy and terror and triumph compounded, with just a touch of wild unholy glee. It reminded Fawn of the loopy look on his face right after they'd slain the malice, actually. He leaned his forehead against Fawn's and whispered, "It's good. It's *done.*"

Lakewalker ground magic of a most profound sort. Worked in front of twenty people. And not one of them had seen it. *What have we done?*

Still sitting, Dag snaked his left arm around her and snugged her in for a proper kiss, though it felt disorienting to be lowering her face toward his instead of raising it. With an effort, they both broke off before the kiss continued at improper length. She thought he just barely refrained from pulling her into his lap and ravishing her right there. She was way overdue for a good ravish. *Later,* his bright eyes promised.

And *then* it was time to go eat.

The boys had set up trestle tables in the west yard under the trees, so there would be room for everyone to sit down who wanted to. One whole table was devoted to the food and drink, which people circled and descended upon like stooping hawks, carrying loaded plates away to the other tables. Women banged in and out of the kitchen after things forgotten or belatedly wanted. With only the four families plus the Sowers present, it was literally a quiet wedding, with no music or dancing attempted, and as it chanced, there were no little ones present to fall down the well or out of trees or stable lofts and keep the parents alert, or crazed.

There followed eating, drinking, eating, talking, and eating. When Fawn hauled Dag and his plate to the food trestle for the third time, he bent and whispered fearfully, "How much more of this do I have to get down so as not to offend any of those formidable women I'm now related to?"

"Well, there's Aunt Roper's cream-and-honey pie," said Fawn judiciously, "and Aunt Bluefield's butter-walnut cake, and Mama's maple-hickory nut bars, and my apple pies."

"*All* of them?"

"Ideally. Or you could just pick one and let the rest be offended."

Dag appeared to cogitate for a moment, then said gravely, "Slap on a big chunk of that apple pie, then."

"I do like a man who thinks on his feet," said Fawn, scooping up a generous portion.

"Yeah, while I can still see them."

She smirked.

He added plaintively, "That dimple's going to be the death of me, you know?"

"Never," she said firmly, and led him back to their seats.

She slipped away soon after to her bedroom to change into her riding trousers and shoes and the sturdier shirt that went with them. She left the lilies in her hair, though. When she came back out to Nattie's weaving room, Dag stood up from his neatly packed saddlebags.

"You say when, Spark."

"Now," she replied fervently, "while they're still working through the desserts. They'll be less inclined to follow along."

"Not being able to move? I begin to see your clever plan." He grinned and went to get Whit and Fletch to help him with the horses.

She met them in the lane to the south of the house, where Dag was watching with keen attention as his new brothers-in-law tied on the assorted gear. "I don't think they'll try any tricks on you," she whispered up to him.

"If they were Lakewalkers," he murmured back, "there would be no end of tricks at this point. Patroller humor. Sometimes, people are allowed to live, after."

Fawn made a wry face. Then added thoughtfully, "Do you miss it?"

"Not *that* part," he said, shaking his head.

Despite the cooks' best efforts, the relatives did drag themselves from the trestle tables to see them off. Clover, with a glance at the addition rising on this side of the house, bade Fawn the very best of luck. Mama hugged her and cried, Papa hugged her and looked grim, and Nattie just hugged her. Filly and Ginger flung rose petals at them, most of which missed; Copperhead seemed briefly inclined to spook at this, just to stay in practice evidently, but Dag gave him an evil eye, and he desisted and stood quietly.

"I hate to see you going out on the road with nothing," Mama sniffled.

Fawn glanced at her bulging saddlebags and all the extra bundles, mostly stuffed with packed-up food, tied about patient Grace; Fawn had barely been able to fight off the pressing offer of a hamper to be tied atop. Dag, citing Copperhead's tricksiness, had been more successful at resisting the last-minute provisions and gifts. After a brief struggle with her tongue, she said only, "We'll manage somehow, Mama."

And then Papa boosted her aboard Grace, and Dag, wrapping his reins around his hook, got himself up on tall Copperhead in one smooth lunge despite his sling.

"Take care of her, patroller," Papa said gruffly.

Dag nodded. "I intend to, sir."

Nattie gripped Fawn's knee, and whispered, "You take care o' him, too, lovie. The way that fellow sheds pieces, it may be the thornier task."

Fawn bent down toward Nattie's ear. "I intend to."

And then they were off, to a rain of good-byes but no other sort; the afternoon was warm and fair, and only half-spent. They would be well away from West Blue by time to camp tonight. The farmstead fell behind as they wended down the lane, and was soon obscured by the trees.

"We did it," Fawn said in relief. "We got away again. For a while I never thought I would."

"I did say I wouldn't abandon you," Dag observed, his eyes a brighter gold in this light than the beads on the ends of her marriage cord.

Fawn turned back in her saddle for one last look up the hill. "You didn't have to do it this way."

"No. I didn't." The eyes crinkled. "Think about it, Spark."

Attempting to exchange a kiss from the backs of two variously tall and differently paced horses resulted in a sort of promissory sideswipe, but it was fully satisfactory in intent. They turned their mounts onto the river road.

It was all a perfect opposite to her first flight from home. Then she had gone in secret, in the dark, alone, afraid, angry, afoot, all her meager possessions in a thin blanket rolled on her back. Even the direction was reversed: south, instead of north as now.

In only one aspect were the journeys the same. Each felt like a leap into the utterly unknown.